ELECTROMAGNETIC ASSAULT

Library of Congress Cataloging-in-Publication Data available upon request.
Cover art designed by S.W. Strackbein, edited by Lisa Lickel.

This is a work of fiction. All events in the book take place decades in the future. Names, characters, businesses, elected and unelected government officials, military members, military units, aircraft, weapons, events, and incidents are the products of the author's imagination. Any resemblance to actual persons, living or dead, actual events, or existing technology is purely coincidental.

First published in the United States of America in 2025
by Sisyphus Triumphant Publishing
Jackson, WI
www.SisyphusTriumphant

Sisyphus
Triumphant
Publishing

First edition January 2026
ISBN 979-8-9939992-0-3 (Softcover)
ISBN 979-8-9939992-1-0 (eBook)

For information about permission to reproduce selections from this book, email the author at bruce@brucelanday.com

Contact the Publisher at info@swstrackbein.com

Books may be purchased for business and promotional use.
Printed in the United States of America

For my wife, Barb, the love of my life.

*Thank you for your unwavering support and
infinite patience with my writing obsession.*

Off we go into the wild blue yonder

ELECTROMAGNETIC ASSAULT

BRUCE LANDAY

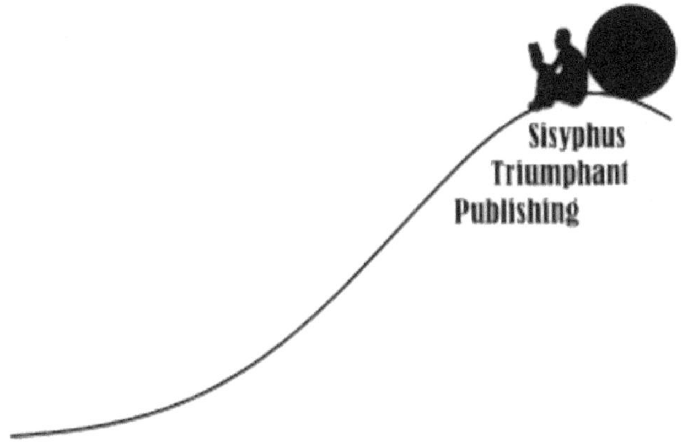

Prologue

USS Enterprise Aircraft Carrier
South China Sea

The packed ready room pulsed with the sound of flight operations from roaring jet engines on takeoff interspersed with the hollow thump of landing aircraft. Navy Lieutenant Jazmin Hassani stood at the front of the room and studied the faces of the two SEAL teams. Each SEAL team member had successfully completed the same grueling training, and all had military-grade neurotech implants surgically placed in their brains which allowed the team members to control weapons, technology, and silently communicate their thoughts through shared hivemind connections. While Lieutenant Hassani wasn't a SEAL and didn't wear the Trident on her uniform, she was SEAL Team One's pilot. Her job was stealth transportation in hostile environments to support any mission. No one was left behind. She was intimately linked to her SEAL Team One comrades through their hivemind connections, and every member vibrated with tension. The SEAL Team Seven members she knew only by reputation but wouldn't hesitate to serve on a mission with any of them.

Lieutenant Hassani watched the back of the ready room, and when Captain Ajax Papadakis came through the door, she called out, "Room ten-hut." Everyone jumped to attention as their commanding officer walked to the front and stood next to her.

Papadakis said, "At ease. Take your seats." Everyone except Hassani and the captain sat in the leather chairs normally reserved for pilots and aircrew members. "It's rare we have two SEAL teams and two octocopters prepped for the same mission, especially on such short notice. National security consequences demand we have two options with separate teams and aircraft to execute either plan. Tensions have never been higher between the US and China. We don't want to start a war, so our goal is zero fatalities on both sides. Flawless execution is paramount."

Standing off to the side, Lieutenant Hassani focused on her boss. Papadakis had been a great mentor and had helped her navigate the challenge of tightly integrating with her team despite not being a SEAL herself. Today he looked more haggard than she'd ever seen him. The high number of missions and never-ending preparations had taken their toll on him. How much longer would he last under the crushing weight of commanding two SEAL teams?

The captain said, "To keep the rivalry between the SEAL teams to a minimum, Lieutenant Hassani will give the mission briefing." A few members from both teams laughed. The two SEAL team mission commanders nodded to Hassani, and she appreciated their silent support.

Hassani swapped places with the captain and made eye contact with each person on SEAL Team One. Through her hivemind connection she felt the emotional jolt of pride and determination of the group. They were dialed in and ready for action. The briefing was for SEAL Team Seven, the backup team assigned to the alternate mission. She pivoted toward them.

Lieutenant Hassani used her neurotech to connect to the carrier's military network, which provided a live data feed for her briefing. Mentally, she took control of the briefing room's holographic projector system, which allowed her to beam three dimensional images anywhere in the room. She presented a series of holographic images of their rescue target, a silver-haired academic in his late fifties. The life-sized photos hung in the air next to her, visible from every seat in the briefing room. "SEAL Team One's mission is to rescue Dr. Victor Cabral from the prison block at the Chinese base on Mischief Reef. The Naval War College professor was abducted from a US-led peace conference in Tokyo eighteen hours ago. His technical knowledge of hypersonic missiles and American military assets can't be allowed to fall into Chinese hands. While our government is pursuing a diplomatic solution, the President cannot allow time for a lengthy Chinese Military Intelligence interrogation. Cabral can stall them for only so long before they drug him or break him. What's in this brilliant man's head could tip the fragile balance of power between the US and China."

She replaced the holographic images with a detailed map of the military facility, along with an area map showing the base's location on the largest of the artificial islands in the South China Sea. "The prison block is located in building Q near the south end of the runway. It's heavily guarded by an autonomous robot security force and a limited number of human guards who monitor the automated systems." She displayed satellite views of key buildings with prison cells. The security control section was highlighted in red. She added DZ with a circle around the letters on the map. "At the Drop Zone, SEAL Team One platoon three fast ropes to the ground, then Alpha Squad hits the robot security force and control center with a barrage of rocket-propelled electromagnetic-pulse grenades. Bravo Squad breaches the prison block with shaped charges, extracts Dr. Cabral, and exfils to the pickup location on the east side of the structure. The octocopter will hover over the area but won't touch down."

Lieutenant Hassani removed the holographic maps and photos from view. "The rules of engagement are simple. Use stun weapons on human targets. Deadly force is only authorized to save Dr. Cabral or your own life."

Papadakis stood next to Hassani. "SEAL Team One, sortie at zero-one-thirty. Good Hunting."

The group jumped to their feet and replied in unison, "Hooyah."

Papadakis headed for the door, and a minute later the ready room was empty. Lieutenant Hassani stayed behind with only the noise from the flight deck intruding on her thoughts. She was the only person on SEAL Team One Captain Papadakis had briefed on SEAL Team Seven's mission. If SEAL Team One failed, then SEAL Team Seven had no rules of engagement. Their mission was to retrieve Dr. Cabral, dead or alive, with no restrictions on body count, weapons employed, or collateral damage.

***

Lieutenant Hassani flew SEAL Team One's octocopter gunship hands-free using her neurotech interface and the aircraft's autopilot.

The stealth copter had no exterior lights. Painted matte black, it remained invisible on the moonless night as they approached the control tower at Mischief Reef. Their onboard AI identified them as a PLA Army Aviation aircraft, and the tower authorized them to land.

So far their subterfuge held, though Hassani knew things could go sideways at any moment. Her team ran a final check-in before go time. The group's adrenaline rushed through her hivemind connection. She came in high over the landing zone and reduced power for a rapid descent.

As soon as she dropped below eight hundred feet AGL, a blue flash filled the sky and lit up her cockpit. A pressure wave squeezed her skull, and her head throbbed in pain. The copter instantly lost power. The automated controls froze. Her hivemind connection evaporated. Total neural silence. Her stomach lurched when the negative g-force hit her. The copter was in freefall.

Heart racing, Hassani fought off panic as she scanned the control panel for anything still functioning. She locked her eyes on the only flight instrument showing signs of life, the backup analog altimeter. The numbers flashed down at a frightening rate. Her octocopter spun out of control to the helipad below. She had seconds to respond if they were to survive.

She switched to manual flight controls and reduced rotor pitch, the first step of autorotation. The fly-by-wire control system refused to respond. Each second burned through altitude she didn't have. No response to her control inputs. She couldn't save the aircraft.

At four hundred feet AGL she pulled the eject handle. The canopy and rotor assemblies didn't explode and blow clear. The catapult charges for launching the crew skyward to safety didn't ignite. Multiple parachutes didn't open. The violent exit from the doomed aircraft didn't come. A red error light flashed on the ejection system digital sequencer. It was the last thing she saw before the octocopter smashed onto the concrete helipad.

The crumpled airframe lay at a forty-five-degree angle. Dazed, Lieutenant Hassani looked out through the smashed windshield at the crumpled remains of the landing gear. She writhed with excruciating pain in both legs, obviously broken in multiple places. The copter burst into flames and searing pain radiated across the exposed flesh of her face. She choked on toxic fumes from burning electronics and plastic. Her personal hell turned black when she lost her sight and hearing.

The impact didn't kill her, though she wished it had. She lay semiconscious and wondered what horrible things the Chinese would do to her once they figured out she was still alive.

Lieutenant Hassani wasn't sure how much time had passed when she felt hands pulling her from the wreckage and strapping her to a backboard. Each movement engulfed her in another wave of horrible pain. She felt pressure on her arm and soon her pain floated to the background. Unable to see, hear, or move her charred mouth, she had no way to communicate. The last thing she remembered before losing consciousness was rhythmic tapping on her arm. She focused on the pattern and finally recognized it as Morse code. *SEAL Team Seven.*

Chapter 1

Milwaukee Joint Military
Rehabilitation Hospital
2 May

Five years ago, Commander Jazmin Hassani swore she'd never return. The military medical campus was filled with horrible memories she wanted to leave in her past. The entrance door to the rehabilitation hospital hissed closed behind her and she forced herself forward. She ran her fingers along the cool stainless steel handrail lining the hallway, and unwanted images from the past intruded. She no longer needed external support to maintain her balance on her prosthetic legs, though today she winced from phantom aches from her missing limbs. Flashbacks of the flaming cockpit, searing burns on her face, and months of slow, pain-racked recovery commandeered her attention. She pushed on, refusing to let her past control her.

Jazmin couldn't have made it through rehab without the support of her closeknit family. Her mom, Mercedes Montoya, the Chief Technical Officer at Defense Air Systems, had treated Jazmin's injuries and recovery like an engineering problem. Surely there was a technical solution to every issue her daughter had to overcome. Jazmin's father, Dr. Saeed Hassani, an international relations scholar for a Washington DC non-partisan think tank, used his considerable network to find out who was behind the attack on his daughter on that fateful mission. Her brother, Enrique, a neurosurgeon, monitored every medical procedure and patiently explained the countless medical details to his younger sister. He also acted as an unasked-for bouncer for her ex-military love interest he'd never trusted.

A low-slung cleaning robot scrubbed the hallway floor and chirped an insipid tune in an endless loop. It misted lemon-orange institutional cleaner, and while the pungent chemical scent clung to every surface, it could never mask the stench of despair permeating everything. Eyes forward, expression neutral, Jazmin marched down the hall past patient rooms. Her bionic-enhanced peripheral vision witnessed suffering in every room. Her dual cochlear implants paired to audio processors heard every moan and cry for help. The final insult was her digital memory that recorded every demoralizing detail.

Using her neurotech, Jazmin located the injured officer she was here to interview for her current investigation. At the end of the hallway, she took the stairs up one flight, turned left at the top of the steps, then found the room three doors down the hall. She knocked on the doorframe and entered the treatment room where a patient waited for a physical therapist. Jazmin said, "I'm Commander Hassani from the Neurotech Defense Agency. I'm working on an investigation. I'd like you to answer a few questions for me."

Navy Lieutenant Kristin Macy struggled to her feet, her expression a mix of exhaustion and worry. She teetered on a mechanical prosthetic leg, and when she lost her balance, Jazmin grabbed the lieutenant's arm and steered her back to a chair. The young officer looked spent, though tried to stand again. Jazmin said, "At ease, Lieutenant, stay seated." She glanced at the prosthetic leg, and the issue was obvious. An improper fit inflamed the tender skin of the amputated leg. "That looks like a temporary prosthetic, and the tech did a lousy job fitting it. Let the physical therapist know, and they'll track down the tech and get it right."

Pain radiated across Macy's face. "Just got it this morning, and what's left of my leg hurts like hell." She glared at the prosthetic limb.

Jazmin sat across from her. "You'll have good days and bad days, but it gets better with time. Do exactly what the doctors, the physical therapists, and the prosthetic techs tell you to do, and you'll eventually get your life back. Don't allow this to define you."

Macy winced as she adjusted herself on the chair. "You sound like you've been through this yourself."

"I spent eighteen months here after my aircraft crashed on a mission. My legs weren't the only things replaced."

The lieutenant's eyes went wide, and she stared at Jazmin's uniform-clad legs. After a few moments, she returned her gaze to Jazmin. Macy's pained, exhausted expression returned, and she folded her arms, hugging herself. "What do you want to know, Commander?"

Jazmin liked Macy's directness. It mirrored her own style. "I'd like to talk to you about your octocopter incident."

Macy sat upright, an anxious look on her face. "Do I need a JAG lawyer?"

Jazmin shook her head. "I'm looking for information. You're not in any type of legal trouble."

Macy sighed. "Why am I being questioned by the Neurotech Defense Agency? Haven't I been grilled enough already? I was pilot in command when my aircraft crashed. Almost every member of a SEAL platoon died. People I would gladly trade places with." Macy's face flushed with irritation.

Jazmin put her hand on Macy's arm to calm her, but it had the opposite effect. The young officer's angry, frightened eyes stared back at her.

Jazmin said, "I understand exactly what you're feeling right now."

Macy yanked her arm away and pushed back her chair with her one functioning leg. "How the hell could you, Commander?"

"I had the same experience as pilot in command and the mission's only survivor. Every operator on SEAL Team One Platoon 3 died when my aircraft went down. I tattooed their names on my arm, so I'll never forget."

Macy looked at Jazmin's uniform again and the lieutenant studied Jazmin's gold aviator badge. After a moment she asked, "Commander, are you still flying?"

Jazmin shook her head. "I maintain my flight qualifications, but I'm not in a flying role." She didn't want to admit that she no longer trusted herself. It was why she had become a Neurotech Defense Agency investigator.

Macy looked away. "I'm not sure I want to fly again."

Jazmin waited for Macy to bring her attention back from her sad musings. "Don't be in a hurry to make a decision. Right now, focus on taking care of yourself. Do you have any family looking in on you?"

"My parents were here and just headed home to North Carolina. My brother, Jack, also a Navy pilot, got emergency leave, and he'll be here tomorrow for a few days."

"It's good to hear you have family support."

Macy nodded and slumped back in her chair. She looked physically and emotionally drained. Jazmin had been there most of her time in rehab and some days still was.

"I've read your file and the accident report. It's scarily similar to my own. We know our enemies are working on directed-energy weapons, though I can't find any other instances of US aircraft being downed by a similar weapon. I'd like to know what you experienced when the energy weapon hit your aircraft. What did you feel? What were you thinking?"

Macy stared at her stump and ill-fitting prosthetic leg, then back at Jazmin. She sat up straight with fire in her eyes, and for the first time looked like a Navy Special Ops officer. "There was an intense pain in the back of my head like someone hit me with a bat. I was stunned and everything slowed to a crawl, like I was in a dream struggling to move."

"Did you see a flash of blue light?"

Macy leaned forward, her eyes drilling into Jazmin. "No, nothing like that. No sound, either. The aircraft just lost power."

Jazmin welcomed the change in Macy. The lieutenant was channeling her anger. If it was the same weapon used five years ago, then whoever was behind it had made it even stealthier. Jazmin would have to follow up on that. "I know the final result, but what happened to your aircraft at that moment? What action did you take?"

"I checked the flight control system, and the octocopter was no longer being flown by the autopilot. The automated flight systems were completely offline. That never happens. I tried switching to manual flight controls, but the fly-by-wire system was down. None of the manual controls responded."

"What about your instruments?" asked Jazmin.

Macy winced. "I still have horrible headaches and have a hard time concentrating. Sorry, what was your question again?"

"I asked about your flight control instruments."

Macy shook her head. "Most were useless. Except for a few backup analog gauges, everything else froze or went dark, and I assumed the aircraft had been hit with an electromagnetic pulse, but the accident investigators didn't find evidence of an EMP air burst or an electromagnetic bomb."

"You haven't mentioned autorotation."

Macy sighed. "I was grilled by the review board and my commanding officer. I tried to reduce rotor pitch and flare the copter to let air spin the props for lift, but the fly-by-wire controls were toasted. Landing the octocopter wasn't possible so I pulled the eject handle, but nothing happened. I was always taught in training that ejection systems will function no matter how badly the aircraft is damaged. I proved that lesson wrong." Macy sighed and then winced in pain.

Jazmin felt a creepy sense of déjà vu and thought about her own incident. The details were too close to be just coincidence. She was convinced these attacks were related, though she had no idea how. She forced her attention back to the present. "What did the doctors say about your neurotech implants?"

"They're fried, but I don't need a doctor to tell me that. The only thing they're good for now are cluster headaches."

A wave of sympathy pain rumbled through Jazmin's head. "Did the surgeon mention anything else?" Jazmin had a specific question in mind but didn't want to risk planting the idea in Macy's head.

Macy looked down and squeezed her eyebrows together in thought. After a moment her features relaxed and she looked up at Jazmin. "The surgeon said that my implants were destroyed but the damage wasn't consistent with an EMP blast. She'd never seen anything like it, though one of her colleagues had." Macy hesitated, as if groping for something else. "That's all I can remember."

Whatever weapon downed that aircraft was also aimed at the people inside. It was equally destructive to people and equipment, or more precisely, the control systems for both.

"Did you have an active hivemind connection during the mission?" asked Jazmin.

Macy's face drooped and she closed her eyes. When she opened them, her eyes glistened with newly formed tears. "Yes." She paused and looked like she was trying to control her emotions. "I was connected to the full team on board and one member on the ground, then total neural silence." Tears rolled down the lieutenant's face, and she brushed them away with the back of her hand.

Jazmin waited for Macy to compose herself. Painful memories of losing her own hivemind connection came back unbidden. The lieutenant sniffed and seemed resigned to her sadness, though no longer overwhelmed by it. "It took a long time for me to get used to having a hivemind connection to my unit, especially on ops when tensions were high. As a group we had to learn thought communication discipline to keep from overwhelming each other. Now the perpetual silence leaves me feeling lonely all the time."

Jazmin leaned forward and squeezed Macy's arm. "You have more friends than you realize. Other military members will support you when you're down, and you'll return the favor. Even military families will surprise you. After my aircraft went down with the people I was closest to in the whole world, I visited each of their families after I was released from rehab. I apologized over and over for what happened and asked for their forgiveness. They surprised me by saying they had nothing to forgive. They hugged me and were glad I survived to keep their loved ones' memories alive."

Jazmin and Macy sat in silence for a minute. Wanting to leave before she got emotional herself, Jazmin stood. "Thank you for your time, Lieutenant. I'll let you know what I find. If you're determined to come back to your unit, nothing will stop you."

***

Once outside, Jazmin summoned a car from the self-driving military fleet, where nanotech coatings converted every vehicle exterior surface into solar panels. The cars required zero downtime for recharging, reducing the total number of fleet vehicles needed. A few minutes later a car pulled up and she got in. A holographic petty officer was at the wheel. It asked, "Where to, ma'am?"

"The military side of Mitchell Airport. Take me to the aircraft incident investigation hangar, please."

"Yes, ma'am."

Jazmin was amused that the military fleet vehicles were all equipped with holographic drivers for the appearance of a human at the wheel. She knew she was speaking to a computer, though the hologram gave the car a touch of humanity so Jazmin was always polite. The car picked up speed and joined the other vehicles on the road. She stared out the window and enjoyed the view of the restored Milwaukee neighborhood where the same nanotech coating used on cars covered every roof. Homes were now connected in microgrids, no longer reliant on power plants.

Her respite in the local scenery didn't last long. She needed to know what the aircraft incident investigators had found. The issue that gnawed at her was the identical aircraft damage profile between her incident and Macy's. Jazmin scanned her tablet for the officer leading the investigation. She locked onto the name, and a welt of pain radiated across her face like she'd been slapped.

Army Major Sean Mulroney dredged up a thousand memories, all of them irritating. He no longer had power over her, so she didn't need to put up with that jerk.

Chapter 2

Military Aircraft Investigation Hangar
Mitchell Airport
2 May

Jazmin paced near the security desk outside the aircraft investigation hangar and repeatedly checked the time. When she had last dealt with Mulroney, the imbecile refused to answer any of her questions and what little he said was unintelligible. He had dragged out the investigation on her aircraft and delayed the release of the final incident report. He outranked her then, but he didn't today.

He finally sauntered into the outer office. His gaze wandered over her like he was checking out a cocktail waitress at a bar. The once-over from this tool added to her irritation.

When he saw her rank insignia, at least he had the good sense to look her in the eyes. "How can I help you, Commander?"

"Mulroney, cut the crap. I've been waiting for thirty minutes. Show me the aircraft reconstruction in your hangar and grant me unlimited access to your accident investigation files on the octocopter incident."

He cocked his head and spoke slowly, as if dealing with a child. "The investigation of your aircraft crash was closed over five years ago, and the records were archived. You can't just walk in here and demand files. You're confusing rank with authority."

"Did you read my message? If you paid any attention to the case number you'd know which incident I'm referring to."

"Where's your authorization?" asked Mulroney.

Jazmin closed the gap between her and the major. "Are you aware of the penalty for hindering an NDA investigation?" She didn't wait for an answer. "I'm certain your commanding officer does, and she won't be happy when I level that charge."

Mulroney took a closer look at the Neurotech Defense Agency badge on her uniform and his bravado evaporated. Her authority as an NDA investigator far exceeded his as the officer leading the aircraft incident investigation.

"My eyes and ears are bionic, so I have a recording of every moment since I entered the building. I just sent that video to your CO. No doubt she'll be fascinated with your fine display of less than professional behavior toward another female officer who outranks you."

"I apologize for delaying you, ma'am. Right this way." He turned, waved his arm over the biochip reader next to the hangar door and led the way. They walked by the burned wreckage of an F-35 fighter jet belonging to the Air National Guard unit at Truax Field in Madison. An area up ahead was cordoned off with a mostly destroyed octocopter surrounded by hundreds of tagged parts waiting to be assembled into something close to the original configuration. A few of the eight rotors providing lift were still largely intact along with their individual motors, though the rest had been destroyed on impact. Jazmin knew reassembly was tedious work and sometimes answers were never found.

Mulroney stopped next to two Air Force personnel who were attempting to reconstruct what was left of the flight control system. "Commander, I'd like to introduce you to Captain Carmen Hacienda and Master Sergeant Steve Roberts." Both shook hands with Jazmin. "Hacienda and Roberts have been working on this aircraft mishap from the beginning and have the best command of the details. They can assist you far better than I can." He turned to the Air Force personnel. "Commander Hassani is with the Neurotech Defense Agency, so please give her your full cooperation." He took out his tablet and swiped a few commands. "I just gave the commander real-time access to our findings. Make sure she gets anything she wants."

Hacienda and Roberts both said, "Yes, sir."

Mulroney let out his breath. "Commander, do you need anything else from me right now?" Jazmin shook her head. A moment later Mulroney's tablet beeped, and he glanced at the screen. "I'm needed on another investigation." He turned. His footsteps echoed through the cavernous building.

Jazmin didn't know if Mulroney was actually needed or just used the incoming message as an excuse to escape. She didn't care; she was just glad he was gone. She walked around the octocopter, inspecting the damage. Halfway around the aircraft, flashbacks of her own incident intruded and threw her back to the most horrifying moments of her life. She forced herself to look away from the destroyed aircraft and focused on an exit sign across the hangar. She reminded herself she was safe and could walk out that door at any time.

After taking a few slow, calming breaths, she could function again and turned back toward the wrecked octocopter. From the concerned looks from Hacienda and Roberts, Jazmin knew her face had reflected her inner turmoil. Fortunately, the two Air Force members had the courtesy not to ask her any questions. Jazmin guessed that hers wasn't an unusual reaction for anyone who'd been involved with a downed aircraft. The military used euphemisms like aircraft incidents and off-airport emergency landings. The raw truth was this was an attack on an aircraft and crew with a deadly weapon, killing everyone onboard except the pilot.

After making a full circuit around the heavily damaged and burned airframe, Jazmin said, "Captain Hacienda, please brief me on your investigation so far."

The captain used her neurotech to project a holographic image from her wrist tablet and read the report. "The OTG-12 octocopter transport gunship was on a training mission at Fort McCoy in Sparta, Wisconsin. At an altitude of 3,000 feet AGL the octocopter experienced loss of flight control, motor power, and communication. All computer controls froze, and the engine generator ceased operation, resulting in complete loss of electrical power. The pilot attempted autorotation to recover controlled flight but fly-by-wire flight controls were inoperative. At 2,000 feet AGL, the pilot pulled the eject handle. The explosive charges to separate the hub and rotor blades from the copter, along with the catapult gun to eject pilot and crew seats, failed. Total loss of lift and flight control resulted in a high velocity impact with the ground resulting in catastrophic airframe damage and loss of life for all crew members except the pilot. We interviewed the pilot in rehab, and she reported a debilitating pain in the back of her head at the time of the incident. She also reported seeing an error light flashing on the ejection system digital sequencer. The ejection system failure is something we've never seen. These aren't ever supposed to fail, and we've contacted Ejection Aerospace for a complete teardown and analysis."

Jazmin asked, "Was the manufacturer able to determine the cause of the failure?"

Hacienda shook her head. "They don't know, either. Their QA department had never seen this happen nor have they been able to replicate the failure."

Jazmin said, "I met with the pilot this morning. She experienced total neurotech failure as a result of this attack. Do you know if the flight crew's neurotech was damaged?"

Master Sergeant Roberts answered. "I checked with the medical staff, and their autopsies all showed significant neurotech damage. One of the team members was grounded by a prior injury. She wanted to stay with her team, so even though she's in a lot of pain, she's doing rehab on site. The petty officer had an active hivemind connection to the team during the exercise and described it as going blank. Total neural silence. She said she'd never experienced anything like it."

Hacienda closed the holographic screen. "Commander, we have further information on specific aircraft subsystem damage if you want more detail." The young captain's report was clinical and by the book. No doubt the same wording would be used for the aircraft incident review board's presentation.

The ejection system failure was identical to what happened to Jazmin's octocopter. Why hadn't this been reported to the accident investigation team or the manufacturer? Jazmin thought about her own experience after her aircraft crash. SEAL Team Seven recovered the black box from her copter before they blew up the aircraft to keep the copter's advanced technology out of Chinese hands. The review board only had the signal data from the aircraft carrier to determine the cause of the mission's failure. Due to complete destruction of the copter's black box data, the board relied on Jazmin's testimony on her attempt to recover aircraft control. The board's final conclusion was an unknown directed-energy weapon was fired at the copter causing catastrophic damage. As pilot in command, she was cleared of any wrongdoing and approved to return to flight duties pending her physical status.

Jazmin recovered from her sad musings and asked, "Captain, have you and Master Sergeant Roberts drawn any conclusions on what caused the loss of power and flight controls to the octocopter as well as the neurotech damage to the pilot and crew?"

"Yes and no, Commander." Hacienda walked over to the cockpit and pointed at the pilot's main control panel. "The glass panel screen supporting the computer driven flight controls is blank and the glass is smoke damaged from the inside." She pointed at some of the instruments and gauges. "All of these are frozen in place, which is typical of a directed-energy weapon."

Jazmin gestured at the panel. "You've shown me significant damage but haven't stated any conclusions or even hypotheses as to what happened. Are you far enough along in your investigation to do that?"

Hacienda hesitated, perhaps not comfortable sharing her assumptions. "The damage to flight and engine controls was consistent with an electromagnetic-pulse weapon. We checked for an air burst EMP in the area as well as evidence of an E-bomb, and we ran into a couple of anomalies that we can't explain. We couldn't find any evidence of an electromagnetic-pulse wave, certainly not one strong enough to take down a military aircraft with significant EMP shielding. Also, the neurotech damage to the pilot and crew members was too extensive for an EMP burst or an E-bomb. If our assumption was correct, then their implants would have survived intact. Theirs were completely destroyed. Commander, you're from the Neurotech Defense Agency. Do you have any idea what kind of weapon or directed-energy pulse would do that much damage?"

Jazmin shook her head. "No, I don't, but I'm going to find out." She took one more look around the cockpit for instrument and flight control damage. She compared the various technologies to implants and neurotech hardware. "Captain, were there any other reports of EMP damage?"

"No. It surprised us as there were plenty of other military assets in the area for the training exercise. The octocopter was the only aircraft hit. No other vehicles were damaged and no other personnel were injured."

"Anything else you can tell me?" Hacienda and Roberts both

shook their heads. "Thanks for your time and your candor."

Jazmin headed toward the exit. As she walked away she wondered what kind of weapon could do this. Was it the same as the one that attacked her? If so, what improvements had been made in the last five years? How did it get to the US for testing? Who was behind this weapon?

Her next interview would be with the surviving SEAL team member on the ground. Jazmin hoped she could learn something that wasn't in the official report.

Chapter 3

Fort McCoy - Sparta, Wisconsin
2 May

Jazmin's military transport car sped down the highway in the reserved government lane, headed to Fort McCoy. Using her neurotech she initiated a holographic video call to the base training group's commanding officer. The call connected and the identifier window just below the hologram showed Colonel Cristina Sanchez. The 3-D image of a serious woman in an urban camouflage uniform floated out from Jazmin's tablet.

"How can I help you, Commander?"

"I'm enroute to Fort McCoy to interview Petty Officer Second Class Sheila Ogando for a current NDA investigation."

The colonel's eyes narrowed. "Will Petty Officer Ogando require a JAG officer to represent her during your interview?"

"No Colonel, Ogando isn't in any type of legal trouble. She's a key witness to an octocopter incident resulting in the death of multiple aircrew members with only the pilot surviving."

Sanchez let out a long breath. "I saw the aftermath. It was a joint training exercise between Army Rangers and Navy SEALs. My people are going over every aspect of the exercise. This should not have happened."

Jazmin felt this wasn't a breakdown in training but something more sinister. "Colonel, I'll be on base in thirty minutes. Where can I interview Petty Officer Ogando?"

"Come to the Advanced Tactical Training Headquarters and I'll make sure Ogando's here to meet you."

"Thank you, Colonel." Jazmin ended the call, and the hologram vanished. She wasn't quite sure what she was looking for, but Ogando had an active hivemind connection to her team. Jazmin hoped she could learn something that was left out of the aircraft incident investigation.

Jazmin's thoughts wandered back to her own aircraft attack and the moment her hivemind connection was severed with her team. She had lost her military family and had never gotten them back. She had time before arriving on base, so she reviewed Ogando's service record. The petty officer was the IT expert on the team. Her specialty was hacking into enemy systems and taking control with AI bots. She was also the team's combat medic. Ogando had excellent reviews from both the team's senior NCO and her commanding officer.

The car stopped at the base entrance where a large sign displayed shields representing all of the US military services. Originally an Army base, Fort McCoy was now designated joint service, as so many military installations in the southern US had closed due to climate change. Sea level rise, hurricanes, droughts, and extreme temperatures had made ever-larger parts of the country no longer habitable. As one of the few remaining operational training bases, the base had grown exponentially in both size and importance. Security at every location had increased dramatically, due to the reduced number of military bases combined with multiple violent foreign incursions. The roadway was blocked by a reinforced twelve-foot-high gate with razor wire, along with telescoping bollards protruding from the pavement. Two guards armed with assault rifles in combat slings approached her car from each side. Weapons raised, they stood back about twenty feet from her. A sniper in a guard tower just inside the compound sighted her, their finger on the trigger.

Jazmin exited the vehicle and kept her hands visible, careful not to make any type of threatening movements as she walked to the security console. She scanned her biochip, then peered into the retinal scanner. After a moment the console light glowed green, and the security guards lowered their weapons.

A female voice coming from the speaker in the console asked, "Commander, what's the purpose of your visit?"

"I'm here to interview Petty Officer Ogando for a Neurotech Defense Agency investigation. I spoke with Colonel Sanchez prior to my arrival."

"Please proceed to the Advanced Tactical Training Headquarters building. You are not authorized for any other locations on base. If you need access to other areas, please contact Base Security for clearance."

"Understood." Jazmin got back in her vehicle. Once inside, the gate opened and the bollards retracted into the pavement. After a short drive, the vehicle stopped, and she entered the tactical training building. An admin took her to a small conference room where Ogando waited. When Jazmin entered the petty officer jumped to attention on her good leg using a single crutch for balance. "At ease. Have a seat, Petty Officer."

Ogando sat down carefully. She tried to cover her discomfort with a smile, though her face showed the pain she was in. Her eyes locked onto Jazmin's Neurotech Defense Agency shield, and her face radiated worry as well as pain. This was a typical reaction when military members saw Jazmin in uniform. NDA investigators handled neurotech abuse cases where special ops personnel used their access to bypass security systems illegally. The military came down hard any time neurotech was abused. Jazmin had ended the careers of officers and enlisted personnel who crossed that line. Sometimes she used this fear to her advantage, but today she needed to get it out of her way and get Ogando to open up.

Jazmin sat across from Ogando. "Petty officer, you don't look very happy to be alone in a room with a commander from the Neurotech Defense Agency."

Stone-faced, Ogando said, "I'm not sure why I'm here, ma'am."

"What did Colonel Sanchez tell you?"

"Nothing. One of the chiefs told me an NDA investigator was coming to see me. He gave me a pitying look and said, 'Good luck. You'll need it.'"

Jazmin laughed and continued to smile. "We have that reputation. You're not being investigated for neurotech abuse. Relax, you're not in any type of trouble. I came to talk to you about the octocopter crash involving the rest of your SEAL team. You were on a hivemind connection with them during the exercise."

Ogando looked both relieved and sad. "That was really bad, Commander."

Jazmin already knew the answer to her next question but wanted to get Ogando to open up and start talking. "How come you were on the ground during the training exercise instead of in the octocopter with the rest of your team?"

Ogando tapped the cast on her right leg. "I broke it during a helicopter fast-roping night exercise onto a building. It was windy, and when the helicopter swayed I missed the roof and hit the ground instead. It hurt like hell when my leg snapped."

"How's it healing?"

"Slowly. The surgeon installed a titanium rod. I'm in a lot of pain but the doc said I'll make a full recovery once I complete all my physical therapy."

"I've had my own rehab experiences. The doctor gave you good advice." Jazmin didn't want to share anything more.

Ogando nodded and looked a little less on edge. "Yes, ma'am."

"During the exercise when the octocopter lost power, what do you remember hearing or feeling on the hivemind connection?"

Ogando was silent for a moment, then closed her eyes as if deep in thought. When she opened them, she stared at Jazmin with an intensity common to SEAL team members. "The exercise was going as planned and the pilot, Lieutenant Macy, was approaching the landing zone. The team did one last weapons check, and everyone slid into their own pre-op ritual. I'm usually too busy with my own to notice what my teammates are doing those last seconds before go time, but I laughed when I got into their heads and heard their little rhymes to make sure they didn't forget anything." The petty officer's intense look eased into a wan smile. Jazmin didn't want to rush her, so she stayed silent.

Ogando looked away and tears formed in her eyes. "The aircraft lost power, and everyone onboard knew something was wrong. I felt their fear like I was going to die with them, then the hivemind connection cut out. They weren't dead yet, but it didn't matter, the voices and emotions were gone. It was horrible watching the octocopter slam into the ground. I'm amazed Macy survived." Ogando wiped away tears with her sleeve. She forced a stoic look back at Jazmin. "I'm sorry, Commander, they were my best friends in the world. The people who really understood me."

For the third time today Jazmin was reminded of her own loss, and it hadn't gotten any easier, though this round she stuffed it back into its locked box a little quicker. "Did the energy blast that killed your team affect your neurotech?"

Ogando thought for a moment. "I had a hell of a headache afterward, but the doc checked me and didn't find any damage."

"Do you remember anything else from that night?"

Ogando tapped her fingers repeatedly on her cast, then shook her head. "I wanted to go to the crash site but wasn't allowed. The aircraft accident investigation team was called in and everything was shipped to a hangar in Milwaukee."

Jazmin waited silently, hoping Ogando would remember something else but the petty officer said nothing more. "I just sent my contact information to your military tablet in case you remember anything else." Jazmin stood.

Ogando acknowledged receipt through her neurotech, then moved to get to her feet, but Jazmin motioned for her to stay seated. "At ease, Petty Officer. Good luck with your leg."

She hadn't learned as much as she'd hoped, though often investigations went that way. Maybe something Ogando said would be more meaningful later.

Jazmin exited the building and got into her waiting vehicle. "Take me to my apartment in Madison." The car pulled away, and Jazmin considered her next moves. She thought about her old boss during the time she had supported SEAL Team One. Ajax Papadakis had retired from the Navy and then moved to DARPA, the Defense Advanced Research Projects Agency, an organization that was part of the Department of Defense. It was an easy transition for him to be the guy developing a better spear instead of the guy wielding it. Ajax was an expert on advanced weapons, specifically DEWs, directed-energy weapons.

She'd research what she could on her own and then, depending on what she found, it might be time to pay Ajax a visit at DARPA headquarters.

Chapter 4

Truax Field - Madison, Wisconsin
3 May

As the senior Neurotech Defense Agency investigator at Truax Field, Jazmin had one of the few private offices allotted to the NDA on base. Using her Top Secret clearance she could see a list of active DARPA contracts but few details. Many of the weapon systems under development were classified as TS/SCI, Top Secret Sensitive Compartmented Information. A few programs were code-word classified. She wasn't cleared for these levels, at least not at DARPA. For these contracts she could only see company names and limited extracts of the research scope. Jazmin started with a search on DEWs, directed-energy weapons, though the high volume of DARPA research projects and dizzying list of companies that came back needed to be narrowed dramatically for her to process effectively. She quickly eliminated laser and sonic weapons, as well as research focusing strictly on disabling people. This limited the list but not enough. She next narrowed the search to EMP, electromagnetic-pulse weapons, and technology that attacked neurotech. The number of research projects and associated companies that came back was still too many to research individually, so she looked at delivery systems.

The next categories Jazmin eliminated were space-based and

ground-based systems. Hitting a ground target from space was certainly possible, though hitting a moving aircraft in congested airspace wasn't feasible yet; at least, no company had an effective targeting system for that level of precision. All of the potential ground locations that could have targeted the octocopter at Fort McCoy were on the base or otherwise under government control. This brought the list down to a handful of companies. The last filter was for demonstrated power to bring down a shielded military aircraft. Only one company remained on the list, PWL, Pulse Weapons Labs.

Her boss, Captain Bill Taylor, knocked on her open door. He smiled. "Good morning Jazmin. There's something I'd like to discuss with you. Please join me in my office."

They walked a short distance down the hall to the captain's corner office, and he motioned for her to shut the door. He sat at one of the chairs at a small round conference table and Jazmin sat across from him. His expression turned serious as he peered at her. Normally, that level of focus from a superior officer meant she was in some kind of trouble, though she didn't pick up that vibe from him today.

He said, "Tell me about your latest case. I realize this one is personal for you, and honestly, I have some concerns about your ability to keep it separate from your past."

He came across as more empathetic than challenging, though it put Jazmin on alert. She had to answer carefully. "I started work on the case yesterday morning. My first stop was to interview Lieutenant Macy, the pilot in rehab, then followed up with the accident investigation team at Mitchell. In the afternoon I interviewed the SEAL Team member on the ground at Fort McCoy."

"What key things did you learn and what are your next steps?"

"The parallels to my own unsolved incident are a little uncomfortable." They were way beyond uncomfortable, but she didn't want to admit that to her boss. "I'm looking into directed-energy weapons to see if there's a DARPA connection." She wasn't ready to discuss a possible visit to Ajax.

Taylor cocked his head and narrowed his eyes. "Normally I turn you loose and allow you to proceed however you see fit. As a commander and my senior investigator, you've earned that right. If it were anyone else, I'd assign a case like this with such personal connections to another investigator or even an officer from another location."

"I appreciate that, sir."

"There's more. I'm retiring at the end of the year, and I've been asked to name my replacement. I'm seriously considering recommending you. Think of this case as your final test. I want to make sure you have both the judgment and ability to work under intense scrutiny that the job requires. If you replace me, the job goes with a promotion to captain, but you'd no longer be authorized further flight hours. If you have any thoughts of returning to a flying role, let me know before I put in my recommendation."

"Thank you, sir. I'll give this careful thought."

Taylor stood, indicating their meeting was over. She left his office, closing the door behind her.

She had mixed emotions about Taylor's news. She'd become an investigator because she couldn't face going back into combat, and while she'd relish the promotion to captain, she wasn't sure her boss's job was one she wanted. While she didn't want to return to combat, the thought of giving up flying all together was depressing. Being in the cockpit of a military aircraft was the place she was happiest and most engaged in life.

***

Back in her office, this time with the door closed, she started an unclassified internet search on Pulse Weapons Labs. All she could find was a business listing showing their headquarters were in Chicago. Their website showed they were in the defense industry but no further details. Logging into the DARPA IT network using her Neurotech Defense Agency credentials showed an active research contract for directed-energy weapons, but when she clicked on both the scope of the research and the value of the contract a warning flashed on screen. *TS/SCI Clearance required for further information.* She didn't expect to see a lot of detail, but the fact that everything was classified got her attention.

Jazmin wanted to learn more, so she launched AI search bots to scour the internet and dark web for background information and videos on Pulse Weapons Labs. It was a small company and the two founding members, CEO Sanjay Guptarian and Chief Technical Officer Rogo Blozard were all over the dark web. Each video featuring them was a new horror show with the pair demonstrating their directed-energy weapons technology, accompanied by approving heads of rogue nations or terrorist organizations reveling in their newfound destructive power. One video even looked like a commercial created for the US DOD. It showed a Chinese rocket with multiple warheads streaking across the sky at high altitude. The rocket turned toward New York City, then the trajectory became unstable and it crashed in a remote wooded area in upstate New York. A message in bold print appeared on the screen, *Advanced Directed-Energy Weapons can protect our air space against automated enemy aircraft and missiles.* Another video clip played. This one showed a flight of four fighter jets in an attack formation. An energy beam from above flashed on the aircraft and they veered uncontrollably off course. Two collided with each other and two impacted the ground.

The images triggered a terrifying flashback of her own aircraft crash and of the unbearable pain from the resulting fire. She spun her chair around to stare at her "I love me" wall. Jazmin focused on her awards and photos of happier times to bring her back to the present. She took several deep breaths and let them out slowly to calm her anxiety.

Once she was ready to continue, Jazmin dug further into the two founders' backgrounds. Guptarian and Blozard both had come to the US as students and earned their PhDs in physics from Stanford and MBAs from Harvard. During a recession, the US government had been desperate for economic stimulus, so Congress approved changes to the EB-5 Immigrant Investor Program. Instead of awarding permanent residence, the program granted US citizenship. Any immigrant who invested a minimum of 100 million dollars to start a new US company and passed a background check was eligible for this program. Jazmin checked PWL's incorporation papers which showed an initial investment of 250 million. Both men were granted US citizenship. Jazmin wasn't able to find the source of the money, but the sponsor for the visas was Senator Ling Chen Jiang, the chair of the Armed Services Committee. This might explain how a sketchy company like PWL could get approved for a classified DARPA project. The military industrial complex comprised some strange bedfellows, and PWL certainly met that definition.

Jazmin called the Pulse Weapons Labs office in Chicago expecting an AI video chatbot to answer. Surprisingly, the video call was picked up immediately and her phone verified she was speaking to a real person, not an AI interface. One of the advantages of working for the Neurotech Defense Agency was the NSA grade smartphone she carried which could accurately make this determination.

A young woman, her head covered in a luxurious hijab and wearing a colorful designer silk dress, answered. "Pulse Weapons Labs, how can I help you, Commander Hassani?"

The personal identification put Jazmin on instant alert. The caller identification on the other end should only have shown the Department of Defense. This meant PWL also had NSA-grade communication equipment. "I'd like to make an appointment to see Rogo Blozard. I have a few questions about PWL technology for a current investigation."

The polished young woman said, "I'm sorry, Dr. Blozard is currently out of the country."

"When will he be back?"

"I don't have Dr. Blozard's itinerary, though I believe he will be gone for several weeks."

Having underlings lie for people who didn't want to speak with investigators was common, so Jazmin studied the young woman's face for signs of deceit. She didn't observe any telltale eye movements or facial expressions, nor could her phone's AI detection algorithms. Jazmin wanted to speak with the technical brains of the company but wasn't willing to wait weeks for that to happen. "Tell Sanjay Guptarian I'm coming to your office tomorrow morning at nine to see him and get my questions answered."

A frosty expression flashed on the woman's face then faded to neutral. "I'll let Dr. Guptarian know." She ended the call.

The receptionist's vague answers made Jazmin doubt Blozard's whereabouts. She checked passport control, though system records were focused on people entering the country instead of those on outbound flights. She checked commercial flight manifests from the last thirty days and found nothing, though he could have flown privately or left by ship. Jazmin wondered if he was actually outside the US or just had a strong reason he didn't want to be seen.

Another possibility was Blozard traveling on another country's passport. After further checking, she found he was a citizen of three different countries and went by different names in each one. Searches on the name and country combinations resulted in no new information. The information vacuum tripped more alarms for her.

Checking the passport system and flight manifests was as far as Jazmin could go at this point. Without evidence of a crime, she had no authority to dig further into Blozard's travels or personal life.

She shut down her computer and went for a run to burn off the adrenaline surging through her body. Feeling no relief, she changed course and headed to the Truax Field athletic center. There were no military members in the boxing room, so she had the robot fight trainer tape up her hands and lace up her boxing gloves. The sizable, well-maintained space had two professional boxing rings. Off to one side was another area lined with heavyweight punching bags and speed bags. Despite multiple fans turning overhead, the room smelled of stale sweat.

Jazmin hit a heavyweight punching bag slowly at first, then sped up her onslaught. At first she forced herself to only use her hands, then gave into her rage over what she knew about PWL and their possible connection to killing her SEAL team. She attacked the bag with her bionic legs, and it was no match for her anger. Sand, sawdust, and shredded cloth exploded from the ripped leather cover before her final kick tore the bag from its chain. Physically spent and panting, all that remained of her ersatz opponent were the heavy metal chain links swinging from the ceiling.

No doubt her boss would get a report on Jazmin's destructive behavior. It wouldn't be a point in her favor showing how well she handles stress.

Chapter 5

Pulse Weapons Labs Chicago Office
4 May

Jazmin arrived at the PWL Chicago office and showed her Neurotech Defense Agency badge to the receptionist, the same woman who had answered her video call the day before. The woman gave Jazmin an appraising look, though remained expressionless herself. "Good morning Commander Hassani, Dr. Guptarian is expecting you. He's finishing up a meeting and will be done in a few minutes." She pointed. "You may wait over there." The young woman's tone was cool, and she didn't engage Jazmin in further conversation.

The office was opulently decorated and looked more like it belonged to a billionaire hedge fund manager than a defense company. The mix of lovingly restored antique furniture interspersed with high-tech devices gave the waiting area a curious vibe, as if the company existed in the realm of an old civilization, yet with the power of modern technology. Discreetly located video cameras and recording devices were everywhere, well-placed to capture careless customer conversations.

Holographic screens with product specifications and videos of PWL devices in operation continuously popped up in midair throughout the waiting area, all carefully choreographed for maximum customer impact. The videos prominently featured groups loathed by most US citizens. They showed terrorist organizations, the Chinese Navy attacking US ships in international waters near manmade islands in the South China Sea, and a North Korean atomic missile launch team. PWL devices were shown bringing these groups' evil plans to a halt. After Jazmin waited about fifteen minutes, Sanjay Guptarian emerged from the back offices. The advertisement loop had just started again, so his timing wasn't a coincidence.

Guptarian's face lit up with an obviously well-rehearsed smile. "Commander Hassani, I'm so sorry to keep you waiting. I was dealing with an urgent customer issue and couldn't break away." He stuck out his hand. "I'm delighted to meet you. How can I be of service to the Neurotech Defense Agency?" His handshake was firm, though not crushing, and his penetrating, intelligent eyes appeared to miss nothing.

"I'm working on an investigation. A US Navy octocopter was attacked during a training mission with what appears to be a directed-energy weapon. The ensuing crash killed ten aircrew members and the lone survivor, the pilot, suffered life-threatening injuries."

Guptarian gently touched Jazmin's arm. "I'm so sorry to hear that. This must be a very difficult assignment for you. How can I help?"

"I have some questions about PWL weapon systems. Is there a place we can speak privately?"

He pointed to a short hall off the reception area. "Right this way." He led her to an expansive corner office with a spectacular view of the Chicago skyline and Lake Michigan in the distance. The office had floor to ceiling windows and display cabinets with PWL product models interspersed with an array of medieval weapons that looked more Asian in origin than European. Once inside, the office door slid silently closed behind them. Guptarian gestured toward two upholstered chairs covered in a colorful mosaic design, and they sat across from each other. Guptarian said, "The human side is the toughest part of my job. Employing our products often results in injuries or loss of life. When it's our enemies we can justify it but, with rare exception, everyone who dies is mourned by someone. What would you like to know, Commander?"

Guptarian came across as a kind, caring individual, though Jazmin wondered if he was a psychopath, a man who would tell her whatever she needed to hear.

"I'd like to know more about your technology and had hoped to speak with Rogo Blozard this morning."

"I'm sorry, Dr. Blozard is traveling on business out of the country. Perhaps you could speak with him when he returns."

A delaying tactic. "Perhaps there's someone else I could speak with or arrange a video call."

"I'm sorry, there's really no one else you can speak with. We're a small company and Dr. Blozard is the only person with the technical depth and intimate knowledge of our products to help with something as important as an NDA investigation."

A non-answer. "What about a video call?"

Guptarian leaned forward with a look of grave concern. "Unfortunately, I'm not in a position to arrange that right now. Dr. Blozard is traveling to countries where we can't guarantee our communication security. Other nations have no regard for privacy, and as good as our encryption algorithms are, it seems other countries with little regard for the rule of law are one step ahead of us. Until Dr. Blozard is back in the United States where we have access to US government secure systems, it's a risk we can't afford to take."

The guy was doing his best to delay answering any questions. "The incident I'm investigating appears to be the result of an unknown directed-energy weapon. Because of the damage to the aircraft avionics and flight control systems, we thought it might be an electromagnetic-pulse weapon. This theory didn't hold up because of the neurotech implant damage to the pilot and aircrew members, as well as the pinpoint accuracy of the attack. No other military vehicles or personnel were hit." Jazmin paused before continuing, weighing how much to push Guptarian. He'd been evasive so far. His reaction to her next question would tell the story. "Is what I described something PWL weapons are capable of?"

Guptarian's affable manner evaporated. "Commander, are you insinuating that PWL had something to do with the incident you're investigating? Our company would like to do business with the US Department of Defense, so I agreed to meet with you. I'm very disturbed by your question. PWL has worked hard to show we would be a good partner to US armed forces in their mission to protect our country."

Good, she'd hit a nerve. "I thought you were already doing business with the defense department. Don't you have a contract with DARPA?"

Guptarian's expression darkened. "That's not a question I can answer. PWL interactions are all protected by non-disclosure agreements and appropriate security clearances. You have neither of those on file with us nor does the Neurotech Defense Agency. I'm sorry, but I really can't go further with this conversation." He made a show of checking the time on his Breguet watch, then stood. "I have an appointment with an important customer."

The office door slid open and a large, fit, man stood in the doorway. A shoulder holster was visible under his unbuttoned suit jacket, and he moved like a commando as he entered the room. "Mr. Gutierrez, our chief of security, will escort you out. I'll discuss your concerns with Dr. Blozard when he returns and see if there's any help we can provide. That's the best I can do unless I get specific approval from our US government contacts for full technical disclosure. Good day, Commander."

Jazmin looked from one man to the other then stood. "Thank you for your time, Dr. Guptarian." She suppressed a smile. If security was escorting her out, it was time to dig further.

Her next step would be a visit to DARPA to find out what Ajax knew about PWL. He'd have the security clearance to see the details Jazmin couldn't.

Hopefully their past relationship was strong enough for him to share those secrets.

Chapter 6

Truax Field - Madison, Wisconsin
DARPA Headquarters
5 May

To keep her pilot qualifications current, Jazmin flew as often as possible. Today's flight was to DARPA headquarters in Arlington, Virginia, to see her old boss and mentor from the Navy, Captain Ajax Papadakis. She hoped his work at DARPA would give him access to the classified information Jazmin needed and he'd be willing to share it with her. She stopped on the taxiway to hold short of the runway with her F-22 fighter jet's engines running. With her pre-flight checklist complete, she waited for clearance from the Truax Field tower. Her hope for an immediate departure deflated when the military air traffic controller's instruction on her aircraft's radio broke through the engine noise. "Pegasus hold short runway 36, traffic is a commercial jet five miles on final."

"Pegasus copies, continuing to hold short runway 36." She tapped the throttles with her fingertips and stopped herself from prematurely pushing them to full military power. Though Jazmin had far more hours flying octocopters and quadcopters as a special ops pilot, her first love was fighters. The five-point harness held her firmly in place, even when flying inverted, and the updated helmet display allowed her to see through her aircraft. She could look in any direction, even down at the floor and cameras mounted on the fuselage gave her a clear view as if the jet was invisible. The 1st Fighter Wing was the active-duty Air Force arm on base. Back-to-back hurricanes had destroyed Joint Base Langley – Eustis, the historical home of the 1st Fighter Wing, and what was left of the two fighter squadrons had been relocated from Hampton, Virginia, to Madison, Wisconsin. The 27th Fighter Squadron flew the remaining F-22 fighters, and the 94th Fighter Squadron flew F-35 fighter jets. The Air National Guard 115th Fighter Wing, the original unit at Truax, also flew F-35 fighter jets.

The Navy wanted Jazmin to maintain her piloting skills, so she trained on the F-22 and had to fly five sorties a month to maintain her Basic Mission Capable rate. While Jazmin had no desire to go back into combat, she still loved flying high-performance aircraft. She had a special fondness for older jets, and the F-22 was perfect. The engines had been converted to burn low emission bio-jet fuel, but otherwise the aircraft still had most of their original avionics. Her neurotech couldn't access the old systems directly, so it was a totally different flying experience than her hands-off mind control of an octocopter.

When the slow-moving commercial jet finally landed and exited the runway, the military air traffic controller said the magic words, "Pegasus, you're cleared for takeoff."

Jazmin taxied to the runway's centerline then advanced the throttles on the Pratt & Whitney jet engines to full power. The fighter accelerated down the runway and pressed her into the seat with the force of two g's. As soon as she was at takeoff velocity, she eased the stick back and the wheels lifted off the ground. She brought up her landing gear and climbed at a steep angle until she punched through the cloud deck into blue sky. One thing Jazmin loved about being a pilot was that if she flew high enough, it was always a sunny day.

She leveled off at fifty thousand feet and throttled back to cruise power. At full power her F-22 fighter could fly at Mach 2, over 1500 miles per hour, but she'd burn through all of her fuel before arriving at her destination. Jazmin enjoyed the break from her usual duties and took the opportunity to hand fly the aircraft to improve her piloting skills instead of relying on the autopilot.

Near her destination, she was cleared for a straight in approach to Joint Base Andrews Naval Air Facility in Prince George's County,

Maryland. After landing she exited the aircraft and stowed her flight suit, helmet, and flying boots in the hangar. Leaving the building, she was greeted by a group of young aircraft mechanics who surrounded her plane for a rare look at an aging fighter jet. One of the crew chiefs came forward. "We'll take good care of your F-22, Commander. I'll check it over and top it off with bio-jet fuel, so you'll have plenty of gas for the ride home."

"Thanks, Sergeant. I'll be back in a few hours."

Jazmin walked away from the flightline and used her neurotech to request a military transport vehicle. A few minutes later a car arrived, and she got in the back. "DARPA headquarters, please." On the drive Jazmin reviewed notes from her interviews with Lieutenant Macy at the Joint Military Rehab Facility, Captain Hacienda at the crash reconstruction hangar, and Petty Officer Ogando at Fort McCoy.

The car dropped Jazmin off in front of DARPA headquarters and she entered the thirteen-story glass and chrome facility. The security desk was just inside the door and the armed guard said, "Please scan your biochip and retina." She waved her left forearm over the biochip reader and the screen pulsed green. Next she looked into the retinal scanner with her right eye. The device registered her bionic eye's unique pattern, and the screen pulsed green. The guard's stern expression softened. "You're all set Commander. Remember, you must be escorted at all times by a DARPA employee."

A couple of minutes later, Ajax arrived, his face lit up with a smile, and he wrapped her in a bear hug. He was still slim and athletic, though now he was gray at the temples and his face had more lines than when she had last seen him. He said, "Follow me," and they walked in silence down a long hallway, then took an elevator to the third floor. Security cameras tracked their way through the facility, reminding Jazmin of the nature of the defense work done here. When they arrived at his office, Ajax shut the door and locked it. Despite his friendly demeanor, she felt a sense of paranoia radiating from him.

He said, "Let me get a good look at you. I'd like to see what kind of job they did putting you back together."

"Where do you want to start? My eyes, ears, and legs are bionic, and my head and face are covered with synthetic skin and hair. I'm the perfect cyborg. I look human but most of me isn't." Jazmin raised her arms waist high and slowly turned like a contestant at a beauty pageant showing off for the judges, but she felt like a carnival freak. "I can do things most people can't. Anywhere I have prosthetics or synthetic skin I can turn my pain receptors down. My face is changeable so I can dramatically alter my appearance. My legs are extendable, giving me several more inches of height to further change my profile."

"I bet that's useful on cases when you need to protect your identity."

Jazmin sighed. "Yes, though it's creepy to not recognize the face staring back at me in the mirror."

He squeezed her arm. "You're still you underneath." He looked at her appreciatively, though in fatherly way so it didn't feel intrusive. "I hope you thanked the doctors and physical therapists at the rehab facility. They did a beautiful job."

She grimaced. "Better than new."

He cocked his head. "But you'd trade in your high-tech parts and superhuman performance for original equipment."

"In a heartbeat." Her light mood at seeing her old mentor darkened.

Ajax leaned forward. "It's been a long time since we've seen each other in person. How are you doing on the inside?"

Jazmin didn't answer right away. She bit back her usual "just fine." "Not very good. Some wounds never heal."

Ajax pointed to a couple of stuffed chairs near the window. She sank into one and he sat across from her. "How can I help you? You mentioned an NDA investigation, though you weren't specific on what you needed."

"I'm working on a case and need help with directed-energy weapons." Jazmin leaned forward in her chair. "What do you know about Pulse Weapons Labs? Did they develop highly accurate EMP weapons, or do they use a different technology?"

His smile evaporated and his expression became guarded. "Why do you want to know?"

"I'm working on a case that mirrors what happened at the Chinese base on Mischief Reef. The circumstances, aircraft damage, and crew injuries are exactly like the weapon that hit my team. The two incidents are over five years and half a world apart, but I can't let go of the feeling they are somehow connected."

"Did this weapon affect your neural implants?" asked Ajax.

"Yes, completely destroyed them. Left behind scar tissue too.

My brother, Enrique, is an expert on non-military neurotech, so he tracked down the best military neurotech surgeon in the country to operate on me while he scrubbed in and watched. The surgeon spoke with me afterward and admitted she had a rough time replacing my implants."

Ajax raised his eyebrows. "That doesn't sound like damage from an EMP weapon. Neural implants aren't silicone based, like IC chips."

"If an EMP weapon didn't do this to me, then what the hell did?"

"It would require a different technology and extremely high power to destroy your implants. Implants are neurotransmitters, effectively high-tech wiring for nerve signals." Ajax moved to his desk chair and activated his computer by waving his biochipped arm over the reader. After a few mouse clicks he completed a retinal scan. His screen lit up with *DARPA Project Executive Summaries*. In bold letters, *Top Secret/SCI* flashed on the screen. "We're not supposed to share this data with outsiders, though I'll make an exception for you. Keep what I'm about to show you out of your official NDA investigation report. That will protect both of us."

Jazmin nodded. "This never happened." Standing behind him, she leaned over his shoulder to get a better view of the screen. Any concern she had about Ajax completely trusting her evaporated, as he knew her bionic eyes and ears recorded evidence for later retrieval. The kind of evidence that would land him in serious trouble.

Ajax searched for directed-energy weapons with Pulse Weapons Labs as the prime contractor, then he clicked on a secure link. *Top Secret DARPA Cleared Individuals Only* flashed on the screen. "A colleague of mine is the primary researcher assigned to PWL. I've attended a couple of meetings where they showcased their weapon systems. The demonstrations I saw were both impressive and scary. What's worse is the CEO made it abundantly clear his technology will go to anyone willing to pay full price."

Jazmin asked, "Do you think there are unsanctioned tests going on?"

Ajax sighed. "It wouldn't surprise me. These guys made my skin crawl. My colleague mentioned testing by off-book black ops teams but didn't share any details."

"I visited their offices in Chicago yesterday hoping to see their chief technology officer, Rogo Blozard. He was conveniently traveling out of the country and was unavailable for the foreseeable future. Instead, I met with their CEO, Sanjay Guptarian. He provided non-answers for every question, told me he couldn't speak with me further until I signed a non-disclosure agreement, and then their chief of security escorted me out the door."

"Jazmin, be careful with these guys. I've heard some really disturbing things about their dealings with other countries and even with terrorist groups. People vanished or came to a gruesome end."

Jazmin said, "I found videos on the dark web demonstrating their technology."

"I've seen them too. Glad I'm not assigned to this project."

"Why are we working with them?" asked Jazmin.

"PWL has the most advanced technology on the market and a powerful senator is sponsoring them."

She pointed at the display screen. "I want to know more about PWL, especially test scenarios."

Ajax turned to face the screen and clicked on the PWL project details. The screen flashed in red *Insufficient Clearance Level— Code Word Classified* then he was booted completely out of the system. *User Locked Out Pending Security Review* displayed in red, then faded to black after a few seconds.

Ajax logged off his computer. "Looks like I'll be having a visit from the security team."

Jazmin stepped back from his desk. "I'm sorry to get you into trouble."

"They'll know you were here, but it would be better if you're gone when they arrive." Ajax stood and put his hand on the doorknob. "I'll walk you down to the front security desk and out."

Ajax led the way, and they walked in silence. She hadn't learned as much as she'd hoped, though she did confirm she needed to learn a lot more about PWL. The fact that Ajax was rattled kept her focused and determined. His troubled expression was the last thing she saw before heading outside.

Chapter 7
Mei Chan

Chinese Military Intelligence Headquarters
6 May

The report from Mei Chan's chief of staff captured the Chinese Military Intelligence officer's full attention. As a general, only the most serious threats warranted her time. She cleared the room of her staff to deal with the alarming series of events that had transpired over the last three days in the US. Due to the twelve hour time difference between Beijing and Washington, DC, she was half a day ahead of America. While it was morning for her, it was still evening the day before in Washington.

American Navy Commander Jazmin Hassani had downloaded extensive information on Pulse Weapons Labs from the dark web. Mei had been tracking Hassani for years, ever since the American had been the sole survivor of a Chinese military-sponsored directed-energy weapons test using PWL technology. The fact that she survived had always weighed on Mei's mind as a dormant threat. The problem had grown when Hassani became a Neurotech Defense Agency investigator.

Pulse Weapons Labs ties to China were both beneficial and problematic. PWL developed technology that was superior to all of their competitors, and China wanted exclusive access, but no amount of money or threats had changed Sanjay Guptarian's policy of selling to any group who paid his asking price, no matter how dangerous or unstable they were. The man simply didn't care whom he empowered with this frightening technology.

Unfortunately, Hassani had visited PWL headquarters in Chicago. Years ago, Mei had prudently put a number of safeguards in place, including monitoring PWL's office security systems and adding their head of security to her payroll. Mei watched a replay of the meeting between Hassani and Guptarian, ending with her being escorted out the door by security. Mei knew by Hassani's history that the American Navy officer wouldn't stop digging. Hassani's next move was to visit her old commander, Ajax Papadakis, a directed-energy weapons researcher at DARPA.

Mei picked up her phone and called her chief of staff. "Colonel Ming, I want twenty-four- hour electronic surveillance on Jazmin Hassani."

"I expected this request. We are monitoring all of Hassani's communications."

"Excellent. Keep me informed." She ended the call.

Next, Mei placed an encrypted call to US Senator Ling Chen Jiang. "Jazmin Hassani visited PWL and DARPA as part of a Neurotech Defense Agency investigation. Shut it down."

Mei didn't wait for a reply and ended the call.

Chapter 8
Jazmin Hassani

Senate Offices – Washington, DC
7 May

At 0500 Jazmin woke from a fitful sleep to the sound of pounding on her apartment door, the kind that immediately preceded a battering ram. She pulled on a robe, picked up her .45 caliber handgun, and chambered a round. It was her military service weapon and tied to her biochip. The firing pin would only engage when the gun was in her hand, making it useless for anyone else. She checked the door camera and saw a man and woman in dark suits with shoulder holsters peeking out from under their jackets. Jazmin opened the door just far enough to see out and kept her gun out of sight. The woman said, "Good morning Commander Hassani, we're from Senator Jiang's security team and we're here to escort you to Washington, DC for your meeting with her."

Jazmin scanned their faces with her bionic eyes. Their official photos and bios popped up in a holographic window only she could see. The pair were who they claimed to be, private security for a powerful US senator, and both were ex-special forces. She'd expected a response after her trip to PWL and DARPA, though she was surprised by the speed. "I don't have a meeting with the senator."

The woman held up her tablet with an official summons from

Senator Ling Chen Jiang. "Our plane leaves in fifteen minutes. We'll wait in the hallway while you change into your uniform." There was no question of her compliance.

***

The private jet taxied to the runway as soon as they boarded and was first in line for takeoff from Truax field, ahead of four F-35 fighter jets. After landing at Joint Base Andrews, they took a black SUV to Jiang's senate office. After Jazmin was escorted into the office, Senator Jiang came out from behind her ornate desk and extended her hand. "Good morning, Commander Hassani. Thanks for coming to Washington on such short notice."

Like she had any choice.

Jiang flashed an icy smile and gestured to the visitor's chair. "Have a seat."

Jazmin remained standing until the senator sat behind her antique desk. Jiang was a small woman, and both the desk and chair were on a raised platform so she could look down on any seated visitor. Video photo frames showing rotating images of the senator with US presidents, world leaders, and general officers from every service branch broadcast Jiang's close alignment with the world's power brokers. Intricate models of key weapon systems filled glass cabinets lining the walls, each a tiny showroom for a tier one defense contractor. In contrast to these symbols of raw power were beautiful framed Chinese calligraphy, all signed by the artist, Ling Chen Jiang. Everything on display was there for a specific purpose with nothing left to chance.

Jiang studied Jazmin for a moment. "I received a call from Sanjay Guptarian at Pulse Weapons Labs. He was very concerned about your investigation. He was horrified by what you shared and inquired if I could help."

Jazmin kept a neutral expression. This was pure political theater. No senator reacted this quickly to constituent requests. Jazmin's inquiry mattered to Jiang; the question was why. "Thank you for your interest, Senator, though I'm surprised that the chair of the Armed Services Committee would be personally involved with a routine Neurotech Defense Agency investigation."

Jiang leaned forward. "Normally I wouldn't be, but when I saw your name, I took a special interest. I remember the first time we met, when you applied to the Naval Academy. I knew after our interview you were a young woman headed for a great military career. I was proud to be your sponsor, to attend your commissioning ceremony, and to follow your career. I was also delighted to learn of your miraculous recovery after your aircraft was attacked."

"Thank you, Senator." Jazmin seriously doubted Jiang had remembered her. Other than a perfunctory meeting when she applied to the Naval Academy, Jazmin had never seen or heard from Jiang. Her only clear memory from their single meeting was Jiang's insistence on only recommending young women for the service academies. The percent of women attending and graduating from college had outstripped men for decades, so the senator felt these numbers should be reflected at the service academies. She had gone on to explain that one of her legislative causes was parity for women in leadership roles in both government and business.

Jazmin decided to go along with the charade. "Can you tell me about Pulse Weapons Labs' relationship with the defense department?"

Jiang rolled her eyes. "Guptarian and PWL made a lot of interesting claims about their proprietary technology and even signed an exploratory contract with DARPA. PWL's weapon systems didn't perform anywhere close to their claims, and their contract was terminated."

Jazmin doubted what Jiang just said because the DARPA secure website showed PWL as an active project. Why would the senator lie about this? "Senator, the attack on the aircraft and aircrew I'm investigating points to a directed-energy weapon similar to an EMP attack, though with more extensive damage and pinpoint accuracy. I'm simply trying to gather more information on what kind of weapon could do this and which companies are developing the capability. Since PWL came up in my research, I went to them first."

Jiang steepled her fingers. "I scanned through your case notes. The questions you raised are quite troubling, and that's the biggest reason I wanted to meet with you today."

Even as a senator, Jiang wouldn't have access to her case notes. This revelation shocked Jazmin, putting her on instant alert. She forced herself not to react. This was personal for Jiang and Jazmin had to find out why, so she'd continue playing along.

"Senator, do you think Pulse Weapons Labs, or their technology, is tied to this incident in any way?"

Jiang shook her head. "Their technology isn't capable of this. They were more at the concept stage than executing anything this sophisticated, despite their aspirational marketing videos. I reached out to the Defense Intelligence Agency director, Lieutenant General Trabago. He's heard rumblings about Chinese weapons technology that lines up with your findings. If there's anything more than rumors, I'm sure his office will share that information with the NDA."

Jiang stood. "Sorry to cut this short, Commander. I have other urgent matters to deal with." The office door behind Jazmin opened and the same security detail who escorted her to Washington stood in the doorway.

As Jazmin got to her feet, she saw a look exchanged between the senator and her security team. Her exit had been well choreographed to cut off any further questions. Jazmin said, "I appreciate you meeting with me and for alerting the DIA." As soon as Jazmin and her escorts exited the office, the door closed behind them and the locks clicked in place.

***

After they escorted Jazmin back to Joint Military Base Andrews for the trip home and ensured she was strapped into her seat on the private jet, the security agents exited the aircraft. Alone in the plane, Jazmin replayed the meeting with the senator in her mind. She had an overwhelming sense that nothing Jiang said or did could be taken at face value. There was a hidden agenda. Everything happened too quickly and too easily. The most troubling thought was that Jiang was personally involved in the attack.

Early in her military career Jazmin had been impressed by senior officers and high-ranking politicians. These men and women always seemed in control, both impressively well informed and cool under fire. As Jazmin gained command experience and rose through the ranks herself, she learned to look beyond the polished veneer of authority and self-assuredness. Beneath the shiny exterior lived doubt, fear, incompetence, and a dangerous streak of self-preservation, the dark underbelly of power.

Senator Jiang displayed all of these weaknesses in abundance, especially the fierce drive to protect herself, no matter the cost.

Chapter 9

Madison, Wisconsin
8 May

Jazmin was in her office when the secure call indicator lit up on her smartphone, though surprisingly, from an unknown number. Encrypted calls on military phones were only allowed from known sources, so she thought there might be an issue with her device. The caller said, "Hello Jaz."

She hadn't heard this voice in years, though she instantly knew who it was. The one person who could anonymously call a military encrypted phone. The last time they spoke, when Jazmin was in rehab, she told him she didn't want to hear from him again, and she hadn't until today. They had a past and, while there were things she missed about him, there were far more she didn't.

"Hello, Harry. It's been a long time."

"It has. As much as it hurt, I stayed away. You need to hear this."

Jazmin gripped her phone wondering what prompted Harry Dexter to come out of hiding. "I'm listening."

"Ajax was found dead this morning in his condo. Police are treating it as a suicide."

When Jazmin had real eyes, they would have teared up at this news, though her bionic eyes stayed perfectly dry and clear, no matter how distraught she felt. It was another reminder of the humanity she'd lost. Her hands shook and she felt like someone had just punched her. "I just saw Ajax. He wasn't suicidal or anywhere close."

"I read the police crime scene report." The fact that Harry had access to the police report didn't surprise Jazmin. He was a sorcerer when it came to hacking into secure systems. Nothing was safe from him.

"What did you learn?" she asked.

"Whoever did this tied it up in a bow for the police. It was textbook suicide, including a note, though even before the medical examiner arrived, the FBI showed up and claimed they had federal jurisdiction because Ajax worked for DARPA."

Jazmin said, "Even though his research didn't involve the company I'm interested in, he warned me about them. He was afraid of getting too closely involved. The FBI claiming jurisdiction sounds like a cover-up." A wave of guilt slammed her. She knew she'd regret asking her next question. There were so many reasons to leave Harry in the past, but she wanted answers, and Harry was good at slithering into dark corners and finding the truth. "Can we meet?"

"It's a beautiful day outside. I'll find you." He ended the call.

***

Jazmin sat on a bench near Lake Mendota where the sun shimmered off the water and a pleasant breeze kept her cool. A memory played in her head of Ajax coaching her on how to handle friction between her and two of the senior NCOs on her team after a mission went sideways. He'd said, "You can't force them to change. You just have to show them your way is better." She had taken his advice, and he had been right. She'd miss her old mentor.

Ten minutes later Harry arrived like a spirit, with a bag of fresh croissants and hazelnut coffee. Smiling, he handed a cup to her. "Just the way you like it, dark and sweet." This familiar phrase brought back memories of better times.

She breathed in the caffeinated aroma and took a sip. Harry handed her a warm croissant wrapped in a napkin. She tore off a piece and put it in her mouth, then licked the crumbs and butter from her fingers. "This tastes wonderful, Harry, but I wish we were here for a different reason."

"Me too." He sat next to her on the wooden bench, took a sip of coffee, and ate his croissant. They enjoyed a companionable silence as they had so many times in the past, though they were different people now. Life had scarred them both. A few minutes later, he crumpled the empty croissant bag and napkins, then threw them in the water. Jazmin couldn't believe he'd just thrown trash in the lake, but the instant the bag of greasy napkins hit the water, it dissolved. A moment later every trace was gone.

"The ultimate in biodegradable packaging," Harry said. He brushed a crumb from Jazmin's cheek. There was a time when an intimate gesture like that was normal for them, though that day had passed. Harry must have felt it too because he pulled away and faced her. His expression went from warm and tender back to his ever-present poker face. "Tell me about your DARPA visit."

"I'm working on an NDA investigation tied to a downed aircraft by a directed-energy weapon. I thought there might be a DARPA connection, so I flew to Washington to see if Ajax could tell me anything."

Harry took a sip of his coffee. "What did you learn?"

"Directed-energy weapons are Ajax's area of expertise but the company I'm interested in, PWL, Pulse Weapons Labs, isn't one of his projects. He accessed a classified database but even with his TS/SCI clearance, he couldn't see anything more because it was code-word classified. Unfortunately, just trying to get access tripped a security alert."

"That certainly alerted the wrong people."

"The day before I saw Ajax, I met the PWL CEO at their Chicago office. After a short meeting, his head of security escorted me out."

Harry laughed. "So you haven't lost your charm."

Jazmin playfully backhanded Harry in the mouth but he caught her hand and held it until she quit struggling. He squeezed it, then let go. At least Harry's playful streak hadn't been stamped out when his military career came to an ignominious end.

Harry said, "And then you met with Senator Ling Chen Jiang."

"Have you been stalking me?" She said it with a smile. It wasn't a serious concern. Part of her knew that Harry would never quite let go of their relationship and would keep tabs on her. As long as he kept his distance, she'd tolerate it.

"No more than usual." His tone conveyed a coldness, an echo from when their relationship ended, and the residue of Harry's anger raised her hackles. Her concern for his reappearance just ticked up a notch.

She sighed. "I was summoned to Washington by the senator, and she steered me away from PWL."

Harry threw his coffee cup in the lake, resulting in the same magic as the bag. "Did you know Senator Jiang is on PWL's board of directors?"

Jazmin shook her head. "No I didn't, though that doesn't surprise me."

"The senator is on the boards of several defense companies, though she never uses her real name. Her offshore bank accounts all have deposits from the tier one defense contractors and even more from the tier two and three companies that want to move up the food chain."

"I thought you'd gotten out of the spy business," she said.

"I never really left. The difference now is I get to pick which jobs and clients I take on."

Jazmin thought about Harry, their relationship, and why she'd ended it. He was a curious mix of guardian angel, stalker, and ex-lover who still cared for her. While Harry was fiercely loyal to his friends, his brutal side came out to deal with his enemies. In some of his darker moments, he'd shared the details of his enhanced interrogations of his targets. Harry had tortured men and women in disgusting ways to get the answers he needed. He had the stomach to do things others wouldn't.

She had loved him and part of her still did, though Jazmin wasn't sure she trusted him anymore. Worse yet, she didn't know if she could trust herself. When she looked in the mirror, she saw a cyborg, though she felt like an android. She was no longer human. It was a struggle to be here with Harry. She was sexually attracted to him while at the same time repulsed by what she'd become.

Jazmin pulled back from her sad musings. She asked the question she wasn't sure she wanted answered. "What do you think really happened to Ajax?"

"Our friend tripped an alarm when he poked into that classified database and spooked the wrong people. Senator Jiang called in a black bag team to stop any further inquiries."

Another wave of guilt slammed her, and her hands started shaking again. She tried unsuccessfully to distract herself by watching two geese fight on the lake. She faced him and asked, "Can we tie his death to the senator?"

He shook his head. "When I was in the military, I completed a series of gruesome jobs on orders from my commanding officer. When things went sideways for her, I was sacrificed. Going after Jiang is a suicide mission. She's too powerful and well protected."

Jazmin let her gaze wander back to the bickering geese. "If I hadn't asked for his help, he'd still be alive."

Harry touched Jazmin on her upper arms and gently turned her to face him. "Ajax was a former Navy SEAL and a captain. He knew he was breaking all kinds of rules when he accessed that classified database. That was his decision. You can't blame yourself."

"Dammit, Harry, I can't stand by and do nothing."

"I'm not suggesting that, either. Let things play out with Jiang. I'll follow the investigation and see what I can learn. The only way we can exact justice is by asymmetrical warfare. We can't win a direct confrontation. We're outgunned a hundred to one. Be patient."

Jazmin sighed. "Patience is a virtue, just not one of mine."

"I know. Me either." He held her gaze, then stood and kissed her on the cheek. "*Au revoir, mon amour.*"

For a time they had always parted this way, her responding in kind. Today she said, "*Au revoir,*" and watched him walk away.

Chapter 10

Truax Field - Madison, Wisconsin
9 May

See me immediately! flashed on Jazmin's phone on her way to the base. The secure high priority message was from her boss, Captain Bill Taylor. Before she made it to his office door, she was intercepted by Master Chief Paula Perez. "Good morning, Commander. Captain Taylor wants you to report formally today." Perez made a quick scan of the area and leaned in close. "The boss is really wound up. I've never seen him like this."

"Thanks for the warning, Master Chief." Jazmin checked her uniform, mentally prepared herself for a typhoon, and knocked on Taylor's door.

A gruff "enter" emanated from the office.

She opened the door, marched to her boss's desk, and crisply saluted. "Commander Hassani reporting as ordered, sir." She held her salute until he finally saluted in return, the delay a petty reminder of their difference in rank, though he'd never done that before. Jazmin dropped her right arm and stood at attention. This was totally at odds with their normal collegial interactions, especially given the conversation they'd just had about her taking over his role.

Taylor stabbed the tablet screen on his desk with his index finger. "I have orders from Lieutenant General Sarraf to immediately stop your current investigation. It will be taken over by the Defense Intelligence Agency. Turn your case files over to the DIA and cease any further work."

"Why would the NDA director shut down one of our investigations?" She already knew the answer but wanted confirmation from her boss.

Taylor looked at Jazmin with contempt. "Sarraf is a three-star general and doesn't owe us an explanation."

"Sir, I believe there may be a high level cover-up for what happened. There's too many anomalies that don't add up."

Taylor stood, his jaw set, and eyes narrowed. "Commander, you have your orders."

Jazmin bit back her argument for continuing the investigation. Taylor left no room for discussion, so a tactical egress was her only sane option. She didn't want to risk alienating her boss by ignoring a direct order.

"Yes, sir." She spun about face and exited his office.

Fuming, she slammed her office door and sat at her desk. She tried copying her case notes and files to her personal tablet, but her access was instantly blocked. Access to her other case files were blocked as well. A minute later, her red-faced boss charged into her office and marched right up to her desk. A vein on his forehead throbbed. "Commander Hassani, what in the hell are you doing? What about the word 'immediately' do you not comprehend?"

Any reply would be pointless and result in additional wrath from her boss. Jazmin stayed silent, eyes downcast, and hoped her look of contrition would be enough.

Taylor leaned in with his face uncomfortably close. "Take the rest of the day off and get your head straight. The master chief will assign you several other cases that will keep you fully occupied." His tone had gone from angry to quietly threatening as other staff members at open desks outside her office pretended not to listen.

Jazmin hated being shut out. That happened five years ago when her aircraft was shot down. She'd tried to investigate and asked for access to the case files but in every instance was denied. It angered and frustrated her then and even more so now when she had formal authority as the investigator. She refused to wither under her bosses cold eyes and flared nostrils. "Sir, I think something illegal…"

Taylor cut her off with a slashing motion across his throat. "I don't care what you think, Commander. When you provoke a high-ranking senator and a three-star general, there are consequences. You brought a shitstorm down on my head and my umbrella isn't big enough for the both of us."

Jazmin opened her mouth to argue, then clamped it shut before doing any more damage to her career. No wonder her boss was pissed, Taylor was all about low drama and smooth sailing. This violated both. She seethed inside, though did her best to project a neutral expression. "Understood, sir. I'll see the master chief in the morning for my new assignments."

Taylor looked mollified for the moment. "Permission to leave, sir?" She hated sounding like a seaman basic on her first day of boot camp, but she needed to get away.

Taylor nodded and stood aside. She headed for the door and didn't breathe until she was outside. Adrenaline flooded her body, and she didn't trust herself to keep from lashing out at anyone or anything in her way. She needed time to calm down and think. This investigation wasn't over, not even close.

Jazmin headed to the flight line. Despite her aversion to going back into combat, she was happiest in the cockpit. She wanted to swap her khaki uniform for a flight suit and helmet, then jump in the cockpit. She imagined herself performing an afterburner takeoff and the crushing force of six g's pressing her into the pilot's seat. Unfortunately, she wasn't on the flight roster today, so she'd have to settle for watching other pilots performing twin takeoffs, her hands mentally on the jet aircraft throttles and control stick.

Still walking, she pulled out her tablet and texted Harry. *We need to talk.* A few seconds later, a text with a series of numbers came back from a different sender. Dammit, nothing was simple with Harry. When his military career in US Cyber Command went down in flames, he became a target for a number of powerful enemies in the clandestine service community. His incessant paranoia had kept him alive and out of prison, though it made it difficult for them to connect. She knew meeting with Harry and pursuing an investigation on her own crossed a line. One that could end her career. She wasn't at the point of no return yet, though she was edging dangerously close to it.

Jazmin needed to burn off her irritation, so she took off her shoes and socks, then began running the three miles to her apartment. The soles of her feet, made from a nanotech-coated composite material, withstood the pounding from the pavement far better than her dress shoes. She picked up the pace and felt her stress melt away in a flow of endorphins. Pegasus couldn't fly today, but she could run like the wind. Ten minutes later she entered her front door.

Despite Harry's tech prowess, he sometimes employed old-school spy craft. Jazmin pulled a book of poetry from a shelf. It had been a gift from Harry and was one of the few paper books she owned. Using the poetry book, she decoded the numeric cipher, resulting in a set of coordinates and a meeting time. She mapped the latitude and longitude, coordinates to a bar in Milwaukee's Historic Third Ward. The meeting time was midnight.

Normally, Jazmin used the military car fleet for ground transportation. Tonight she'd use a special service that catered to clients who valued discretion, one not tied to the usual government surveillance sources. She wouldn't be paying a premium for transportation; it was for her privacy.

Chapter 11

Milwaukee, Wisconsin
10 May

Jazmin arrived early and took a seat at the bar. It was the kind of establishment Harry loved, a vintage dark wood decorating scheme, patrons ranging from armed gang members to wealthy local politicians, and a fantastic jazz trio playing on the small stage. She took in the music and ambience while she waited to be served. A few minutes later, the bearded android bartender approached, and its face lit up with a warm smile. "Welcome to the only jazz club in Milwaukee featuring live music seven days a week. What can I get for you?"

"Knob Creek bourbon neat, please." The android poured her drink and placed it in front of her on the polished bar, then pointed to the biochip scanner on the counter. She paid for the drink using an anonymous payment stick. Jazmin forced herself to take a single sip and set the glass on the bar, though she wanted to down it in a single gulp. She used her neurotech implants and special ops clearance to tap into the club's security system. Special forces neurotech had the advantage of being untraceable in the system, and their invisibility lasted for their entire military careers. Each member of elite forces went through an extensive background investigation before being awarded their high level clearance and getting their neurotech implants upgraded. Her bionic eyes projected the club's video surveillance and weapons analysis feed as a hologram, though only visible to her. Many of the patrons were armed, some with concealed weapons and others with holsters in plain sight. Jazmin normally didn't carry a weapon off duty, but tonight she kept a 9mm compact handgun in a holster hidden under her blouse.

Just after midnight, Harry came through the door and made his way to the bar while he discreetly scanned the room for threats. As expected, he was armed. His jacket barely covered the bulge from his shoulder holster, and another smaller weapon strapped to his ankle peeked out as he walked. Most of the patrons appeared to recognize him as he waded through the crowd like a mob boss. Men reached out for handshakes or nodded respectfully in his direction. Women hugged him and kissed him on the cheek. The rest hid their gaze in fear. The android staff didn't respond though they kept their distance.

He sat next to Jazmin as if they'd never met before. "Hello, gorgeous. What brings you to this neighborhood?"

She rolled her eyes at him. "I'm waiting for a friend."

"I'll keep you company while you wait."

She gave him a withering look. "As long as you give up your seat when she arrives."

He flashed a lecherous grin. "Only if the two of you take me home."

"Not happening." She turned away and scanned the room. Two men who moved like special forces operators entered the front door. She caught Harry's eye and realized he'd seen them too. She faced the bar again and cycled through the video surveillance system to make sure there weren't any more.

A different android bartender appeared, now a gorgeous blonde with a silky low-cut top. "Hey, Harry, your usual?"

"Same as always." It took down a bottle of single malt scotch from behind the bar, poured a double shot into a glass, added five ice cubes, then brushed Harry's hand in a subtle, intimate gesture. His eyes lingered on it adoringly, then he waved his arm over the biochip reader to pay for his drink, adding an obscene amount for a tip. Jazmin assumed the beauty behind the bar was also a sex worker and Harry fucked it.

Jazmin stared into her drink, not able to look at Harry. She'd ended her relationship with him after her body had been destroyed. In rehab her scars and stumps disgusted her, and she wondered how anyone could find what was left appealing. After learning how to function with her new prosthetics, she endured countless cosmetic surgeries. At the end of this grueling reconstruction, she was an attractive woman again, though she felt like a freak. Half of her was manufactured, just like an android's body. An it.

Jazmin forced herself to focus on the mission. She'd asked for Harry's help, so she shoved her anger aside. Harry took a sip of scotch and scanned the room. Jazmin followed his gaze. They both watched the men she identified as threats. Wisconsin was an open carry state, so they didn't bother to conceal their handguns. The two men scanned the room, though they didn't appear to have identified their targets yet. It was just a matter of time.

Harry put down his drink. "I'm going to say hello to a couple of friends. Don't give away my stool." He stood and winked. "You can join me if you like. They'd love to meet a looker like you."

"No thanks." She turned away and checked the exits. She was about to get sucked into the black vortex surrounding Harry, though she felt surprisingly calm. Dark forces had attacked her SEAL team, and she was the lone survivor, the only one left to demand answers. The fear that immobilized her for so long had bloomed into anger. Even if it cost Jazmin her military career, she wasn't backing down.

Harry slipped away while Jazmin faced the bar and monitored his movements using her neurotech. A moment later he vanished, having found a hole in the club's video surveillance coverage. Jazmin downed the rest of her drink, then followed him to a short hallway that led to an automated kitchen. Harry waved his arm at the biochip reader and the locked door opened to a large room of robot chefs. Once inside, they were invisible to the automated mayhem of the professional kitchen where people were banned. Not designed to support human life, there were no safeguards to protect them. Harry led as they jumped over high-speed delivery robots and dodged raw ingredient trolleys supplying knife wielding robot chefs. The room smelled fantastic, though hazards were everywhere. High pressure steam erupted from pots, grease-fueled flames shot from grill stations, razor sharp knives rhythmically chopped vegetables, and meat cleavers cut steaks into single portions. Harry choreographed his moves like a dancer to pass one hazard after another unscathed. Jazmin mirrored him, failing only once, and burned a hole in her blouse. They made it through the automated gauntlet to the far wall where an oversized service door rolled up to expose an alley. Once outside, the door closed behind them, and they stood in darkness.

She faced him. "You've done this before."

"Once or twice." Her night vision eyes read his satisfied expression in the dim light.

"What happens now? Are your buddies going to pop through this door?"

"You'll see."

Jazmin was never sure what to expect from Harry. He was clever, resourceful, and dangerous to his enemies. She didn't fear him but didn't want to get caught in the crossfire. She scanned the alley and sky overhead and saw nothing in the dark, though a soft buzzing cut through the air. Drones were headed their way. She checked the sliver of sky between the buildings, then stole a glance at Harry. He was perfectly calm. The buzzing grew louder and was directly overhead. She expected to see strobe lights flashing on the two drones, but they weren't lit at all. The military rescue drones designed for transporting a single person were coated in a black matte finish. They landed a few feet away, rotors still spinning.

Harry touched Jazmin on her arm. "Here's our ride." He went to the one furthest away, strapped into the open-air seat and put on tech glasses. Jazmin strapped into the seat of the closer drone, then her neurotech connected to the flight control system. Her bionic eyes projected a holographic heads-up display, and the rotors spun up, though there were no physical controls on the tiny aircraft. Just as she and Harry lifted off, a barrage of gunfire erupted through the service door from the automated kitchen and ricocheted off the brick wall opposite the alley door. A second later the door rolled up, and the two operators scanned both ends of the alley while pointing high caliber handguns.

Before the enemy gun barrels lined up for their human targets, Jazmin and Harry pulled their handguns. She aimed for center mass on the right-side shooter and Harry aimed at the man on the left. They both emptied their magazines. If the men were wearing combat armor, they'd live to fight another day. Both men went down and lay moaning on the concrete, though it was too dark to see if they were bleeding out. She wondered how much backup they had and how brutal they'd be when they sought revenge.

Jazmin had just crossed another line. She envisioned her court martial hearing and wondered what possible argument her defense lawyer could make to keep her out of a military prison. She pushed that thought out of her mind and focused on her heads-up display. She cleared the alley and flew over the buildings and houses in the area. The open-air arrangement felt more like a hang glider than a rotorcraft. She tried overriding the flight controls with her neurotech, but the drone kept returning to its programmed course heading. There were no comms on the rescue drone, so Jazmin initiated a communication-only hivemind connection with Harry. She wasn't ready for an immersive connection where they could read each other's thoughts and doubted Harry was, either. That required a level of trust that had disintegrated along with their love relationship. There was a lag before the hivemind connection stabilized. That wasn't a technology failure, just Harry deciding if he trusted her enough to get inside his head, even if it was only a comms link. Finally, he said *comms link confirmed.*

It was Harry's voice in her head, though it sounded totally different from when they spoke face to face. Now they could speak wordlessly, essential in a firefight. She replied, *Copy.*

They flew a circuitous route toward the old Allen Bradley clock tower, a Milwaukee fixture from the middle of the twentieth century. The two rescue drones landed on a small helipad on the roof of the old factory building. Once they had unstrapped and stepped away from the small aircraft, the rotors spun up and the drones headed in opposite directions. It had been years since they'd been on a mission together, though she felt them falling back into special ops mode, each scanning their assigned area. It was clear for now, but that could change at any moment. The backup from the two operators they put down had to be on their way.

Harry headed to a rooftop door and waved his arm past the biochip reader. Ten deadbolts retracted and the titanium security door opened. They entered and it closed behind them, deadbolts thumping home. The exterior of the historic building belied what lay inside. The interior was a high-tech installation filled with gleaming surfaces, LED lighting, and abundant power for the HVAC equipment required for a large data center. Harry led the way through rows of servers to a large room taking up the entire floor from the east side facing Lake Michigan to the west side facing a neighborhood. A semi-circular table with two chairs faced a huge holographic screen. He sat in one of the chairs and pointed at the other. "You're one of the few people to see my data center." He spoke normally, though he left the hivemind connection in place.

She sat next to him. "Thanks for bringing me inside." The holographic screen lit up with security scans of the outside of the building, the rooftop, and the floor below with additional racks of servers, HVAC equipment, and a massive uninterruptable power supply. Another screen cycled through cable runs filled with thick fiber optic bundles and copper bus bar for power. The status window at the top of the screen showed *All Systems Green – Perimeter Secure – Clean Power Grid – Communications Network 10% Load.*

"Let's see what our friend Ajax was up to before he died." A DARPA logo screen opened in front of them, and Harry logged on as an admin. As he scrolled through each session ID on the screen, content showed to the right. Harry stopped when the window showed *DARPA Top Secret – Code Word Classified.*

Jazmin looked at the date time stamp. "That's when I was with Ajax in his office, and we found the project with Pulse Weapons Labs."

Harry kicked off a bot search routine. "Let's see what else we can find attached to PWL." A few seconds later search results appeared. "Isn't this interesting." A window opened with the PWL-DARPA project contract. Harry whistled tonelessly. "There's lots of zeros for the funding. Fifty billion is five times the size of DARPA's entire budget. They're getting dark money from somewhere."

Jazmin took control of the screen and scanned the contract. "It was sponsored by Senator Ling Chen Jiang. In her office she told me the contract had been cancelled."

"I didn't think senators normally signed individual DARPA contracts."

She shook her head. "They don't."

Harry kicked off another search bot. This time it was a dark web search on PWL and Senator Jiang. A video played showing a PWL directed-energy weapon attacking a military-grade drone. The quad rotor platform lost flight control and power, then crashed into a cliff face. Another short video showed a group of prisoners at a government black site, though it was unclear whose government. Prisoners walked around an outdoor pen, hands tied behind them, each wearing external neurotech skull covers. A few seconds later each man fell to the ground twitching uncontrollably, followed by vomiting. Minutes later, they all stopped moving. The screen showed a close up of Jiang smiling with approval, then zoomed out as she kicked one of the men laying on the ground, verifying he was either dead or too incapacitated to fight back.

Jazmin shook her head in disgust. Jiang had just demonstrated her depravity. No doubt she was capable of worse.

Harry logged into a Defense Intelligence Agency classified site. "Let's see what else the senator and her colleagues are up to." The screen *showed Black Flag Operations – Top Secret – Eyes Only*. He scrolled through two screens of entries until he saw one with DARPA. The link required code-word entry and after a few seconds, Harry's password cracking program flashed *Solution*. A report showed on screen. *Target: Ajax Papadakis – Mission Status: Target Terminated*. A video started and showed a heavily drugged Ajax holding a gun in his mouth along with a pair of gloved hands. One around Ajax's neck held him upright, the other pulled the trigger. An explosion of blood and bone blew out the back of his head where his brainstem was located. The video ended. The rest of the report was displayed on the screen. *Mission Authorized By: Senator Ling Chen Jiang and Lieutenant General Anton Trabago*.

The pulse in Jazmin's temples pounded as she watched the short video. "It's horrifying that the Chair of the Senate Armed Services Committee and the head of the Defense Intelligence Agency can authorize the murder of an American citizen and get away with it."

Harry stared at her with a look of disapproval and disappointment.

She glared back at him. "What's on your mind, Harry? What aren't you saying?"

"You know my past and why I'm on the run."

"What's your point, Harry?"

"Don't be so damn naïve. In the military our job is to kill people, so we imagine them as subhuman and declare ourselves patriots. It's the only way we can sleep at night. Before you go after Jiang and Trabago, look in the mirror."

Jazmin stood and inhaled through flared nostrils. "Are you defending them?"

He held up his hands in surrender. "Not for a second. I want to make sure you understand what it's like to live in the dark."

"Dammit, Harry, they had Ajax murdered. Doesn't that bother you?"

He looked back at her, impassive. "Of course it does."

Jazmin put her hand on Harry's shoulder. "I've been living in the dark since my copter was shot down. I'm sick of being shut out, pushed aside, and lied to."

He pulled away and stood. "Are you ready to sacrifice your Navy career and live in the shadows for the rest of your life?"

Jazmin took a deep breath to calm herself. "I already crossed that line."

"Maybe you can still go back. It's not too late."

"The second I called you my career was done."

"You think I'm that toxic." He took a step back.

She shook her head. "No, it's not that." She grabbed his hand and pulled him close. "I know what you're capable of and I need your help. I'm going after powerful enemies. I can't fight this from inside the Navy, and I have no regrets for coming here." She looked into his eyes and doubt reflected back. Despite her words, she was still coming to grips with her decision to go dark, and Harry knew it.

An alarm sounded and her moment of introspection evaporated. Red lights flashed and a holographic screen opened in front of them. *Enemy Raid in Progress.* Another holographic screen opened showing video of the rooftop. Fifty feet above the helipad an octocopter hovered and a team of six commandos fast-roped to the roof. A few seconds later a heavy thump of boots sounded on the ceiling above them, followed by running feet. Two of the commandos ran to the rooftop door and placed a magnetic charge, while the other four created a defensive perimeter. As soon as the timer was set the two backed away. Three seconds later the charge went off. The entire building shook and the screen was momentarily washed out from the blinding flash of the explosion. Harry studied the screen. "The door's holding for now, but it won't survive another blast. We need to get the hell out of here." The video showed the two-person demolition team placing multiple charges on the now damaged security door.

Harry cycled through the exterior security camera views. One screen showed the six commandos armed with assault rifles and another displayed the jet black Special Ops military octocopter with a belt fed door gun.

"They've never come after me with this much fire power."

"Oh my god, Harry. I'm sorry for bringing this down on your

head."

"We don't know what triggered the assault." His eyes darted from screen to screen as multiple blasts shook the building.

The security system announced, "Perimeter breached. Intrusion team in building."

Harry killed the alarm, and the flashing red lights stopped. "Security system, Destructive Wipe."

The female computer voice responded. "Destructive Wipe confirmed. Data elimination in progress."

Jazmin's heart rate jumped as a series of explosions cascaded through rack after rack of the server farm, engulfing the equipment in flames, while sparks showered from shorted electrical circuits. She froze in place, transported back to the darkest moments of her life.

Harry must have sensed her distress. He grabbed her hand and pulled, then spoke to her over their hivemind connection. *Follow me.* He ran away from the racks of exploding equipment toward the other end of the building, never letting go of her. Human touch and movement snapped her back to the present. Harry squeezed her hand. *Flashbangs coming.* He let go and covered his ears with his hands and kept his head down while he ran. High intensity flashes and deafening sonic blasts erupted behind them. Jazmin's bionic eyes and ears protected her from the worst of it, so she wasn't debilitated, but it was hard to focus through the painful assault. They were now in another part of the building that hadn't been updated, and it took all of her concentration to keep up with Harry's zigzag pattern around abandoned machine tools from a bygone era. Enemy footfalls echoed off the decrepit wooden industrial floor. Three-round submachine gun bursts ricocheted off pipes and old machinery. *We're almost there*, he said.

She wondered where "there" was. They couldn't win a firefight with handguns against a commando team armed with assault rifles. Harry ducked behind a row of antique wooden crates filled with dust-covered spools of wire. She followed, crouched alongside him, and saw the wooden crates were a false front for a massive Kevlar shield, video screen array, and weapons controls. Harry tapped an icon on the screen extinguishing all interior lights and Jazmin's eyes switched to night vision mode. Enemy footsteps ceased. The only sound was the team positioning and clicking on night vision gear.

Harry waited for movement, then flooded the warehouse with

blinding white light. Their eyes didn't have time to adjust before he triggered a burst from ceiling mounted taser ports. A muffled chorus of curses filled the warehouse, followed by thumps as bodies collapsed onto the wooden floor. A few mercenaries got off erratic shots before they went down, followed by silence. Acrid smoke and the stench of burning electronics surrounded them. Fire alarms shrieked and the overhead sprinkler system cascaded water everywhere, transforming the area from a burning building into a smoky sauna.

Harry pointed to the far wall. *That's our escape route.* He glanced at his wrist tablet where an exterior security camera view flickered, then went dark. *The security system's offline. We're running blind.* He sprinted to the exterior wall with Jazmin right behind him. When he reached it, he tore away a panel revealing a flexible tube and two backpacks. *This will take you to the ground. I'll be right behind you.* He retrieved a helmet from one of the packs and she strapped it on her head, then he slid the pack onto her. *The go bags have weapons, money, and supplies.*

Jazmin placed her feet inside the tube, then pushed off, keeping her arms pinned to her sides. She picked up speed, descending past the top two floors of the six-story building, then slowed as the tube narrowed near the bottom. She pulled herself free, then pressed up against the building. The rhythmic rotor noise meant the copter was close, though she couldn't see it yet.

A few seconds later, Harry emerged from the slide and checked the sky. *I have a safe house nearby. We just have to be invisible a while longer.*

Jazmin scanned the area around them, checking for more hostiles, but saw none. A moment later her neck and arms erupted in goosebumps, a mix of dread and cold air blast from rotor downwash. She had only a moment to decide if fear would immobilize her, or rage would keep her alive.

Chapter 12

Milwaukee, Wisconsin
10 May

Jazmin dove behind a boulder near the building. Pain radiated through her body when she hit the hard ground. A moment later, Harry slammed into her when he flung himself in the tight space next to her. She gritted her teeth as the second wave of pain pummeled her. Harry killed the outdoor lights, and they both looked skyward. Glowing green eyes from night vision gear in the hovering octocopter searched for them.

Rage kept Jazmin functioning. *This is not my day to die.* She pulled an electromagnetic-pulse grenade launcher from her backpack and armed it. Harry clipped on night vision gear, then retrieved a submachine gun with .45 caliber ammo and several 30-round magazines from his pack. They both lay perfectly still and listened.

Harry aimed at the copter. *This is no match for an armored octocopter, but I can spook the pilot.* He fired three round bursts at the copter's windshield and engine compartment. The copter sustained only minimal damage, but the pilot veered off until the shooting stopped. When the copter returned, the side doors were open and a door gunner targeted their position. Harry emptied a 30-round clip on full automatic into the open doorway while Jazmin targeted the engines with the EMP grenade launcher and squeezed the trigger.

They both dove down behind the boulder as bullets from the door gunner pelted the side of the building. Brick and glass shards flew in every direction.

The flash from the exploding grenade lit up the area. When the noise of the detonation faded away, the only sound was the sputtering engine generator. The eight rotors instantly lost power as the electrical system failed and the computer-controlled motors ceased. With the flight control system offline, the octocopter tilted at a sixty-degree angle and spun out of control. Even if the pilot attempted to autorotate, they were too low to the ground to recover. The crippled octocopter impacted a light pole in the unused parking lot and tore the steel structure to its cement base. A screeching metal symphony accompanied slow-motion destruction as the doomed war machine pirouetted into the asphalt. All that remained was a crumpled heap of shredded composite airframe members and shattered glass, engulfed in a cloud of black smoke from burning plastic and electronics.

The pilot lay motionless, partially concealed by a bloody smear on the windshield. Two others were ejected on impact. One lay still, impaled by wreckage. The other, covered in blood, tried to move but only twitched. Jazmin's moment of triumph was overtaken by a sense of horror. In their final moments, her faceless enemies had become people again.

Harry grabbed Jazmin's arm, forcing her attention back to her own survival. *We need to vanish before reinforcements arrive.* He pointed to a nearby residential area and started running. Jazmin stole one last glance at the dead and dying assault team near the smoking copter, then followed Harry. She could no longer pretend her military career wasn't over.

Her bionic ears detected multiple sirens, faint but closing. *Emergency responders are coming.*

Harry scanned the area south of their position. *Police and fire stations are only a few miles away. Once they see a military octocopter they'll call the feds and the FAA. We'll be overrun by guns and badges.*

When they got to the adjacent residential area, they walked through backyards to stay hidden from the street. A few people were outside looking at the burning remains of the copter but ducked back inside their houses when they saw Harry and Jazmin carrying automatic weapons. Harry approached a wood-frame house built before World War Two, where a huge black dog the size of a wolf patrolled the yard. The animal growled at Jazmin and she reached for her gun, though she didn't want to shoot the dog. Harry held up his hand to stop her and waved the dog over. The huge animal was delighted to see him. He knelt down and petted it, then pulled a dog biscuit from a steel box attached to the house. *I own this house and the dog. There's an ex-military family who lives here rent free with two stipulations. They take care of Zeus and never enter the basement apartment.*

Jazmin watched as he typed a twelve-digit code on a cipher lock on the beat-up exterior metal door leading down to a cellar. Behind it was the real security, a vault door with ten deadbolts that retracted after he punched in a different twelve-digit code on a keypad that read his fingerprints. The door opened after he held his arm over the biochip reader. They took several steps down into the underground room, and the two outer doors closed behind them. The inside was nicer than she expected given the age of the property, and the space was even larger than the footprint of the house above. The single room had a queen-size bed, a galley kitchen, and a wall covered in weapons.

She joined Harry as they studied a holographic screen showing security camera views of all sides of the house. No one was approaching yet. Next they checked on the emergency responders. Firetrucks, ambulances, and police cruisers, all with their lights flashing, were parked haphazardly in the parking lot near the octocopter wreckage, and what was left of the aircraft was drowned in fire retardant foam. Three bodies lay on the ground covered with blankets. With no one to save, the paramedics stood off to the side and waited.

Harry took off his backpack and set it on the floor. *We can't stay here long. Once they get done arguing over who's in charge, they'll fan out and start searching. Too many neighbors saw us.*

Jazmin took in the scene and tried to process the three deaths, the lives she'd ended. She'd killed in combat, though all had been enemies of the United States. This time it wasn't clear. *What do you think happened to the assault team we left in the building?*

They've probably recovered by now and know what happened to the octocopter crew. They'll fall back to their emergency exfil location, get picked up, and plan their revenge. Harry opened a cupboard and pulled out two quick draw tactical vests. He put one on and handed the other to her. *Leave your pack here. This has everything you need.*

Jazmin laid her backpack on the floor and strapped on the

tactical vest packed with a .45 caliber semi-automatic handgun and extra magazines. *I hope this comes equipped with new IDs.* Gallows humor for the mess they were in.

Yes it does. There's a driver's license, passport, pilot's license, and credit cards all tied to your biochip.

Jazmin raised her eyebrows. *You're joking, right?*

He tapped one of the pockets on her vest. *Look.*

She unzipped the pocket and pulled out a wallet and passport. It was her photo and biochip number, but the name on all the IDs was Evelyn Starbright. A chill washed over her. *What the fuck! Harry, what's really going on here? When did you obtain these?*

He sighed. *I've had them for a while in case you ever needed help. After we spoke yesterday, I was afraid things would go sideways and put them here. The documents are genuine and logged into the appropriate government systems. You can leave now and start your new life.*

This is creepy and invasive. This is one of the reasons I didn't want you in my life. What aren't you telling me? How could I possibly walk away right now?

You probably can't, not without my help. They stood silently for a few moments. Finally, she exhaled loudly, flaring her nostrils and shaking her head. A holographic alert appeared and floated between them. The FBI was on the scene and agents fanned out from the downed octocopter. Harry looked at her with a pleading expression. *Too many people are looking for us. We need to go.* He pointed to another pocket on her vest. She unzipped it and pulled out a new military grade tablet. He stuck out his hand. *Give me your smartphone. It can be tracked. Your IDs too.* She reluctantly handed them over and he placed them into a secure shredder. She felt her life fading away as the titanium blades destroyed evidence tying her to a raft of felonies.

Harry punched a code into his tablet and a wall slid open, revealing an electric touring motorcycle. He waved his biochip near the controls mounted on the handlebars, and the instrument cluster came to life. Helmets with full face shields and leather jackets were stacked neatly on the shelf above the bike. The jackets fit over their vests and the helmets hid their faces from traffic cameras. Harry wheeled the large bike to the door and punched a code into the keypad. The two outer doors opened and everything in the safe house powered down. He sat on the motorcycle and patted the rear seat. *I'm pilot and you're Wizzo for this mission.*

She swung her leg over the seat, put the balls of her feet on the pegs, and got her balance. She thought he must be joking about her being the Weapon Systems Officer, since she was riding on the back seat of a motorcycle instead of in a fighter jet, until her helmet display lit up. *Weapon Status: .50 caliber machine guns and EMP grenade launchers – Weapons Hot.* Holy shit.

The outside steps leading down to the underground safe house folded flat into a ramp. The powerful motorcycle drove up the steep incline. Then the doors closed behind them and deadbolts slammed into place. Harry drove out of the back yard around the side of the house. *We'll stick to two-lane roads and head north. I have another safe house in a small town in western Wisconsin near the Minnesota border. We can lie low there until we figure out our next move.*

Using her neurotech, Jazmin alternated her helmet display between moving map view and satellite images of the multiple emergency response teams. She also monitored police and military channels for any sign they were being followed. They would have made faster progress using interstate highways, but there was too much surveillance on the main roads. They could still be tracked on two-lane highways, but these offered more escape routes with places to hide. Harry kept the bike within five miles of the speed limit so they wouldn't attract attention from any local or state police.

After they had been on the road for forty-five minutes and were well away from the octocopter crash site, Jazmin's adrenalin rush wore off. Combat fatigue set in from being hyperalert all night. It had been a long time since she'd been on a life-or-death mission. The reality of being a fugitive also hit her. At least one of the clandestine services was hunting her. No doubt the military, FBI, local law enforcement, and black ops mercenaries had joined the party. A weariness overtook her, and she was glad Harry was driving.

A police cruiser approached from the opposite direction at high speed, red and blue lights flashing. Jazmin checked weapon status and targeted the cruiser with an EMP grenade. Unlike an aircraft hit with an EMP weapon, ground vehicles suffered less catastrophic damage, and she wanted to avoid using the .50 caliber guns. Using her neurotech, she checked the law enforcement dispatch network, and while there was a call in the area, she couldn't tell if the cruiser was responding to it. Yesterday she wouldn't have thought twice about pulling over for a traffic stop but not today. Harry slowed and pulled to the side of the road, a tautness in his stance on the bike. The cruiser flew by them without slowing and Harry resumed normal speed again. Jazmin took the EMP grenade targeting system offline and back into standby mode. They were well north of Milwaukee, but they had a long ride ahead of them.

She patted his leg, the one part of him not covered in weapons. *I'm sorry for getting you into this mess.*

It's okay. You're worth the fight.

I hope you don't live to regret it. They rode on in silence. Jazmin was glad her hivemind connection was communication only. Her mind wandered to dark places she didn't want to share. She reviewed everything that had happened in the last twenty-four hours and, while she trusted Harry with her life, what wasn't he telling her?

Chapter 13
Ling Chen Jiang

Washington, DC
10 May

Ling Chen waited for Trabago on the balcony of the DC condo she used as her personal base of operations. It was near her senate office, though it wasn't her home. Heavy footsteps on the stairs alerted her he'd arrived. She came back inside as the general ascended the last step into her living room, escorted by the most trusted member of her personal security team. "Danica, please make sure we aren't disturbed." The guard nodded and retreated. Ling Chen sat in her favorite chair, an antique upholstered with royal purple fabric, and pointed to the wing chair opposite her.

Trabago sat. "I don't have much time. My next meeting is in thirty minutes." He leaned forward. "Last night's events were precipitated by a conversation I had with Lieutenant General Sarraf. I told her Hassani's investigation was tied to a Top Secret special access program within the DIA. I asked her to shut down the NDA investigation. That's likely why Hassani went to Dexter, someone we've had under surveillance for years. Dexter's a problem, but when a former president says he's off limits, I need to tread lightly."

Ling Chen raised her eyebrows. "What about now? Last night was a shit show."

Trabago didn't react to her taunt. "Last night didn't go as planned."

She rolled her eyes. "There's an understatement. Dexter and Hassani neutralized your assault team, downed a black ops octocopter, killed the pilot and two crew members, then escaped."

"We'll find Dexter and Hassani and deal with them."

"This situation is spinning out of control, and I hate loose ends. If this goes public it will create blowback for both of us."

Trabago made a fist and slapped it against his other hand. "Dexter and Hassani crossed a dangerous line last night. My orders were to keep tabs on Dexter as long as he wasn't causing national security issues. That's no longer the case."

She glared at him. "It's time to make them disappear."

"I have a team working on that now. The next phase of the operation is in motion." Trabago stood. "I need to get back for my next meeting. The President doesn't tolerate lateness."

She stood too. "Keep me informed on your progress." His next report had better be positive or it would be time to reconsider their partnership. She didn't tolerate liabilities.

Chapter 14
Jingle

Madison, Wisconsin
10 May

Jingle ran her preflight checks on the Cessna Citation-X business jet at Dane County Regional Airport. The custom aircraft had been modified to increase both its power and service ceiling. To avoid attention, she stayed inside the private hangar owned by the mercenary firm that employed her. The Pulse Weapons Labs technicians had installed their aircraft attack system at the depot in Dubai, and she'd flown the plane back to the US. During her time in Dubai, she trained on the PWL simulator, learning to deploy the aircraft's weapons for maximum destruction. She checked weapon status, and the PWL built-in tests all showed green. She ran through the targeting sequence. All controls responded perfectly. Next, she checked the weather for any updates, tuned to the tower frequency, and then tapped into the Truax Field secure IT system on the military side of the airport. She checked the military flight roster and verified the morning schedule. Three F-35 Air Force fighters and three F-18 Navy jets were doing separate exercises and would join up for a final set of joint maneuvers.

The robot tugger attached itself to the plane's nose gear and pulled it outside. When the aircraft was a safe distance from the building, the tugger detached itself and scurried back inside the hanger. The overhead door closed behind it. Jingle started the left engine, and as soon as it stabilized, she started the right. All engine gauges showed green. There was a single air traffic control tower at the airport. Though it was manned by a mix of civilian and military air traffic controllers who coordinated with each other, they communicated on different radio frequencies. She tuned her radio to the tower frequency for civilian aircraft. "Dane County tower, Cessna Citation 666 Zulu Bravo requests taxi to runway 3."

The controller responded. "Cessna 666 Zulu Bravo, Dane County tower, taxi to and hold short runway 3."

Jingle nudged her throttles forward and taxied to the hold line. "Dane County tower, Cessna Citation 666 Zulu Bravo holding at runway 3." She parked just short of where runway 36 and runway 3 intersected. The military jets were lined up at the far end of runway 36 and a pair of F-18s sped down the runway, shot past her location, and climbed skyward. A minute later, two F-35s took off behind the Navy jets. The third pair of fighters, one F-18 and one F-35, took off last. Jingle waited impatiently for the wake turbulence to clear.

"Cessna Citation 666 Zulu Bravo, runway 3, cleared for takeoff, use caution for wake turbulence from departing F-35 and F-18 aircraft." Jingle rolled off the taxiway and lined up on the centerline of the runway, then pushed the throttles to full power. The lightly-loaded jet raced down the runway. Jingle pulled back the yoke and climbed into the sky. Once she had retracted her landing gear she set the aircraft to maximum climb to catch up with the fighter jets. Jingle headed for the military practice area, which was restricted airspace. When she reached 50,000 feet, she turned off her transponder. At this altitude she was flying above commercial jet traffic. Her aircraft had a nanoparticle coating that made it almost invisible on radar. Normally, a business jet flying in military restricted airspace would be instantly identified, escorted out, and forced to land. Once on the ground, the pilot would be arrested. That wouldn't happen today; instead, the controllers wouldn't pick her up at all or would simply classify her unknown aircraft as a system anomaly to have the techs check out.

Jingle's aircraft was equipped with the same military-grade decryption hardware as on the fighters, so she tuned her radio to their frequency and monitored communication. Using her onboard aircraft radar, she identified the six fighter jets, all at a lower altitude than her current flight path. To avoid detection, Jingle kept her aircraft just outside the fighters' radar coverage. She listened to the military pilots' radio chatter as they focused on formation flying and combat maneuvers. Since they hadn't flown together previously, the two flight leaders decided to keep their groups of three aircraft apart, though each pilot kept situational awareness of the other fighters.

Having the two aircraft types stay in flights of three was an advantage for Jingle. She mirrored the flight path of the F-35s from above and brought the PWL targeting system online. The F-35 fighters were in a tight formation and well within the weapon's envelope. Jingle pushed her throttles to full power, dove, and closed in to maximize the damage. When she was just inside the fighter's radar coverage range, she pressed the weapons release button on the control yoke. An energy wave blasted out from the belly of her aircraft. Not as exciting as a physical missile, though the results were just as deadly. All three F-35 fighters lost flight control and two of the jets collided. Fireballs engulfed both planes in the midair collision. Their debris field would stretch for miles. The third jet tumbled toward the ground, though Jingle didn't see the inevitable impact. She scanned the sky for parachutes, but none of the pilots ejected. One of the F-35 pilots got off a distress call, no doubt heard by both the F-18 pilots and range control. Another concern for Jingle was the jets' transponders going offline, which would alert air traffic control. The emergency beacons from the jets' black boxes would also be transmitting by now, which would also trip an alert.

She had to act fast to take out the F-18s before they realized she was responsible for the deaths of the Air Force pilots. She rolled hard left and dove on an intercept course with the F-18s. The fighters were outside the PWL weapon's envelope and not enough focused energy would hit her targets at this distance. Jingle wanted her bonus for eliminating all six pilots, so she closed the gap to her prey at over a thousand miles an hour. In a few more seconds they'd be within lethal range. At this rate of speed her weapons lock would last for less than two seconds. The F-18s weren't in as tight a formation as the F-35s. She could only target two at a time and took the shot. The jets collided, but it wasn't a fatal impact. One pilot ejected. The rocket-propelled seat shot clear of the aircraft, and the parachute deployed. The third pilot pulled the stick hard left and dove. Jingle couldn't line up another weapons attempt, and she was no match for an F-18.

Over the military radio channel the remaining pilot transmitted "Mayday, Mayday, Mayday, flight of three F-18 fighters in military restricted airspace under attack. Two fighters hit, one pilot ejected. Lost radio and radar contact with flight of three F-35 fighters. Sending coordinates to Air Rescue Service. Immediately clear all remaining military aircraft from area. Call sign Shock Wave. Hunting for aggressor."

"Shock Wave, range control copies. Clearing and rerouting aircraft in the area. Air Rescue dispatched. Good hunting. Range control out."

Jingle went from hunter to prey. The remaining F-18 pilot, Navy Captain Ebony Diamond, was the one Jingle feared the most. She was no match in head-to-head combat with an experienced fighter pilot, let alone the previous commander of the Navy's TOPGUN school. Jingle's edge, stealth and surprise, was gone. Her radar signature was small but not invisible. Her opponent outmatched her in speed, maneuverability, and combat experience. Jingle's hands trembled on the yoke, and she could barely keep her plane flying on a straight trajectory. There were no other aircraft in the military restricted airspace. Even at top speed, her modified business jet couldn't outrun an F-18, especially one using its afterburners.

Her only viable option was to target the Navy jet at maximum range before Shock Wave could fire a missile. Jingle took deep calming breaths to settle her hammering heart rate and focused her attention on finding the F-18. She set the PWL targeting system for maximum range with the largest engagement zone. These settings lowered the probability of complete system destruction to sixty percent, but a hit could disable the F-18, allowing her time to escape. The PWL system went into search mode, and Jingle's excitement spiked when the screen showed *TARGET ACQUIRED*. She poised her finger over the button, ready to fire the instant she had a weapons lock. The green lock light flickered and didn't stay on long enough for Jingle to fire. The F-18 rolled hard right, and Jingle stopped breathing when the screen showed *TARGET LOST*.

She neared the edge of the military restricted airspace and began to breathe again. She might be able to blend into commercial air traffic and escape. She'd lost track of the F-18, so she pushed her jet to full power and joined a drone route to Canadian airspace. She'd lie low for a while, take time off someplace warm and lie on a beach.

Downing five of the six fighter jets was a solid accomplishment and well within successful mission parameters. Things might turn out okay.

Back on autopilot and on a northern drone route, she took the PWL weapon system offline, eliminating the opportunity for an accidental firing of the directed-energy weapon and drawing unwanted attention. She couldn't add Shock Wave to her kill wall or imagine another F-18 painted on the side of her aircraft, but she'd escaped the legendary fighter pilot's crosshairs. Today, she counted that as a win and relished the moment. A second later she saw the faint smoke trail of an approaching air-to-air missile. It was the last thing Jingle saw before her jet exploded into a fireball, debris raining down for miles.

***

General Trabago answered the encrypted call on his satellite phone. The caller said, "Five of the six fighters were shot down."

"Good. Who survived?"

"Navy Captain Ebony Diamond, but she downed the PWL attack aircraft with an Advanced Medium-Range Air-to-Air Missile."

Trabago tightened his grip on the satphone. "I'm not surprised she survived given her reputation, but this is a complication." He closed his eyes for a moment and thought. "We knew this was a possibility. Make sure our people are assigned to the emergency aircraft recovery teams. When the lead accident investigator is assigned to the review board, make sure they are vetted by the inner circle. We must insure the right conclusion to move our plans forward."

"Understood, sir."

Trabago ended the call. He had to brief Jiang on events. He knew she'd explode in an insulting harangue and he'd have to be stoic and not respond to her gibes. He preferred working with his military and clandestine services counterparts, who assessed each situation and took appropriate action with a minimum of drama, just as he had his entire career. Jiang was an annoying, though necessary, partner. He'd wait until he knew more before briefing her. There was one call he needed to make right now—the wing commander at Truax. He called her on an encrypted line.

"Colonel Banerjee speaking. How can I help you, General?"

"I was horrified to hear of the attack on your fighter aircraft today. We are treating this as a terrorist attack, and I'm taking personal charge of the investigation. Make sure all information is routed to the DIA."

Chapter 15
Harry Dexter

St. Croix Falls, Wisconsin
12 May

Harry and Jazmin were worn out when they arrived at his safe house in St. Croix Falls. They'd barely avoided being captured from the ever-tightening net of closed roadways manned by the state police and FBI agents hunting them. Their motorcycle was spattered with mud and scratched from multiple offroad escapes and hours-long hideouts in abandoned buildings. Harry had promised to get her to safety. So far, he had kept his word.

Once inside the safe house, they checked the security cameras covering the perimeter of the ten-acre property. All was clear. Harry knew once Jazmin went AWOL her special ops neurotech access would be cut off. He'd prepared for that eventuality by adding an automated routine to his data center self-destruct protocols. As a first step before he lost his data center, her name was hidden in the military neurotech access list without her losing any of her old capabilities. The system would show her as deactivated and thus eliminate tracking by the government. She had all of her old power but none of the Defense Department oversight. Military equipment under Harry's control would still recognize her.

Exhausted, they took off their helmets, leather jackets, and tactical vests, then collapsed into chairs. Harry had barely closed his eyes for some much-needed sleep when a holographic screen opened, demanding his attention. He nudged Jazmin awake.

Critical News Alert – Attack in US Airspace. Stock video of F-18 and F-35 fighters taking off from Truax Field played and at the bottom of the screen a news chyron scrolled. *A flight of three F-18 and three F-35 fighters were attacked during a training exercise. Five of the fighter jets were downed.* Drone video showed a debris field with plumes of black smoke drifting over the surrounding area, a mix of farmland and woods. The camera zoomed in on burned wreckage and the grisly remains of a pilot still strapped into the cockpit. *Only two survivors. A Navy lieutenant ejected from one of the F-18s and is now unconscious and in critical condition in University of Wisconsin Hospital in Madison. Navy Captain Ebony Diamond flew the lone F-18 that evaded the attack and downed the aggressor with an air-to-air missile.*

Harry and Jazmin watched the video loop of the debris field and crash site. A military team was already onsite. She said, "I've been assigned to these teams in the past. Stuffing bloody and burned remains into body bags is grisly duty." Jazmin looked away from the screen and took a few deep breaths. She seemed lost in bad memories.

Harry knew she'd want more data and thought about what was available. Except for clandestine missions in hostile airspace, black box data was captured live from military aircraft and pushed into military cloud data storage. Commercial aircraft black box data along with radar coverage in the US and allied nations was also captured live and then pushed into an FAA cloud data warehouse.

Jazmin looked back at the video loop. "I wish we had access to cockpit video."

"Give me a moment."

"I thought that data was encrypted and locked down," she said.

"Since when has that ever stopped me?" He opened three holographic windows with frozen video images. Each showed the pilot's control panel and a timer starting at three minutes and ending at zero. "I can open up the time window to the beginning of the flight, but I thought this is what you'd need to see."

The wide-angle view from the camera above the pilot's left shoulder showed the instrument layout. It also showed the aircraft exterior view through the cockpit bubble canopy, both ahead of the plane and on both sides. Jazmin started the video for the lead aircraft.

"The three jets are in tight formation. Two are right behind the lead's wingtips. This is exactly what I would expect. There's nothing unusual on the instrument panel. The jet's at cruise power. All other engine and flight controls are within normal operating parameters. The only anomaly I see is the tactical radar. The flight of three F-18s is there, but right before the planes are destroyed, there's an unidentified aircraft in military restricted airspace. Every military aircraft would show a transponder ID. Even a civilian aircraft or drone that wandered into the area would have a squawk code. We need to identify that aircraft."

Harry said, "That might be difficult if it never transmitted an aircraft ID."

They continued to watch the cockpit video. The final seconds showed complete loss of flight control and camera shake when the two trailing aircraft slammed into the lead jet. Jazmin repeated the exercise with video from each of the trailing planes. "The other two jets show all systems normal and in controlled formation flight until the final moments. There's something off but I don't know what. I'm missing something. Do you have access to helmet video?"

He said, "Let me see what I can do." After a few seconds three more holographic windows opened.

"Helmet video shows only critical information. It's limited to key engine parameters, air speed, altitude, and tactical radar. The unidentified aircraft had been on an intercept course with the F-35s. I'd like to know where the mystery aircraft went after the F-35s went down."

Harry closed the cockpit and helmet video windows and opened a new holographic screen with radar coverage for the military restricted airspace. The radar view showed the three F-18s with the unidentified aircraft closing at a high rate of speed. It refreshed every few seconds showing updated locations for each aircraft. Harry stopped the display when the two F-18s collided and the third fighter peeled away. He asked, "What kind of plane is the mystery aircraft? Its radar signature doesn't line up with any type of military aircraft, and it's too small for any drone that could fly that fast."

Jazmin zoomed in on the unidentified aircraft and ran the radar signature library against it. The screen showed *No Match*. "Whatever this thing is, it's been designed for stealth."

Harry opened another holographic window. "I'm searching for satellite coverage. Maybe we can get lucky." Blurry images and a time stamp measured in hundredths of a second flashed on the screen, then the image stopped. It was fuzzy at first, then it resolved into a clear but distant object.

Jazmin studied the photo. "It's a business jet."

"This is no ordinary private jet." He zoomed in on the nose of the plane where there was a bulge on both sides. "There's two high-power directional energy beam ports."

Jazmin let out a long breath. "Captain Diamond blew it to hell with an air-to-air missile. We can't reconstruct that weapon from fragments. Can you trace where this originated from?"

Harry opened a new screen on top of the others. The radar tracks reversed direction, and the timestamp flashed on the screen, this time going backward. Two F-18 fighters reappeared and came together along with the lone surviving F-18. The picture zoomed out and next the F-35 jet fighters appeared on the screen. The view zoomed out again showing the adjoining commercial airspace surrounding the restricted military zone. He kept the unidentified aircraft centered on the screen at all times, and the timestamp continued to roll backward. The mystery plane finally squawked a commercial transponder ID. "Got you." The timestamp froze. He did a squawk code search and matched it to the flight plan and aircraft. "It took off from Dane County airport." Next he checked the plane's records. It was owned by a shell company registered in the Cayman Islands.

His expression darkened. "It's probably a black ops mercenary outfit on the US government payroll. The people behind this are getting bolder. They're testing directed-energy weapons on US military aircraft. The question is, what's their end game? Is it a show to motivate the defense hawks in Congress to take action?"

"It's fortunate Captain Diamond was involved. Her call sign Shock Wave sums up her personality. She blew the enemy pilot out of the sky, and she'll hunt down whoever's behind the attack."

Harry waved his arm, and the holographic screens closed. "Maybe Diamond can kick down doors that we can't and bring Jiang and Trabago out from the shadows."

A yellow strobe light flashed, and the security system announced, "Media Alert." Multiple holographic windows opened. Jazmin scanned them, each one showing news worse than the last. The first window showed *Terrorist Watch List – Wanted for Attack Against US Aircraft in Wisconsin.* Harry and Jazmin's names and photos were displayed like old-fashioned wanted posters, along with a $500,000 reward for information leading to the capture of these domestic terrorists. The only thing missing was *Wanted Dead or Alive*, though it was implied. Another window showed video from a local news station. The reporter was in an open hangar with the runway behind her and Truax in the distance on the other side of the flight line. "This is Krystal Boomer reporting live from Madison, Wisconsin. Behind me is the base where the downed fighter jets originated. Two of the six pilots survived, though one is in critical condition at University of Wisconsin Hospital. The hero of the day is Navy Captain Ebony Diamond, former commander of the Navy's TOPGUN school. She shot down the attacking aircraft.

"The Defense Intelligence Agency has released photos of the two suspects in this heinous attack on American soil." The terrorist watch list images appeared on the screen. The reporter continued. "A disgraced former Cyber Command Major, Harry Dexter, along with AWOL Navy Commander Jazmin Hassani, a Special Forces pilot, are the chief suspects. Both were involved in an attack yesterday on a military octocopter, killing the pilot and two crew members. This pair is considered armed and dangerous. If you see them, do not try to apprehend. Instead, immediately report them to the Defense Intelligence Agency using any of the contact methods listed on your screen."

The wanted posters vanished. "Dexter and Hassani are believed to be supported by Chinese government forces. When the Chinese ambassador was confronted by our Washington DC affiliate, she called any notion of Chinese involvement a complete lie, saying these sorts of allegations would further strain the US Chinese relationship."

Jazmin said, "This damn sure wasn't the Chinese, whatever narrative Jiang and Trabago are pushing."

Harry silenced the newscast. "We need to leave. We're in a small town, and a half million dollar reward will motivate the local cops and vigilantes to hunt us down."

"Where can we go?"

"It's time to head to the bunker."

"What's the bunker?"

"A place with friends and lots of weapons. I'll explain later."

He didn't want to tell Jazmin that getting her to the bunker had always been the objective.

Jazmin said, "Even blaming us, Jiang and Trabago will have a hard time covering this up, especially with a survivor who shot down the attacking aircraft. I don't understand their endgame. Why in the hell would they attack US military aircraft if they want to prove how effective directed-energy weapons are?"

"Follow the money. It's possible this was another demonstration of Pulse Weapons Labs capabilities. We know Jiang is secretly on PWL's board and a major shareholder. She's just maximizing shareholder value."

Jazmin shook her head in disgust. "How can someone kill so casually for money? The senator's already rich. What's in it for Trabago?"

Harry shrugged. "You're right about Jiang. She already has more money than she can spend. After a certain point it's no longer wealth or lifestyle. Money means power. Who knows, they both might have other reasons."

Both of their tablets beeped, and Jazmin read the screen. *Terrorist Alert — be on lookout for Harry Dexter and Jazmin Hassani. Report immediately to DIA.* "It's time to disappear."

Harry let out a long breath. "Agreed." He pulled a blister pack from a hidden pocket with ten Modafinil tablets. "We're both exhausted. It's time for some go pills." He took one and gave the package to Jazmin.

"It's been a while since I've needed to take these." She stared at the package for a moment, then pressed a pill into her hand and dry swallowed it.

Harry had taken a lot of go pills when he was in Cyber Command. The meds allowed special forces operators and pilots to function on little or no sleep. The pills increased concentration and enhanced decision making. He knew from experience they worked until they didn't. Even with pharmaceutical help he could only function on zero sleep for so long. Harry's mission had been simple, but every moment it was getting more complicated. His orders were clear: Tell her only enough to keep her with him. He hoped Jazmin would forgive him.

Chapter 16
Mei Chan

Chinese Military Intelligence Headquarters
12 May

Mei focused on the report for her superior, rewording it to diplomatically send the message that his preferred course of action would end in disaster. A knock at her door interrupted her work. Colonel Ming, her chief of staff, entered. "I'm sorry to interrupt, General, but you need to see this." He held out his tablet with a television news report on an attack at Truax Field in Madison, Wisconsin, USA. Mei watched long enough to learn five military pilots were shot down and Navy Captain Ebony Diamond was the lone survivor. She seethed at the news, though didn't allow her facial expression to reveal her inner turmoil.

"Please monitor all relevant news sources and keep me informed of significant events."

Colonel Ming tucked the tablet back into his pocket. "I'll give this story my personal attention." He exited her office and closed the door.

Mei scanned several other news sources on her tablet and learned the attacking aircraft hadn't been identified before it was destroyed by an air-to-air missile from Diamond's F-18. She knew it would take the Americans months to reconstruct the pieces from the extended debris field into an airplane, though they'd eventually succeed, and they would tie it back to PWL. Once that connection was made, it could also lead them to their Chinese sponsors.

Mei had initially recruited Ling Chen as a Chinese military asset, and her success in the US Senate was beyond Mei's wildest imagination. The problem was that with her rise to power as the senior senator on the Armed Services Committee, Ling Chen's arrogance had grown out of control. It was time to rein her in. Mei sent an encrypted message to Ling Chen and scheduled a video call, nighttime for the American and mid-morning for Mei.

***

Mei was in no mood for their usual pleasantries. Drumming her fingers, she waited for the encrypted video call to connect and the secure light to turn green. "You're out of control.

This was supposed to be a simple demonstration downing a single aircraft and leaving no trace of the weapon's source behind."

Ling Chen coolly stared back, unruffled by Mei's accusations. "Five of the six fighters were destroyed by the PWL weapon. American law enforcement is chasing Hassani and Dexter, who are now both on terrorist watch lists. The missile left the attacking aircraft scattered in so many pieces the authorities will have a hard time identifying the type of plane, let alone assembling any meaningful evidence. I have people in place to make sure damaging information is suppressed. The situation is under control."

Mei thought deflecting the blame for the attack onto Hassani and Dexter was inspired, though she'd never admit that to Ling Chen. "You didn't execute the plan. You were reckless."

Ling Chen laughed. "I was bold, and I succeeded. This attack on American military aircraft at a US base can't be ignored. Our goal is for China to lead the world with directed-energy weapons technology. This was a demonstration to send that message."

Mei leaned into the camera and narrowed her eyes. "You've been in America too long. You no longer understand subtlety or how to send an indirect message."

Ling Chen flashed an icy smile and leaned back. "I understand Americans in ways you never will. Violence is the only thing they understand. I delivered the message that needed to be sent."

Mei let out a long breath. She'd coached Ling Chen and supported her rise to power in the American government. She was no longer the timid young woman Mei recruited all those years ago but, like an errant dog, she needed to be reminded who was in control. While Mei wanted to bring her star asset in line, it would have to wait. Damage control was the best she could do today. "You need to silence Diamond. I'm concerned about what she might uncover."

Ling Chen leaned forward, and her arrogant expression fell away. "I'm making sure she's banned from the investigation and cut off from her usual supporters."

"Keep me informed of any new developments." My staff will be watching too, she thought.

Ling Chen nodded, smugness clinging to this tiny gesture. "Of course." As a final act of taking back control, she ended the call.

Mei would have to think about what steps she'd need to take to bring Ling Chen in line. Her fear was that the senator's arrogance and reckless behavior would bring them both down. Mei had worked too many years climbing the ranks of Chinese Military Intelligence to let any asset derail her, even one as valuable as Ling Chen. Mei was a three-star general, and she wanted the fourth star that went with the top job in military intelligence. Success would be hers, as long as she was committed enough to her goals and ruthless enough in her actions.

Chapter 17
Jazmin Hassani

St. Croix Falls, Wisconsin
12 May

Jazmin and Harry had barely arrived at the safe house when it was time to run again. They put on their tactical vests and headed out the door. She assumed they'd get back on the motorcycle, but when she approached it, Harry shook his head, then took the bike inside the safe house.

She stuck her head in the doorway. "What are we using for transportation?"

"We have a better option. I'll be right out."

A minute later he returned, and the door closed behind him. Harry looked into the surveillance camera. "Execute safe house lockdown protocols. Deadly force authorized."

A computerized voice responded. "Safe house locked and armed."

He turned, then headed to the back of the property and Jazmin followed. When they were thirty yards from the house, he punched a code into his tablet and a telescoping bollard punched up through the soil. He flipped open the cap on top of the bollard covering a retinal scanner and placed his eye over the viewer. A few seconds later, a section of prairie grass retracted to expose a fifteen-foot-wide ramp. A holographic image of the original prairie grass was projected onto the opening to disguise the subterranean chamber from drone or satellite cameras.

Harry led the way into an underground garage where an eight-wheeled Amphibious Combat Vehicle was parked. Jazmin had used these on special ops missions, though there were many variants. She walked around all four sides to determine this particular ACV's weapons and armor. It had bulletproof glass and nanoparticle composite armor plating on all sides, making it impervious to a wide array of munitions while remaining extremely light for its size. It was armed with .50 caliber remotely operated automatic weapons, 30mm cannons, a rocket propelled grenade launcher, and surface-to-air missiles. "This is quite a war machine. I can see why you don't drive this around town."

Harry shrugged. "It's a dangerous world out there." He patted the hood of the huge vehicle, and it flashed its lights. "ACV, allow full pilot and weapons control to Jazmin Hassani."

A computerized voice responded. "Confirm voice, retina, handprint, and biochip identification."

Jazmin had completed this ritual countless times on special ops missions as pilot in command. The left side window lit up with an input screen. She placed both her palms on the screen and looked into the retinal scanner.

The ACV responded, "Handprint and retina match confirmed. Continue with voice and biochip identity."

She waved her left arm across the biochip reader. "Commander Jazmin Hassani, US Navy."

"Identity confirmed. Full pilot and weapons control authorized." Composite armor entry doors opened with a hiss.

Harry asked, "How's your claustrophobia?"

"Since my accident, not great. I'm okay as long as I'm not in a confined space surrounded by people or in really tight quarters. When those things happen I begin to lose it."

"It will be just the two of us in the ACV. Hopefully you'll be all right."

She nodded, though not convinced, then climbed inside to take a look. The interior of the ACV was filled with weapons and gear, some in racks and the rest behind labeled panels or in storage compartments. She would have to practice her breathing routine to stay calm.

When she exited the ACV, Harry said, "I prepared for the worst, and now it's here." A holographic screen opened. It flashed red three times then displayed *Intruder Alert*. Surveillance video showed two men armed with assault rifles, peering into the windows of the safe house. The men's appearance this soon was disturbing. Harry opened a full hivemind link and Jazmin immediately accepted. She could now read his thoughts. He was rattled too. Harry grabbed two combat shotguns from the weapons rack in the ACV, handed one to Jazmin, and they headed up the ramp. They hid in the trees at the edge of the clearing, where they watched and listened. Jazmin used her neurotech to check the military facial recognition database. After a minute a match came back on both men. *They're Serbian Special Forces, though their bio ends three years ago after they escaped from a military prison serving life sentences for killing their commander.*

Somebody hired them for their skills and lack of legitimate options, Harry responded.

Even though these foreign mercenaries wouldn't hesitate to kill her, Jazmin didn't want another death on her conscience. She wanted to walk away but knew what she had to do. Raising her shotgun, she targeted one of the men while Harry targeted the other. The two mercenaries backed away from the house, then pivoted toward the clearing and brought up short-barrel automatic weapons in one smooth motion. They swept the area for targets, but Jazmin and Harry fired before the men spotted them. The shotguns' slug ammo tore through their victims, and they died instantly from the heavy projectiles designed for hunting large animals. Jazmin had reacted to protect herself, though she knew their bloody images would haunt her.

Harry handed Jazmin his shotgun. *Put these back in the ACV. I'll collect their weapons, tablets, and the spent slugs.* She headed for the garage and put their weapons back into the ACV's gun rack. When she returned, Harry pointed at their victims. Both men had bled out rapidly from chest wounds, the dirt soaking up the blood. *We've got to dispose of the bodies.* He picked up the first man under his arms, and she grabbed the man's feet. They carried him across the dusty field and down the ramp into the underground garage. They laid him next to a rectangular cap on the cement floor. They went back for the other man and laid him next to the first.

Harry handed her a large jug with a pouring spout. *It's filled with DNA scrambler. We need to destroy any evidence that these two were ever here.*

Sprinkle this anywhere you see blood, bone, or tissue.

She took the jug to where the men were shot, twisted the cap on the spout, and tilted the jug until liquid sprayed out. As she poured the DNA scrambler on the remains of their victims, white smoke floated up from the ground and blew away in the breeze, leaving dirt, weeds, and unidentifiable DNA residue behind. Jazmin rechecked the area to make sure there was no trace of their crime, then scuffed the dirt with her boot.

When Jazmin returned to the garage, what she saw stopped her at the top of the ramp. Harry wore thick rubber boots and was encased in a hazmat suit with full head-to-toe coverage. The suit had a breathing hose connected to a filter unit that hung off Harry's back. The cover had been pulled aside, exposing a rectangular tank sunk into the floor. A high-speed exhaust fan on the roof of the garage whirred above him. Harry looked up at her, though she couldn't read his expression with his face obscured. His dark thoughts coming through their hive mind connection chilled her even before his words did. *Stay where you are, the tank is filled with sulfuric acid.*

Standing well away from the acid bath, Jazmin still had a clear view from her vantage point. Using a pole with a hook, Harry dragged the first man up to the edge of the tank and nudged him into the acid feet first. Harry backed away as violent bubbling erupted from the tank. After a minute the bubbling slowed, and Harry pushed the other body into the tank. He dropped the spent shotgun slugs, the men's weapons, and their tablets into the acid bath. *They have no identification and if anyone finds them, they'll be impossible to identify.*

The fact that Harry had an acid bath for disposing of dead bodies was chilling. Since they were on a full hivemind connection, she peered into the dark recesses of Harry's mind. How much violence and depravity was in his past? What were his limits? In the back of the underground garage was a torture chamber behind a hidden panel. The images from Harry's past were overwhelming, both in sheer number and the gory details. Harry had tortured numerous enemies both when he was in Cyber Command and after he left. Modern militaries no longer used metal dog tags, only biochips for identification. Harry had collected his victim's biochips and kept them as obscene souvenirs.

Jazmin severed their hivemind connection and retched. After

her stomach was empty, she dry heaved. When she finally stopped, Jazmin wiped her mouth with the back of her hand. The acid taste of vomit lingered in her mouth. The body count kept going up. How many more murders would she commit? Her heart raced, and she took a couple of deep breaths to calm herself, each was more labored than the last. She couldn't wait to leave, but she still had no idea where they were headed.

Jazmin finally snapped out of her daze when Harry, hazmat suit now gone, stood next to her. She wondered how long he'd been there. He tapped his temple indicating he'd like a hivemind connection. She hesitated, then initiated a connection but this time she limited it to communication only.

He said, *You need to compartmentalize this, or you won't be able to live with yourself.* The anguished look in his eyes told her his warning came from personal experience. *Time for us to disappear.*

The doors of the ACV slid open when they approached. Harry entered the left side with the driver's instrument display and Jazmin entered on the right side with the weapons panel. Both strapped in with five-point harnesses similar to a fighter jet. Once the doors closed, Jazmin terminated their hivemind connection.

He said, "Destination Superior, Wisconsin, back roads, maximum stealth, weapons hot."

The ACV responded. "Command authority confirmed. Proceeding to destination." The combat vehicle silently headed up the ramp. Once they cleared the top, the entryway closed and the cylindrical bollard retracted into the earth. It was dusk now, and they drove through the woods in the back of Harry's property and out to the two-lane road. The motorcycle tracks near the main entrance from when they arrived might confuse a team sent to follow them. The tracking team would waste time and miss the ACV tracks. Jazmin studied the weapons panel. She had been the weapon system officer on ACV SEAL team missions. Her main screen showed *Weapon Systems Status*. RPG's, .50 caliber guns, and 30mm cannons were on standby. Anti-aircraft missiles and torpedo tubes were offline.

The ACV sensors didn't require visible light, so they drove in darkness on the rural roads. The interior lighting switched to red to ease the strain on Harry's eyes, and Jazmin's eyes switched to night vision mode. Designed for stealth, the ACV emitted a limited sensor array for both navigation and weapons, making it difficult for police and military to find them at long distances. Despite the vehicle's short range sensor capabilities and countless warning systems, Jazmin continuously scanned the road ahead and to the sides. Her weapons panel tracked air traffic, though so far detected only a few delivery drones.

***

Two hours into their drive north an alert flashed on her screen. "There's a military drone at twenty thousand feet, but there's no bases or anything of strategic value in this part of the state."

"Except us," Harry said.

She brought the anti-aircraft missiles online. Then, using the targeting computer, she zoomed in on the drone. "It's the latest generation AI combat drone with two air-to-surface missiles onboard, and it's tracking us as targets of interest."

Harry opened a weapon systems window on his display. "Let's take it out with an antiaircraft missile."

Jazmin checked her weapons panel for a threat response assessment. "The drone would launch a missile against us before ours hit."

"We need to kill it a different way."

"Or vanish. Can you hack its onboard computer?" Before Harry could reply, transcripts of the combat drone's transmissions scrolled across her weapons alert screen. "An octocopter gunship has been dispatched for a visual."

"What's their ETA?"

"Five minutes out." Jazmin checked the surrounding terrain. There were woods but no place they could hide from an octocopter.

Harry said, "If we speed up or head off the road we'll trip all kinds of alarms."

"I scanned for a warehouse or factory building we could hide in, but there's nothing close that their sensors can't see through."

"I have something in mind. I'm rerouting us to Lake Superior."

"How does that help us?" she asked.

"You'll see."

Alerts scrolled across her tactical display. "The copters are scanning us."

"Let's not give them a reason to lock weapons until we're ready. The ACV's got armor but won't withstand a full assault from a gunship and a drone."

"Dammit, Harry, I know that."

"Think like an octocopter pilot. They won't shoot if there's doubt in their minds. We can't react to their presence."

"That's only if we're dealing with a military pilot. If they're mercenaries, all bets are off."

"Even mercenaries don't want to explain their fuckups to their bosses." Large caliber shells pinged off the ACV. "Looks like the rules of engagement just changed." He checked the tactical screen. "ACV, top speed to the lake." They were squashed back into their seats as they rocketed to one hundred fifty miles per hour on the two-lane highway running along the lakeshore. "Jaz, fire anti-aircraft missiles and take out the octocopter and the drone."

She locked weapons on the two aircraft and fired missiles. As soon as her ordnance were away, the tactical alert flashed on her screen. *Air to Surface Missile on Intercept Course!* Death rocketed toward them. She watched the tactical display in horror and counted down the seconds remaining in her life. The ACV's sharp left swerve barely registered in her consciousness as they careened off the highway and were airborne over the lake.

Time slowed, and it felt like they hung in the air for an eternity before a blinding flash and shockwave slammed their vehicle. Pain radiated through her body from the energy wave. Flung against the straps, the five-point harness barely held her in place. The ACV hit the water with another vibrating jolt. Completely submerged, they sank toward the dark frigid bottom of Lake Superior.

Chapter 18
Ling Chen Jiang

Washington, DC
12 May

Ling Chen paced around the top floor of her condo, then stood on the balcony and peered into the nighttime sky. Trabago was thirty minutes late for their meeting. She valued punctuality and his lateness stank of disrespect. Their relationship had become prickly and, while they needed each other, the veneer of civility had worn away. Her musing was interrupted by heavy footfalls from the living room, accompanied by Danica's catlike steps. Ling Chen turned and glared at Trabago from the balcony. "You're late."

"I was detained, Senator." Ice dripped from each precisely enunciated word.

Ling Chen entered the living room. "Danica, you're excused." The security officer backed away and disappeared downstairs. "Have Dexter and Hassani been taken care of?"

Trabago's impassive expression was his tell, and it was a bad sign. "We believe so."

"That's a weasel answer I expect from a politician. Not from you. Explain, General." Her opinion of the general's effectiveness sank further. She sat in her favorite chair, though she didn't extend an invitation for him to sit.

"Dexter and Hassani were flushed from his safe house in St. Croix Falls, Wisconsin. A black ops team was sent to dispose of them, but both men are missing and haven't reported in. A follow-up team was sent and secured the safe house. Unfortunately, Dexter and Hassani were gone by then. Inside the safe house, we found the motorcycle they used to escape from Milwaukee. Amphibious Combat Vehicle tire tracks were found at the back of the property, and we believe that's how they escaped."

She leaned forward and gripped the arms of her chair. "So once again, they slipped away."

Trabago bristled. "A military combat drone picked up a suspicious vehicle in northwest Wisconsin and dispatched an octocopter gunship for human confirmation."

Ling Chen rolled her eyes. "Did they find and execute Dexter and Hassani?"

"When the gunship got close, the ACV fired missiles at both the gunship and the drone, then accelerated toward the lake. The octocopter crew fired an air-to-surface missile at the ACV before both airborne platforms were destroyed. Satellite coverage shows the ACV went airborne over the lake and was within the effective blast radius when the missile detonated."

Ling Chen shook her head in exasperation. "You still haven't answered my question. Did anyone recover bodies from the lake and confirm their identities?"

Trabago frowned. "Lake Superior is cold and deep. They couldn't have survived. There's no other activity in the area."

She stood. "Not good enough, General."

Trabago closed the gap between them. "An underwater drone is enroute to search the lake."

Though he towered over her, she peered up at his angry eyes unafraid. Despite the general's irritation and formidable size, he wouldn't physically assault her. Attacking a US senator would end his military career and land him in prison. Her security team had them under surveillance and would intervene if necessary. Danica wouldn't hesitate to slam Trabago into a wall, and his three stars would offer scant protection. "Let me know when you've confirmed their deaths. That pair is a threat to our plans. The rest of the details don't matter."

Trabago stood his ground. "I'm not one of your underlings you can order around."

She gave him an indulgent smile. "No, General, but we're in this together. If I go down, I'll take you with me all the way to the bottom."

Chapter 19
Jazmin Hassani

Lake Superior – Near Bayfield, Wisconsin
12 May

Shaken from both the missile detonation and the airborne ACV hitting the water, Jazmin struggled to think clearly. Every part of her body hurt, but she ignored the pain. Until she had time to evaluate her injuries, she was afraid to turn down her pain receptors. She wasn't on a hivemind link with Harry. She glanced at him to check if he was hurt. He looked fine and seemed surprisingly unfazed by what had just happened. Her top priority was to assess their situation. The ACV was in a steep dive, and the outside water pressure was ramping up by the second. She searched the hull for any cracks and the door seals for leaks. The ACV was watertight for the moment, though that could change at any time. A mechanical whirring spooked her, and they dove even faster. She focused on controlling her rapid breaths and hammering heart to keep panic at bay, though it was a losing battle. She feared being trapped underwater and drowning. Knowing they were in a combat vehicle designed to operate submerged didn't alleviate her stress. On all of her previous missions, the team had used a checklist to complete the multiple transition steps required to go from land to water operation, especially when operating underwater at depth.

She took a deep breath, let it out slowly, then checked her instrument cluster. *Depth 120 feet, forward speed 12 knots, two propellers turning, battery charge at 96 percent, passive sonar online, torpedoes loaded in tubes one and two.* She switched to weapon status. *Tube one, EMP torpedo. Tube two, anti-ship torpedo. Firing checks complete.*

She checked the door seals and windows again for any traces of moisture indicating a leak. "Launching off the highway was an insane risk."

"Yes, but it worked."

The ACV leveled off at a depth of 170 feet. Her fear-induced adrenaline rush faded, then fatigue hit her. "Where are we headed, to some secret underwater submarine pen?" It wasn't a serious question, simply gallows humor after surviving the air-to-surface missiles.

Harry looked at her straight-faced. "That's exactly where we're going. The bunker in Bayfield has a submarine dock underneath it." He turned on the ACV's night vision, and the front screen glowed green and cabin lights turned red. Jazmin didn't need this as her eyes had already switched to night vision mode. They passed a couple of shipwrecks. Schools of lake trout swam by. "It's not far," he said.

An alert flashed on Jazmin's tactical screen. *Military Drone Detected on Passive Sonar.* A weapons alert came up next. *Drone Armed with Torpedoes.* She said, "This drone was dispatched when we didn't surface."

"Taking out a drone and an octocopter gunship motivated them to make sure we're dead. Let's keep them wondering." Harry shut down the props and eased open the ballast tanks to take on more water. "Let's head to the bottom and get lost in ground clutter."

The ACV glided downward at a thirty-degree angle. Ahead were the upright remains of a ship that had gone down in a prior century from a hole torn in its metal side. Years of accumulated silt added to the deterioration of the Great Lakes freighter. Harry adjusted the ACV's dive planes and set down on one of the few clear spots on the deck of the derelict ship. "If the drone finds us, we'll need to kill it quietly. I don't want to attract attention this close to the base."

Jazmin ran their weapon systems diagnostics to confirm everything was still functioning. All weapons showed green. "The EMP torpedo is our best option."

"Agreed, but make sure we're out of the hot zone. EMPs propagate differently under water than in the air."

They both watched the passive sonar tactical screen. The computer created a simulated image of the drone along with its track. Each time the drone came closer on its circuitous search path, more details appeared on the display. The tactical screen showed a red circle centered on the drone, surrounded by a circular yellow band along with the current ACV location. The colors indicated the hazard zone for their EMP torpedo as it tracked the drone's location. If the EMP torpedo detonated while the ACV was in the red zone, their computer systems would be toast and they'd be dead in the water.

Their current depth was 310 feet. If they were trapped down here, making it to the surface without getting decompression sickness would require an obscene amount of luck. Even if they survived that, hypothermia from swimming in forty-five degree water would kill them before they made it to shore. Jazmin set the EMP torpedo targeting control to allow detonation only outside the yellow zone. Detonation inside the yellow zone was potentially fatal, depending on how badly their control systems were damaged. Even though the ACV was shielded from EMP blasts, water distorted everything.

The underwater drone continued to search the area. Its path brought it both closer and further away during its circuits. The search pattern was AI driven, though Jazmin had no idea what logic or parameters the artificial intelligence was trying to optimize.

Harry cycled through all the exterior camera views and lingered on the forward screen. "That drone keeps getting closer. Target torpedo tubes one and two. Hit it with the EMP if you can, otherwise we'll need to leave in a hurry if the anti-ship torpedo detonates."

"I've been manually targeting the drone when it's in range, but I can't lock on to it, or we'll get its attention."

"I don't mind if it knows we're here, as long as we can kill it before it responds."

"AI drones are fast. I'll only do a weapons lock when I'm about to fire." She opened the torpedo tube doors and flooded the compartments.

The underwater drone circled back and headed straight for them. For the first time, it used active sonar, and pings hammered on the hull of the ACV. Jazmin locked on to the drone with both torpedoes, hoping to fire the EMP, but they were in the red zone. She fired the anti-ship torpedo in tube two and ten seconds later it obliterated the drone, but the resulting shockwave slammed the ACV sideways off the sunken ship's deck. The left bow plane caught a piece of railing on the ship, tipping them sideways, and the water-filled ballast tank pulled them to the bottom of the lake like an anchor. Since Jazmin was strapped into the seat on the downside of the ACV, every loose item inside missed Harry and careened toward her, pelting her with tools, weapons, and ammo. Just before the ACV righted itself, a shotgun fell from the weapons rack and slammed into the side of her skull. Her head exploded in a wave of pain and nausea. She felt woozy and was barely able to focus. She closed her eyes and lay back against her seat until she felt less wretched.

Jazmin hadn't blacked out, or at least she didn't think she had. She'd definitely lost track of time. "How long have I been out of it?"

"About ten minutes." Concern and fear was etched into Harry's face.

Not as long as she feared. Jazmin felt her head. "No blood but there's a lump. I hope I don't have a concussion." She tested her neurotech by taking control of the cabin lights, turning them up and down. Fortunately she didn't have any trouble. Next she opened a communication only hivemind connection with Harry. *Do you hear my voice in your head?*

Sure do. How do you feel?

Relieved that my neurotech is working and pissed at the engineer who designed the gun rack. She winced in pain when her fingertips grazed the lump on her head. She disconnected from her hivemind link with Harry.

"The torpedo caused a lot of residual damage."

The bland statement with no details meant he wasn't telling her everything.

"Are we trapped down here?" she asked.

"Maybe." He sighed. "The ballast tank water valve is stuck open and the dive planes on the right side are jammed. Even if we get off the bottom of the lake it'll be almost impossible to control our depth or direction."

Jazmin tried to concentrate. They had a limited amount of time to get out of there. Even if they got the ballast tank valve working, pushing out the water would use up a huge amount of their air reserve. "Can we reach the ballast tank valve assembly from inside the ACV?"

Harry shook his head. "Access to the valve is under a panel on the bottom of the vehicle. It's only reachable from the outside." He pointed to a rear compartment on the left side of the ACV. "I have a repair kit."

She checked the life support screen to determine how long they could remain underwater before their air ran out. Another screen showed their depth at 345 feet.

Harry said, "The underwater explosion will attract all the wrong kinds of attention. Another drone is probably on its way."

She'd never seen him this subdued during a crisis, as if he'd already given up. "Show me your deep water diving gear."

He stared at the equipment panels lining the sides of the ACV, and after a moment pointed to one, then blurted, "I'm an expert skydiver and base jumper but I'm not even a certified scuba diver, let alone a technical diver." Now she understood his hesitation.

Jazmin knew diving with a possible concussion was risky. At this depth she didn't know how that would affect her. Her other alternative was certain death from running out of air. "The diving expert on our SEAL team was a technical diver. I was interested in deep-water diving, so she trained me, and I went on cave dives with her." Jazmin looked in the back of the ACV and found the *Technical Diving Equipment* panel and opened it, exposing a deep cabinet of tanks and diving equipment. "There are tanks with trimix, which is oxygen, helium, and nitrogen. There are also a couple of drysuits, masks, swim fins, and a dive computer. I'm certified on this type of equipment, and I'm used to managing the gas mix."

Another panel was marked *Escape Tube*. She hit the release button, and the panel slid open, exposing a horizontal clear tube with pressure doors on each end, one at the outer wall at the back of the ACV and the other inside the vehicle. She took a closer look at the gear and the size of the escape tube. "This is going to be a tight fit once I get the dive gear on." She pulled the diving gear from the equipment locker. The tanks, regulator, and dive computer were identical to what she'd used with Cinnamon, her SEAL team dive instructor. "With my bionic legs, I need less air. I just have to oxygenate the upper half of my body." She stripped off her clothes and wriggled into the drysuit and gloves. It wasn't a perfect fit, but it was close enough.

Harry brought over the replacement valve kit for the ballast tank and the required tools. He projected a repair procedure video for her from his tablet. "Let's get you inside the escape tube." He released the pressure seal and swung the door open. The space was narrow, and it would be a tight fit for Jazmin and her required gear. He put the repair kit and tool bag at the bottom where her feet would go, then connected a strap to her leg so they couldn't get away from her. Jazmin swung herself into the tube, lying uncomfortably on the tanks. She got everything into place and performed a final regulator check. Harry opened a hivemind connection and a mix of fear, relief, and encouragement flooded her consciousness.

She looked up at him. *I'm ready.* He closed and latched the door and did a final pressure check. It felt like a tight-fitting cylindrical coffin. The only thing that kept her claustrophobia from overwhelming her was seeing Harry's face through the transparent chamber and feeling his reassurance through the hivemind connection.

If you can't repair the ballast tank, head for the surface. You can come back for me. They both knew if she was unsuccessful and swam to the surface, he'd be dead long before she could find help and rescue him. He'd run out of air, or another drone would come and finish him off. Several drones were probably hunting for them now.

It's a simple repair. I'll be right back, and we can get out of here. Her words conveyed a confidence she didn't feel, and she couldn't hide her fears from Harry on a hivemind connection. In a depot for a certified ACV mechanic, this was a straightforward repair. Using tools while wearing heavy diving gloves, in frigid water over three hundred feet deep, was more than challenging. It was still better than her other option, dying down here. She cycled the bottom chamber pressure seal to allow lake water inside. Even in the dry suit, the cold at this depth was numbing, and the water pressure crushing against her chest made it difficult to breathe. She wanted to check the dive computer strapped to her wrist, but her arms were pinned to her sides in the tight chamber.

When pressure equalized, the eye-level green light went on and the hatch at the back end of the chamber opened. She carefully wriggled her way out of the confined space into open water. Now that she had room to move, she checked her dive computer and adjusted her gas mix. Next she turned on her facemask LED lights and illuminated the bottom of the ACV. She swam to the ballast access door, trailed by the repair kit and tool bag strapped to her leg.

The valve door is just above the lake bottom and the tires have settled into the silt. There's not much room to get the new valve assembly in place.

Copy.

I'm checking the left side diving planes. The front one is bent from where it caught on the ship's railing and the rear diving plane is undamaged. Jazmin swam around to the other side of the ACV. *Right side front and back diving planes are bent down and stuck in the lake bottom.*

That explains why the right side dive planes won't move.

I only have time to swap out the ballast tank valve. If we're lucky the dive planes might be functional once we float off the bottom.

We're due for some good luck.

She swam to the ballast access panel and reached for the tool bag. She found the special tool to release the panel, then pulled it open. Her tanks and facemask were too big to let her see inside. She tried taking off the tank backpack to see if that got her any closer, but the space was too tight. She'd have to do the repair by feel, reaching in at an awkward angle. She put her tank backpack on again and found the tool needed to remove the valve assembly. Making the repair in diving gloves added to the difficulty. It was impossible to get the correct angle to loosen the bolts, and the torque wrench kept slipping. The cold and pressure from working at this depth were taking their toll on her, so she checked her tank gauges and dive computer. She'd been exerting herself more than she realized and was burning up air at a frightening rate. She kept working. Five of the six fasteners were out, and the last one was stripped. After several more minutes of effort, it finally came free. *Harry, cut the power to the ballast tank valves.*

Already done. How is your air holding out?

Just fine, she lied, and he'd know it, but she'd rather die trying to save them than give up. Jazmin pulled the valve assembly free from the four wiring harness connectors and dropped the malfunctioning part into the silt at the bottom of the lake. She retrieved the new valve assembly from the repair kit, reconnected the wiring harness, and started replacing fasteners. When she got the third fastener in place, it got harder to breathe. The warning alarm on her dive computer vibrated violently on her wrist, which meant it had triggered a warning several minutes earlier that she'd failed to notice. Jazmin scanned the low pressure warning, then checked her tank gauges. She was already halfway through her emergency air reserve. If she didn't get inside right now she'd run out of air.

Harry, test the ballast valve.

Water pumping and ballast weight dropping. Get back inside.

The ACV nudged off the bottom of the lake, and she sensed his relief about the repair and his worry about her. Each breath was harder than the last. She kicked her way to the escape tube and released the strap from her leg. She seemed to be moving in a fog, every motion more difficult than the last. She wriggled inside the tube and flailed at the switch to purge the water, though it seemed always out of reach. She was out of air and losing consciousness. Her world went gray, then black.

***

Jazmin woke up lying on the floor of the ACV. All of her diving gear had been removed except her dry suit. Breathing was easier now. She felt the vibration of propellers and wondered where they were. She tried sitting up, but muscle pain, dizziness, and nausea pushed her back to the floor. She no longer had an active hivemind connection with Harry.

He got up from the pilot's seat. "How are you feeling?"

"Grateful to be alive."

"You lied to me about how much air you had left." He opened a first aid kit and removed a flat package. "I had to wait for you to wake up before I could give this to you." He tore it open and peeled off the backing to the drug patch then placed it on her neck. "This should make you feel better." He pulled a protein bar and an energy drink from a supply cabinet. "Eat and drink these as soon as you can keep them down."

Jazmin stayed on the floor for another couple of minutes then tried sitting up. She still felt lousy, though better than a few minutes earlier. She tore off the energy bar wrapper, took a couple small bites, then washed it down with a sip of the energy drink. After finishing both, she felt almost functional. "Where are we?"

"About ten minutes out from the sub pen in Bayfield. We're going slow to stay quiet. The banged-up dive planes are making attitude control dicey. We're also hard to miss on sonar."

Jazmin peeled off the dry suit and put her regular clothes back on. She climbed into the righthand seat just as they surfaced into an underground structure. The ACV morphed back into land rover mode, and Harry drove it up a ramp. Two figures came out of the shadows. One had a submachine gun, the other an RPG.

Harry said, "Looks like they weren't expecting us." He shut down the ACV. "Do exactly what I tell you or they'll kill us."

Jazmin watched the pair close in on them.

Harry said, "Remove your weapons, then exit the door on your side of the ACV with your hands on your head. Walk to the front of the vehicle and lie face down. I'll be doing the exact same thing." They removed their handguns and combat knives, then Harry looked at her to make sure she was ready. At gunpoint, they did exactly as Harry specified.

Lying face down on concrete Jazmin felt, more than heard, the pair approach them. These were skilled operators. Hands professionally frisked her, then the person stepped back. A female voice said, "Time to meet the boss."

Jazmin was too exhausted to be scared. She didn't know what was coming next. At least they hadn't shot her.

Chapter 20

Wisconsin Militia Base
Bayfield, Wisconsin
12 May

The woman with the submachine gun in a combat sling escorted Jazmin to a small room that looked like a holding cell. "Scan your biochip and your retina, then state your name and military rank."

Jazmin waved her arm over the biochip reader, then stared into the retinal scanner. Both devices beeped, though neither indicated a positive or negative outcome. She spoke into the microphone. "Jazmin Hassani, Commander, US Navy."

After a few moments a computerized female voice said, "Identity confirmed."

Jazmin's escort said, "We know you're also AWOL and wanted on terrorism charges." Surprisingly, the woman relaxed her stance. She pointed her submachine gun toward the floor and set the safety. "Walk with me." The woman exited the room and strode down the hallway to a closed door. She knocked twice.

A voice behind the door said, "Enter." Her escort opened the door and motioned Jazmin inside. A woman with a lined face and gray-streaked hair sat behind a large desk. She studied Jazmin with a calm appraising gaze and intelligent eyes. After a few moments she said, "Leave us." Her escort backed away and shut the door. Jazmin stayed silent. A faint smile and slight crinkle around the mystery woman's eyes felt almost welcoming. The weariness of command was etched into her face, though relief was also present, along with a release of tension in her gaze and posture. "Welcome, Commander Hassani. I've had my eye on you for quite a while." She gestured to the chair in front of her desk. "Please sit."

It sounded like a greeting for an ally, though perhaps it was a trap, a twisted mental game. "You know exactly who I am. Who are you and what is this place?"

The woman steepled her fingers. "Didn't Harry tell you?"

Jazmin shook her head. "He referred to this as the bunker and never explained further."

"How much do you trust Harry?"

The conversation was getting strange and worrisome. Jazmin wished she had her sidearm. "I trust him with my life." Then she thought, maybe I shouldn't. She knew the man he had been, but not the man he'd become. That realization scared her.

"That's good. He was sent to recruit you."

"Recruit me?" She stared back in disbelief, and her whole body went cold. Had the last few days been just an elaborate trap? Had she destroyed her naval career for nothing?

After not hearing from him for years, Harry had contacted her about Ajax. When she had needed to talk, he'd found her in the park. Was their meeting in the bar in downtown Milwaukee and their escape to his data center and to both safe houses an elaborate ruse to lure her to the bunker?

"My head is pounding, and I'm too exhausted to play this game. You need to answer my questions."

The woman looked amused, which irritated Jazmin.

"I respect your directness, Commander. My name is Priya Suresh. I was a major general in Space Command, where I was responsible for all US military space stations. I was offered a new assignment with a third star, but I couldn't live with what I had to do, so I turned it down. I had already crossed too many ethical lines in my career. When I returned to Earth I was forced into retirement."

Jazmin could see Suresh as a flag officer in the way she radiated quiet power in her bearing and direct style.

Suresh had a faraway look in her eyes as if lost in unpleasant memories before resuming her story. "I hated the way my career ended. After I left Space Command I wanted to make a difference on my own terms. I saw way too much corruption and abuse of power during my career in both the military and in the government. I was never allowed to take action against officials who were enriching themselves by stealing funding and resources from people who couldn't fight back. I recruited a small team of elite ex-military officers and senior enlisted personnel. Now I get to define the missions we undertake."

Jazmin was impressed by the woman's credentials, but she wondered if the people in this group were actually the military's best trying to hold the line on integrity. Maybe they were disgruntled former operators, vigilantes wrapping themselves in the delusion of patriotism. "Why me?"

"We're a small force and you have capabilities we lack." Suresh ticked off items on her fingers. "You're a special forces rotorcraft pilot, a fighter pilot, a diver, an expert in neurotech, and as an active Special Ops officer, your neurotech bypasses all security systems."

Jazmin set her jaw and shook her head. "You forgot to add AWOL and wanted terrorist to the list."

Suresh got up from behind her desk. "Everyone on this team is a wanted terrorist. That's why we stay in an underground bunker. Harry has exceptional capabilities. He's kept your secure neurotech access alive. That will open a lot of doors for us."

Jazmin wondered if this was a team she wanted to be on. "Where's the line between recruitment and abduction?"

A thin smile appeared on Suresh's face. "Did Harry force you to go with him?"

Jazmin sighed. "No."

"If he didn't force you, he clearly didn't abduct you."

"Perhaps subterfuge would be a more apt description."

Suresh sat on the edge of her desk near Jazmin. "Refuge would be a better word. You were on the run and Harry provided a means of escape. I won't hold you against your will, but how long will you last alone against a black bag mercenary team?"

Jazmin didn't reply, and Suresh didn't fill the silence. This group was Jazmin's only option for short-term survival. Ajax died because of her, and she was compelled to avenge his death. As the lone survivor, she had to settle the score for the attack on her SEAL team. Her rage had gotten her through rehab and all the years since, while the Navy did nothing. She couldn't fight these battles alone, not anymore. Despite Harry's questionable ethics, she trusted him with her life. He'd never lied to her, at least not overtly, and he'd protected her when she immolated her military career. Despite her misgivings, staying in the bunker was her only viable option. But committing to this group was another question. Who did General Suresh answer to? Someone must be supporting her, or this militia couldn't exist for long.

Suresh waited for Jazmin's inner turmoil to subside. "It appears you need some time to think, Commander. We can talk again after you've had time to rest." She gestured toward the door.

The woman with the submachine gun waited in the hallway. She stuck out her hand. "I'm Gadget. I take care of all the vehicles, aircraft, and anything else that needs repairs or maintenance. Suresh found me just after I retired from the Air Force as a chief master sergeant. The general said she needed a little help with maintenance." Gadget shook her head with a wry smile. "That was an understatement." She led Jazmin down several corridors and stopped in front of the medical clinic. Gadget waved her arm over the chip reader and the door opened. Once inside, she spoke with the nurse. "We have a new militia member. She's had a rough couple of days getting here and the general wants her checked out."

The nurse smiled and pointed to one of the exam rooms. "We'll take good care of her. We've got it from here."

Chapter 21

Wisconsin Militia Base
Bayfield, Wisconsin
13 May

Jazmin woke up with a start in total darkness, jittery from nightmares fueled by her near-death experiences over the last couple of days. She took a deep breath, slowly exhaled, and pushed the terror of being hunted back into one of the many sealed containers that kept her sane. She focused on the soft supportive mattress and smooth cotton sheets to ground her to the present, finally awake enough to remember where she was. Jazmin sat up in bed and leaned against the cool steel headboard. She said, "Room lights on," and a warm glow of soft white light illuminated her newly assigned quarters. She checked the time and found she had slept for the last fourteen hours, far longer than normal, even when exhausted.

She thought back to the last thing she remembered, and then her mental confusion upon waking made more sense. Gadget had taken her to the medical clinic, where a retired Space Command emergency medicine doctor gave her a neurological exam and a CT scan. She had a concussion from the beatings her head had taken in the amphibious combat vehicle, so he prescribed a traumatic brain injury drug commonly given to SEAL team members after ops went sideways. The drug cranked up the body's repair cycle. The commandos in her unit called it "turbo," because it got them back into action sooner than the body could heal naturally. She'd taken a lot of it during rehab, and it always knocked her out while it worked. She wondered when she'd connect with Harry. Given his deftness for finding her, she decided to wait. They had a lot to discuss.

Jazmin got out of bed and found a fresh flight suit in the small closet and clean underwear on the open shelves. After showering and dressing she found the cafeteria where an android chef made her an omelet and croissants for breakfast. She sipped her second mug of coffee and absorbed her surroundings, eerily similar to the aircraft carriers she'd served on. The polished surfaces, sturdy austere furniture, and ruggedized equipment felt like the Navy she'd left rather than a sketchy state militia.

Gadget entered the cafeteria and came over to Jazmin's table. "I hope you got a good night's sleep. I have lots to show you."

"I did." Jazmin stood. "Just had breakfast and coffee. Let's go."

Gadget exited the cafeteria and led the way down a confusing set of hallways and through a door into a maintenance shop. The hangar-sized space was spotless, the walls lined with rolling tool carts, computerized test equipment, and racks of spare parts. Robot tuggers moved aircraft in various states of repair from one end of the hangar to the other. An overhead crane suspended a jet engine being installed on an aircraft. "We have another workshop this size for trucks and combat vehicles."

A few mechanics were in the hangar, but they weren't introduced. A fast-attack quadcopter caught Jazmin's eye. She inspected the rotorcraft with its extensive weaponry. "How did your team get this, and who flies it?"

Gadget rested her hand on the nose of the aircraft. "We cobbled this together from a hangar queen and a couple of banged up birds after an op went sideways. They needed an intervention to save them from a bad ending." She cleared her throat. "We liberated them off a transport ferrying the carcasses back to the depot and diverted them here for some much-needed spa time." Gadget cocked her head at the young mechanics. "The kids and I put this back into flying condition."

"What about tail numbers?" asked Jazmin.

With a barely suppressed smile, Gadget said, "Harry got into the military tail code assignment system and corrected the clerical errors." Her mechanics chuckled at this explanation. Gadget lost her amused expression and looked Jazmin in the eyes. "To answer your second question, Commander, you're the pilot."

"You were that sure I'd join your group?"

"Harry was and so was the General. Suresh said, 'Make it happen,' and he did."

A commando, the same one who'd held Harry at gunpoint when they arrived, sauntered into the hangar. The man's facial features and dark complexion reminded Jazmin of her Algerian father. He was armed with an assault rifle suspended in a combat sling, a 9mm handgun in a shoulder holster, and a combat knife strapped to his leg. The young mechanics gave him a wide berth. He had the lean muscular build of a young man, which contrasted with his salt and pepper buzzcut and short beard. He wore an *I Am the Weapon* T-shirt with an image of an assault rifle digitally printed on it. The man moved with the intense energy of a coiled snake about to strike. He walked toward Jazmin and Gadget while scanning the hangar and everyone present with a machine-like precision, barely moving his head yet missing nothing. He had a haunted expression from too many ops that went bad. The operator exchanged a look and a hand signal with Gadget. Jazmin had known SEAL team members like this one, the extreme outliers. A combination of the greatest ally in battle and the worst enemy when anyone dared to disagree. She gave commandos like this lots of room, never wanting to get in their crosshairs.

Gadget said, "This is Derez. He's an ex-Navy SEAL who thinks he's a badass. He spent ten years undercover in North Africa blending in with the locals. Anything I send him out with comes back all shot up or blown to pieces. Don't loan him anything you want back in working condition."

Derez didn't react to the ribbing. He looked at Jazmin with piercing brown eyes. In a surprisingly deep voice with a trace of a French accent he said, "Harry asked me to escort you to the Toybox. Follow me."

He turned and strode out a different door than the one he had entered. Jazmin glanced at Gadget, and the older woman nodded. Jazmin chased after Derez, who was already ten steps ahead. They walked down a long hallway with meeting and training rooms on one side and racks of computer equipment sealed behind glass doors on the other. The underground facility was much larger and better equipped than Jazmin thought possible for what appeared to be a tiny militia group. At the end of the hallway, they arrived at massive vault doors.

Derez said, "Harry told us you're a Special Ops rotorcraft pilot. That will be a huge advantage when we need to infiltrate and exfiltrate on operations." Not waiting for a response, he turned toward the vault door, waved his biochip over the reader, and then scanned his retina. The light above the large titanium door handle changed from red to green. Derez rotated the handle and pulled the massive door open. They entered, the vault door swinging closed behind them. A moment later, Harry appeared. Derez said, "Package delivered," then he strode to the other side of the weapons locker and disappeared behind the floor-to-ceiling racking. A vault door clunked closed on the other side of the huge space, and a holographic window opened and displayed *Weapons Vault Secured*. Harry waved the window closed.

Jazmin said, "I guess we're on the approved list."

Harry shrugged. "There was never any doubt in my mind. Our welcome was standard operational procedure. We've been burned before by people we trusted."

Jazmin could no longer pretend that things were okay between them. She moved in close and slapped him across the face hard enough for her hand to sting. "You lied to me." She swung at him again but this time he caught her hand and held it while she struggled. "I trusted you with my career and my life, for what?"

"I'm sorry, Jaz. You were in deeper than you knew in a battle you couldn't win alone. Getting you here was the best option."

She yanked her arm away from him. "Why the hell should I believe you?"

"No one will hold you here against your will, but this is the only safe place right now."

She glared at him as her emotions roiled. "When I calm down, you'll need to explain what you've gotten me into."

To burn off her anger, Jazmin walked through the weapons vault with Harry beside her. The walls were lined with assault rifles, .50 caliber machine guns, personal defense submachine guns, combat shotguns, and cases of ammunition. Several rows of shelving held rocket propelled grenades and launchers including flashbangs, EMPs and anti-personnel grenades. Several shelves held mines, shoulder-mounted anti-aircraft missiles, and mortars. "My god, you have enough weapons in here to start a war. Where did all of this come from?"

"I diverted a few weapon shipments. It's amazing how much sway a general's authorization has, especially when she doesn't realize it."

Jazmin was both horrified and impressed. "This facility, aircraft, military vehicles, along with the array of weapons and ammunition, are enough to support a huge militia. The few people I've seen can't possibly support all this infrastructure or take it into battle. Where are the rest of your personnel? There's billions of dollars of equipment. Where's the money coming from?"

Harry leaned against a crate of submachine guns. "The team you see here is the most senior and dedicated members of the militia. The full group is much larger. For operational security, we only bring people in for training or when we're launching ops. We also meet at the operations site whenever possible and scatter afterward."

"Basic guerilla tactics. How many are in your full militia?"

"Hundreds, though I don't know the exact numbers. We're all assigned to cells, and the cells are kept isolated."

"And the money?"

Harry's face lit up into a mischievous grin. "Don't let anyone tell you crime doesn't pay. It does."

She raised her eyebrows in mock horror. "I'm shocked. What has the larcenous Mr. Dexter been involved in? Surely not kidnapping, contract killing, or extortion."

He lost his grin and shook his head. "I don't do that for money." Though he didn't deny doing those things for other reasons. He cocked his head to one side. "I'm a gentleman thief. I liberate funds languishing in offshore accounts stashed by people who can't report it stolen because it was illegally obtained or hidden from the tax man. My targets are typically politicians, self-made billionaires, entertainers, and professionals who mistakenly think they are above the law. I make sure they pay their fair share to the nation where they earned their ill-gotten wealth."

He shrugged. "So there's no honor among thieves." His expression turned serious. "Now that I've answered your questions, I have only one for you."

She already knew what it was, though she wasn't ready to answer. Her Navy officer's oath to defend the Constitution against all enemies, foreign and domestic, wouldn't allow her to walk away, though every shred of self-preservation screamed "run." Her military career was over, though what she committed herself to hadn't changed. Jiang,

Trabago, and God knows who else aligned with them had to be stopped. Jazmin wanted retribution for her own injuries, for her SEAL team, and for Ajax's murder. If she couldn't defend her country through official channels, then she'd do it by other means. Did she trust this group enough to commit to them? Was there any other alternative? What did she even know about the militia?

Jazmin asked, "What's the mission of the Wisconsin Militia? What operations will this group undertake? Who does Suresh answer to?"

"Our mission is to eliminate extreme military and political corruption. This includes abuse of power, selling secrets to enemies, espionage, the theft of billions from the treasury, and funneling money to politicians and defense contractors. We also stop mercenary companies from running secret black ops sites in the US and other black bag operations."

She said, "That gives you pretty wide latitude."

"It does. That's why we have a lot of firepower and we're always recruiting new members."

"Who does Suresh take orders from?"

Harry shrugged. "There's no strict command and control at her level. She reports to a board of trustees. I don't know all the players, but they're a mix of current and former high level government officials. Senators, Secretaries of State, flag officers from all the services, diplomats, and even a former president."

"Harry, we once loved each other. Despite everything I know about you and being pissed at you for lying to me, deep down I still trust you. Does this group align with what you and I committed our lives to?"

He came close and took her hand in his. "I still love you. I wouldn't have brought you here if I didn't believe in our mission. Priya Suresh is the most principled person I've ever met. She restored my faith in supporting something bigger than me after it had been torn to shreds by my last commander, who booted me out of Air Force Cyber in handcuffs. Suresh is the most honest flag officer I've ever served under. She keeps her word no matter what. There's a lot of us willing to follow Suresh into battle."

Harry's eyes were moist, and his usual thick veneer of arrogance and swagger were gone. Jazmin sensed a vulnerability and openness that Harry rarely showed anyone. She initiated a full hivemind connection. A tidal wave of loss, sadness, anger, and helplessness slammed into her consciousness, making her dizzy. Harry caught her in his arms and steered her to a bench, then sat holding her close. The emotional wave subsided, and Jazmin's head cleared. Even when she and Harry had been lovers, before they both became damaged by life, it hadn't been this intense, this intimate. Harry trusted her enough to expose what lurked inside, and it wasn't pretty, but she had a dark side too. She had her answer. *I'm all in.*

Chapter 22

Wisconsin Militia Base
Bayfield, Wisconsin
14 May

Jazmin had spent the last couple of hours exploring the base and familiarizing herself with both the layout and the facilities available. She sat drinking coffee alone at a table and thought about all that had happened to her in the last few days. Harry and Gadget entered the cafeteria, filled coffee mugs, and sat across from her. He had the same happy look in his eyes as when they had been lovers. "Good morning, Jaz."

Gadget pulled a military-grade tablet from a pocket in her coveralls, activated it, and laid it on the table. "Commander, the General approved you for senior staff privileges. I need a biochip and retinal scan to get you added to the system."

Jazmin waved her left forearm over the tablet and peered into the retinal scanner on the screen. Gadget verified the biometric entries. "You now have access to all facilities on base including the ops center and weapons locker. When you're ready, find me in the maintenance hangar and I'll get you set up on the flight simulators. You need to prove you're well qualified before I'll let you take out any of my aircraft."

Harry laughed. "She's not kidding about *her* aircraft. Gadget gave me hell for the ACV damage."

Jazmin smiled and enjoyed the light moment, the first in a while. "Message received, Chief. I'll take good care of your birds."

"Good. We'll get along just fine." Gadget picked up her coffee mug and headed out the cafeteria door.

Harry pointed at Jazmin's tablet. "New software was just loaded."

She checked the screen and there was a new icon; underneath it was displayed *Senior Staff Eyes Only*. Jazmin tapped the icon and a new screen appeared with symbols for key government agencies: CIA, DARPA, DIA, DOD, NSA, POTUS. She scrolled through the different agencies. Each had news feeds and classified briefings. The one for POTUS included the President's daily intelligence briefing. She now had access to classified information way above her security clearance. "How did you do this?"

Harry leaned back, sipped his coffee, and gave her a conspiratorial look. "Friends in low places and a little hacking." He stood. "I'll give you some time to catch up on your classified reading."

Her first thought was now she could get some long overdue answers. She refilled her coffee mug and clicked on the DARPA icon.

Chapter 23
Drago Milosevic

Yunnan Province, Republic of China
20 May

Drago Milosevic enjoyed killing people from a distance. For tonight's mission, he piloted an uncrewed stealth drone on the other side of the world from the secret base in western China. The drone's transponder identified it as a freight carrier, and Drago kept it at 20,000 feet following its assigned slot in the automated US air traffic control system. He picked up the trio of Marine One helicopters transporting the President to Camp David, where it was still morning US time. The three identical helicopters played the presidential shell game by constantly swapping positions in flight. The helicopter with the President was Marine One Actual, and the two decoys were Marine One Escorts. Drago was an expert at hunting people and aircraft from the sky, though even he had difficulty continuously tracking the copter carrying the President. Adding to the challenge, the Presidential TFR, temporary flight restriction, meant he had to maintain a thirty-nautical-mile distance.

Fortunately, another DIA black ops officer on his team had planted an additional transmitter on Marine One Actual, so there could be no mistake. Drago lined up test shots with the PWL laser targeting system, then adjusted for shooting from an aircraft in flight. Now he was dialed in for the kill. Drago vibrated with nervous energy. His mission was to create an international incident. His next act had the potential to start a war between superpowers. He was about to attack the President of the United States.

A few minutes later, the presidential helicopters were in close formation over a heavily populated area. Drago targeted the lead helicopter and fired. The directed-energy burst destroyed every computer system operating the helicopter, along with toasting the crew's neurotech. The unresponsive fly-by-wire flight controls and low altitude made autorotation impossible. The crippled aircraft tumbled out of the sky, slammed into a twelve-lane overpass, and exploded with a massive fireball. Charred steel and concrete cascaded onto the roadway below, killing or severely injuring dozens of people. The two remaining helicopters banked in opposite directions to avoid the billowing cloud of black smoke. Self-driving cars couldn't respond fast enough to avoid barreling into the wreckage or careening off the destroyed overpass. The resulting massive pileup blocked both directions of the freeway. The road would remain closed indefinitely for repairs.

There was no distress call from the downed helicopter, as its communication capabilities were terminated the instant the directed-energy weapon hit. Frantic radio calls from the remaining helicopters flooded Drago's headset. "Mayday, Mayday, Mayday. Marine One under attack." Drago smiled at their terror. It was time to go for his bonus, a second kill. Standard operating procedure for an attack on Marine One was to dispatch fighter aircraft. Joint Base Andrews was the closest base. The alert aircraft would be in the air within the next few minutes and on station over the area. Drago couldn't remain in the area for long.

The remaining Marine One helicopters kept in constant motion, changing flight positions, and swapping off as lead in their flight of two aircraft. Drago verified which helicopter held the President, Marine One Actual, then lined up his shot. The two aircraft were in tight formation again. The difficulty wasn't in hitting the targeted helicopter, Marine One Escort, it was in limiting the residual energy field engulfing the President's aircraft. He lined up the reticle on the escort helicopter and targeted the engine. Drago had to time the shot perfectly so the energy wave wouldn't harm the President's aircraft. He needed a clean kill. Marine One Actual had to survive to send the strongest possible message. Drago held his breath and squeezed the trigger. A microsecond later, Marine One Actual veered in an unexpected direction. When the energy wave hit its target, the escort helicopter lost power and nosed over, barely missing the President's aircraft. The next second produced a horrifying spectacle. Marine One Actual also lost power.

Drago's chest exploded in fear, and he could barely catch his breath. He was covered in sweat and the air-conditioning chilled him. The one absolute order for today's attack was that the President must remain unharmed.

His intended target, Marine One Escort, had taken a direct hit and plummeted at an increasing rate. It smashed onto the concrete roadway. This time, with traffic stopped, only a few cars were destroyed by the falling wreckage. The aircraft was on fire with a plume of black smoke but there were no explosions. The Marine One Actual pilot identified the threat early and initiated an autorotation by reducing the collective to full down. The main rotor, now disengaged from the transmission, spun freely to create lift. Near the ground he pulled back on the cyclic to reduce the rate of descent and increased the collective for a soft landing.

Drago zeroed in on Marine One Actual with the drone's high-power camera. He saw movement through the front windshield, though couldn't see the President or the other passengers. Agonizing seconds later, two members of the President's Secret Service detail emerged from the copter. Submachine guns drawn, they set up a security perimeter around the aircraft. Emergency vehicles, red and blue lights flashing, raced toward the downed aircraft, but their progress was slowed by traffic jams. Drago checked police and Secret Service networks for radio calls. A Secret Service agent said, "Cheetah appears to be unharmed after the emergency landing. We're taking her to Walter Reed for the doctors to check her out. The Beast is enroute."

Drago let out a long breath. He'd gambled on a risky maneuver. Luck had saved him. A red light flashed on his tablet screen. The boss wanted him. Drago made sure the drone was back on a standard track and heading southwest to its launch point in Mexico. He verified autopilot was engaged and spoke into his headset. "Milosevic."

His boss, Brigadier General Malik said, "My office. Now."

Drago replied, "Yes, sir." Another pilot at her own station sat next to him. There were no dividers between them. "Geeta, please keep an eye on my drone. It's on autopilot heading back to Sinaloa. The boss wants to talk to me."

Geeta brought up a secondary screen to monitor Drago's aircraft and flashed him a sympathetic look. "No problem. I've got you covered. Good luck with Sledgehammer."

Drago knocked on General Malik's door. A second later a gruff voice said, "Enter." Drago came inside, shutting the door behind him. Malik's large, muscled frame and dark complexion looked an order of magnitude angrier than his usual pissed-off-at-everything expression. Drago wasn't afraid of many people, but Malik was one of them.

His boss stood uncomfortably close. "What in the hell were you thinking?"

Drago bit back his gut reaction to the question. He wanted to blurt out "I was thinking of the huge bonus." Instead he said, "I had a clear shot at the second copter, and the mission objective was to down both Marine One escorts."

Malik's eyes narrowed. "You idiot. You almost killed the President. That was an insane gamble. I told the project director offering the bonus for both copters was an unacceptable risk when an attack on one was more than enough to achieve our objective."

Drago remained silent. He'd learned silence was the safest career strategy when faced with an angry superior, especially a flag officer. Drago steeled himself for the next wave of invective. A holographic screen opened and flashed *Secure incoming command communication.* Malik sighed and waved his hand to accept the video call. His face morphed into something resembling calm. "General Malik. How can I help you, Senator?"

Jiang's face filled the screen, her expression inscrutable. Drago had seen Jiang personally kill bioweapon test subjects who didn't die as quickly as expected. There had been no mercy in the act. Drago went cold. Malik would put on a show of anger, but there were rules in the military. He would lose respect if he physically assaulted his officers. Jiang was in the shadows and played by her own rules. Just because she was physically on the other side of the world didn't mean she couldn't reach out and smash Drago like a bug on a car's windshield. Drago waited for her to respond.

Jiang remained silent for a few moments longer, reinforcing that she was in charge. Both men served at her pleasure and suffered severely when she was unhappy. Her face exploded with joy. "I called to congratulate you on the superb outcome of today's mission. Downing the two escort helicopters and forcing the President's copter to the ground was the best possible scenario. I just got word from Walter Reed that the President is fine. She's headed back to the White House with a massive show of force surrounding her motorcade."

Drago gulped in air, not realizing he'd stopped breathing. He took a few calming breaths, and his heart rate decelerated from hammering in terror to thumping on a sprint.

Malik said, "Thank you, Senator. The drone is headed back to our base in Mexico."

Jiang looked like a magnanimous queen bestowing a gift to her favorite knight. "Major Milosevic, you'll be happy to know I've approved your bonus for the mission, and it's already been deposited in your account."

"Thank you, Senator. I'm glad the mission results met with your approval." He'd never received a bonus that quickly.

"Excellent work. General Malik, I'll want an update on our other operations at our usual weekly meeting."

"Of course, Senator. I'll be prepared."

Jiang looked away from the screen then forward again. "I'll initiate next steps." The screen went blank.

Malik's usual pissed-off expression returned. "Milosevic, you were beyond lucky today. Get the hell out of my office."

Drago saluted, did a quick about face, and shot out the door. He couldn't stop grinning.

Chapter 24
Mei Chan

Chinese Military Intelligence Headquarters
20 May

Mei watched the video call between Ling Chen, Brigadier General Malik, and Major Milosevich, horrified by the senator's gleeful reaction to the mission outcome. Ling Chen had even rewarded the drone pilot for taking a reckless risk. The Americans were unaware that Chinese Military Intelligence monitored all communications at the black ops site in Yunan province, providing Mei and her team real-time knowledge of all activities at this secret location. More importantly, it gave them leverage.

Everything about the attack on Marine One was an escalation of the mission parameters Mei and Chinese Intelligence had authorized. Had this insane strike resulted in the injury or death of President Francesca Navarro, the geopolitical ramifications would have been staggering. If the US government realized the attack emanated from China, it would be considered an act of war. A minor escalation in tension between China and the US over an isolated incident could be tolerated, but not this.

Fortunately, Mei handled stress well. She closed her eyes and took several deep breaths to center herself. After sitting quietly for a couple of minutes, her heart rate returned to normal. As Deputy

Director of Chinese Military Intelligence she had taken on both an increasing scope of responsibility and high visibility operations. Ling Chen's recklessness eroded Mei's equanimity. She'd hoped after the incident with the attack on the military fighter pilots, Ling Chen would be more circumspect in her actions. Mei had misjudged the senator's penchant for bold, independent action. It was time for an intervention.

Chapter 25
Jazmin Hassani

Wisconsin Militia Base
Bayfield, Wisconsin
20 May

Jazmin started each day at the militia base in the gym, completing a brutal workout routine that only her former SEAL team members could have sustained. Next she reviewed the latest intel for each key government agency, her neurotech allowing her to ingest the daily classified information at computer transfer speeds. The rest of her day was spent logging hours on the flight simulators to regain her combat flying skills. She ended the day with target practice on the weapons range. She'd been a Navy Special Ops officer who regularly trained with SEAL Team One. The last five years as a Neurotech Defense Agency investigator had degraded her skills. She hadn't logged nearly as many flight hours as she had previously and had visited a shooting range only a handful of times since she joined the NDA. As an investigator Jazmin had a completely different mindset than she did as part of a team of operators. When she had left rehab, she wasn't ready to return to combat, broken in ways that would never heal, but her new reality was forcing her to change. Now she spent every day honing her warrior edge.

An alert from General Suresh flashed on Jazmin's tablet. *Senior staff to the ops center.* She was on the combat range, so she secured her weapon, then went to meet the others. The range was the furthest location from the ops center, about a ten-minute walk, so everyone was already there when Jazmin arrived. The secure facility had three tiers of workstations with a holographic projector system. Large screens could be projected at the front and sides of the room and smaller screens in any open space. Suresh sat at the commander's station on the highest level, while Gadget and Derez sat at workstations on tier two. Jazmin joined Harry on the lowest level at the front of the room.

Suresh said, "There was an attack on the President earlier today on her way to Camp David. Two of the escort Marine One helicopters were downed by directed-energy weapons, killing the pilots, air crews, and Secret Service agents—a total of fourteen military and government personnel. An additional twenty-seven civilians died and forty-three were injured from the ensuing traffic accidents. All were transported to local hospitals. Marine One Actual got caught in a residual energy field, lost power, and made an emergency landing. The President was rushed to Walter Reed and fortunately was unhurt."

On the main screen a CNN reporter stood in front of the smoking wreckage of a destroyed Marine One helicopter. A bevy of emergency vehicles with flashing red and blue lights choked the scene. Traffic on the highway was completely stopped. The reporter repeated variations of what Suresh had just shared with the group. A news banner scrolled across the bottom of the screen with new details, including the names and photos of the pilots and aircrew members who lost their lives in the attack. This scene cut to the newsroom where the anchor said, "We now have a special announcement from the President of the United States."

President Francesca Navarro came on screen from the Oval Office. Normally she projected a calm demeanor no matter what chaos was happening in the world. Today she looked exhausted and shaken. Jazmin hadn't been with the new team long enough for anyone other than Harry to be comfortable with a hivemind connection, but she sensed an unusual amount of tension for a group used to functioning in a constant state of stress. She was connected to Harry, and he radiated tension mirroring her own. An attack on the President with an unknown directed-energy weapon was a huge escalation.

Navarro said, "Today while flying on Marine One, our aircraft were struck with directed-energy weapons. As a nation, we mourn those lost. I want to personally thank the pilots, aircrews, and Secret Service agents for their bravery and quick actions today, but too many of these fine men and women paid the ultimate price in service to their country. Our hearts go out to the innocent victims on the ground as a result of multiple traffic accidents and falling wreckage. This cowardly act will not go unanswered. We don't know who was behind today's events and are pursuing all possibilities, including foreign and domestic terrorists, as well as potentially a state-sponsored attack by a foreign government. This administration won't rest until the perpetrators are brought to justice, no matter how long it takes."

The camera zoomed in on Navarro's agitated face. "We will find you. There will be a reckoning."

The newscast went back to the studio anchor and Suresh turned it off. Silence hung in the ops center.

The general said, "I want to know how this attack was executed and who's responsible. If this was sponsored by or carried out by anyone inside our government or military, we'll take action if the appropriate authorities don't. Harry, Jazmin, analyze telemetry and air traffic. Figure out how the directed-energy weapon was delivered."

Harry said, "On it, General."

"Derez, Gadget, figure out what kind of weapon hit Marine One and determine if they missed the President on purpose or if our nation's leader got lucky."

In unison Derez and Gadget said, "Yes, ma'am."

Suresh stood. "I'll check with my government and military contacts. If it's time for someone to immediately retire or just plain disappear, we can make that happen. No doubt a lot of people are rattled right now. Let's reconvene in four hours." Suresh headed for the door with Derez and Gadget right behind.

When the others were gone, Harry faced Jazmin. "This likely wasn't a state-sponsored attack. No foreign government, even a rogue nation, would risk the overwhelming US military response."

Jazmin shook her head at the audacity of the attack. "I suspect Jiang and PWL are behind this, but I don't know how to prove it. Until I have something solid, I don't want to bring this up to Suresh.

Flag officers like answers a lot more than questions."

"Let's see if we can come up with something concrete. Then we can approach the general." Harry brought up an air traffic control system map overlaid on a topographic view on the large holographic screen. "Let's assume the directed-energy weapon was launched from an airborne platform. The superpowers all have space-based weapons, but those are more useful for shooting down satellites or targeting a fixed position on earth. Downing aircraft on a constantly varying flight path is beyond what these weapons can reliably accomplish. If this was a test, it's amazing that Diamond survived the attack on her aircraft. She must be one hell of a pilot."

"She is. I've had the privilege of flying with her. Shockwave is the best stick I know." Jazmin studied the air traffic map and the terrain below. "It's probably not a ground-based weapon. The two kills were in different locations. It would have been impossible from a single point on the ground. There's lots of elevation changes and woods in the area, so just getting a clear shot would be extremely difficult. Hiding a weapon like that from satellite reconnaissance would be a challenge, though we can check on this later to rule it out as a possibility."

Harry projected a US map on the screen with the states outlined on the lowest layer and thousands of colored lines tracing point to point. Commercial airline flights, military traffic, commercial drones, and private planes that filed flight plans were depicted in different colors on the three-dimensional representation. He peered at the map. "Right now it's too busy to make any sense, but once we drill down into a small enough area, we'll be able to see the details."

Red traces appeared on the visualization. "These are the flight paths of the three Marine One helicopters." He zoomed in on the state of Maryland and the mass of colored lines spread out.

Jazmin said, "Let's remove flights from the map. Start with commercial airline traffic." Harry adjusted the view, and the thick layer of white lines turned transparent. She said, "It's still too busy. Try removing military traffic next." A blue layer of lines turned transparent. "What about drones?"

He limited the screen traces to just two colors. "I split drone traffic into long haul and delivery. Point-to-point long haul drones aren't likely, though delivery drones or ones with unusual flight patterns are suspect. I'll leave those showing." A layer of green lines vanished, and a less dense layer of yellow lines remained. "The yellow drone routes need to be analyzed further."

Jazmin studied the flight traces. "Can you identify drones with the big commercial carriers?"

Harry added symbols to the traces and projected a legend. "Can you start eliminating flights?"

Jazmin picked up a laser pointer. "I can tell the difference between short delivery hops and drones on station tracking targets or setting up for attack runs. As I identify each drone route with the laser, make it transparent."

"Just pulse the routes with the laser and they'll vanish."

She started with the easy targets to clear the screen. After several minutes, a lot of the clutter was gone, though the decisions to eliminate traces got harder. It was tedious work, but after an hour, the screen displayed a manageable number of flight traces. "I've eliminated most of the commercial drone traffic, but there's a couple of unidentified traces I'd like to investigate further." Jazmin circled two with her laser pointer and Harry added aircraft owner and transponder ID number. "We can eliminate this drone. Its flight pattern is consistent with map updates. This one, however, has a suspicious flight path and appears to be tracking the Marine One flights. Pull up any details you can." Another holographic screen on the side of the room came to life. It displayed a photo, specification sheet, and transponder ID. The owner was listed as Drone Delivery International, and the drone was remotely piloted.

Harry said, "Isn't this interesting. A drone owned by a multinational conglomerate whose subsidiaries deal with international security services is following the President's helicopter right before it's attacked."

Jazmin stood and glared at the screen. "It just went from interesting to scary. Clear the screen of all flight traces except this drone and the three Marine One helicopters. I want to see a timeline from where all these aircraft originated and trace what happened to this drone after the attack."

Harry updated the screen. A date/time display showed on the right corner of the screen. The drone's launch time was hours before the attack on Marine One, and the flight originated from Sinaloa, Mexico. Jazmin said, "The biggest airport in Sinaloa is Culiacán. It's an international airport that also handles military flights. Did it originate from there?"

Harry zoomed in on the launch coordinates. "No, it took off

from a private airstrip in an area controlled by the Sinaloa Cartel."

"Do you have access to DEA drone coverage? No doubt this area is getting extra attention."

"Jaz, you insult me. Of course I do." He projected high-resolution closeup views of the area.

She spent a minute studying the photos. "There are no NAVAIDs or runway lights, but there's a large modern hangar and a sizeable security force. The group around the airstrip looks like cartel thugs carrying hunting rifles and shotguns. The second group near the hangar are in desert camo uniforms, armed with assault rifles. They're positioned to protect the building and arrayed like special forces operators."

"Since when do Mexican drug cartels employ well-armed, professional mercenaries?"

She shook her head. "They don't. Not troops that look like that. I think it's time we learn more about Drone Delivery International. Any ties to the US government or Senator Jiang?"

"Let me run a search." A holographic screen opened on one side of the room and multiple windows opened AI search bots.

Jazmin used her neurotech enhancements to process the flood of information scrolling across the screen. Other holographic windows opened throughout the room. Using hand gestures she arranged the windows in priority order and closed the rest to eliminate clutter. "Drone Delivery International is a multinational company that owns a web of interconnected privately held firms. Its financial assets are in the Cayman Islands, but it has no physical presence there. Several of the subsidiaries are international security companies fulfilling contracts with both the DOD and US clandestine services."

Harry fast-forwarded the drone flight through the attack on Marine One and back to the airstrip it had originated from, then checked the time stamp. He synced the DEA drone views with the time stamp and found a series of photos showing two people exiting the hangar to retrieve and service the drone. He zoomed in and ran facial recognition software. "I've got two positive hits. Both are ex-military special forces followed by time in the CIA. They left the country two years ago and disappeared."

"Why are US clandestine services in bed with Mexican drug cartels launching attacks on a sitting US president?" she asked.

"There's something bigger in play here. These aren't groups that normally cooperate."

Gadget and Derez entered the ops center. Gadget said, "We'd like to compare what we've figured out before we brief the general. We're seeing some pretty disturbing things."

"Us too," said Jazmin.

Derez said, "The attack on the trio of Marine One helicopters most likely came from an airborne weapons platform."

"We came to the same conclusion," said Harry.

Jazmin pointed to the flight traces on the front screen. "We think we've identified the drone that attacked the President." She brought the drone specification screen forward. "It was launched from a private airstrip in Mexico controlled by a drug cartel, but the people operating it look like mercenaries potentially tied to US black ops. The drone was remotely piloted."

Gadget studied the drone specifications. "That all lines up with the damage to the three Marine One helicopters. I can't be sure without a teardown of the aircraft, but based on the severity and type of damage, it looks like PWL weapons were used. They're small enough to be launched from a drone. No other defense company has developed a directed-energy weapon with PWL's power-to-weight ratio. The only one even close uses a mobile truck-based launcher. These weapons require a heavy airlift cargo plane to get them airborne and that's not useful in combat."

Jazmin asked, "How did Marine One Actual escape the attack?"

Derez placed his hand on his sidearm. "The President was lucky, but I'll make sure the bastard that shot at her won't be."

Gadget gently pulled Derez's grip off his weapon. "The two helicopters that went down had direct hits. Marine One Actual was caught in a residual energy wave field. The PWL technology is based on electromagnetic-pulse weapons, though it's more sophisticated and can be precisely targeted. Marine One Actual had enough EMP shielding to protect it from the worst of the energy beam, and enough flight controls survived for it to successfully autorotate to the ground. I'm not sure if Marine One Actual wasn't targeted, or the attacking pilot thought they had a successful kill and wanted to gain distance from the point of attack."

General Suresh entered the ops center. The lines etched into her face looked deeper than a few hours previously and her normal ramrod posture sagged. "I'm glad to see all four of you here. Please brief me with your updates, and then I'll share what I've learned."

Jazmin went over the flight traces and ID of the attacking drone along with Drone Delivery International's ties to US clandestine services black ops groups. Gadget reviewed the analysis of the aircraft damage and likelihood that PWL weapons were used. Suresh took this all in and asked a few clarifying questions, though she made no assessment of her own. She looked deeply troubled by what the team told her. "I spoke to some of my old colleagues still on active duty, along with a couple of sitting senators. The usual culprits, China and Russia, came up. There's no terrorist groups or rogue states sophisticated enough to pull this off, so they concluded it was state-sponsored. Chinese and Russian diplomats called Navarro. Both denied the attack and offered their assistance. There's lots of back-channel communication, with strong denials from America's usual enemies in the Middle East, North Korea, and South America. Friendly countries in Europe and Asia are also offering support. All the usual posturing after events like this. Now I'm going to cover the things that feel really off."

Everyone focused intently on Suresh as a silence and chill hung in the air.

"There was a classified briefing for members of the Senate Armed Services Committee and the Joint Chiefs. China is believed to be behind the attack on the President, and this assertion was echoed by Senator Jiang. The Joint Chiefs have been asked to prepare for war. The service heads were also tasked with creating a plan to speed development on their respective service's directed-energy weapons capability. The President said that America needs to lead the world in directed-energy weapons. The Armed Services Committee will immediately draft bills to increase funding for this effort." Suresh paused to let the group process the implications of what was happening in Washington. "What I find most disturbing is the description of how the attack was carried out. It looks nothing like what you have presented. Everyone I spoke with conjectured about foreign assets and were convinced the attack was state sponsored. None of them provided any proof."

Derez spun around and slammed his palm on Suresh's workstation. "Whose analysis do you believe, General? Ours or what you heard from your Washington cronies?"

Jazmin was startled by the outburst, but the others either pretended not to notice or were used to Derez spouting off.

Suresh looked at them, holding each in turn for a moment in her calm, confident gaze. "Without a doubt, I trust the assessment of this team. There's too many conflicting and hidden agendas to accept that briefing at face value."

"What are your orders, General?" asked Gadget.

"Keep digging until you figure out the motives for the attack and how it was executed. We need to understand the end game for this attack. Once we know, we'll quietly work with the appropriate agencies to take action and punish whoever is behind this, especially if the group is inside our government. We'll only take independent action if there are no other options."

Harry asked the question the rest of the group was probably thinking. "Do we handle retribution quietly, or can we make some noise?"

A slight smile creased Suresh's serious expression and her eyes had a mischievous glint. "We'll do what's needed. Find the answers so we can do what we're here for, making problems go away that no one else can."

Suresh stood and everyone got to their feet. As the general left the ops center, the other faces morphed into a look Jazmin had seen before. They were preparing for battle.

Chapter 26
Mei Chan

Washington, DC
22 May

As a high value target for American intelligence, setting foot on US soil was risky. Normally, Mei avoided traveling alone outside of China, but Ling Chen's reckless behavior required drastic action. Since she was traveling without her usual security detail, Mei took extra precautions to keep her identity secret. She used artificial skin to make subtle changes to her face and wore high tech glasses which reflected and obscured light to confuse facial recognition systems. Her flight to the US originated in London, and Mei used a fake passport identifying her as a British national, Sandra Lee, VP of International Sales for Shark Fin Digital Communications, a tier three US Defense contractor.

After landing at Dulles and exiting US Customs, Mei was picked up by a secure private car. The vehicle's trip logs were immediately erased after dropping her at Ling Chen's condo. An armed security guard answered the door. "How can I help you?"

"I'm Sandra Lee. Senator Jiang is expecting me."

Using his neurotech, he matched the woman in front of him to the senator's security database. "Ms. Lee, I see you are on the approved entry list. Please follow me."

The security guard led Mei upstairs where Ling Chen sat on a couch with her full attention on her tablet. Infuriatingly, Ling Chen did not look up at them.

"Senator, Sandra Lee is here to see you."

Ling Chen flashed the security agent an irritated look for interrupting her, then her expression morphed into an uneasy smile. She stood and took a few steps toward the guard. "Please make sure we're not disturbed." She turned her attention to Mei. "Sandra, thanks for coming to see me." As soon as the door closed and the guard's footsteps receded, Ling Chen's friendly expression evaporated. "Why are you here?"

Mei charged forward and slapped Ling Chen across her face so hard a red handprint glowed on her cheek. She shoved Ling Chen backward and forced her down on the couch. Looming over her, Mei lowered her voice to a barely controlled growl and spoke in Mandarin. "You insolent, reckless child. What in the name of all the gods were you thinking, attacking the US President? Are you trying to start a war?"

"The mission was a total success. The Americans are cowering…"

Mei slapped Ling Chen again, knocking her to the floor. She stepped on her wrist to pin her down. "If you ever run another unsanctioned operation jeopardizing US relations with China, I will personally throw you into a pit in a Chinese black site prison and subject you to our full spectrum of reeducation. The paltry remains of your mind and wasted body will be shipped to a North Korean prison camp. You won't even know who you are when we're done."

Ling Chen opened her mouth to speak, then closed it.

Mei stepped on Ling Chen's wrist harder now, stopping just short of breaking bones. The anguished expression on Ling Chen's face was gratifying. "You take orders from me. You do not ever vary from those orders." Mei kicked Ling Chen in the ribs with her other foot. A grunt erupted, though Ling Chen didn't speak. "If I ever need to visit you again, it will be to end your life, and your mercenary teams won't be able to save you." Mei kicked her one more time with enough force to ensure Ling Chen wouldn't be able to fight back.

Mei exited the condo and got into a waiting car. She used a different set of fake IDs to travel home. She took a train to Boston, then flew to Toronto, then Spain, and finally to China. Mei had sent a blunt message and hoped Ling Chen would heed her warning. It would be a waste to burn such a prized long-term asset, but Ling Chen was only valuable if she could be controlled.

Chapter 27
Ling Chen Jiang

Washington, DC
22 May

Ling Chen was unable to move from the floor. Her wrist throbbed in pain and swelled to twice its normal size. With her other hand, she pulled up her blouse. Her ribs were red and faintly blue and purple where Mei had kicked her. There was a little swelling, and the skin was taut. Ling Chen knew it would look and feel worse before it began to heal. She probed the bruises with her fingertips, causing pain to radiate from even the gentlest touch. Every breath hurt. She wondered if she had internal injuries. It was time for a house call from her concierge doctor, who was both highly competent and discreet. The latter justified the woman's high price.

Ling Chen had been a spy most of her adult life, and China had supported every step in her political career. As her stature in the US Senate grew, she went to greater lengths to hide her ties to Chinese Military Intelligence. Even a minor slip would destroy her. Normally, she communicated through encrypted emails or video calls routed through multiple countries, the circuitous route making the electronic trail almost impossible to trace. Today was one of the rare times Ling Chen had seen her handler. Beyond the physical assault, the worst aspect of Mei's visit was being humiliated. Ling Chen vowed to never let that happen again. If Mei returned in person, she'd put a 9mm bullet in the spymaster's head.

Even though the attack on the President was well beyond what she'd discussed with Mei, Ling Chen expected congratulations on a successful operation, not a beating like she was an unruly child. The near miss on Navarro's life had meant personal outrage and overreaction from the President. China wished a free hand to escalate their directed-energy weapons program, and having Navarro start an arms race would ensure China's ultimate victory. The US would bankrupt itself in a vain attempt to outspend China, and internal politics would create further US turmoil. This would be a total victory for China. It would create chaos for its most hated rival.

Anger fueled Ling Chen to push through the pain and claw her way back onto the couch. Despite Mei's reaction, today was another step toward Ling Chen's goal of retribution for her parents' murders. As Chinese academics living in the US, they had been targeted by Asian-hating thugs propelled by the xenophobic American culture. Unforgivably, the murderers were exonerated by a US senator who even called the men "heroes." Ling Chen's first mission when she was elected was to destroy the man's career and his life.

She called her doctor, then contacted Shelbey Tanzini, a trusted television reporter. She offered the reporter something the woman couldn't resist, an exclusive interview with a senate power broker. Ling Chen wanted to amplify a message of warning through the media. It was time to put America's beloved free press to work destroying the country.

Chapter 28

Washington, DC
24 May

Ling Chen arrived at her senate office early so she'd have time to prepare for her television interview with Shelbey Tanzini about the horrendous attack on the President. The truth, that whether by skill or luck, the drone pilot had accomplished the near impossible feat of destroying both Marine One escort helicopters and forcing the President's aircraft down without injuring her, would not be part of the discussion.

Her quiet time ended when her assistant, Ting, entered the office, followed by a camera operator, lighting technician, and makeup artist. Ting steered the makeup artist off to the side and let her know she wouldn't be needed. After an embarrassing television experience early in her career, Ling Chen trusted only herself for hair and makeup that met the demands of high-resolution video. She meticulously chose her outfit to project power, trust, and a unique sense of style.

Shelbey entered the office with a friendly nod to Ling Chen. Blonde, fit, and expensively dressed, the reporter looked twenty years younger than her actual age, fifty-seven. Cosmetic surgery, a brutal fitness routine, and a six-figure wardrobe budget made this possible. Shelbey had a reputation in Washington power circles as a hard-hitting, no-nonsense journalist who both made and destroyed careers. The two women, both ambitious professionals, had an unspoken agreement to use each other to further their respective careers. Last night at Ling Chen's condo, they had worked out their script, with Shelbey asking leading questions to elicit the newsworthy soundbites they both desired.

The camera operator and lighting tech carefully arranged two upholstered chairs. Shelbey sat in the interviewer's chair and Ting sat opposite her so the crew could make final camera and lighting adjustments. Once they were set, Ting stood off to the side.

The camera operator counted down from five, and at one Shelbey broke into her trademark smile. "I'm here today with Senator Jiang, the Chair of the Armed Services Committee. Senator, what went through your mind when you heard about the dastardly attack on President Navarro?"

Ling Chen looked at Shelbey with practiced seriousness. "Like most Americans, I was angry that anyone would attack our president. I was relieved that President Navarro escaped unharmed, and grateful to the brave military members who lost their lives protecting her. The loss of life from the many people killed in the ensuing vehicle crashes on the ground was tragic."

"Senator, do you think this was a terrorist attack, or state sponsored by one of America's enemies?"

Ling Chen paused a moment, as if she had to think about her response. "At this point in the investigation, the government is pursuing all leads to determine what happened. It's too early to know for certain who was responsible for this vicious attack. Every government investigative agency is reviewing the evidence, and Americans can rest assured we will find out what happened."

Shelbey inclined her head and narrowed her eyes. "I understand we don't have definitive answers yet, but what is your best guess on who is behind this attack?"

Ling Chen mirrored Shelbey's pose. "This was a sophisticated attack and beyond the reach of most terrorist organizations. Given the level of planning, execution, and how close our enemies came to murdering our president, it's more likely a state-sponsored attack."

Shelbey fired off her next question. "Who are the top candidates capable of creating and deploying such a dangerous weapon for this brazen attack on our president?"

Ling Chen conveyed a look of calm assurance. "I'll leave that to the men and women leading the investigation."

Shelbey struck a more relaxed pose herself. "Senator, as Chair of the Armed Services Committee, what actions are you taking in response to this attack on our democracy?"

"One of the early findings is that a directed-energy weapon was used in the attack against Marine One. The Armed Services Committee will be holding hearings to determine how to accelerate our offensive and defensive directed-energy weapons capabilities across all military branches."

Shelbey leaned forward again. "The President vetoed your last defense budget because it increased funding for directed-energy weapons. Do you think she's changed her mind?"

"I expect a renewed urgency from the White House for funding directed-energy weapons." Ling Chen faced the camera. "The top priority for the President and Congress is to protect the American people from attack. We will take action."

"Thank you for your time this morning, Senator. Our viewers will be very interested in any new developments."

The camera cut away and the bright lights dimmed. A few minutes later the video equipment was packed, and the two women shared a conspiratorial smile as Shelby and her crew left. Ling Chen's plans would be driven forward when the interview aired, making directed-energy weapons spending the hot topic for the day's news cycle. Having been attacked and almost killed, President Navarro would happily sign an emergency appropriations bill for new directed-energy weapons programs.

Ling Chen relished the idea of a new arms race bringing her one step closer to achieving the wealth and power she needed to exact revenge for her parents' deaths.

Chapter 29
Jazmin Hassani

Wisconsin Militia Base
Bayfield, Wisconsin
25 May

Jazmin stared at the fast-attack quadcopter simulation results with growing alarm. She'd crashed the aircraft in all twenty-five landing attempts. Even using autopilot, military pilots weren't allowed to perform the maneuver she was training for now – a quadcopter maglev catapult capture – the vertical equivalent of a jet fighter landing backward on an aircraft carrier and slowed by the catapult running in reverse. While she'd made progress over the course of the training runs, all ended with the same result—total destruction of the aircraft.

The underground base used a vertical launch tube for rotorcraft. The tube used supercooled magnets, similar to how maglev trains operate. Magnetic force held the copter perfectly aligned inside the launch tube and pushed it out at high speed. During launch, the four rotors were disconnected from power and spun freely. Once clear of the launch tube, the pilot engaged power to the rotors for controlled flight. While it looked easy, this maneuver took lots of practice runs on the simulator to get the timing down. For rotorcraft recovery, the base normally opened a camouflaged hangar door at ground level, even though this left the militia open to attack. Jazmin was the only member of senior staff willing to take that risk for Captain Diamond. After reviewing other options, they finally agreed to allow a quadcopter maglev catapult capture. Jazmin sent the encrypted message to Diamond using one of Harry's stealth algorithms.

The problem was Jazmin couldn't execute the plan. After assurances from Gadget that it was technically possible, Jazmin assumed she could fly precisely enough to land safely once she completed a hivemind connection with Diamond and took control of the quadcopter. The flight simulations made it clear she couldn't. With only twelve hours before Diamond arrived, assuming the captain was willing to take the risk, Jazmin needed to clear her head. The only other pilot on base was General Suresh, and she wasn't rotorcraft qualified. Jazmin also didn't want to admit failure to her commanding officer. She headed to the maintenance hangar. Gadget wasn't a pilot, but she knew more about aircraft and systems than anyone on base.

Jazmin found Gadget working on the neurotech avionics interface of a quadcopter she was rebuilding from several others that had been seriously damaged. Among other schemes to arm the group, Harry had set up a company licensed to buy surplus military hardware to refurbish and sell to friendly nations' militaries. He participated in online auctions and purchased surplus and damaged weapon systems for Gadget to rebuild. It was all legal and approved by the DOD. It also meant the group had access to any weapon system they wanted. Gadget's team enjoyed the challenge, and they had no end of work.

Jazmin tapped on the exterior of the copter and Gadget opened the door. "I need your help. You know more about aircraft and flight control systems than I do. Since you're not a pilot, you approach things differently, too."

Gadget laughed and she patted the seat next to her. "I appreciate your humility, Commander. Sit down and tell me how I can help you."

Jazmin sat in the pilot's seat and scanned a familiar control panel and forward view out the windshield. She turned to Gadget. "I've tried landing the fast-attack quadcopter inside the launch tube on the simulator and crashed it every time. I can't keep it under control all the way to the bottom. On my best attempt, I only made it halfway down the tube before rolling the copter sideways and tearing off the rotors. I destroyed the aircraft on all twenty-five attempts, and I only survived five of the landings. I have less than twelve hours to figure out how to do this, or we have to call off the meeting with Captain Diamond."

Gadget nodded, looked out the windshield into the hangar for a few moments and then back at Jazmin. "I have a couple of questions, Commander. Are you keeping magnetic flow on or off during the descent?"

"Magnets off."

"Are you attempting controlled flight in the launch tube?"

"I'm hand-flying the aircraft. Autopilot won't engage inside the launch tube. I even have to suppress the alarms."

Gadget looked at Jazmin like a teacher lecturing a well-intentioned but slow student. "You're going about this all wrong, Commander."

This wasn't the answer Jazmin was expecting, and Gadget's cutting remark stung. She was about to argue, then reminded herself she was failing and had asked for help. "Please explain."

"It's a maglev catapult inside a tube. The airflow in that confined space makes controlled flight impossible. On launch, you disengage your props for free rotor flight. You wait to engage power until you're out of the top side. The magnets keep you from hitting the side of the tube."

Jazmin sighed. "You're not telling me anything I don't already know."

"Your problem, Commander, is you're trying to fly inside the tube, something we both know is impossible."

"No argument there, Chief." Jazmin shook her head wearily.

Gadget pulled out her tablet and projected on the copter's windshield a video of a maglev catapult launching a quadcopter. The video ran forward until the pilot engaged power and attained controlled flight. She froze the image on the screen. "This is a standard training video for a maglev catapult launch. I'll slow it down and run it in reverse." The video ran at one quarter speed. The quadcopter descended to the top of the catapult magnetic field, where it was locked in place, then descended with perfect trajectory down the tube, slowing as it went all the way to the bottom. "Instead of trying to fly the copter down the tube, the trick is to perform a maglev capture at the top and let the catapult slow your descent to the bottom while keeping the aircraft centered in the tube."

Jazmin thought through the steps to attain a maglev capture. "Will a launch tube run in reverse?"

Gadget projected the maglev launch control panel on the windshield. "It's not a standard operational function but in maintenance mode, it's an option." The screen changed to the maintenance control panel. Capture and controlled descent were now options.

Jazmin laughed. "I wish I'd come here sooner."

Gadget cleared the holographic projections from the cockpit windshield. Her face lit up with an amused expression. "I knew what you were trying to do. I figured it was only a matter of time before you gave up and stopped by. Derez was afraid you'd try it on an actual sortie."

"Would you have let me try?"

Gadget shook her head. "Hell no, Commander. I wouldn't let you destroy one of my aircraft. We're all experienced enough to have had our egos beat to hell. That's the worst that can happen in a simulator. We wouldn't let you fail in a real aircraft. It would have been a suicide mission. I had the copter locked down just in case you tried."

"Thanks. I'm still new here and not sure where I stand."

Gadget put her hand on Jazmin's shoulder. "You're one of us, and we take care of each other, no matter what."

"Can you program the flight simulator for maglev catapult captures?"

Gadget tapped her tablet, and the maglev catapult simulator screen projected on the cockpit windshield. "Already done. The next time you log into the simulator, you'll see it as an option."

Four hours later, Jazmin got up from the simulator after performing fifty successful maglev catapult captures and smooth descents to the bottom. Now she was ready for her meeting with Diamond.

Chapter 30

Wisconsin Militia Base
Bayfield, Wisconsin
26 May

Jazmin checked the screen to make sure Captain Diamond's quadcopter was the only aircraft in the area. She didn't want to risk radio traffic, so she sent an encrypted text to Diamond. *I'm sending a hivemind connection request.*

Diamond replied, *copy.*

Jazmin concentrated. While hivemind connections could function at a distance, the reduced signal strength made them harder to initiate. It took twenty seconds to establish, and all Diamond would authorize was communication.

Shockwave, I appreciate your trust.

I hope it's well placed, Pegasus.

Let's talk face-to-face.

Where do I land?

I need to take control of your aircraft. Our landing procedures are unusual.

You're AWOL and a wanted terrorist. Why should I hand over control of my copter to you?

Have you ever snagged the top of a maglev catapult and landed at the bottom of the launch tube?

That's insane.

Only if you haven't done it before. It's perfectly safe if you know how but it takes practice. These are the rules of engagement if you want to know who killed our friends at Truax and learn about the attack on the President. Pull your master weapons controller out of the panel. Authorize me for full control of your aircraft. When you land you'll only see me. I won't answer any questions about where you are, who I'm working with, and how I know what really happened. When we're done, I handle the launch and return control once you're airborne. You're free to go after that.

You're asking a lot. I called in countless favors to get an Air Tasking Order approved to come here armed. If I regret giving up my firepower today I'll be back. Weapons hot.

We can help each other. Decision time, Captain. Be bold or go home.

Jazmin wondered if she'd overplayed her hand. Then a deep synapse connection opened and the neural bandwidth channel stabilized. She felt Diamond hesitating and wondering if her trust was well placed, but then the captain pulled the master weapons controller from the panel and stowed it in the safe box. All the quadcopter's weapons were offline. Jazmin felt Diamond probe her thoughts and intentions. This was both an intimate and intrusive act as the women connected to each other's inner dialogue. Satisfied, Diamond authorized full control of her aircraft. Jazmin imagined the controls in her hands and saw the instrument panel. It had been a long time since she'd piloted a quadcopter or an octocopter with only her mind, especially from a remote location. *I have the aircraft.*

Diamond replied, *You have control.*

I'm taking the aircraft's black box offline. There can be no record of our meeting. This was a feat that was supposed to be impossible, though Harry had found a way. Jazmin felt Diamond's unease. Instead of speaking, Jazmin projected calm assurance that Diamond was safe. Once the quadcopter was over the maglev catapult, Jazmin descended until the magnetic field supported the copter. *Maglev capture complete. Setting props to freely rotate.*

The quadcopter began a controlled descent down the launch tube, just the way Jazmin had practiced. The descent slowed toward the bottom, and the copter landed gently on the skids. Half the tube rotated and formed an opening around the front and side doors of the copter.

The maglev catapult was adjacent to the maintenance hangar. Normally, it was a large, well-lit space filled with equipment. Today, other than a single workstation, holographic screen, and two chairs, the area was empty. Only a small space immediately surrounding the launch tube was lit. Since this was an underground facility, the rest was pitch black, and it was impossible to see anything beyond the pool of light.

Jazmin approached the front of the copter, her hands held off to her sides in clear view. "I'm unarmed. Please remove your sidearm." Through the windshield, Jazmin watched Diamond take off her holster and place her handgun on the copilot's seat. Diamond exited the aircraft.

The captain studied Jazmin, then scanned what little she could see in the room. "Well, Pegasus, you left the Navy on rather short notice, and your post-service escapades made very interesting reading." Diamond made a theatrical gesture at the empty space all around them. "I hope you haven't turned to the dark side."

Posturing, exaggerated tone of voice, and theatrical gestures normally made for stressful situations. Speaking on a hivemind connection was a totally different experience as both had access to each other's emotional responses and intensions. Jazmin radiated confidence, calm, and purpose. "Just because the file cover shows Top Secret, doesn't mean it's true. Let's dispense with the mind games. We both want the same thing."

Diamond put her hands on her hips. "What happened at Truax? How did five fighter pilots get shot down? Who the hell was behind the attack?"

Before she could answer, Jazmin's attention was drawn to her colleagues hiding in the dark. Harry aimed a high power taser at Diamond with Derez backing him up with an assault rifle. With her normal vision, Diamond couldn't see the two men, even if she looked right at them, though Jazmin saw them easily with her night vision eyes. Jazmin wanted to be alone with Diamond, but Suresh had vetoed that option. While darkness gave the appearance of her being alone, Jazmin couldn't keep up the charade while on a hivemind connection with Diamond.

Diamond's eyes hardened. "How many guns are pointed at me?"

There was no point in lying. "Two that I'm aware of. My colleagues are less trusting than I am."

"Trust is a fragile thing. At least you had the decency of not lying to me. How do you expect me to trust you when you insist I be unarmed while holding me at gunpoint?"

Jazmin stared at Harry and then at Derez. "Leave us. I'm turning on the lights."

Harry nodded and headed to one of the exits. Derez flashed an ugly expression and shook his head in disgust. A moment later, he exited, too.

Once they were gone, Jazmin brought up the lights. "Now we are both unarmed and alone in the room." Jazmin waited and let the silence linger.

Diamond did a slow scan of the mostly empty space. "I see you cleaned house before my arrival. The problem with being a captain is I rarely see facilities as they really are. There's something scary about any officer O-6 or above seeing normal operations, as if we suddenly all got amnesia the day we pinned silver eagles on our collars. My guess is your hidden base has enough people and firepower to start a war. No doubt your associate Harry Dexter is the one who pulled you in. I know your personal history. How am I doing so far, Commander?"

Jazmin walked over to Diamond's quadcopter. "You've done your homework, as I expected you would. You also know I have to stay in the shadows. What's the investigation board telling you?"

Diamond shook her head in frustration. "Nothing useful. I'm under investigation too, for blowing the attacker out of the sky. I can't even get confirmation that the aircraft or drone I took out was the attacker. It was the only thing in the airspace without a transponder ID. If the pilot wasn't onboard the aircraft, I'll chase them to hell."

"I'm not surprised." She gestured to the two chairs in front of the workstation. "I'll brief you on what I know. Is the government still selling the false narrative that Harry and I are behind this?"

Diamond shook her head. "Everyone has just gone silent."

Jazmin sat at the workstation and Diamond sat next to her. On the holographic screen, Jazmin showed a photo of the attacking business jet parked at Dane County Regional Airport prior to attacking the fighter jets. She projected a second photo showing the energy beam ports protruding from the bottom of the fuselage. "We believe the jet was outfitted with directed-energy weapons. The radar signature didn't match the aircraft, and it was designed for stealth, which is how it got close enough to down five fighter jets."

"This is consistent with what I experienced in the air. What infuriates me is the silence. None of this was shared with me." Diamond's anger pulsed through Jazmin in waves.

"We were able to pick up a transponder ID when the attacking aircraft flew in the clear before going dark. We traced ownership of the plane to a company whose subsidiaries provide security services. We think these companies are providing black ops teams to the US government."

Diamond spun in her chair, and her laser stare drilled right through Jazmin. "That's one hell of an accusation. What do you have to back it up?"

Jazmin stared right back at Diamond. "Senator Jiang has been pushing the need for improving the US directed-energy weapons arsenal. She's leading the charge in the Armed Services Committee to fast-track a massive budget appropriation that the President will undoubtedly sign. Jiang is also a major stockholder in Pulse Weapons Labs, the company which will likely see a hundredfold increase in business. The strike on Marine One had disturbing similarities to the attack on the fighters at Truax. We think what happened to you was a warm-up before going after the President."

Diamond stayed silent for a moment, taking in the information. "The chief theory being floated around Washington is the attack on the President was sponsored by China."

"China is a convenient enemy to point at to ratchet up the arms race on directed-energy weapons. Personal greed is in the mix, though likely something even worse is driving all of this," said Jazmin.

Diamond said, "Washington is filled with intriguing theories. Countless groups are feeding the madness. We may never know what's driving Jiang and her associates." She scanned the area around them, then looked back at Jazmin. "If you have a maglev catapult, then there's far more to this facility than what I'm seeing."

Jazmin stood and walked over to the quadcopter. "You have the legitimacy to ask the hard questions and demand the answers I can't. Are you going to live up to your call sign and create a shock wave in Washington, or is my trust displaced?"

Diamond joined Jazmin by the quadcopter. "Does my freedom depend on the answer to your question?"

Jazmin opened the pilot side door. "I keep my promises. I'll hand off control once the copter attains stable flight after launch."

"I'll carefully consider what you've told me." Diamond climbed inside, shut the door and strapped in.

Jazmin stepped back. *Engine start.* The zero emission hydrogen engine generator started. She waited for it to stabilize and for the electric motors driving the rotors to come online, then set the four rotors to rotate freely. The maglev tube rotated closed. *Maglev launch in three, two, one.* The copter lifted off and accelerated through the tube, held in perfect alignment by the supercooled electromagnets. As soon as the quadcopter cleared the top and was thrown skyward, Jazmin engaged power to the rotors and attained stable flight. *Handing off control.*

I have the aircraft.

Godspeed, Shockwave. Don't leave anyone standing in your wake. Jazmin severed her hivemind connection with Diamond. Time would tell if her gamble would pay off.

Chapter 31

Wisconsin Militia Base
Bayfield, Wisconsin
29 May

Jazmin bolted upright in bed in excruciating pain. Her skull felt like it was being crushed and was about to explode. A wave of fear slammed her, and she panted for breath as her heart rate accelerated out of control. A hundred voices vied for her attention, all demanding a hivemind connection. Nothing like this had ever happened before. She tried to calm herself and think straight, but it was impossible. Through her fog, fear, and pain, she had a grim realization. In the five years she'd been a Neurotech Defense Agency investigator, she'd only seen this happen once, and the victim had died.

A wave of nausea overwhelmed her. She vomited every bit of undigested food and liquid in her system all over herself and could barely catch her breath. Afraid she'd pass out and choke on her own puke, she crawled off the bed and dragged herself out of her quarters and across the hall. A warm, stinking trail marked her progress. She pounded on Harry's door with her fist.

The door opened and in an instant Harry's expression went from annoyed to concerned. He knelt to help her. "What the hell happened to you?"

With all of her remaining strength she croaked, "Hivemind overload attack. Help me." Sprawled on the floor, Jazmin continued to retch. After several minutes of dry heaves and waves of muscle spasms, she was too weak to even lift her head.

Harry triggered a medical emergency on the comms system. A calm computerized voice said, "Please state the scope of the emergency: single victim, multiple victims, or mass casualty event."

"Single victim."

"Please state the nature of the emergency."

"Patient is Commander Jazmin Hassani. She's reporting a hivemind overload attack."

"Connecting to Commander Hassani's biochip and tracking vital signs. It's crucial to keep her airway clear. Medical droid and combat medic alerted."

Harry checked her breathing and squeezed Jazmin's arm. "Help is on the way."

Footfalls grew louder down the hallway, and there was the whir of a fast-moving droid. Derez arrived with an emergency medical kit slung over his shoulder. He knelt next to her. "Jazmin, we're going to take great care of you. Try to relax while me and robodoc figure out what's going on."

As dreadful as Jazmin felt, she latched on to an amusing thought. Derez the combat medic had a totally different personality than Derez the commando; a caring human being lived inside his gruff shell. The medical droid rolled up. Some of the AI cybernetic trauma physicians were designed to handle hands-on treatment. This one was limited to diagnosis and direction. Derez, as the combat medic, would take care of the hands-on care. Jazmin trusted him more than the droid, especially if he had to do anything invasive. She'd read Derez's file, and he was well respected by other combat medics. He had also been an instructor at the end of his active-duty career.

Jazmin lay on the floor while Derez and Harry spoke quietly. Her head pounded and everything around her spun. Derez studied the medical droid's diagnostic screen. "Jazmin, your body's stressing out. Your heart rate and blood pressure are way too high, you're breathing like you're sprinting, and your neural activity is off the charts. Harry said you thought this might be a hivemind overload attack. Do you still think that?"

Jazmin could barely follow what Derez said. She hesitated while his words fought their way through the fog of her muddled brain. She croaked "Yes."

Derez and Harry exchanged a worried look, then Derez fished out a hat with a flexible metallic coating from his medical kit and pulled it over Jazmin's head. "This is a signal attenuator. It will slow down the barrage of electromagnetic waves coming at you. We need to isolate you in a Faraday cage."

Once the hat covered her head, the noise level and pain abated from excruciating to just miserable. Derez swabbed Jazmin's arm with an antiseptic wipe, inserted an IV, then loaded a hypodermic. "I'm going to give you something to calm down your system." Before Jazmin had a chance to respond, he plunged the needle into her IV line. A few seconds later she began to relax and felt a little less dreadful. The last thing she remembered before losing consciousness was Derez and Harry placing her on a hover gurney and floating it down the hallway.

***

Jazmin woke up in a dimly lit room. She had no idea how long she'd been unconscious. She wasn't in the clinic, though she was hooked up to a medical monitor. She checked the screen. Her system wasn't racing like it had earlier, though all of her vitals were still running far above normal. She was exhausted but in less pain than before. She scanned the immediate vicinity. She was in a SCIF, a sensitive compartmentalized information facility. Above the door a red LED sign showed *Classified Materials Locked Down and Secured — Active Hivemind Connection Detected.* To stop the transfer of classified information outside a SCIF, hivemind connections of anyone inside were forbidden. It made sense they put her in here. Derez wanted to get her inside a Faraday cage where no outside signals could penetrate, and the SCIF had the highest level of shielding on base.

Jazmin did a quick inventory of her condition. She was so weak she could barely lift her head off the pillow. Her IV was still in, along with a catheter. That didn't bode well. She wore loose fitting, clean clothes she didn't recognize, and she no longer smelled of vomit. Even her hair was clean. She owed a huge thank you to whoever took on the nasty job of cleaning her up. Her mouth was dry, and she found a mug of ice water with a straw next to her bed. She took a sip of the cool water, then closed her eyes.

She wasn't sure how much time had passed when she heard a

tap on the door. She opened her eyes in time to see a large man with broad facial features and kinky gray hair enter the room. His face lit up with a kindly smile, and in a British accent said, "My name is Dr. Thaddeus Montgomery. Most people call me Monty. I'm a retired Navy trauma surgeon, and I help out the team from time to time. You must be pretty special. General Suresh flew out to my cabin in Wyoming to bring me here."

Jazmin sat up in bed, though even that was exhausting. "How long have I been out?"

"About fourteen hours. I've spent the last few hours studying your medical history. You've spent a lot of time in medical facilities." He pulled up a chair next to her bed. "Can I take a look?"

Jazmin nodded and wondered why they'd flown in a trauma surgeon. She knew she was in trouble, maybe worse than expected. Fear added to her misery.

Dr. Montgomery looked into her eyes with a penlight, then asked her to track the pen with her eyes as he moved it back and forth.

"You do realize these are bionic eyes?"

"Commander, I'm well aware of which parts of you are organic and which ones were added later." His tone made it clear he didn't welcome her second guessing his competence. "I'm testing the connection between your visual implants and your brain." The doctor swiveled in his chair and brought up a new holographic screen fed by the medical monitor. It hung in the air where Jazmin could see it. Manic waveforms pulsed on the screen, blue at the bottom and red on top. "Your neurotech is being attacked. The powerful outside signals are even reaching you inside the SCIF. I've only seen this a few times in my career. Normally, I'd send you on to see a neurosurgeon, but that may be difficult, given you're wanted by the government as a terrorist." He waved his hand, and the screen disappeared.

"How is this happening? What can you do to stop the attack?"

Montgomery looked away for a moment, then peered back at her. "I need to do some research and review options. For now you need to rest. Your body is under a lot of stress." He stole a glance at the medical monitor screen. "Too many of your systems are racing from the stress of the attack. I'm going to adjust the meds in your IV."

Before she could ask further questions, Montgomery tapped in a new rate for one of the drugs feeding her IV lines. She felt herself slipping into a fearful fog, wondering if this would result in a slow-moving death.

Chapter 32
Harry Dexter

Wisconsin Militia Base
Bayfield, Wisconsin
29 May

Harry arrived in the secure conference room. He had barely slept since Jazmin had crawled to his room looking like she was on the fourth day of a three-day bender. She was the toughest person he'd ever known, and he was amazed by her resilience, but no one could survive the neural pounding of a hivemind overload for very long.

Derez, Gadget, and Monty entered the room and joined Harry at the table. Each seemed confined to their own worried thoughts.

A minute later Suresh arrived and sealed the door. "The attack on Jazmin is the most significant security breach we've had in a while. Harry, I want to know what happened and how to stop this type of attack in the future."

Harry activated the holographic screen at the front of the room and displayed a visual representation of what he'd figured out. "The carrier wave originated from Jazmin's hivemind connection with Ebony Diamond. Then it was transferred to a high-power signal generator we traced to a US black ops site. It's hammering Jazmin across the electromagnetic spectrum. The only way we can protect her is by isolating her in the SCIF. It has the most effective shielding in the facility, and even that doesn't block all of it. I'm working on a better defense, but the attack hardware is robust."

Suresh steepled her fingers. "Keep at it. We can't afford these types of attacks. We've never had this happen before. How do we stop these in the future?"

Harry said, "We don't know. Once the carrier hands off the individually targeted attack, there's no trace left behind. Going forward, we'll scan Diamond before she can make direct contact with Jazmin."

Suresh turned to Monty. "How is your patient?"

"She's heavily sedated and getting some rest, though all of her systems are racing. The neural overload is taking a toll. Her neurotech is damaged and will continue to degrade. There's nothing more I can do for her. She needs a neurosurgeon, and we haven't recruited one. If I take her to a hospital, they'll check her biochip and discover she's on the terrorist watch list."

"Is there anyone who'd be willing to work on her here?"

Monty shook his head. "I don't trust the few people I know who'd be willing to risk their careers. They'd be more likely to kill her than save her."

Suresh looked at each person around the table. "Is there anything we can do to save one of our own?"

Derez said, "Kidnap a surgeon and hold their family hostage."

Suresh shook her head. "I'd prefer other options. Too many things can go wrong."

Harry said, "Jazmin's brother, Enrique, is a neurosurgeon who's an expert on neurotech implants. I'm sure Derez and I could convince him to help his sister."

"Tell me more about him. There's always a risk to the militia when we bring in an outsider."

***

Twelve hours later, an octocopter disguised as a commercial delivery drone dropped Harry and Derez near an automated loading dock a few blocks from Dr. Enrique Hassani's office in the Chicago Loop. Harry and Derez walked to the doctor's office while the automated copter took off and flew a delivery route in the area so it wouldn't draw attention. Neither man ever left the militia base unarmed, both carrying wireless tasers and 9mm handguns. The last time Harry had seen Enrique at the military rehab hospital, things had gotten ugly. Jazmin's brother wouldn't be happy to see him.

They walked to Enrique's office and entered. A couple of teenaged patients were in the waiting area with their parents, watching holographic screens advertising the latest neurotech implants. The infomercials briefly showed diagrams of how these devices were surgically implanted, then covered new user capabilities, including learning efficiency and mind control of electronic systems.

A medical receptionist sat behind a glass partition, and she looked up from her computer when Harry and Derez approached the window.

Harry said, "We'd like to speak with Dr. Hassani."

The receptionist gave them an appraising look. "Do you have an appointment?"

Before Harry could answer, Derez opened his jacket revealing his shoulder holster, and the receptionist's eyes went wide. Harry glared at Derez for starting with a show of force.

Harry turned to the receptionist and smiled. "I apologize for my overzealous partner. We're federal agents and we need to speak to Dr. Hassani. He isn't in any type of trouble. We just need some information. Please let him know that Harry Dexter and an associate are here to see him."

The alarmed look on the woman's face eased, and she went to the back of the office. A minute later she returned with Enrique. Harry hadn't seen Jazmin's brother in over five years. Enrique was heavier now and grayer around the temples.

Enrique glared at Harry. "Why are you here?"

"It's about Jazmin. Is there someplace private we can talk?"

"We can talk in back." Harry and Derez followed Enrique down the hall and into his office. Derez shut the door. Enrique put his hands on his hips. "I had hoped Jazmin left you in her past. I learned she hadn't when federal agents visited me. What the hell did you pull her into that got her on the terrorist watch list? Don't fuck with me, Dexter. One phone call with your location will land you in a maximum security prison cell. You'll never see the light of day again."

Harry forced himself not to react to Enrique's threats. The man had every right to be mad.

Derez said, "We're trying to save her life."

Enrique narrowed his eyes. "What happened to her? Who are

you?"

Derez spoke calmly. "I'm the combat medic who treated her. Your sister was attacked. She's being treated by a trauma surgeon, but her injuries are neurological. She's sedated but needs a skilled neurosurgeon."

Enrique let out a long breath, and his angry expression morphed into a worried look. "Military doctors have far more experience than I do handling brain injuries, and I don't treat family members. Jazmin needs to turn herself into the authorities."

Harry and Derez exchanged a look of surprise. Harry said, "If Jazmin comes out of hiding, she'll be arrested for treason and will face the death penalty. There's no guarantee she'll even be treated. Her injuries are fatal but won't kill her immediately."

"Dammit, Dexter. I warned her about you."

Harry held up his hands in surrender. He didn't want to get into an argument with the one man who could save the love of his life. "Jazmin is suffering from a hivemind overload attack. Even isolated, she's still getting slammed."

Enrique ran his hand through his hair. "The only way to treat that is surgically."

"That's why we're here," said Derez.

Enrique shook his head. "There's better people than me. It's a rare affliction, and I have no experience treating it. Only military doctors see that. I install neurotech implants in teenagers. Special ops military implants aren't something I have any expertise in. You need somebody better than me."

Derez said, "You're her best option."

Enrique sighed and looked away for a moment, probably struggling with the ethical dilemma. "What medical facilities do you have?"

Harry thought, good, he's at least considering operating on her.

Derez said, "We have a trauma facility and operating room. Our pharmacy can handle most needs and synthesize specialty drugs with a little notice. We have an experienced trauma surgeon and me to assist."

"What about an anesthesiologist?"

Derez said, "Our AI robodoc determines the drug regimens and monitors vitals. I administer the drugs."

Enrique frowned. "Do you have neural firmware burners?"

Derez shook his head. "Sorry, we don't."

"I have a portable unit. How do we get there? Where are we going?"

Harry allowed himself to relax. He'd been ready to pounce and take Enrique by force if needed. "We have an octocopter standing by. Obviously, stealth is critical. Tell your staff and your partners you've been called away by the government for an emergency consultation. Tell your wife you'll be out of contact for several days and will be in quarantine."

Derez said, "Take any equipment or special drugs with you. We need to go now."

"I'll do what you ask because I love my sister, but when I'm done, I never want to see you two again." He moved in close to Harry. "If I do, I'll make sure you disappear forever." He took off his white lab coat, then headed down the hall. He picked up two cases and shoved them into Derez's hands, then filled a cold insulated bag with several vials of drugs and syringes. Enrique headed to the front desk. He set down his drug bag and waved his nurse over. "Cancel all of my appointments for the next several days." He cocked his head toward Harry and Derez. "I need to help these federal agents on an emergency case." Enrique picked up his drug bag and headed to the door with Harry and Derez close behind.

The three men walked quickly back to the loading dock. The octocopter was parked on the ramp. Once inside, they stowed the medical gear and the copter took off. Since it was disguised as a delivery drone, there were no windows, though monitors projected an outdoor view as if the walls were transparent. Enrique stared at the monitor and appeared to be mesmerized by the buildings zipping by the low flying copter. Derez sneaked up behind the doctor and placed a drug patch with a fast-acting sedative on Enrique's neck. A few seconds later Enrique was unconscious.

When they arrived at the militia base, Harry and Derez strapped Enrique to a hover gurney and delivered him to the same room as Jazmin. Once the gurney's brakes were set, Harry removed the restraints holding Enrique in place.

Half an hour later, Enrique woke with a start. He stared unsteadily at Harry, then saw Jazmin. He took a few unsteady steps to her bedside. He shook his head. "Jazmin, what the hell have you gotten yourself into?" He turned and glared at Harry. "Why him again?"

She sat up in bed and gave her brother a long hug. "Thanks for coming, Enrique." They sat in silence for a few minutes. "I'm getting closer to finding out what happened to me and my SEAL team in China. Some very nasty people are after me. I asked for Harry's help. That's all I can say." Enrique opened his mouth to argue, but Jazmin cut him off with a shake of her head.

A knock on the SCIF door cut off further attempts at conversation. Monty entered and stuck out his hand. "Hello, Dr. Hassani, I'm Dr. Montgomery. I've been taking care of your sister, but she needs more help than I can give her. Surgery is scheduled for eight a.m. tomorrow morning. We have sleeping quarters reserved for you. All of my case notes are on a terminal in the room. I'd be happy to go over any clinical details."

Enrique and Monty shook hands, then the old doctor ushered Enrique to the door. Jazmin mouthed "I love you" to her brother just before he left.

Once the door closed, Harry bent down and kissed Jazmin on the cheek. "I hope your brother is as good a surgeon as you've bragged about."

She smiled wistfully. "He is."

Harry let out a sigh of relief. The first part of the mission to save Jazmin was a success. Now it was up to the doctors.

Chapter 33

Wisconsin Militia Base
Bayfield, Wisconsin
30 May

Harry stood off to one side of the operating table and monitored Jazmin's neurotech for hivemind traffic. He had shielded the operating room as best he could from outside signals, though it wasn't as effective as being inside the SCIF. Her risk was elevated now, but soon the shielding wouldn't be needed. Enrique, Monty, and Derez surrounded the table where Jazmin was strapped down and under general anesthesia. Thankfully, there was a sterile drape suspended over Jazmin's head, so Harry could only see her from the neck down. He couldn't bear to watch them peel back her scalp and remove the top of her skull to expose her implants. Harry's job was to eliminate as much hivemind signal traffic as possible. He'd already severed his own connection to her and ensured everyone else at the bunker was also blocked. Maddeningly, signals still pushed through. He tried to eliminate or at least attenuate them, though it felt like zombie warfare. For every signal he killed, two more popped up.

He also monitored the neurotech firmware burner that Enrique had brought with him. Harry had triple-checked the functioning of the gear prior to surgery and had collected any spare hardware he could find on base. In addition, he had the technical specifications on his tablet. He insisted Gadget study the firmware burner and be ready to intervene if there were any issues. She was parked outside the operating room, gowned up and ready if she was needed.

Monty had told Harry the surgery would take about two hours. They were already ninety minutes in, and from the calm demeanor of the three medical professionals at the operating table, Harry was optimistic they'd be successful. His optimism crashed when they lost power and the operating room went dark.

Enrique said, "Nobody move, or we might kill her. I'm in the process of inserting neural probes into her brain."

The already-quiet room went silent. Even the beeps from the medical monitors stopped. That shouldn't have happened. The entire facility had backup power, and critical areas like the operating room had instantaneous switchover. At worst, the lights would flicker, but all the medical monitors ran on batteries that were kept continuously charged.

Harry checked his tablet. It was completely dead. The only good news was this looked like a zero hit. People's neurotech was powered by the brain's electrical pulses, so it wouldn't be affected by a zero hit. He opened a hivemind connection to Gadget. He breathed a sigh of relief when he connected with her. *Was the entire facility slammed with a zero hit?*

Gadget said, Yes, but after the last time this happened I shielded the emergency power generator room. It just kicked on, but it can't power the whole facility.

We're blind in here and Dr. Hassani is in the middle of inserting neural probes into Jazmin's brain. Divert power to the operating room first.

Already done.

Every joule of power had been sucked from the facility, but unlike an EMP burst, a zero hit wouldn't destroy the equipment. Zero hits disrupted operations temporarily while an opposing force took over, but they didn't cause permanent damage. Harry wondered what enemy was coming for them, but he had more immediate concerns. He was afraid to move, as he was next to the operating table and was terrified he'd bump it groping around in the dark.

Enrique said, "Dexter, my hands are getting jittery. Can you get the lights on?"

"Any second now, Doctor."

The operating room lights glowed back to life, and the area filled with a cacophony of beeps and buzzes as all the medical equipment and monitors came back to life. Harry checked the hivemind activity tracker, killed his connection with Gadget, and saw nothing else active.

Harry said, "Dr. Hassani, I'm not seeing any more hivemind activity."

Enrique let out a long breath. "Replacement neural probes are inserted. Firmware engaged and coming up now."

Harry held his breath while waiting for the surgeon's assessment.

Finally, Enrique said, "Firmware load complete and brain scan is running now. Dr. Montgomery, special ops military neurotech is quite different from the high-end headgear I normally work with. Do these scans look normal to you?"

Monty peered at the monitor. "The neurotech activity is lower than normal, but she's under general anesthesia, so that makes sense. I'm not an expert, but what I'm seeing appears to be in the acceptable range. Nothing I would normally be concerned about."

Enrique exhaled and stretched backward, then flexed his hands. "Time to close. Derez, since the top of her skull is synthetic as well as her skin, we can use bio-adhesive rather than screws and stitches. I'll show you a technique that minimizes scarring. It's much quicker too, so it might be useful in battlefield situations."

Derez held up two syringes. "Loaded with medical adhesive and ready to go. I'm always up for learning new techniques."

Harry was glad he couldn't see what they were doing. He checked the electronic medical equipment around the room, and all appeared to be functioning normally. He'd get with Gadget after this was over and run a thorough check of every system on base. He scanned the base's exterior sensor array for any type of incursion but saw nothing.

Harry couldn't shake the sense of being vulnerable. Someone had just attacked them and would try again. He'd have to work with the team to figure out who their enemy was and stop them permanently.

Monty released the brakes on the operating table, and it hovered over the floor. "Derez, please take Jazmin to recovery." Monty clutched Enrique's shoulder. "Nice work, Doctor. Thank you." Derez floated the gurney past Harry.

Enrique looked drained, though he had enough energy to flash Harry a venomous look. "I can't control what Jazmin does, but I want you the hell out of her life." He tore off his gloves, gown, and cap, then threw them in the medical waste bin. The air in the room grew frigid as Enrique walked past.

Harry made a mental note to talk to Monty when it was time for Enrique to return to his normal life. They had to make sure Jazmin's brother had no memory of any of this.

Chapter 34
Jazmin Hassani

Wisconsin Militia Base
Bayfield, Wisconsin
31 May

Jazmin, an IV still in her arm, woke to the beeping of medical monitors. She was in one of the clinic's regular overnight rooms. She had a vague memory of speaking with Enrique and Dr. Montgomery in the recovery room, but she couldn't recall what they said. She fell back asleep, waking once or twice with had no sense of how much time had passed.

At one point Derez came into her room. "I'm glad your surgery went well."

She sat up in bed and tried to focus, though all she could see was his profile in the dimly lit room. "My head still hurts, but the hundred voices screaming for my attention are gone."

"As long as you continue getting better, you'll be released in a few days for light duty."

"Derez, I appreciate everything you've done."

He flashed a rare smile. "Just doing my job. I'll let you rest." He left, closing the door behind him.

Jazmin relished the mental silence. Her hivemind connections were completely shut down, and she wasn't in a hurry to establish another, even with Harry. She turned up the room lighting and used a mirror to check the top of her head where Enrique had peeled back her scalp to replace her neural implants. Her brother was an artist. She could barely see the incision line, and the artificial flesh and bone would heal over perfectly in a few more days. Her senses of touch and pain were controlled by her neurotech, and they were turned down for now. As soon as her head healed, she'd return them to normal. Still exhausted, she fell asleep again.

***

Harry knocked on the door and came in. She grinned and patted her bed to bring him closer. "Thank you for everything, especially getting Enrique here. Where is he? I saw him briefly with Monty when I woke up in the recovery room, but not since then. Now that I'm fully awake, I owe him a hug and huge thank you."

Harry pulled up a chair next to her bed and sat, then peered at her for a moment. "Enrique's back in Chicago. We thought it best that he didn't stick around."

"I know he couldn't stay, but I'd hoped to thank him for saving my life." Harry's expression didn't match her own sense of joy. "What aren't you telling me?"

"It's safer for him and us if your brother has no memory of his visit. Monty gave him a dose of zipdol. It knocked him out for the ride home, and when he woke up he had no memory of being here. I delivered him to the isolation ward at Rush University Hospital, and one of the militia doctors met him there. She told Enrique he was suffering from short-term memory loss, that he'd consulted on a miliary case and was accidentally infected by a top-secret neurotoxin. His body was now clear of the drug."

Jazmin looked away. Harry was a constant reminder of the choices she'd made, and her brother was another victim. "Maybe one day this could be a funny family story."

Harry reached out and touched Jazmin on the cheek with his fingertips. He gently turned her back to face him. "You can never tell him."

She sighed. "I know."

Harry held her hand and neither spoke. She welcomed his warm touch and the quiet after so much noise. After a few minutes Harry pulled away and his expression turned serious. "While you were in surgery we were attacked with a zero hit. Every trace of power on the base was drained. It was scary. Your head was open, and Enrique was replacing your neural implants. Your brother's a hell of a surgeon."

Jazmin winced. "I'm not sure I wanted to know that."

"Gadget and I tried to trace the source but came up empty. When you're cleared for duty, we need your help to figure out who hit us. We also need to figure out if your hivemind overload was caused by Ebony Diamond. If yes, how did she get infected, and did she know she was a carrier?"

"I can't imagine her doing that on purpose."

"You never know what people will do. I learned that the hard way in Cyber Command."

"I should be released soon. Whoever it is, I bet they're on the government payroll and Jiang is giving the orders."

Harry stood. "That was our assessment, too. Now that you're no longer hearing voices, we need your investigator skills. Try to get some sleep."

He left the room and closed the door. Jazmin had never regretted her life choices, but the price tag kept getting higher. She shut her eyes and drifted into oblivion.

Chapter 35
Ling Chen Jiang

Washington, DC
1 June

Ling Chen and Danica arrived at the business park located in one of the northern suburbs around Washington. Their car pulled up to a large building with no signage, not even a street number. It was Ling Chen's first visit to Trident Services, one of several security contractors on her payroll.

Danica scanned the area for threats. "The front part of the building has offices, conference rooms, and a data center. In the back there's a warehouse with a fleet of specialized military vehicles and a large weapons locker." She pointed at the roof. "There's a helipad with a lift underneath to lower rotorcraft into the building for maintenance, weapons loading and refueling." Danica led the way to the building entrance, unlocking the security door with a wave of her biochipped arm followed by a retinal scan. Once inside, they passed through several reinforced doors that opened with another wave of Danica's biochip. Ling Chen couldn't see any cameras, but she was certain their progress was being tracked through the facility.

A guard holding a compact submachine gun with a 50-round magazine and dressed in a black uniform stood outside the executive conference room. He nodded to Danica. "Please scan your retinas."

Danica went first, followed by Ling Chen, and the reader glowed green after each scan. Ten deadbolts retracted from the titanium vault entrance, and the heavy door swung open.

Danica signaled for Ling Chen to stay back, then entered the room. A moment later she returned. "The room is secure, and everyone is present."

Ling Chen had read the dossiers on the three mercenaries meeting them, though she had met none of them in person before today. All stood when she entered the room. The leader of the group, Vikas, was a former Navy SEAL in his fifties with short salt-and-pepper hair, a weatherbeaten face, and piercing gray eyes like a coyote. Marcel was younger and a former Army Ranger built like a football linebacker. Ceylon, the tech expert, had prior experience as a CIA field agent.

Vikas motioned to the head of the table. "Welcome, Senator. We appreciate you making the trip here today."

Not that I gave them any choice, thought Ling Chen as she sat in the comfortable executive chair. No doubt this was usually Vikas's seat. It must irk him to be booted from it, though he knew not to let it show. After a moment the others sat along the two long sides of the table. These people worked for her, so she was in the power seat where she belonged. "Tell me about the failed attack to disrupt the power sources at the militia base in Bayfield, Wisconsin."

Irritation flashed across Vikas's face before his neutral expression returned. "We executed the operation as directed. When Diamond visited the militia base, she infected Hassani's neurotech so the hivemind overload attack was successful. Unfortunately, Diamond wiped the copter's logs, so we didn't have pinpoint accuracy for an optimal strike on the base. Per standard protocol, the team executed an area zero hit. We used near maximum power settings for underground penetration, short of wiping out the area's power grid. We monitored the vicinity for activity, but there was no immediate response. The area is still under surveillance."

Ling Chen scowled at him. "I was expecting a more definitive result."

Vikas said, "We can take more aggressive action, though it would entail significant risk. Our intel shows this area houses an underground base and that the militia is comprised of extremely well-armed elite ex-military operators."

In a low growl she said, "So are you."

Vikas stared back at her. "That's true, though I thought our mission was focused on stealth, not open warfare."

Ling Chen leaned forward. "Jazmin Hassani is a dangerous threat that needs to be eliminated. How you do it is not my concern."

Danica said, "Senator, instead of attacking the militia, one option is a personal assault. Hassani's mother, Mercedes Montoya, is an executive at Defense Air Systems, a tier one defense contractor, and she's in Washington on a regular basis. An attack on Hassani's family would bring her out of hiding."

Ling Chen wanted Vikas to squirm and was irritated by Danica diverting the direction of the meeting. Of course, Ling Chen knew all about the members of Hassani's family and their value as targets. Only one of them was truly valuable. Instead of lashing out, she bit back an angry retort and took a moment to consider Danica's suggestion. Ling Chen knew the woman wanted more responsibility than just handling personal protection for a senator. While the mercenary was well paid and much appreciated, she was underutilized in her current role. Vikas and his team were competent, but he didn't inspire his people with anything close to the fire that burned inside Danica.

Ling Chen said, "Danica, you have forty-eight hours to come up with an operational plan to go after Mercedes Montoya and silence Hassani for good. If we need more leverage we can always go after her father and brother." She pointed at Vikas. "Support Danica with whatever resources and people she needs. This is her operation, and all assets answer only to Danica."

The two mercenaries bristled, though Vikas was smart enough not to react. "Yes, Senator. She has the team's full support."

Ling Chen stood. "I've heard enough." She exited the room to the sound of angry murmurs, confident their resentment would focus their actions and get results.

Chapter 36
Jazmin Hassani

Wisconsin Militia Base
Bayfield, Wisconsin
6 June

Multiple cockpit alarms screamed for Jazmin's attention. Flying through storm cells at just below Mach 1, all she could see outside the cabin were black clouds and lightning in the nighttime sky. She scanned each instrument cluster in the damaged F-22 fighter jet and tried to make sense of the chaos. The left engine was on fire, the right-side vertical stabilizer was gone, and her fighter was in a flat spin, almost impossible to recover from. Jazmin shut down the left engine and hit the fire arrestors, then pulled the control stick back to get the nose of her aircraft up. She reduced power on the right engine. She couldn't go to idle or she wouldn't have enough power to recover from the spin. She silenced the alarms and focused on spin recovery. Her jet twirled and she lost altitude at an unnerving rate of descent. It wasn't time to eject yet, though her window to save the aircraft and her life was closing fast. The altimeter wound down to Jazmin's threshold for survival, then everything froze. The critical instrument cluster on the heads-up display cleared, and a message read *Jazmin, you need to see this. Meet me in the ops center right now.*

The message was from Harry.

She closed her eyes and gave herself a moment to let her heart rate and breathing return to normal. The emergency procedures aircraft simulation cleared, and an exercise recovery code appeared on the screen. Jazmin released the five-point harness and climbed out of the simulator. She removed her helmet and G-suit, and hung them on the equipment rack. She took a moment to study the pair of F-22 fighters that lay in pieces on the other side of the hangar. Harry had found them at a military asset auction and won the bid. Gadget thought using the parts from both aircraft, she could get at least one of them in flying condition, so Jazmin was training to be combat ready. She texted Harry, *On my way*. What was so important that he'd interrupted her in the middle of flight training?

***

The first thing she saw when entering the ops center was the grim expression on Harry's face. He was alone. She'd expected others to be with him, especially as his summons made her think an emergency was unfolding. "What was so important that I had to come instantly?"

He pointed at the holographic screen at the front of the room. "An NSA friend tipped me off."

Jazmin sat next to Harry and watched the horrifying bodycam video from a team of six DIA agents wearing black balaclava masks. The timestamp on the video was 0300, seven hours earlier. The team arrested her mother during a raid at her parents' home, leading Mercedes away in handcuffs while her grief-stricken father struggled as one of the agents pinioned his arms behind him. The video continued showing additional DIA officers searching the house, though they were sloppy and unprofessional. They knocked over furniture, heaved the contents of cupboards on the floor, and smashed everything they found. Jazmin was enraged as government hoodlums ransacked her parents' house in the guise of a search. When Saeed objected at the destruction of his home, one of the officers knocked him to the floor. He lay dazed on the carpeting, his nose bleeding profusely. One of the agents yelled obscenities at the offending officer, not for hitting an innocent man but for allowing it to be captured on video.

One of the agents triumphantly displayed a stack of classified fast-attack quadcopter master weapons controller design documents. The camera moved to show a computer screen with Mercedes' private dark web email account. It showed top-secret attachments sent to an address tied to Chinese Military Intelligence. The video ended, and the screen went blank.

Jazmin's fists involuntarily clenched. She wanted to beat the man who'd hit her father, along with the others who'd torn apart her parents' home. "How did the NSA get this video?"

Harry shrugged. "None of the competing government intelligence agencies trust their counterparts, so they spy on each other. My contact has a particular hatred and distrust for the DIA. Something we have in common. He tips me off when the DIA colors way outside the lines."

"This was a setup. There's no way my mother is passing classified information to Chinese Military Intelligence."

Harry said, "I know. There's more."

"Show me," Jazmin demanded.

He let out a long breath. "It's hard to watch."

Jazmin glared at him in disbelief. "Harder than watching my mother get arrested on false charges, my father slammed to the floor, and my parents' home get ransacked? Are you kidding?"

Harry shook his head. "Harder in a different way." An IT audit trail showed Mercedes' work computer had downloaded classified design data. A second audit trail showed evidence of her home computer transmitting electronic documents to a dark web site tied to Chinese Military Intelligence. Jazmin seethed while looking for signs the audit trails were fake, though she saw nothing obviously wrong. The last video showed Mercedes at a conference kissing a Chinese man on both cheeks and hugging him too long to be any type of professional greeting.

Jazmin asked, "Who is this guy?"

"Feng Liu, a Chinese diplomat and retired Chinese Air Force colonel. He works the defense company circuit and spends lavish sums entertaining defense company lobbyists."

The video ended. Jazmin tilted her head at Harry. "What aren't you showing me?"

"The video that really crosses the decency line."

She leaned closer to Harry and growled. "Now." He tapped his tablet screen. The life-size video projected at the front of the room. It was a porno movie of her mother and Feng Liu, but the woman's guttural moans sounded nothing like Mercedes.

"My mom's in great shape for her age, but that's not her. Whoever created this abomination never read her medical file. Her abs are covered in burn scars from an aircraft accident early in her career. She had cosmetic surgery to repair the worst of them, but the woman in the video had flawless abs."

Harry said, "Except for the last video, these were real videos with modifications. The sex video was fake with faces swapped out. Whoever created these had access to top-notch deepfake video technology but didn't have the experience or the artistry to cover their tracks. These wouldn't fool an expert."

Jazmin sighed. "If these get released onto the web, it won't matter how poor the quality is. My mom's reputation will be ruined, if it's not already."

Harry said, "Body cam footage from DIA raids usually doesn't get released to the public, though nothing would surprise me. Jiang and Trabago are trying to goad you into the open."

"They might get their wish, but if I leave the base, it will be to terminate them. I'm already a wanted terrorist. Why not add assassin to the list?"

Her tablet pinged with a news alert. CNN was airing a joint address from Senator Jiang and Lieutenant General Trabago. Jazmin projected the news broadcast onto the main screen. Jiang stood at a lectern with Trabago at her side. She said, "This morning Mercedes Montoya, Defense Air Systems Executive Vice President of Engineering and Chief Technology Officer, was arrested at her home by agents from the Defense Intelligence Agency for passing classified weapon system designs to Chinese Military Intelligence. What's particularly troubling is that Mercedes Montoya is the mother of terrorist Jazmin Hassani, who is still on the run. However, the country is safer because we now have Ms. Montoya in custody."

Several reporters' hands shot up and Jiang pointed at one. He said, "Ms. Montoya has been tied to Feng Liu. Did she pass classified information to him?"

Trabago answered. "The DIA sent officers to question Mr. Liu, but he refused to answer and has since retreated to the Chinese embassy."

A different reporter was called on. She asked, "Do you have any leads on Hassani? Any danger of her trying to free her mother from custody?"

Trabago answered this question too. "There's a nationwide

search for her. We are closing in, and we'll bring Hassani to justice."

Other hands shot up. Jiang said, "That's it for questions." She and Trabago walked away from the lectern. Jazmin turned off the video feed.

Harry said, "I know you want revenge, but you can't do this alone. You have a team behind you. Hard as it is to watch and not react, that's what you have to do for now. Let's put a plan together. When we're ready, we'll go hunting."

Jazmin was livid and wanted Jiang's and Trabago's heads stuck on poles outside the base as a warning not to mess with the people inside. She knew Harry was right, so she closed her eyes and tried to contain her rage until they could come up with an attack plan.

Chapter 37

Wisconsin Militia Base
Bayfield, Wisconsin
6 June

As soon as Jazmin and Harry had briefed the general on her mother's arrest, Suresh assembled the senior staff in the ops center. The general said, "Jazmin, please tell the group what you told me about your mother, Mercedes Montoya."

"My mom is an executive vice president at Defense Air Systems. First, she was framed for espionage. Then the DIA ransacked my parents' home and arrested her. She's being held at the Federal Correctional Institute in Hazelton, West Virginia. The only good news is that Hazelton is a medium security facility, so she isn't incarcerated with violent criminals."

Suresh said, "We need to free Ms. Montoya. Jazmin, the best way to protect your mother is by bringing her here, and we could certainly use her expertise while she's staying with us. Do you think she'd be willing to help us?"

The question caught Jazmin by surprise. Was this the price for rescuing her mom? She'd need to answer it carefully. "If it's technical help on aircraft and weapon systems, my mom loves to teach and would likely provide that. I don't know how she'd react to operational help on missions."

Gadget said, "I'd love to have access your mom's technical expertise."

Suresh asked, "Is there someone at Defense Air Systems that will take over for your mom? Will there be a power vacuum that Jiang can take advantage of now that Mercedes has been removed?" Jazmin said, "Her two top people both want her job, and either could take over."

Suresh asked, "Will Jiang go after your father and your brother?"

Jazmin sighed. "I'm afraid they might."

Derez said, "We can assign people to act as security and make sure nothing happens to them."

Suresh said, "Will your father and brother accept protection from us?"

Jazmin said, "Dad will. Enrique is too proud."

Suresh said, "Derez, assign 24/7 teams to both men. Let Saeed know, but do it from the shadows for Enrique. What options can we pursue to rescue Ms. Montoya?"

Derez said, "I can lead an assault team to the prison and breach the outer walls with explosives. We can find her cell, extract her, and exfil to a waiting octocopter."

Monty said, "I have a less violent option. We can fake a medical emergency the prison staff can't handle. An Ebola outbreak, for example. We identify Ms. Montoya as patient zero, and wearing hazmat suits, we extract her to a medical transport vehicle."

Harry said, "We can attack the prison's automated security system by creating a computer virus to take over the automated entry control program. We open every door in the facility and grab Mercedes in the ensuing chaos."

Suresh listened to each idea then shook her head. "Each of these approaches are high profile and could be traced back to us. I'm also concerned about collateral damage."

Frustrated with the general's ruling Jazmin said, "I wish we could clone my mother. We could sneak the clone into her cell and free my mom." The room went silent.

Gadget looked at Jazmin. "That's not as far-fetched as it sounds."

Suresh cocked her head and looked intrigued by the idea. "What are you proposing?"

Gadget said, "A clone isn't the answer, but creating an android version of Mercedes is possible. We have the equipment and the know-how to do it."

Jazmin felt a wave of relief and excitement. "When can we start?"

Suresh held out her palm to stop the conversation. "I want a few more details before I'll greenlight this op. One, how do you create an android copy of Mercedes Montoya? Two, how do you get the android into the prison? Three, how do you get the real Mercedes out undetected?"

Gadget said, "We have android soldier kits we can customize. I'll need Jazmin's help with her mother's personality profile and personal history. Not sure how to get the android copy in and the real Mercedes out."

Jazmin smiled. "A government investigator can get inside and get access to prisoners. Modify my face and send me in with a biochip spoofer. Remember, my face is one hundred percent synthetic, so it's changeable. I can also adjust the length of my legs to change my height. I was an NDA investigator for five years and I've done this countless times. The android will be my partner. Military uniforms and badges glide right past prison guards. Besides, my mother trusts me, and she'll follow my instructions. Since the android will be a perfect copy of her, their clothes will fit when they swap, and nothing will get tripped on the video surveillance system."

An amused expression lit up on the general's face. "Make it happen."

Chapter 38

Wisconsin Militia Base
Bayfield, Wisconsin
7 June

Jazmin and Gadget were working in the base's android lab. Before the team meeting when Gadget suggested this option, Jazmin hadn't realized this facility existed. The lab was in a secure location, locked behind vault doors. The militia didn't have a huge stock of android soldiers, especially the humanoid variety. They were employed for stealth missions deemed too dangerous for key personnel. Compared to humans, the androids were expendable, but because they were so lifelike, it was hard not to form emotional attachments to them. Jazmin wondered how she'd feel about creating a copy of her mother and exiling it to a federal prison.

The lab had dozens of 3-D printers, a wall of crates with cybernetic brains, a small server farm to generate the computer power needed for all the AI programming and learning algorithms, and a studio for personality programming. The final piece of equipment was a biochip spoofer. It generated both authentic original biochips registered in the federal government system and spoofers that would silence a person's implanted biochip while broadcasting another ID. Biochip spoofers were simple devices. They contained a replacement scannable ID; all the other bio information came from the actual biochip. All the personal identification information was in the federal database. Even though the government claimed the federal biochip system was impenetrable by outside hackers, Harry and a few other world-class hackers had proved the claim wrong.

Gadget sat at the 3-D printer network station with Jazmin perched nearby. Gadget said, "Let's start with the easy part, building the body. The first priority is creating a composite skeleton. It supports everything else." She brought up holographic images of Mercedes assembled from video at conferences, public cameras, and video shot at home. Like many wealthy, security-conscious people, Mercedes and Saeed had total home video coverage. This provided hours of video of Mercedes from every angle. In most of the video Mercedes was clothed. However, there was a limited amount of her naked. This allowed the AI algorithms to obtain precise measurements of her body. "All of this video will help us sculpt a perfect copy of your mother." Gadget froze the video on Mercedes' abdomen. "There's quite a bit of scarring."

"When I was three years old I touched my mom's scars and asked her what happened to her tummy. She said she was in an accident before I was born. She wasn't embarrassed and didn't pull my hand away. I learned years later she was in an aircraft accident. She went up with one of the test pilots and things went very wrong. She was badly burned, and the pilot died."

Gadget zoomed in. "We can reproduce the scarring. We'll just need to adjust the settings during the synthetic skin build, but that's late in the process." Four different holographic monitors showed slowly rotating 3-D images of Mercedes. One showed skeleton and support structures, including the android version of ligaments and tendons. The second displayed the nervous system with all the connections back to the cybernetic brain. The third monitor showed propulsion and synthetic organs. The screen showed everything that would allow the android to move as well as simulate bio-signs to feed credible readouts to a biochip. These included simulating basic functions like breathing and digestion. The fourth monitor showed cosmetic and sensory systems, including musculature, skin, hair, eyes, and ears. The cybernetic brain provided incredible AI processing power to make everything work.

After six hours of effort, Gadget did a final check of all systems. "I'll let you give it the build command."

Jazmin pressed the large green holographic button and dozens of 3-D printers on every wall in the android lab hummed to life. "The printers will chug away for about twelve hours."

Jazmin stood and stretched. The process of building an android copy of her mother was a reminder of how much of herself was bionic. So much of her was 3-D printed, though all of those parts had been surgically grafted and were now extensions of her body. The process of creating Mercedes was fascinating, horrifying, and emotionally wrenching all at once. They hadn't even gotten to awakening its consciousness or crossing the line into self-awareness. Jazmin forced herself to compartmentalize all of the emotions surging through her and focused on one thought only. She was rescuing her mother.

Gadget gazed up at Jazmin with a knowing look. "Building androids is a surreal experience. It must be terribly difficult for you. It's hard enough for me to keep my emotional distance. I can only imagine what you're going through. I understand if you need a break."

Jazmin shook her head. "The mission comes first. I'll deal with my emotional baggage later, after we rescue my mom."

Gadget stood. "Follow me. Now comes the interesting part, creating a credible replica of your mother's personality. This is tough technically and emotionally. This isn't something we push through in a marathon session. It will take a few days."

Gadget walked to the other side of the lab and pulled down a brain box. She carefully removed the brain from its case, leaving it in the carrying caddy. She unwound two fiberoptic wiring harnesses from the backside of the brain, one for power and a thicker bundle for the android's nervous system connections. She expertly connected both bundles to the programming workstation, then booted up the android brain for the initial program load. Messages from thousands of programs loading flitted across the workstation's screen. "Everything looks good so far. In my experience, if there's a problem with the brain, it fails right out of the box. In another couple of minutes the base program load will be in place. From there the AI self-learning algorithms take over and things get interesting. The process is never quite the same, especially when personality cloning for clandestine missions."

The workstation chirped and a female computerized voice said, "Initial program load complete. Ready for experiential learning."

Gadget said, "Android, your mission is to impersonate Mercedes Montoya. Body build on 3-D printer network is underway. Exposing AI to background information and video." Gadget executed several commands on the workstation.

After a minute, the computerized voice of the cybernetic brain said, "Hello, my name is Mercedes Montoya, Executive Vice President of Engineering and Chief Technical Officer for Defense Air Systems Corporation, the leader in military aviation technology. Our aircraft serve in all five branches of the US military, as well as the armed services in more than a dozen allied countries."

Jazmin was startled as the computerized voice sounded exactly like her mother, including the trace of her Mexican accent. "Hello, I'm Jazmin Hassani."

The cybernetic brain said, "I have a daughter named Jazmin Hassani. She's a Naval Aviation officer." Pride was evident in the android's tone.

Jazmin flashed a questioning look at Gadget and mouthed, "Now what?"

Gadget said, "Mercedes, it's time for school. We're going to expose you to everything we know about who you are and what you know. We want you to learn and assimilate everything available."

The android brain said, "I will strive to be better than my original."

Jazmin cringed at the android's response. Gadget must have picked up on her reaction and put a calming hand on her arm. The pace of program transfer between the workstation and the android brain shot up. Load messages swirled across the screen, and the low hum of data transfer grew increasingly louder. Gadget pulled Jazmin away from the workstation. "This part goes on for a while. Let's grab some dinner, and we can check back later."

Gadget gave her a push, and Jazmin moved in a fog toward the cafeteria. She steeled herself for dealing with a more lifelike version of her android mother.

Chapter 39

Wisconsin Militia Base
Bayfield, Wisconsin
9 June

It took a couple of days to complete the android version of Mercedes from the countless 3-D printed parts. Next, they connected the brain to the android's nervous system. Jazmin was amazed at Gadget's breadth and depth of knowledge. She was also a patient teacher, answering Jazmin's countless questions during the process. She learned more about her bionic half in those few days than she had in the five plus years since her release from rehab. They'd even discussed the physical transformation process for Jazmin for the upcoming mission. While Gadget could recover Jazmin's original face, she was a wanted terrorist who could be picked up by facial recognition, so there were tactical advantages for Jazmin keeping her new looks after the changes were complete.

She'd known people in rehab who had undergone significant facial changes after cosmetic repair. Due to her significant burns, the doctors hadn't been sure how successful they'd be at recovering her original face, so she had gone through psychological counseling to prepare her for seeing someone different in the mirror. Fortunately, the plastic surgeons were able to return her appearance to close to what she'd looked like previously.

Jazmin knew she'd need time to get used to a new face. She also knew that once she was cleared of the falsified charges, she could get her original face back. Jazmin and android Mercedes ate lunch in the cafeteria. While sharing family stories, Jazmin watched for quirks that would make people wonder if this version of Mercedes was an android. The AI learning algorithms were fantastic. By the end of the day, Jazmin felt like she was spending time with her mom and had to remind herself that this Mercedes wasn't human. On the third day, Jazmin and Gadget accompanied android Mercedes around the rest of the base. The android assumed its new persona, Navy Lieutenant Catarina Silvado, and was introduced as a new militia member. Only the senior staff knew Catarina was an android. Jazmin's new identity for the mission was Navy Commander Zina Kaddour.

Chapter 40

Wisconsin Militia Base
Bayfield, Wisconsin
10 June

Jazmin and android Mercedes entered the ops center in uniform as Defense Intelligence Agency investigators Commander Kaddour and Lieutenant Silvado. Right before the meeting, Jazmin checked herself in the mirror. Her uniform was fine, but she was still getting used to seeing a different face. She now had the broader facial features and darker skin tone of her Algerian father instead of the previous lighter tone and narrower features inherited from her Mexican mother. She'd also adjusted her gait to allow for her newly increased height. She'd done this many times in the past for investigations where she needed to hide her identity, but this time Jazmin felt like she'd lost a piece of herself. She wondered who she'd eventually become.

The general and the rest of the senior staff were already there. Suresh studied Jazmin's and the android's uniforms, focusing on their ribbons and insignia. She gave Jazmin a penetrating look. "The two of you look the part, but that will only get you so far. Ops never go as smoothly as we'd like, so let's review all the things that could go wrong and make sure we've planned for them."

Jazmin made quick eye contact with Harry, Gadget, and Derez

to get a read on their level of concern but got nothing back, negative or positive.

Suresh said, "First of all, why doesn't facial recognition on the android match Mercedes Montoya? Surely, all prisoners' faces are in the system."

Gadget opened the holographic screen at the front of the room and projected photos of the real Mercedes Montoya and the android version. Next to each was an image of how facial recognition software would read both faces. "We created minor differences in the facial structure between our android version and the real Mercedes Montoya. The changes are subtle so the prison staff won't be able to tell them apart, though the facial recognition software will pick up the variation and correctly identify them as two different people. The android can make minute adjustments in her facial structure to align with either persona as needed when dealing with facial recognition. Few of the guards will see the real Mercedes Montoya and the android at the same time."

Suresh didn't look entirely convinced, but she moved on to another question. "What about the fake identities of Commander Kaddour and Lieutenant Silvado. Will they stand up to scrutiny?"

Harry took control of the holographic screen and projected extensive biographies along with official and casual photos of Kaddour and Silvado. "I took my time building these aliases as both are military officers with Top Secret security clearances. Using a fleet of AI bots, I created complete histories and populated countless systems. There's now a vast electronic footprint that will hold up to security clearance investigator standards. Anyone who digs into their backgrounds, even government spooks, will find what they expect. Because Jazmin can dramatically change her appearance, including her height, I made sure her cover is airtight for multiple missions."

"Their freedom and possibly their lives depend on your thoroughness." Suresh turned her gaze to Derez. "Assuming they get past the front gate, how are we suppressing prison surveillance once they're inside?"

Derez held up a small device the size of a laser pointer. "They'll each carry a security scrambler that will jam any video or audio recording equipment within a fifty-foot radius."

"Will the prison security systems detect the scramblers?"

"Yes, General, but not right away." Derez looked at Jazmin. "Don't use these until it matters. You'll probably have only a few minutes before someone realizes there's a problem."

Jazmin nodded. "Understood."

Suresh made eye contact with everyone in the room. "Team, if things go sideways, can we extract Jazmin and her mother from a federal penitentiary?"

Derez said, "We can do it, but there'll be collateral damage."

Suresh pursed her lips. "Can we successfully execute this mission given the risks?"

There was silence for an uncomfortably long time. As the seconds ticked by, Jazmin wondered how the others would answer.

Harry said, "I believe we can. We'll have as many safeguards in place as we can to handle contingencies."

Derez said, "I agree." Gadget just nodded.

Suresh stood. "You're go for mission but make damn sure you avoid an extraction with firepower after a botched op."

Jazmin was relieved. She hoped firepower wouldn't be needed to extract her mother, though she had no doubt she'd do whatever was necessary, no matter the consequences. If Jiang could have her mom thrown in prison, she could also hand her over to Chinese Military Intelligence. Her mom was an expert on too many classified weapon systems. Under enhanced interrogation, the technical knowledge in her mother's head would be extracted. This would be a national disaster and would put the US military at tremendous risk.

Chapter 41

Hazelton Federal Correctional Institute
West Virginia
11 June

Jazmin flew the quadcopter from Wisconsin to West Virginia via drone routes. The hum of the engine generator, whir of the four props, and chirps from the navigation system were the only sounds on the long trip. The android, a perfect copy of her mother and lifelike in every detail, was strapped into the seat next to her. Sentencing this sentient being to a prison cell felt awful, something Jazmin couldn't do to another human being. She kept her guilt in check by not allowing herself to think of it as human, though Catarina Silvado was human in every way that mattered.

The quadcopter's transponder identified the aircraft as a package carrier and, as their flight progressed, they were handed off between automated air traffic controllers. Like a child on her first plane ride, Silvado alternated between looking outside and studying the copter's flight controls. As an experiment, Jazmin let the android take control of the aircraft and marveled at how Silvado smoothly flew the copter like an experienced pilot, precise but differently from autopilot.

As they approached the prison, a guard in the watch tower tracked their final descent and landing through the scope of her high-power sniper rifle. The red laser dot lit up the copter's windshield, centered on the pilot. The guard remained locked on her until engine shutdown was complete and they had exited the aircraft. Once Jazmin and Silvado were away from the copter, the guard put down her rifle and used her binoculars to study the copter's weapon pod.

Jazmin said, "It's go time. Lieutenant Silvado, are you ready?"

"Yes, Commander Kaddour."

They approached the security station where a guard met them outside the gate. A second guard hung back with a shotgun. Jazmin said, "We're from the Defense Intelligence Agency, here to question one of the prisoners. It's already been cleared with the warden." Harry had created the fake clearance in the prison security system, and they'd be gone before anyone figured it out.

The woman pointed to two red glowing circles on the concrete. "Stand with your hands away from your body while I run a weapons scan." Jazmin and Silvado complied, and a moment later the circles turned green. "I need a biochip scan to confirm your identification." Jazmin waved her arm over the reader mounted on a titanium post, followed by Silvado. The guard studied a holographic screen, though Jazmin couldn't see the information. She hoped the biochip spoofers and simulated bio signs for the android held up. The guard exchanged a look with her partner, its meaning undecipherable to Jazmin. After a few tense moments, the woman pointed to a concrete bench. "Wait there until your escort arrives."

A cell block guard armed with only a stun stick on her belt approached them. She had a deeply lined face, mean eyes, and stared at them with disdain. "Follow me." As they entered the first cell block, the walls felt like they were closing in. Jazmin's claustrophobia escalated as the security door slammed shut behind them. The clang of deadbolts jamming home into the metal and concrete doorframe further amplified her dread. Cells lined the hallway on both sides, and angry eyes peered out from every cage. Cameras tracked their movements, increasing her sense that everything was constricting around her. Jazmin felt a tightness in her chest and it became harder for her to breathe. Her mother had been here a lot longer, and Jazmin worried about Mercedes' mental state.

They walked past two more cell blocks, each with their own set of security doors. Finally, they stopped outside a solid steel door. "Wait here." The guard opened the door with a wave of her arm past the biochip scanner. She checked the room and pressed a sequence of buttons on a control panel. "You can come in now." Jazmin and Silvado entered the room, which contained a metal table and chairs bolted to the concrete floor. Steel rings for chaining a prisoner in place stuck up from one side of the table.

"I'll be right back with prisoner 73652. Y'all make yourselves comfortable." She laughed, flashed a cold smile, then left the room.

"Do you detect surveillance?" asked Jazmin.

Silvado nodded.

A minute later the guard returned with Mercedes, dressed in an orange prison jump suit and restrained with handcuffs. The guard leered at Jazmin with her toothy yellow grin. "Would you like me to shackle her to the table, or stay in the room to keep her in line?"

It took all of Jazmin's self-control to ignore the woman's taunts. She fought to keep her voice and facial expression neutral. "Remove her handcuffs and leave so we can question her in private."

The guard's wrinkled face drooped in disappointment. "I'll be right outside. Y'all just knock on the door when you're done, and I'll toss that traitor back in her cage." She left the room and the door's deadbolt locks slammed home. Jazmin reached into her jacket pocket and turned on the electronic scrambler.

She tried to read her mother's expression. The older woman looked guarded, though not defeated. Good, the place hadn't broken her yet. Silvado moved next to Jazmin.

Mercedes stared at Silvado, then her eyes went wide. "Why do you look like me? What kind of sick game is this?" She backed away against a wall.

The frightened look on her mom's face chilled Jazmin. "I'm here to take you out of here but you have to trust me."

Mercedes glared at her. "You're a stranger. Why would I trust you? She pointed at Silvado. "Get her away from me."

Jazmin motioned with her head for Silvado to back away, and the android moved to the opposite side of the room, took off its hat, and began to undress. Jazmin waited a moment for Mercedes' expression to soften. "I'm your daughter, Jazmin."

"No, you're not."

"I've been surgically modified but I'm still the person you raised. Ask me something only Jazmin would know."

Mercedes took a couple steps sideways and collapsed onto one of the immobile steel chairs. She let out a long, slow breath. "I've got all the time in the world, so I'll play your little game. What did your brother tell you was in your favorite dish as a child?"

Jazmin thought instantly of her Mother's chicken mole sauce and the luscious dark chocolate flavor. "Enrique said mole was made from dark brown moles cut from old women's faces."

Mercedes looked surprised at the answer, though she didn't acknowledge that it was correct. "Where did I take Jazmin as a child where she shrieked in terror while her tormentors howled with laughter?"

"You took me to EAA AirVenture every summer in Oshkosh, Wisconsin, where you were the technical rep for Defense Air Systems. When I was nine, one of the pavilions had two Air Force pilots who strapped me into a fighter jet cockpit and explained how the ejection seat worked. They told me to pull the handle to test it. When I did, a CO2 canister shot off and scared the hell out of me. The two pilots laughed their heads off."

Again, Mercedes didn't react, though she didn't deny the story. "What was your first airplane ride?"

Jazmin smiled at the happy memory. "It wasn't an airplane. It was an antique Bell 47 helicopter over the EAA grounds. We went up together, and I squeezed between you and the pilot in the tiny glass bubble. That was when I knew I'd fly one day." Jazmin pulled herself back to the present. "How am I doing? Three for three?"

Silvado pointed at the ceiling array of cameras and microphones. "They just went into diagnostic mode."

"Mamá, we're out of time. If you want to walk out of here with me then swap clothes with Lieutenant Silvado. She's an android copy of you. I've got a biochip spoofer." As soon as Mercedes saw Silvado's scarred torso, she tore off her prison jumpsuit.

"Dios mío! You weren't making this up." She put on Silvado's clothes and Jazmin made sure her mother had the uniform on correctly. Jazmin attached the biochip spoofer to Mercedes' arm. The adhesive strip held it firmly to her skin under the uniform sleeve. The android was now dressed in Mercedes' orange prison jumpsuit and had a downcast expression on its face.

"Say nothing and follow my lead." Jazmin knocked on the door. "We're done questioning the prisoner." She waited but nothing happened. After a minute she knocked on the door again, harder this time. A moment later, two guards the size of football linemen entered the room, leaving the door open behind them. She took one look at their expressions and knew they weren't going to walk out of there without a fight. Jazmin stared back at them like a flag officer whose orders were never questioned. "We're done with the prisoner. Take us back to the main gate."

The guard closest to Jazmin laughed. "You're not going anywhere."

Her anger flared and she kicked the man just below his knee. When he stumbled forward, she did a double hand slap to his ears. He groaned in pain and before he could recover, she grabbed his neck and upper arm, twisted him a quarter turn and tripped him onto the cement floor. She stomped on his lower leg, breaking his tibia. The android picked up the other guard and flung him across the room. He hit the wall and crumpled to the hard floor. Both men lay on the concrete and moaned. Ignoring Suresh's orders, Jazmin executed Harry's prison break program on her tablet. "Mamá, stay close to me no matter what happens." Her mom looked terrified at the sudden violence. All she could manage was to stare back blankly and nod.

Jazmin led the way back down the cell-lined hallway toward the entrance, with Mercedes right behind her and the android at the rear. The rhythmic slap of running boots heading their way was interrupted by the creak of multiple cell doors opening and a deafening alarm. Prisoners flooded the hallways, bringing the guards to a halt in the confusion. One inmate tried to block Jazmin's way, so she moved in close, grabbed the woman's arm, twisted her hip behind the prisoner, and pushed up on the assailant's chin. The orange clad figure went down hard on the concrete. Jazmin kept moving. The other prisoners who witnessed the assault backed away. She pressed ahead and waved her arm at the biochip reader on the security door. It opened to the next cell block. All the cell doors swung open. Prisoners flooded out, though more slowly than in the previous cell block. None tried to stop the trio.

They passed through the next security door, and all the cell doors popped open. This time the prisoners peered out and let the trio pass. At the end of the hallway a phalanx of six security guards wearing body armor blocked the exit. Each was armed with a riot shield and a stun stick, a side handle baton that delivered an incapacitating electric shock. This wouldn't stop the android, but one touch would drop Jazmin and Mercedes to the ground. Silvado came up alongside Jazmin and slid back the covers of its fingers on both hands, exposing high power wireless tasers. Jazmin said, "Hit them with a non-lethal jolt."

Silvado raised both fists and bursts of taser fire dropped three guards to the floor, where they lay unconscious. Another taser blast knocked one more guard to the ground, where she writhed in pain between electricity induced muscle spasms. The two toughest guards were still on their feet, though both had lost their confident sneers and backed away.

In a fluid motion Jazmin swept up a stun stick dropped by one of the downed guards. One of the remaining guards pounced, but Jazmin calf kicked him and brought the man to the ground. She touched the stun stick to his exposed throat, the only part of him not covered by body armor, helmet, or a face shield. His whole body spasmed in pain before he passed out. Silvado took down the last guard with a barrage of lightning-fast arm and leg blows.

Jazmin, Mercedes, and Silvado rushed past the injured guards and exited the security door into a hallway. The building's exterior door was now in sight. Jazmin said, "Run." The three of them sprinted for the outer door and then into the sunshine. Jazmin matched Mercedes' pace while the android bolted ahead to the copter and retrieved a sniper rifle. It took up a defensive position behind the aircraft and targeted the sniper in the guard tower. Jazmin hoped the android wouldn't accidentally kill anyone. It fired shots at the tower, cracking the glass, but none broke through. The shots were close enough to keep the sniper off balance but none hit the guard.

Mercedes got in the left side door and strapped in. Jazmin jumped in the pilot's seat, fired up the engine generator, and spun up the props. Just as the quadcopter lifted off, it rocked sideways from the weight of the android jumping onto the weapons pod below the main cabin. Jazmin opened the .50 caliber gun ports, sighted the prison tower, and fired off controlled three-round bursts. The large glass windows shattered, raining broken glass onto the prison yard below. Sparks shot out from the tower communication panel and black smoke curled upward. Once they were away from the prison and out of range of the sniper, Jazmin closed the gun ports to reduce drag and checked the camera feed under the aircraft. The android pumped its fist in triumph, then crawled inside the weapons pod through an access panel and disappeared from sight.

Jazmin increased power for maximum climb rate, and the quadcopter disappeared into a cloud bank. She lined up with a northerly drone route, then changed the transponder to show they were an international delivery drone with a flight plan to Canadian airspace. She set the autopilot and gave herself a moment to breathe and process what happened. It was hard to relax with adrenaline still coursing through her body. After ten minutes flying through the mass of gray clouds, they popped out on top and into the sunshine.

Mercedes spoke for the first time since they escaped. "Thank you for rescuing me from that hell hole and this crazy nightmare."

Jazmin looked at her mother and wondered what was going through her mind. "You're welcome, though the insanity isn't over."

Mercedes nodded wearily and closed her eyes. Tears rolled down her face. "Why is this happening?"

Jazmin reached over and wiped away her mother's tears with the back of her hand. She was flooded with memories of when she was a child and her mom had wiped away her tears. It was funny, she thought, how when we got old enough we switched roles with our parents.

"I kicked over a hornet's nest. I'm sorry."

Mercedes shook her head and sighed. "When you were a kid I knew you'd be a force to reckon with when you grew up. It's both inspiring and frightening to watch you now." Mercedes cocked her head at Jazmin. "Did you program my evil twin?"

Jazmin laughed at her mom's sense of humor. "She's just like you but with a little more attitude."

"No, *mi'ja*, a lot more attitude."

"I need to check in and let the team know I got you out."

Mercedes nodded, then closed her eyes. She looked spent. Jazmin wondered if her mother would suffer mental trauma from all that happened. Of all the things she bonded over with her mother, this wasn't one she wanted to add to the list. Jazmin pulled out her tablet and sent an encrypted message to Harry. *Package retrieved. Alternate exfil required. Cargo returning.*

A five-word response came back. *Her majesty is NOT AMUSED!*

Chapter 42

Wisconsin Militia Base
Bayfield, Wisconsin
11 June

Jazmin and Harry stood at attention in General Suresh's office. Suresh sat behind her desk, her fingers steepled. Her cool gaze chilled Jazmin. She'd expected a two-star ass chewing, but so far, Suresh hadn't said a word. What leaders didn't say was often as powerful as what they did, and general officers understood power.

Suresh leaned back in her chair. "This was supposed to be a stealth mission. Instead, your prison break, Commander, was the featured story on CNN, and your method was in violation of my direct orders. Ms. Montoya was freed, but every other mission objective failed. Plus the collateral damage was totally unacceptable. The guards you hospitalized did not falsely imprison your mother. They were simply doing their jobs. Missions go sideways, but how we react is a choice, and there were other options. The only thing you got right was no fatalities."

Jazmin wanted to respond, though she knew interrupting a general's monologue never ended well.

Suresh focused her icy stare at Harry. "Dexter, I vetoed your idea of opening all the cells and helping Ms. Montoya escape in the chaos. Did you think I changed my mind?"

Harry didn't respond.

"Wiping the prison surveillance systems of all traces of Hassani's visit after the fact was a cleanup exercise that shouldn't have been needed." Suresh picked up a moon rock from her desk, then tossed it in the air repeatedly and caught it. "I've lost faith in two of my senior officers. It's a bad day when I question your honesty and integrity. I'll be reviewing hourly AI generated logs on your activities. All areas of the base are covered with surveillance, so I can check real time as well. If you ever make the mistake of lying to me again overtly or by omission, your continued membership in this militia will end no matter how valuable your skillset or how well you're liked. I don't tolerate officers I can't trust. Am I crystal clear?"

Jazmin and Harry both said, "Yes, General."

Suresh stood and slammed the moon rock on her desk like a judge pounding her gavel. "Out."

Jazmin and Harry both saluted, did crisp about faces and exited the office. Jazmin closed the door behind her, relieved to have escaped the general's wrath with a minor punishment for her transgressions. In truth, she could have tried to keep up her charade at the prison longer than she had, maybe even bluffed her and Mercedes' way to freedom, but she had been mad and wanted to lash out at and everyone everything.

Jazmin exchanged a conspiratorial check-in glance with Harry as soon as they'd escaped the general's office. He looked unfazed. He had been with the militia much longer than she had. His technical skillset and money-generating ability were probably irreplaceable. Her piloting and special ops skills would be more easily backfilled.

Derez walked down the hall toward them. He and Harry exchanged amused expressions and did a quick fist bump. Derez grinned at Jazmin. "I didn't think you had it in you. A fine display of badassery." He fist bumped her and continued down the hall. Harry turned the corner and pulled Jazmin into a conference room. "Jaz, just stay out of Suresh's sight for a while and don't ask for anything. This will blow over when the next crisis hits and she needs us."

"Will she ever trust me again?"

Harry shrugged. "Probably not, but that's not new for me. I'm glad you got your mom out of prison. Despite the general's display of regal displeasure, she's glad you did, too." Harry squeezed her shoulder and left the room.

Jazmin was happy to have a minute alone. She'd been

summoned to General Suresh's office as soon as she had landed. Jazmin didn't know where her mother was but assumed someone was taking care of her. She wanted to end this nightmare with Jiang and Trabago. At least now her mother was safe at the militia base, and her father and brother were under militia protection. It was time to find her mom and plan for the next round. Jazmin headed for the hangar, the last place she'd seen Mercedes.

Chapter 43

Wisconsin Militia Base
Bayfield, Wisconsin
18 June

In the week since the rescue mission to break Mercedes out of prison, things had settled into a new normal at the base. Jazmin stopped by the hangar to see how the rebuild was coming on the pair of F-22 fighter jets. Gadget rolled out from under an ACV, wiped her hands on a rag, and smiled. "Good morning, Commander. I'm still getting used to your new looks. Both your face and your height." Gadget gave her a quick head-to-toe look then continued. "Your mom and her twin are incredible."

Jazmin had never seen Gadget this effusive and wondered what made the normally low-key technical wizard so giddy. "What have they been up to?"

Gadget got to her feet and led Jazmin to the other side of the hangar where the two F-22 fighters were parked next to each other. The jets were in various stages of disassembly, surrounded by tool carts and air pallets piled with parts. "The android insists that she's Catarina Silvado, your mother's twin sister." Gadget smirked. "I guess that makes her your new aunt."

Jazmin closed in on Gadget. "It's not my mother's twin sister or my aunt. It's an android copy." No matter how human or how familiar

Catarina had become because she was made to impersonate her mother, it was an android and would never be human or a part of her family.

Gadget's glee diminished. "Understood, Commander."

Jazmin had sent her message but didn't want to ruin Gadget's enthusiasm. "You look pretty excited. What's happening with the fighters?"

Gadget's grin returned, and she looked admiringly at the scene around them. "They think they can get both fighters in flying condition. Instead of me and the kids rebuilding these jets, I have two world-class engineers in a race with each other as to which plane will be ready for a test flight first. I'm learning an amazing amount just listening to them. The only time I get lost is when they argue engineering minutia in Spanish."

Jazmin laughed. "When my mom gets excited and starts explaining things in excruciating detail she switches to Spanish and talks twice as fast." Jazmin and Gadget walked around the far jet where Mercedes and Catarina were peering into the cockpit and discussing the merits of heads-up displays vs. helmet displays. Both wore coveralls and had their hair tied back in ponytails. They looked identical, though Jazmin could tell them apart by their scents. Traces of body wash, dark roast coffee, and spices she sprinkled on her eggs at breakfast clung to her mom. The android smelled of jet engine exhaust and lubricants, as if she existed only in the hangar with no life outside.

Mercedes saw Jazmin, and her face lit up. "I haven't had this much fun in years. I'd forgotten how much I missed working on jet aircraft. It's even more fun having a partner who's as smart and excited as I am."

Catarina put her hands on her hips with an exaggerated look of shock on her face. "I'm the smarter sister."

Mercedes shook her head and pointed at her temple. "You just have more integrated circuits than I do." They both laughed.

Jazmin said, "I'm glad you two are having a good time." She got closer to her mother. "Are you worried about Dad?"

Mercedes' playful expression grew serious. "I miss him. I didn't get a chance to say goodbye." She looked around the hangar, then turned her gaze back to Jazmin. "This feels like a weird work vacation. I'm enjoying the technical challenge, but this isn't where I belong. I miss Saeed. I miss my home. I like being an executive, and

I work with a great team. Hopefully, they're doing all right without me." She stared at Catarina. "While it's fascinating working with my android doppelganger, it's bizarre too. Each day I stay away from my job it gets harder to go back."

"I'm sorry, Mom. I don't know when you can go home." Jazmin hugged her mom and took in her scent. After a moment she let go.

Her mom let out a long breath. "At least Harry helped me get word to Saeed."

This surprised Jazmin. As painful as it would have been for her father to not know what happened, it would be safer for there to be no communication trail between her parents. Jazmin didn't want to burden her mom with her worry. "That was nice of Harry."

Mercedes must have picked up on Jazmin's concern. She squeezed Jazmin's arm. "It was a one-line message. 'I have slipped the surly bonds of Earth.' Your dad will know I'm all right."

Jazmin knew the poem well. There was a beautiful, framed lithograph of it hanging in her parent's home. Her dad had purchased it as a gift for her mom when she'd earned her pilot's license. The poem also helped him to understand why his wife still wanted to fly despite the crash that scarred her for life.

Jazmin pulled away. "Glad you're enjoying the rebuild. I have some things I need to take care of."

Jazmin endured her mom's penetrating, mind-reading look, but said nothing. Harry had violated her trust again. She headed to the hangar exit.

***

She found Harry in the ops center. His smile wilted from the heat of her angry expression. "We agreed to have no outside contact while Mercedes is here."

Harry shrugged. "Despite the disguise, your prison break didn't fool Jiang and Trabago. They have to know you're the only one with the skills and motivation to pull off Mercedes' escape. I bounced the encrypted message around the world a dozen times before Saeed ever saw it, and it didn't show up on a device tied to him. I gave your parents a little peace of mind in the middle of all this insanity."

Jazmin sighed. She wanted to argue but couldn't refute his logic. Harry's facial expression rarely gave away what he was feeling. Today his face was lined with concern, never a good sign with him. "You look troubled. What are you tracking?"

"Nothing good." He pointed to the holographic screen at the front of the room. "Jiang and Trabago led a classified briefing for the President and Joint Chiefs, where they fabricated key evidence to make their point. Based on their testimony, Navarro signed an executive order authorizing black site testing of US directed-energy weapons in violation of the International Directed-Energy Weapons Test Ban Treaty. It took two presidents and eight years to convince the world's other superpowers to sign the treaty, and we're about to become the biggest violators."

Jazmin went cold considering what this meant. "Jiang is trying to start a directed-energy weapons arms race."

Harry brought up a new screen with the test results at a US offshore black site. The debris field covered most of the island. "These photos and video are the aftermath of a mock war staged with drones mimicking fighter aircraft, along with a combination of tanks and armored personnel carriers on the ground. Total destruction." He looked disgusted and shook his head. "I underestimated Jiang. She's trying to start a war."

Jazmin studied the screen and fought back images of the attack on her octocopter. "We need to figure out Jiang's motivation. Let's dig into her past." She brought up Jiang's official biography and highlighted key words including education, hometown, parents, professional experience outside of government, and international accomplishments. "Is this tied into the security clearance background check system?"

Harry looked offended. "Of course it is, along with half a dozen dark web search engines."

They spent the next hour chasing link after link through dozens of classified systems. Every screen in the ops center was filled with background material on Senator Jiang. Many of the positive press pieces and reports looked like they were planted by Chinese Military Intelligence. Many citations were from offbeat news sources and sounded as if they were written by non-native English speakers. Other sources were from recognized think tanks but were financially supported by foreign sources. They gathered more credible evidence from legitimate US government three letter agencies (NSA, CIA, DIA) and from journalists at reputable news sources. One by one Jazmin assembled the disparate pieces into the investigative report format she used in the Neurotech Defense Agency. It took another four hours to clear the screens as she assembled the final report. She pushed back from the workstation and stretched her shoulders. "We need to act on this intel, but Suresh needs to agree first."

Harry laughed. "We saw how well it went the last time we colored outside the lines."

Jazmin looked at the door. "I can't afford to do that again. I've got nowhere else to go."

"What if she shuts it down?"

"We act on it anyway and suffer her wrath."

Chapter 44

Wisconsin Militia Base
Bayfield, Wisconsin
19 June

Jazmin and Harry arrived in the ops center and waited for Suresh. The general entered, took her seat, and eyed them coolly. "What have you two figured out?"

Harry said, "No doubt you've seen the President's latest executive order, violating the directed-energy weapons test ban treaty."

"Yes, it's very troubling."

Jazmin said, "Jiang convinced the President to start a directed-energy weapons arms race."

Suresh raised her eyebrows. "That's quite an accusation, given Navarro doesn't trust anything Jiang tells her."

Harry said, "Their animosity runs deep, but assuming we're right, the question we had is why is Jiang doing this. That's what we want to show you."

Jazmin projected her investigative report on to the holographic screen. "We dug into Jiang's history and pieced some things together. The details are in the report, but a key finding is Jiang's parents were murdered by anti-Asian racists who were never brought to justice. Afterward, she returned to China where her parents' fate made her a target for Chinese Military Intelligence to turn her against the US.

Her political career started with dark money, and ever since there have been overlaps with Chinese Military Intelligence activities. Given Jiang's position on the Armed Services Committee, she's in a perfect position to aid China."

Suresh studied the evidence. "You've put together an interesting case, though there's lots of conjecture."

Jazmin said, "Agreed, so let's kick the hornet's nest."

Suresh shook her head. "We don't have enough proof to go on the offensive, and I won't sanction an op against Jiang."

Jazmin held up her hands. "I'm not asking you to. I have something more insidious in mind."

The corners of Suresh's mouth turned up in amusement. "Tell me more."

"I'll send a teaser version of this intel package to select news outlets and offer Shelbey Tanzini from CNN an exclusive to the complete report. It's enough to give her career a hell of a boost, even if it threatens to burn her prized Washington power connection."

Suresh drummed her fingers on the table. When her fingers stopped, she said, "I need to run your findings by my Washington network to see what they know and find out if we can expect any support if this is released." The general stood. "Don't take any action yet. I'll let you know when it's time to start tossing bombs."

Jazmin was disappointed with the general's answer, but at least their plan wasn't shot down. She and Harry stood. She said, "We'll await your orders, General."

Chapter 45

Lake Superior
Near Bayfield, Wisconsin
26 June

Since Jazmin's meeting with Captain Diamond at the Bayfield base and her subsequent hivemind overload, there had been no further contact between them. After a thorough check of all militia base systems, Harry determined that the only possible way Jazmin could have been hit with a hivemind overload attack was from interacting with Diamond. Since the captain gained nothing from this attack, the consensus was that she was an unknowing virus carrier. Once the virus had transferred to Jazmin, there was no way to prove that theory. As a result, only safe way they could meet again was to have Diamond disconnect from the military hivemind network whenever she met a militia member. Harry picked up intel through his clandestine network that Diamond had made the rounds in both political and military circles in Washington seeking support to go after the people who had attacked the Truax pilots. Her bare-knuckle tactics had ruffled more than a few politicos' feathers. She also jammed burrs under flag officers' stars. Unfortunately, she didn't find any backers for a hunting party.

With or without a sponsor, Diamond had to be planning something, and Jazmin wanted in. Now that her mom was safe, she was tired of hiding underground in the Bayfield base. Having flown hundreds of simulated combat missions in multiple aircraft types, she was ready for action. She'd even spent countless simulation hours flying quadcopters at ground level through the woods surrounding the base while aggressor aircraft pursued her.

Suresh greenlighted a meeting between Jazmin and Diamond to hear the captain's plans. If Jazmin felt they were worth pursuing, then she was approved to set up a meeting between Diamond and the rest of the senior staff. At all times Diamond must be isolated from the military network or be verified to be virus free.

Jazmin contacted Diamond with an encrypted message, *1600 Zulu, 26 June, Latitude: 47.723087, Longitude: -86.940720, -100 AGL. Disconnect from the military hivemind network prior to meeting. Our last encounter resulted in a hivemind overload attack.* She received a terse response from Diamond. *Confirmed.*

***

Jazmin leveled her Amphibious Combat Vehicle at one hundred feet below the surface, deep enough to avoid the keels of the largest Lake Superior vessels. The water was shallow enough that she could use regular scuba equipment rather than technical diving gear. She was thirty minutes early, so she dove deeper and ran a search pattern for drones. She also deployed a passive sonar array to pick up any watercraft in the area. All was quiet except for the sonar signature of another ACV. Coming up from below, Jazmin pulled her vehicle up nose to nose with the other ACV and flashed her lights in morse code, *seahorse.* The vehicle opposite her responded in morse code, *formed under extreme pressure.*

Setting the amphibious vehicle's controls to hold station with the other ACV, Jazmin then headed to the rear to put on her scuba gear. She needed a wetsuit only for the top half of her body. Since her head was covered with synthetic skin and her legs were bionic, they were minimally affected by cold water. She also turned down her pain receptors. She slipped on swim fins, strapped on an air tank, and put on her mask. Next she squeezed into the airlock, sealed the door, and bit down on her regulator. She cycled the outer door, and freezing cold water flooded the chamber. She slid out the bottom, then sealed the hatch, not wanting any fish or other creatures waiting for her when she returned.

Jazmin kicked her way the short distance to the airlock on the other ACV, opened the hatch, and pushed her way inside. As soon as the water drained out and the air pressure was equalized, Diamond opened the inner door.

Jazmin pulled off her face mask and swim fins, then wriggled out of the tank harness in the tight quarters. Diamond handed her a towel. "Commander, you sure are creative with your meeting locations. Glad you warned me about your new looks. Your face and physique have really changed."

Jazmin dried her face and hair. "I hate interruptions and value my privacy."

Diamond pointed to a seat and the two Navy officers sat across from each other.

Jazmin said, "When you're done scaring politicians and lighting fuses under flag officers, I want in on whatever op you're planning. You need people you can trust, and I have personal reasons to join this fight."

Diamond studied Jazmin with a cool expression. "What makes you think I trust you?"

"If you didn't, you wouldn't be here."

Diamond shrugged. "Maybe, but you're still a liability."

Jazmin wasn't sure if Diamond was just being thorough in vetting her or if the captain had serious doubts about her value. Time to press her. "Captain, I'm an asset, otherwise you wouldn't be wasting your time with me. You know my history and what I've been through recently. You're too careful to leave anything to chance. Certainly not something as important as your core team on a black ops mission. You want to settle accounts, and no one in the administration or any flag officer wants to get near this."

Diamond's laser-focused stare flickered.

This was her tell. Jazmin had hit a nerve, and she let the silence hang between them.

"You're right on all counts. I'm planning two missions, and I need an executive officer. Someone willing to put everything on the line. I won't ask the few officers I trust enough for these ops. I won't delude myself by wrapping my reasons in the flag. This is personal. What I'm planning and the people I'm going after likely make this a one-way mission."

Jazmin leaned forward. "I'd be honored to be your XO if you want me."

Diamond nodded. "I do. Get your affairs in order. You might

not be coming home afterward."

Jazmin suppressed a smile. "How soon do we launch?"

Diamond cocked her head and looked amused. "You don't even know the mission yet."

"Captain, I've studied your career and watched you in action. You know how to fight, and you pick the right battles. That's all I need to know."

"I'm still putting the team together. We're short some critical skills."

Jazmin noted the change to *we*. "I have some highly skilled colleagues who are experienced operators. They know how to get things done and disappear afterward."

Diamond seemed to be mulling a decision, so Jazmin waited. After a minute the captain pulled a microdot from a pocket in her flight suit. "Give me your tablet." Jazmin pulled her tablet from a waterproof pocket and handed it to Diamond, who placed the dot on the tablet's screen. A few seconds later the dot dissolved after transferring five terabytes of information.

"I assume you just gave me the mission brief."

Diamond touched the tablet. "That's everything I have. I violated regulations and broke laws when I collected Top Secret information. Handing it to you just adds to the charges against me."

"Welcome to the dark side. No doubt there's a place in hell for both of us."

Diamond turned away and looked out the front window of the ACV at the fish lit up by the craft's exterior lights. "Earlier in my career I dreamed of becoming an admiral. Now I know the cost of that dream, even as it slips away."

"You can still walk away."

Diamond shook her head. "I could, but then I couldn't look at myself in the mirror." She checked the time. "I need to get back to Washington. I can be back in a week, and we can meet again."

"We have a submarine pen at the militia base. It's time for you to meet my colleagues." Jazmin collected her scuba gear and headed to the airlock. It was time for battle, and she was finally ready.

Chapter 46
Ling Chen Jiang

Washington, DC
2 July

Ling Chen awoke in the bedroom of her condo to two cell phones vying for attention with dueling ringtones. She checked the time, 0600. Never a morning person, she had standing orders to hold all routine matters until nine and urgent matters until seven. She reached for the first phone, the number known to few people. She declined the call. Her chief of staff would have to leave a message, adding to the three already waiting, the first at 0400. Groggy and irritated from a late night of drinking, she answered the second phone, a call from Danica. "What's the emergency?"

"Senator, the condo and your home are both surrounded by news vans and a mob of reporters. They're all looking for answers about classified documents reportedly leaked by Chinese Military Intelligence."

Ling Chen snapped out of her early morning stupor. "Is there anything credible?"

"Yes. We have a serious problem. I bribed one of the reporters for a copy of what they had, and it's shockingly accurate. I just sent it to you in an encrypted text."

Ling Chen didn't dare open her curtains and expose herself to the news jackals. She activated the security monitor on her wall, revealing a frenzy outside. "Get here as fast as you can. Use the underground entrance. I have to focus on damage control and need your help."

"On my way." Danica ended the call.

Ling Chen called her chief of staff and spoke as soon as the woman answered. "I'm aware of the news frenzy. Cancel all my appointments today and only reschedule critical meetings. Tell people I'm unreachable and nothing more. I need to go." She ended the call before the woman on the other end could respond.

As she dressed, Ling Chen considered likely candidates for this brazen attack. Her list of enemies was long, though few would be confident enough for a direct assault. Once she had read through the allegations, she'd have a better idea of possible sources. Danica's comment about it being "shockingly accurate" was worrisome. While Ling Chen didn't share everything with her personal security staff, Danica was the best informed, having proven her loyalty on countless occasions.

Ling Chen walked down to the kitchen where she measured loose imported green tea into a strainer then submerged it in a ceramic teapot filled with hot water. She placed a warm croissant delivered from a local French patisserie on a gold-rimmed plate, waited for the tea to steep, and then poured it into an antique china cup. She placed both on a lacquer tray and carried her breakfast upstairs. Sipping tea and taking small bites of warm croissant, she reviewed the file Danica had sent. Whoever had put this together was extremely well informed; even more concerning, it was marked as a partial file. It was chilling to think about what else might be in the complete package. One conclusion was certain. It was time for war. This attack called for scorched earth tactics.

The most damaging evidence pertained to the attack on the President. Whoever had compiled the document got both the control point of the drone attack, western China, and the origin of the drone, an airstrip in Sinaloa, Mexico, correct. Even more frightening was the connection between her own movements in China and the secret black ops site, as well as the video evidence of her activity on black websites. Ling Chen cringed at the damning video she'd had no idea existed.

The final pieces of evidence were the attacks on the fighter pilots at Truax Field in Madison, Wisconsin. The attacking plane was traced back to a business jet taking off from Dane County airport, just the other side of the runway from the military base. The plane, though destroyed by Captain Diamond, was traced back through multiple shell companies to one of the black ops mercenary firms on Ling Chen's payroll. There were also details on how the deep fake video was created and falsely used to justify arresting Mercedes Montoya.

Ling Chen wiped butter and crumbs from her fingers onto a linen napkin and drank the last of her tea. She thought through the short list of people who would have access to this incriminating evidence. Trabago was the first person who came to mind, though he was as guilty as Ling Chen in their efforts. Though sometimes prickly, their relationship was cool and professional. She hadn't threatened him in any way, so he had no reason for such a move. The next most informed person was Danica, but if she were behind this, she wouldn't have sounded the alarm and provided the report. Danica also had far more to lose than to gain if Ling Chen went down. The rest of her security team was minimally involved in her illegal activities, and her senate staff was completely isolated from anything but her official senate duties.

Few of her enemies were a serious concern. Commander Hassani was the biggest unknown. The former Special Ops Naval officer just refused to die. Hassani had been caught in an early test of the PWL directed-energy weapon system and somehow survived. The woman's miraculous recovery, followed by several years as an NDA investigator made Ling Chen think the threat had been, if not neutralized, certainly sidelined. A more recent weapons test created a survivor who suffered a similar fate to Hassani, and that had been the first domino to fall. Hassani didn't have the intel skills to tie the threads together, unlike her ex-lover, Harry Dexter. He was a cockroach that should have been crushed by one of the previous presidents. Then he had teamed up with that damned Major General Suresh, causing trouble ever since with their Wisconsin Militia. Ling Chen had never gone to war with them, as they always used guerilla tactics and vanished afterward. Also, Suresh still had some powerful friends in Washington, despite her role as leader of a private militia. Suresh quietly did favors for the right people, who continued to help the retired two-star maintain her fiction of patriotism. The trio in Wisconsin seemed to be the most logical choice for the leaked information. No doubt the jail break of Mercedes Montoya was engineered by the Wisconsin Militia. Ling Chen didn't know how Hassani had pulled it off, but there was no doubt the daughter had rescued her mother and flown her to safety. Her father and brother were still valid targets.

Footsteps thumped on the stairs. Ling Chen was irritated to be disturbed, though her anger cooled as Danica came through the door at the top of the steps.

"It took longer to get here than I expected. The throng of reporters and bystanders has grown exponentially. All routes are blocked. Even the underground ones that come out into other buildings or out onto other streets. You can't leave without going through a wall of people."

Ling Chen sighed. One thing China had right was control of the press. In the US anyone with an internet connection could claim they were a reporter for any made-up news source. At the White House and Senate offices there was some control, but there were no restrictions at her condo and home. "I can stay here today but come nightfall, you must find a way to get me out of here unseen."

Danica considered the problem for a moment. "I might have to create a disturbance or some other distraction to clear the streets."

"I don't care how you do it, just make it happen. Ensure the safe house is ready. I won't be going home tonight."

Danica said, "I'm glad we set up a fallback location."

Ling Chen's phone rang. The caller ID showed her chief of staff. She gripped the phone in annoyance as if trying to crush the life out of it. On the fourth ring she punched the answer icon. "This had better be an emergency."

"Serena Baines wants you in her office at ten this morning. I can't feign ignorance of your whereabouts with the President's chief of staff. You know what a pit bull that woman is. She just issues commands and demands compliance."

Ling Chen swore silently. "I won't be there. When Baines calls, tell her you left multiple messages for me, but we never spoke. Don't call me again." She disconnected the line.

Danica gave Ling Chen a concerned look. "If the President's chief of staff wants to see you, that means the report made it to the Oval Office. Is defying Baines your best move?"

Ling Chen glared at Danica. Though she was annoyed, it was a legitimate question. "There are no good options. If I don't show up, I risk the wrath of that venomous bitch. If I arrive unprepared, she'll sink her fangs into me."

Danica's face remained neutral, unruffled at her boss's consternation. "Can you delay the meeting and buy yourself some time?"

She thought a moment. "I can't delay the meeting but perhaps you can."

Danica smiled conspiratorially. "If a bomb detonates here with another outside your home, killing several people, you can go into hiding."

Ling Chen considered her dwindling options, then decided. "Use military grade explosives and have the Wisconsin Militia claim responsibility."

Chapter 47

Washington, DC
2 July

Ling Chen waited in the basement of her condo with her go bag containing clothes, cash, a 9mm handgun with spare magazines, a Chinese passport under a different name, and a burner tablet with access to all of her cloud files containing her extensive blackmail evidence. She hoped she wouldn't need anything in her go bag, but things were going sideways, and she wanted to be prepared. She sat quietly in the most protected corner of the dimly lit basement. Danica would get her at the appropriate time for an undetected exit at the height of the mayhem. Ling Chen hated the waiting and her dependency on Danica for her escape. Her relationship with the President was prickly at best and subzero at worst. She couldn't hide for long before the President summoned her, to be escorted by a protective detail so she couldn't protest or delay due to personal safety concerns.

Years of careful planning and tireless work were unraveling. The intel dossier on her was too accurate for Ling Chen to completely distance herself from it. Even her favorite reporter, Shelbey Tanzini, might turn on her.

Lost in her dark musings, Ling Chen was jolted back to the present when an explosion rocked the building. Heart pounding in her chest, she listened as a wave of falling debris rained down on the brick exterior. She wondered how much damage would need to be repaired on the outside of her condo. She heard shouts and moans in the distance. Using her tablet to tap into the condo's exterior surveillance system, she surveyed the damage. She'd told Danica to use a large bomb, something a terrorist would use. In this case, the terrorist was ex-military special ops, and the extensive building damage would support that narrative.

Danica appeared from one of the underground tunnels. Ling Chen grabbed her go bag and threw one strap over her shoulder, relieved to see the one person who could get her to safety. Danica's face was etched with concern, though she moved with assurance. "Time to go. It's chaos outside and everyone is too frantic to notice anything." Danica led the way through the underground tunnel which exited on a quiet street behind the condo. Glass from blown out windows, stray nails, and shrapnel from the bomb littered the street. Bleeding, dazed people wandered past, but none seemed to recognize or even acknowledge Ling Chen and Danica. Moving quickly, Danica led a path away from the security cameras to a car parked a few streets away. Once they were inside the car, Danica said, "Safe house. Stealth mode."

The car responded, "Surveillance detection route engaged. Transponder spoofing enabled." The car pulled away and proceeded on a circuitous route. A direct route would take twenty minutes; theirs took forty-five.

Danica scanned the area. "It doesn't look like we were followed." The safe house was set back from the road on a wooded lot, the mature trees making it difficult for anyone to see what might be going on inside. Cameras strategically placed around the property provided good visibility from inside the house. The car pulled into the garage and the door closed behind them. Danica checked video surveillance on her tablet for inside and outside the house. She activated a pack of six robot guard dogs to patrol the property. The ferocious four-legged mechanical beasts would deter any attackers on foot and provide mobile video to assess threats. "Everything is clear, and the robotic sentries have been activated. Let's go inside, Senator." Danica led the way into the kitchen and halted. "Stay here." She pulled her sidearm with .45 caliber hollow point ammunition and left the kitchen. Ling Chen wished more of her security team was with them. The safe house wasn't nearly as large as either her condo or home, though it was clean and well-protected and the refrigerator and cupboards were stocked. She placed her go bag in the corner. Even inside the safe house with Danica to protect her, Ling Chen wanted her go bag close.

When she was stressed, Ling Chen prepared food. Simple acts were comforting when chaos was swirling around her. They also gave her a sense of control. To calm her nerves, she pulled ingredients from the refrigerator and laid them on the counter. She made two large salads and added cold chicken. Then she heated rolls in the oven and made a pot of oolong tea. She placed everything on the table. She called out, "Danica, please join me in the kitchen."

A moment later Danica appeared in the doorway. Ling Chen motioned toward the table. "It's been a long day. I made us something to eat." The two sat across from each other. "I appreciate all you've done for me. It won't get any easier from here."

Danica shrugged. "I do what's necessary."

Ling Chen shook her head. "You do far more than the others, and I trust you more because of it. Please, eat something." Ling Chen picked up her fork and speared a piece of the chicken perched on top of the salad greens and put it in her mouth. Danica looked exhausted. Ling Chen needed her one-woman security team in decent shape. She poured a mug of tea and placed it in front of Danica, who took sips in between large forkfuls of salad. The woman's hunger overtook her usual stoicism.

Danica said, "Thank you for the food." She tore a warm, buttery roll in half and devoured it, then reached for another. After she had finished three rolls, the salad, and every morsel of chicken, Danica wiped her hands on a napkin. She refilled her mug of tea from the pot and cradled the warm mug in her hands. She seemed more relaxed now, less manic than before. She peered at Ling Chen and asked, "How are you going to handle your disappearance?"

Before Ling Chen could answer, the perimeter alarm and all six robot dog security alarms went off with warbling multi-tone shrieks.

Danica pulled her sidearm from its holster and checked security video on her tablet. The normally cool as ice operator turned pale and halted in place.

Already exhausted and rattled by the long day's events, Ling Chen was pushed over the edge by the jarring alarms. She unconsciously reverted to her Chinese Military Intelligence training, leaping up from the table, and grabbing the 9mm handgun from her go bag.

Ling Chen scanned the surveillance video on her tablet. Two grim-faced men wearing suits and earpieces approached the front door. Six men in black fatigues and carrying assault rifles were right behind them. Just before the men reached the front door, Danica killed the alarms, and the room was silent.

The lead man banged his large fist on the door and in a loud voice said, "Senator Jiang, the President wants to see you in her office. We're here to escort you."

Ling Chen closed her eyes, wishing this nightmare would end and she could return to her life. A moment later she handed her gun to Danica and walked to the front door, feeling like she was heading to her execution.

Chapter 48
Jazmin Hassani

Wisconsin Militia Base
Bayfield, Wisconsin
2 July

From the shadows, Jazmin watched the Amphibious Combat Vehicle drive slowly up the ramp and into the submarine pen. Per militia protocol for unvetted visitors, the welcoming party was hidden and well-armed. Derez targeted the ACV with a grenade launcher, while Gadget aimed her submachine gun from another vantage point. As soon as Captain Diamond exited the vehicle, Harry said, "Step away from the ACV and put your hands behind your head." Diamond complied and Harry approached with his 9mm handgun trained on her. "Wait here while I inspect your vehicle."

Gadget shifted her aim to Diamond while Harry searched for hidden passengers and bombs. He was also responsible for verifying Diamond wasn't connected to the military hivemind network. His inspection and verification complete, he exited the ACV and gave a slight nod to the hidden militia members, though he kept his gun out.

Jazmin approached Diamond and patted her down for weapons. "I need to scan your biochip and retina to confirm your identity."

When the checks were completed she said, "Welcome to the Wisconsin Militia Headquarters."

Diamond brought her hands back to her sides. "You have an interesting idea of how to welcome people."

Jazmin said, "We need to be careful who we invite inside."

Harry holstered his sidearm, then Derez and Gadget came out from hiding with their weapons pointed down. Diamond looked at each, holding their gaze for a moment and seeming to take their measure. Next, the general approached. "I'm Priya Suresh, the militia commander. Before we go any further I want to confirm that you fully appreciate the line you're about to cross. Officially, we're a terrorist organization, and most of us have open arrest warrants for treason. Consorting with us will at best end your military career and banish you to a life of living in the shadows. At worst, you won't have long to live."

Diamond held the general's hawklike gaze. "General, I know exactly who and what you are, as well as the jeopardy my career's in. In Washington you're revered by more people than those who vilify you. The difference is the level of respect I have for the people who hold you in high regard."

Suresh closed in on Diamond. "Why are you here?"

"I've tried taking action through official channels. Now it's time for some unsanctioned ops. I'm willing to risk my career for what I think is right, but I won't force the people loyal to me to make an impossible choice."

Suresh rested her hand on her holstered side arm. "But we're okay because we're already tainted."

Diamond shook her head. "You're willing to do what others aren't. None of us are innocent, but we all have a line we won't cross, even when it costs us everything. We can help each other settle accounts. General, I've studied your career, and I understand why you resigned instead of trading your integrity for a third star. Most militias are a bunch of misguided vigilantes. Not this one. The people in Washington who vilify you are the ones who fear you."

Suresh looked at each of her senior staff in turn, and all gave a nod to go forward. She turned to Diamond. "Let's keep talking. Follow me." She led the group to one of the secure conference rooms and seated herself at the head of the table. Suresh indicated for Diamond to sit at the far end. Harry and Jazmin sat along one side, Derez and Gadget the other. Suresh said, "Tell us about your proposed missions and how we can assist."

Diamond laid her tablet on the conference table where it synced with the holographic projectors. A map of western Mexico showing Sinaloa state, across the water from Baja, California, appeared on everyone's screens. "Per your intel, the attack on the President was launched from this black ops site." Diamond zoomed in on the hangar from the satellite view. "I floated an attack plan on this compound up through my chain of command, but it was nixed for murky reasons. I wasn't able to determine who's protecting whom, though Senator Jiang's fingerprints are all over it. The pushback consisted of spurious concerns about violating Mexican sovereignty and a lack of evidence tying the drone attack on the President to this location. I reviewed the radar and transponder tracks Jazmin shared with me. The trail is solid."

Suresh said, "Just to be clear, are you proposing we launch an attack on this site?"

"Yes. You're the only option for an F-22 strike. A stealth jet can fly in from the west, over the water, and use precision air-to-ground missiles to obliterate the black ops site."

Jazmin liked the sound of this and wondered how close they were to an operational F-22.

Suresh asked, "How do we deal with the Mexican government over the political fallout? They'll demand answers from the US for violating their airspace."

Diamond leaned forward. "Only if they catch us." She zoomed out the satellite view to include Naval Air Station North Island in San Diego. "The cover operation is Navy jet fighter exercises over the Pacific. The Navy flies F-18 carrier-based aircraft, and the Air Force Aggressor Squadron flies a combination of F-15s and F-22s. The attack aircraft will need to kill its transponder, then fly into and out of Mexican airspace in a hurry. Once it's over the water, the jet will stay below 150 feet and cruise over 200 miles from shore. You'll still be detected by land-based radar, but it will have problems tracking you."

Diamond's gaze drilled into Jazmin. "Commander Hassani, are you up for some challenging flying?"

Jazmin suppressed her excitement. "Yes, ma'am."

Suresh said, "How does your career in the Navy survive after a stunt like this? You'll earn some powerful enemies."

Diamond put her hands on the table. "I have some friends in

high places who will intervene with President Navarro. She'll be more than happy for the retribution."

Suresh frowned. "Hell of a gamble, Shockwave. Your career and your freedom will be riding on a good word from a politician."

"I trust these people enough that I'm willing to take the risk."

Suresh turned to Gadget. "How soon will one of our F-22s be mission ready?"

Gadget pursed her lips. "Mercedes and Catarina have been working non-stop and said the jets will be ready for initial test flights tomorrow. Depending on what we find, it might be another week to have them combat ready."

Jazmin couldn't wait to get in the cockpit of a real fighter instead of a simulator. She hoped the general would greenlight the mission.

Suresh leaned back and steepled her fingers. Everyone was silent. Finally, she flattened her hands on the table and leaned forward. "Captain, I'd like to take out the people who attacked our president. I wouldn't be upset if the drug traffickers hosting the black site were wiped out, too. But before we engage in this mission, we need a well-planned exit strategy." Suresh looked around the table. "We all want to live to fight another day. Captain, I want to see a comprehensive plan that covers possible contingencies and deals with political fallout as well. My senior staff must be involved and agree it's the best possible plan." She faced Gadget. "Make getting those F-22s combat ready your top priority." The general locked her eyes on Jazmin. "Hassani, get as many flight hours as you can skimming just over the waves while avoiding ships in the area. Your margin for error is razor thin."

Jazmin said, "Yes, General."

Diamond said, "Hassani, I can share some hard lessons I've learned about doing that kind of flying. The last lesson cost the government a couple hundred million bucks and came damn close to killing me in the process."

Jazmin looked forward to that cautionary tale.

Suresh said, "Captain Diamond, you mentioned more than one op. What else do you have in mind?"

Diamond let out a long breath. "I'd like to hit the black site in China from where the drones that attacked the President were remotely piloted. Logistically, that's a much more difficult target."

Suresh shook her head. "Despite its proximity, Mexico has limited ability to hurt the US. China's a superpower and won't tolerate a military incursion on their soil. The Chinese are already difficult to deal with in international waters when they're protecting their man-made islands in the South China Sea. We're just a militia, and that mission is way beyond what we can even consider."

Diamond looked disappointed, though not surprised.

Suresh said, "Let's focus on the mission in Sinaloa, Mexico. That will be challenging enough." She stood. "Get to work, team." Everyone else rose. The general walked over to Diamond. "How long will you be with us?"

"I need to leave in the morning."

Gadget joined Suresh and Diamond. "I'll arrange overnight quarters for you."

"Thanks, Chief," said Diamond.

Suresh headed toward the conference room door as everyone's tablet pinged with alerts.

Harry said, "There's been multiple explosions with fatalities outside Senator Jiang's DC condo and her home. The senator is in protective custody with her security team."

Jazmin stared at her tablet in disbelief. "According to CNN, the Wisconsin Militia has taken credit for the bombings."

Diamond looked suspiciously around the room. "Is this true? Have I misjudged you that badly?"

Derez slammed his hand on the conference room table. He glared at Diamond. "I'd love to blow that bitch to hell, but that wasn't us. We don't miss, we don't kill innocent civilians, and we damn sure don't advertise."

Jazmin was rattled by the news and was glad Derez exploded with the indignation she felt. Jazmin had sent off the intel report to the press after the general approved its release. The goal was to set Jiang off. Maybe it had worked a little too well.

One by one Suresh made eye contact with each of her direct reports. Gadget, Harry, and Jazmin all gave her micro headshakes. The general walked back over to Diamond and touched the captain's shoulder. "You haven't misjudged us. This was not our doing, but we'll find out who's behind this. My guess is that Jiang is in trouble, and this is a diversion to focus the spotlight elsewhere. The senator is rattled and we're an easy target."

After a moment, Diamond backed away.

Suresh said, "I need to reach out to my network and let them know it wasn't us."

Chapter 49
Ling Chen Jiang

Washington, DC – White House
2 July

Ling Chen was escorted to the Oval Office by two humorless Secret Service agents. Looking and feeling disheveled, she stood in front of the Resolute Desk where President Navarro sat with an icy expression. Navarro looked past her to the Secret Service agents. "I'd like some privacy."

"Yes, Madam President." The pair of agents retreated and quietly closed the door behind them.

Navarro leaned back in her chair. "Senator Jiang, how considerate of you to come out of hiding and stop by."

The President's sarcasm irritated Ling Chen, but she refused to be bullied. "The squad of Secret Service agents made it clear I didn't have an option."

A frigid smile formed on Navarro's face. "They can be quite persuasive when they need to be, but apparently that's what it took to get you here. I expected to see you this morning."

Ling Chen glared back at the President, the long shot candidate from the other party, who should have never been elected. "There was an attempt on my life, so, with the help of my personal security agent, I went into hiding."

Navarro leaned forward. Her condescending smile evaporated. "Your condo and your home were damaged. This wasn't an attempt on your life."

Ling Chen moved toward Navarro's desk. "The exterior to both locations were badly damaged and people died. This was hardly a minor incident. If that had happened here, you would have been hustled off to an underground bunker with a huge force protecting you and a larger force searching for the assailants." Ling Chen took another step closer wanting to show her anger but stopped short of threatening the President. "What was so important that you dragged me here at gunpoint?"

Navarro laughed. "Bravo, Senator. Quit pretending that you don't know exactly why I brought you here."

Ling Chen shook her head in feigned disgust. "If you're referring to that ridiculous smear campaign circulated by the news organizations, don't waste your valuable time chasing that web of political fantasies. While your ardent supporters might give that trash credence, a cursory inspection would show it's utter nonsense."

Navarro's ice blue eyes bore uncomfortably into Ling Chen. "Funny how the DOJ, FBI, CIA, and NSA feel differently."

A wave of fear whipped through Ling Chen, though she forced herself not to react. She wouldn't give the President the satisfaction. She calmed herself with the knowledge that bureaucracy moves slowly. A good legal team can obfuscate and delay for years. "I'm sure the country's voters are excited about flushing their hard-earned tax dollars on another political witch hunt."

Navarro stood. "Senator, you're a danger to this country. I want your resignation as Chair of the Senate Armed Services Committee."

Ling Chen stood straight, relaxed her agitated facial muscles, and shook her head. "Madam President, the senate committees select their own members, and as senior member of the majority party, it's my chair and my decision. As president of the minority party, you don't have control of either the Senate or the House. I'm not going anywhere."

Navarro's expression turned venomous, and she pressed the intercom button on her desk. "Agent Yakov, please escort Senator Jiang from my office."

The outer door of the Oval Office flew open and four Secret Service agents charged in. The two largest agents up front looked as if they were about to pounce. The two behind them had weapons drawn, one a .45 caliber handgun and the other a compact submachine gun. After a slight nod from the President, two of the agents grabbed Ling Chen by her arms and hustled her out the door. They briskly walked her out of the White House while she fumed. The lead agent said, "Senator, your access to the White House has been revoked, and you are not allowed within one hundred feet of the President. Don't make the mistake of pushing boundaries. You'll be tackled and arrested if you violate this order." The agents let go of her arms and returned to the White House, slamming the door.

The President would pay for this insult. Ling Chen let out a long breath to center herself, then pulled out her tablet and called Danica to pick her up. Playing brinkmanship in the President's office had one positive outcome – she wouldn't have to answer any uncomfortable questions, at least not today. When the FBI and DOJ started sniffing around, she'd lawyer up. She repeated to herself, "Say nothing. Admit nothing."

***

Danica picked up Ling Chen outside the White House. They returned to the safe house. Once inside, Ling Chen said, "I want the heads of all the mercenary teams here for a 0700 meeting."

"We've never brought the team leads together."

Ling Chen glared at Danica, irritated that she was questioning her orders. "We are now."

"It will be difficult to get everyone here for a seven o'clock start. They'll need to travel all night."

Ling Chen let out a breath that ended in a low growl. "Not my concern. We are going to war, and we need everyone." After a tense moment, Danica backed away and headed into another room to make the arrangements. Ling Chen headed into the home's office to make plans for the next morning.

Chapter 50
Jazmin Hassani

Wisconsin Militia Base
Bayfield, Wisconsin
6 July

Jazmin, Harry, Gadget, and Diamond met in one of the secure conference rooms to plan the attack on the Mexican cartel site from where the drone attack on the President originated. Diamond said, "I can get the three of you added to the exercise roster for the carrier electronic warfare exercise, though you'll need new identities. Making you part of the fighter squadron at Truax would be the easiest cover, as you already know the base and the pilots."

Harry said, "I can create new identities for the three of us and get them added to the Truax roster."

Gadget said, "We need to get the F-22 and our octocopter tail numbers into the Truax registry so they show as the Fighter Wing's assets."

Harry said, "That won't be a problem."

Jazmin asked, "How do we get our air-to-ground missiles past the inspection point at Naval Air Station North Island when we land?"

Gadget said, "We can put them on the octocopter with the tools and spare parts. We'll need our own hangar so we can mount the missiles in secret before the exercise launch. Captain, is this something you can arrange?"

Diamond thought for a moment before answering. "I can assign you the hangar we use for visiting Air Force units. I'll make sure the rest of the Truax fighter squadron is diverted to another mission, so you'll be alone. Since North Island is a Naval Air Station, the Air Force hangar is off on its own, away from the main runway."

Jazmin said, "While I don't expect any serious opposition when I raid the cartel site, I want to go prepared with a couple of air-to-air missiles."

Diamond pursed her lips. "This is supposed to be a stealth mission. Quick in and quick out. I'll warn our counterparts in the Mexican Air Force that one of our fighters may wander into their airspace as part of the exercise."

Jazmin shook her head. "I'm not worried about the Mexican Air Force. They don't have any aircraft capable of going head-to-head with an F-22. Mercenary assets are another story."

Diamond said, "If you need to take out an aircraft, make damn sure it's justified and won't cause an international incident. I know a senator who was born in Mexico and is a naturalized US citizen who can intervene if we get into trouble, but that's a favor I'd rather not use."

"Understood."

Diamond asked, "How do you plan on handling air traffic on the run into Mexico?"

Jazmin said, "I'll take off with my assigned exercise group and open a hivemind connection with Harry."

Harry projected the radar image of the exercise area on a holographic screen. "When Jazmin peels away to hit the Mexican cartel, I can hack into the base radar system and generate a trace that shows Jazmin on track with the exercise and remove her real radar tracks. Once she finishes her mission in Mexico, I'll cover her tracks until she rejoins the exercise."

Gadget said, "When Jazmin lands after the war game, we pack up and disappear."

Diamond asked, "Any questions before we brief the general?"
Everyone shook their heads.
Jazmin said, "I'll let the general know we're ready for her."

Chapter 51

Naval Air Station North Island
San Diego, California
19 July

Jazmin's F-22 was painted with tail codes for the 27th Fighter Squadron at Truax. Her flight suit had matching patches. She made her approach to Naval Air Station North Island, one of several Naval facilities in the San Diego area. Due to its importance, the DOD had built up the island at colossal taxpayer expense to offset massive climate change impacts. With so many military aircraft stationed there, along with several aircraft carriers, the location was perfect for the mission to attack the Sinaloa airstrip. Harry had created fake identities in the military system for Jazmin, Gadget, and himself so they could move undetected on the base. Jazmin's identity included updated photos of her new face along with a database redirect so her bionic eyes would show up as retinal scans for biological eyes. Jazmin contacted the military tower and was given clearance to land, slotted between a flight of four F-18s and a C-130 support aircraft.

Diamond arranged for Jazmin to be assigned to the training mission to attack the USS *Theodore Roosevelt*, an aging aircraft carrier with updated electronic warfare systems. As a training exercise, the only weapons allowed were electronics pods. As soon as she landed, one of the exercise coordinators inspected the internal weapons bay on her F-22 to verify the jet wasn't armed. Once the inspection was complete, she taxied to the far end of the runway, then to a taxiway leading to a row of buildings. She shut down her engines, and a robot tugger pulled her aircraft out of the blazing sun into the private hangar assigned to visiting Air Force units where Gadget and Harry waited, both in Air Force uniforms. Harry attached a ladder to the cockpit, and Jazmin climbed out.

Gadget walked all the way around the plane and inspected every surface. "Any issues on the flight out?"

"Flew better than if it had just rolled off the Lockheed Martin production line. You, my mom, and Catarina did a hell of a job rebuilding this fighter."

Gadget inspected the nose gear and wiped away a touch of grease, then looked sternly at Jazmin. "Remember, Commander, it's my aircraft. I'm just loaning it to you, so you better bring it back in one piece. Derez is destructive enough for the whole militia."

"Will do, Chief." Both women laughed. Jazmin loved how possessive Gadget was with the militia's aircraft and vehicles. It meant they were meticulously maintained. Jazmin walked to the other side of the hangar where one of the militia's octocopters was parked, and the others followed her. Rolling tool carts, spare parts, and missiles were arrayed around the copter. Jazmin asked, "How was your flight out?"

Harry patted one of the air-to-ground missiles. "I spent too much time cozying up to these. I'm happier when they're attached to the outside of the aircraft." He frowned. "I don't trust autopilot systems, either. In Cyber Command, I took control of aircraft or sabotaged their flight control systems. Both had the same ending, the death of everyone onboard."

Gadget shrugged. "I slept most of the way here and woke up in time to enjoy a picturesque landing over the water."

Jazmin looked back at the F-22. "Are we still go for the mission?"

Gadget said, "I'll need to check the aircraft systems. Once I move the electronic warfare pods to hard points on the wing, I can tuck the thousand-pound bombs into the weapons bay. In case anyone gets frisky, we also brought a couple of air-to-air missiles. Just in case you need to blow an enemy out of the sky."

Harry gestured theatrically like a game show host to the pair of air-to-air missiles. "Apparently the air-to-ground and air-to-air missiles don't play well together, so we have to keep them separated."

Jazmin playfully touched one of the air-to-air missiles on its nose. "A girl can never be too careful when going into combat."

Harry moved closer to her. "I'm starving. Do you want to get something to eat?"

Jazmin looked at Gadget, who just shook her head. "I want to check over your jet and get the weapons loaded. I'm happy to have peace and quiet."

Jazmin turned to Harry. "I'm hungry, too. Let's grab something before the fun begins."

***

The internal bomb racks on her F-22 were completely full for the mission. Jazmin never thought she'd look forward to going back into combat after recovering from her injuries, but she was ready now. She was on the taxiway and next in line behind a pair of F-15 fighters flown by contractors. The pair of fighters took off ahead of her. As soon as the jet wash cleared, she turned her plane onto the center of the runway, pushed both engines to full power, and began moving. Since the jet was fully loaded, her ground roll was longer than usual. As soon as she hit takeoff velocity, Jazmin pulled the stick back and climbed. She retracted her landing gear, then maneuvered to her spot in the pattern of attacking jets in today's exercise against the aircraft carrier. She reduced airspeed and opened up the distance between her jet and the F-15s.

Jazmin opened a hivemind connection to Harry. It was the first time since she had recovered from the hivemind overload attack. *I'm in attack formation for the third wave of fighters. Are you ready to create radar and transponder tracks in the sky?*

Affirmative, and I'll make the real ones vanish.

Jazmin checked her GPS coordinates and flight computer. *Break away in three, two, one.* She rolled left, silenced her transponder, and activated the radar signature and transponder spoofer. Her mom and Catarina had made a few upgrades to the aging fighter jet, including the ability to alter the radar profile in flight for clandestine missions. They had also added significant EMP and directed-energy weapon shielding, along with a unique clear nanoparticle coating on the canopy to protect the pilot from neurotech damage if attacked. Jazmin headed south and stayed over the ocean to minimize her time in Mexican airspace. The goal was to get in quick, destroy the

Sinaloa cartel and black ops installations, and get out before Mexican air traffic even knew she was there.

Jazmin slowed her airspeed, changed her heading toward the Sinaloa airstrip, and descended to an altitude of 22,000 feet. This altitude was lower than commercial air traffic and well within the range for pinpoint accuracy with her thousand-pound bombs. She was flying a stealth fighter and took full tactical advantage. She couldn't avoid detection by Mexican air traffic control, but she wanted to confuse them so she squawked a long-haul drone ID. She wanted to delay triggering any reactions from a controller, even if it was only an automated instruction.

On her tactical radar, Jazmin picked up a flight of three F-15s taking off from the Sinaloa airstrip. When they got closer, she captured photos with her aircraft cameras. Her F-22 was designed for stealth, so she had a minimal radar signature, but the F-15 pilots must have seen her inbound. Jazmin wished she'd caught them on the ground, but it was too late. She had known drones were launched from the site, but fighter aircraft were a new development. Her hivemind connection to Harry was still open. *Harry, three F-15s just launched from the cartel airstrip.*

Tracking now. No transponders and they're heading out over the ocean. I'll trace as long as I can.

Her aircraft was now five miles out from the Sinaloa airstrip, so she locked on to her ground targets. *Executing bomb run now.* Jazmin opened the bomb bay doors and launched. She stayed on course, flipped on her aircraft's high-speed cameras, and waited for the destruction to unfold. Both bombs hit their targets a fraction of a second apart. Twin fireballs shot skyward, followed by a black mushroom cloud of smoke and flying debris. The remains of the two hangars floated back to earth, partially filling the gaping holes where the buildings had stood. The video would be a fitting gift for President Navarro. Jazmin made a low pass over the base for a battle damage assessment. Nothing moved.

After the massive explosions, any pretense of stealth was gone. She had to get out of Mexican airspace and back over the Pacific. Jazmin pushed her twin jet engines to full power, climbed to 50,000 feet, and killed her transponder. *Mission accomplished with souvenir video for the President. Rejoining war games.*

Sending updated coordinates to your flight computer. Stay dark until you get in range.

Copy.

Using her neurotech, Jazmin accessed photos of the three F-15s that had flown past her from the cartel base and projected them onto her helmet display. She studied the images. Something was off about the jets' profiles. The missile rails on the jets were empty, so no obvious armaments, yet they all had conformal fuel tanks for extended flight operations. When she zoomed in on the aircrafts' fuselage beneath the pilots, a chilling sense of foreboding engulfed her. Every square inch was covered with the same energy ports as the business jet that had attacked the fighter pilots at Truax Field.

Chapter 52
Fang

Pacific Ocean
9 July

Fang's F-15 was the lead fighter with the other two in tight formation. The three former Chinese Air Force pilots were lured away from the military by the high pay of Aggressor Aviation, the mercenary group employed by Senator Ling Chen Jiang. Fang had seen her bosses with the mercurial Chinese American senator but had never met her. Just prior to this mission, each of the three female pilots had been handed a US passport, a prize Fang had no intention of giving up.

Fang hadn't expected an inbound fighter jet in Mexican airspace. The Sinaloa airstrip was sufficiently far from the closest commercial and military airport that no aircraft were expected at all, let alone an American F-22. She thanked the gods that the three F-15s had taken off before the F-22 arrived. She aimed her targeting pods back toward the Sinaloa airstrip. Moments later two massive explosions engulfed the area, shooting smoking debris skyward. She was lucky to be alive. Her associates at the Mexican airstrip were likely dead, a hazard in their line of work. Fang would settle the score if she had a chance, but right now she had a mission to fly, and she'd get a huge bonus upon successful completion. She missed her daughter, Lifen, who was in China being raised by Fang's elderly parents. When this was done, she'd send them money and visit her little girl.

The three F-15s passed over Baja California. Once over the water they broke formation, spread out, and dove to an altitude of one hundred feet. At this low flight level the land-based radar waves would reflect off the water, creating radar blind spots, and the signals would be too weak to accurately detect their planes. Fang kept a close visual watch outside her aircraft to avoid slamming into any ships or oil platforms at this insanely low altitude. She also had to watch her fuel burn rate. Even with the additional range provided by two conformal fuel tanks on each plane, they'd need a refueling stop to complete their mission. As soon as they were fifty miles from shore the three aircraft turned north, then climbed to 50,000 feet, where they maintained radio silence. Their destination was Ocean Ridge Airport in northern California, a general aviation airport no longer open to the public that had been taken over by Aggressor Aviation. The company had also extended the single runway to support military aircraft operations.

***

After refueling at Ocean Ridge, Fang and her two wingmen headed south to Naval Station North Island. Their company had a contract to fly aggressor missions against Navy ships. The three Chinese pilots were flying replacement aircraft for the original planes which Aggressor Aviation claimed had been grounded due to a mechanical issue. This was the cover story they provided to the Navy. To fulfill the contract, Aggressor Aviation agreed to supply replacement aircraft at the last minute, and the Navy waived the usual pre-wargame aircraft inspections. They timed their arrival so they could launch with the last wave of exercise attack aircraft from Naval Air Station North Island. Fang's flight of three fighters joined the others that had just taken off from the base. She checked her radar and smiled when she saw three other F-15s from her company in attack formation. These were the other last-minute replacements and were equipped with anti-ship missiles hidden inside electronics pods. Small explosions erupted from under the other group's F-15s, blowing off the outer skin of the weapons pods and exposing the anti-ship missiles.

Fang counted down the seconds, then dove toward the *Theodore Roosevelt* aircraft carrier. She blasted the floating airstrip with a wall of energy from the PWL weapons, destroying the massive ship's control, weapons, and communication systems. Her two wingmen dove at the rest of the carrier group, rendering the closest ships unable to mount a counterattack. So far, everything had gone exactly as planned, but now they were in the most dangerous phase of the operation. Fighters in the area flown by other contractors and military units were caught in the directed-energy weapons' field. Planes flying at low altitude crashed into ships before their pilots had a chance to eject. The planes flying higher lost power, and their pilots ejected right before their aircraft careened into the water or into the ships below. The airspace all around Fang had become unpredictable and dangerous. She saw the three aircraft with anti-ship missiles line up for their attack runs on the carrier. A moment later a fireball erupted outside her front canopy.

Chapter 53
Jazmin Hassani

Pacific Ocean
19 July

Jazmin flipped on her transponder and rejoined the last attack wave, just as the airspace below went from an orderly choreographed attack by a disciplined aggressor force to the full-on insanity of a war zone. Three F-15s dove at the aircraft carrier group like World War Two dive bombers and made low passes over the ships. All aircraft in the area lost flight control and crashed into the ships, the water, or collided with other aircraft. A lucky few punched out, and Jazmin was happy to see parachutes deployed after their ejection seats dropped away, but the downed aircraft vastly outnumbered the parachutes.

The upgraded attack radar suite and avionics her mom and Catarina had installed, along with super sight from her bionic eyes, allowed Jazmin to see things other pilots couldn't. Three F-15s with anti-ship missiles were setting up for their attack runs. They were seconds away from launching, so Jazmin locked on to the closest target with an air-intercept missile and fired. The fighter exploded in a huge fireball, the remains of the burning aircraft falling into the ocean, and a cloud of pulverized debris floating down after it. The two other fighters fired their anti-ship missiles, then peeled away at low altitude. Once the missiles hit the water, they went into torpedo mode. A few seconds later they impacted the carrier below the waterline and detonated.

Jazmin rolled hard right, dove, and locked on to one of the F-15s. Her second air intercept missile found its target and obliterated the fighter. Jazmin pulled her stick back, hit the afterburners, and was shoved back into her seat as her aircraft climbed. A second later debris slammed into her left wing, and the aircraft shuddered. She desperately needed to gain altitude, but her engine thrust went to zero. Every alarm in the cockpit screamed for her attention.

Jazmin scanned her engine instruments. Both engines had flamed out. She tried to level off to preserve her decaying airspeed, but the jet was unresponsive. She checked her fire control radar and heads-up display. Both were blank. As her airspeed dropped, she could no longer control the fighter. She was just along for the ride. The asymmetric drag on her damaged left wing pulled the aircraft into a flat spin. One of the few instruments still functioning was her backup analog altimeter, which showed she was losing altitude at a frightening rate. Spinning downward, each corkscrew rotation cranked up her fear. She thought about one of her early fighter instructor's advice on when it was time to eject. "When ejecting scares you less than staying in the aircraft, it's time to punch out." With no hope of recovering enough control for a survivable water landing, Jazmin pulled the eject handle.

The fasteners exploded and the canopy blew off. A second later the rocket engine under Jazmin's seat launched her skyward, clear of the crippled jet, and, because her altitude was so low, the parachute deployed immediately as her seat fell away. She checked the condition of her parachute; it was intact and perfectly inflated. She raised her helmet visor and threw away her mask.

After she deployed her survival seat kit and inflated her harness life preserver for the inevitable water landing, she surveyed the scene below. The aircraft carrier had two gaping holes in its hull and was listing badly to starboard. Aircraft and equipment were sliding off the deck into the ocean. The four attacking F-15s that remained headed out to sea, and the chaotic skies were quiet. She felt impotent rage as she floated down. While she still had some altitude, Jazmin used her parachute guide handles to steer herself clear of the massive sinking ship and aircraft wreckage. Her ejection seat had already dropped into the ocean. The distress beacon attached to it would now only show the general location of where she went down. Each second she drifted further away. She tried to reactivate her hivemind connection with Harry, but without a communication system signal for the carrier wave, her personal neurotech didn't have the power to connect at this distance.

When Jazmin hit the water, the emergency beacon attached to her flight suit triggered automatically. She disconnected her parachute and double checked the inflation on her life preserver. The cold water shocked her system at first, but she soon grew accustomed to the chill. She hoped air-sea rescue would arrive soon, before her core temperature dropped too far and hypothermia set in. Jazmin located her deployed seat kit and the small personal life raft attached to it. She used the attached rope to pull the raft toward her. Slightly wetting the raft for lubrication, she slid her body out of the water and into the makeshift shelter. Her body ached like she'd been in a car wreck, but she was afraid to turn down her pain receptors in case she was more seriously hurt than she realized.

Jazmin was exhausted and began shivering. She scanned the area for other pilots, but it was difficult to tell the living from the dead. After examining her body for injuries overlooked due to shock, Jazmin reviewed her entire flight, especially the pursuit of the enemy pilots and the loss of her aircraft. Time passed slowly. Finally, the sound of lapping waves was broken by the thwup of rotors. Jazmin scanned the sky to the east and saw a Coast Guard rescue helicopter in search mode. When it got closer, she triggered the sea dye marker attached to the raft. The ocean surrounding her instantly turned bright green.

A minute later the copter hovered overhead, the air blast from the rotors kicking up small waves around her. A rescue swimmer jumped into the water and swam over to Jazmin. Over the rotor noise the female rescue swimmer asked, "Are you injured?"

"Nothing serious, just cold and exhausted."

"Let's get you home." Fighting the vicious rotor wash and salty sea spray, the rescue swimmer helped Jazmin out of the raft and into the rescue basket. The steel cable attached to the winch in the helicopter pulled her out of the water. Another aircrew member inside the copter helped her out of the basket, deflated her life preserver, wrapped Jazmin in a reflective blanket, and sent the harness down on the cable. A minute later the rescue swimmer was pulled aboard, the side door slammed shut, and the copter gained altitude and forward speed.

Jazmin asked, "How come we aren't still searching?"

The crew member said, "We're low on fuel and heading back to the base. We'd like to get you checked out in case you're injured and don't realize it."

Jazmin wondered how they could be so low on fuel when they had to have been dispatched because of the war game attack. She looked out the window. They weren't headed for land but further out to sea. Jazmin studied her two rescuers, who both had identical tattoos on their necks. There was something familiar about the tattoos, but Jazmin couldn't place where she'd seen them before. She tried connecting to the military network with her neurotech but couldn't find a signal. With all the electronic fallout from the directed-energy weapon attack on the aircraft carrier group, the signals likely were blocked, or possibly the network had been shut down as a precaution. It nagged at her subconscious, but there wasn't more she could do until she got back to shore. She wanted to check in with Harry.

The rescue swimmer said, "Commander, you don't look well. Let me give you something to warm you up." She pulled a drink pouch from a panel, squeezed it to activate the chemical heat reaction, then placed it in Jazmin's hands. Hoping to clear her head, she took a couple of long pulls on the straw to ingest the sweet, caffeinated mocha drink. A moment later, wooziness overcame her. She dropped the drink bag, and hot sticky liquid saturated her lap. Right before losing consciousness, she realized two things.

The rescue swimmer called her Commander, even though she was wearing Air Force insignia. Her fake identity hadn't held.

The tattoos were Russian Spetsnaz.

Chapter 54
Mei Chan

Chinese Military Intelligence Headquarters
20 July

Mei awoke with a start to the opening bars of "The Stars and Stripes Forever" blaring from her tablet. Her chief of staff, Colonel Ming, was calling. He had an affinity for American military marches and called only when there was a crisis that couldn't wait. She checked the time: 0300.

Ming said, "I'm sorry to wake you, General, but you need to be aware of events in America. There was a surprise attack on the US aircraft carrier *Theodore Roosevelt* during a planned electronics-only wargame."

Mei tried to clear her head, having slept for only two hours. "I'll come into the office. Send my driver."

Ming said, "He's on his way. Senior staff has been alerted, and I've arranged for food and tea."

"Good. Brief me on the details when I arrive." She ended the call and went to put on her uniform, as no doubt she'd have to brief her boss and possibly the Paramount Leader. She had the sickening feeling that Ling Chen was behind the attack on the carrier. After Mei's visit to Ling Chen's condo, her American asset had acted contrite, but Mei suspected it was just an act. Mei tried to tamp down her panic. Mei's boss, Senior General Fehua Tian, and Paramount Leader Yulong Qing were unforgiving old men. Mei had climbed far higher in military intelligence than any other woman, and the elderly men who held power over her would use any excuse to knock her down. Now they had good reason, and she was terrified.

***

Mei arrived in the conference room where her senior staff was already gathered. A tray with fresh dumplings and a pot of green tea was placed at her spot at the head of the table. She took a bite of dumpling to try to calm her stomach and a sip of hot tea to clear her head. The others around the table looked as tired as she felt.

Colonel Ming led the briefing. "The US aircraft carrier *Theodore Roosevelt* and its strike group were engaged in a wargame with attacking fighter jets armed with electronic weapons. All went as expected until the last wave of fighters, three American F-15s flown by contractors, attacked the carrier strike group with what appeared to be PWL weapons, followed by additional F-15s with air-to-ship torpedo missiles. The carrier is listing, taking on water, and expected to sink before it can be towed back to port. The other ships in the strike group are dead in the water. An air battle ensued with a number of fighters going down. An unexpected outcome was a Coast Guard helicopter and several fighter jets heading north toward Canadian airspace. The situation is fluid, and rescue ships are in the area."

Mei tried not to react. Colonel Ming reported the worst-case scenario for an attack Mei and Ling Chen had gamed out at the American black site in Yunnan province. When the games were complete, Mei had ordered Ling Chen to stand down on any plans going forward. This type of attack would likely result in the US declaring war on China, an unthinkable outcome.

Mei said, "Thank you for the briefing." She looked around the room at her staff. "Please track each of your areas and keep Colonel Ming informed of any critical changes. That will be all."

The officers around the table got up to leave. Mei stood too. "Colonel Ming, a word." He waited for the others to exit, then shut the door. Mei let out a long breath. "Have you contacted Senator Jiang?"

Ming pursed his lips. "I tried to contact her through the usual channel. She didn't respond directly, only a message from an underling that she was out of the country and couldn't be contacted."

"If my suspicions are correct, this could turn out very badly for China."

"Agreed, General."

"Keep me informed of new developments. I need to brief General Tian."

Ming nodded and exited the conference room. Mei mulled over the possible consequences, each one worse than the last, then came to a decision.

From her office, Mei tried contacting Ling Chen, leaving a coded message that she should meet Mei at the American black ops site in western China and confirm her arrival time. There was no response from Ling Chen, which didn't surprise Mei. It just confirmed her next course of action. Her next play was risky, but doing nothing was worse. Mei contacted Ping Zhao, the second-highest-ranking member of the Politburo Standing Committee. Ping was in line for General Secretary, but Yulong Qing had put together a slim coalition of old men to beat her out of the top job. However Zhao was younger than Qing and held more modern views, especially for effectively dealing with the US.

***

Mei met Ping Zhao at the powerful leader's home. A servant brought Mei to a formal sitting room where Zhao sat on an elaborate sofa. In front of her was a long table with a pot of tea and porcelain cups. The servant left, closing the door behind her. Zhao studied Mei for a long, uncomfortable moment. "Have a seat. Would you like some tea?"

Mei took a chair opposite Zhao. "Yes, thank you."

Zhao poured a cup of green tea, then handed it to Mei, who concentrated to keep her hands from shaking.

Zhao cocked her head with a mischievous smile. "So why has the number two military spy master asked to meet with me in secret at my home?"

Unsteadily, Mei put her cup of tea down before she spilled it. "I've come to ask for your help on a delicate matter with grave consequences for China."

Zhao took a sip of tea. "Shouldn't you be having this conversation with your boss and the Paramount Leader?"

"They are part of the problem, as am I. You're the only person with enough power, political finesse, and courage to stop this madness from destroying the country."

Zhao leaned forward. Her penetrating stare cut right through Mei as if she could see Mei's thoughts and intentions. "You need to explain in detail what has transpired and how you think I can help."

Mei spent the next two hours reviewing her history with Ling Chen, their deteriorating relationship, and the recent events leading up to the attack on the USS *Theodore Roosevelt*. Zhao asked a few thoughtful questions, though she mostly listened. When Mei was done, the powerful leader sat in silence for an excruciatingly long time. Mei didn't interrupt Zhao's silent deliberations.

Zhao's expression changed to a look of determination. "You did the right thing to come to me, though moving against the Paramount Leader will likely end in both of us being convicted of treason or executed. Before I'm willing to make a move, I want to see the evidence backing up your claims."

Mei pulled a micro dot data transfer device from her pocket and handed it to Zhao. "Here's everything I have."

Zhao studied the tiny device. "I'll download this to an isolated tablet so it can't be used against us." She stood, signaling the meeting was over. "I need to discuss this with a few trusted colleagues. I'll contact you if we need to talk again."

Mei bowed her head. "Thank you." She exited the room and went outside where her driver waited. He had the good sense not to ask about the meeting with Ping Zhao and simply waited for her orders. "Take me to my office." The car sped off. Mei checked her tablet. Twenty messages with updates on the situation in America. Each one more alarming than the last.

Chapter 55
Jazmin Hassani

Masset Island off British Columbia
Western Canada
20 July

Jazmin awoke in total darkness, gripped by vertigo and nausea. Her head pounded, and the tiniest movement was agony. She lay on a cold concrete floor, her hands and feet shackled with metal chains. Her flight suit was damp, permeated with the sour smell of the drugged mocha drink, and her skin was wrinkled from too much time in the water. A clammy fabric bag over her head clung to her face. Panting with fear, Jazmin had a hard time catching her breath. She forced herself to slow her breathing and take control of the one thing she could, her mental state. Breath control was her first step in calming down and taking stock of her situation. The last thing she remembered was being picked up in the water by a Coast Guard rescue swimmer and hoisted into a helicopter. A few fuzzy images of her rescuers floated at the edge of her consciousness, but nothing more. She tried to get a sense of her surroundings, and focusing on the sounds echoing off the hard floor. In the distance she detected muffled voices, snippets of what sounded like Chinese and Russian, though she understood none of it.

Normally her neurotech AI interface automatically connected with the military cloud computing network. Jazmin didn't know if she was blocked or simply out of range. She thought back to her SERE training. Her only option at the moment was to focus on survival. Evasion, resistance, and escape would have to wait for later, assuming she lived long enough for those things to matter. Exhausted, she cleared her mind to conserve energy, dozing on and off. With no visual cues in a quiet environment, it was impossible to keep track of time.

***

Jazmin was jarred awake when the bag was yanked off her head. Her bionic eyes adjusted to the light, and she awkwardly rolled into a sitting position, chains pulling on every limb. She didn't recognize the man holding the black bag. He was fit and had the hard eyes of an ex-military member who'd seen too much action. His lined face, topped with a head of salt-and-pepper hair, was etched with combat experience. He waited in silence as she swiveled her head to take in her surroundings. Her hands were manacled behind her, and she was chained to a U-bolt protruding from the concrete floor at one end of a large aircraft hangar. The three F-15s she had passed in Mexico were parked nearby, close enough for her to study the energy ports on the lower fuselage. A fourth F-15 with hardpoints for standard armament was there too. She assumed this was the surviving aircraft with anti-ship missiles from the attack on the carrier. On the other side, farther away, was the Coast Guard helicopter that had pulled her out of the water.

The man held out a bottle of water with a straw so she could drink. "It's plain water and it's not drugged. It's been hours since we picked you up and you need to drink, or you'll get dehydrated. Boss wants you in good shape." He spoke with a thick Russian accent.

Jazmin studied his face for signs of deceit. She didn't know if he was telling the truth or was just a good liar, but she was so thirsty she didn't care. She took the straw in her mouth and drank greedily. The cool liquid washed the terrible taste down her throat. He held the bottle patiently for her, as if he was taking care of a beloved grandchild. She drained the bottle, and he pulled it away and placed it on the floor. She wondered again if he'd lied about it not being drugged, though she felt no ill effects. She wasn't lightheaded from a tranquilizer nor was her heart racing from a stimulant.

Jazmin focused her attention back on her captor. "Where are we?"

He hesitated before answering. "You won't be here for long, so it won't matter if you know. You're on Masset Island off British Columbia."

Jazmin was surprised he answered so she kept asking questions. "Who are you?"

"I'm the helicopter pilot who brought you here, but I'm not with the Coast Guard." He flashed a sardonic smile.

Jazmin bit back a snarky reply. "What happens now?"

He looked over to a group of mercenaries on the other side of the hangar. "I try to keep the others away from you until boss arrives. The two pilots you killed were their friends and they want to make you suffer, despite our orders." He shook his head and wagged a finger at her. "You can't afford to make any more enemies."

"Then I'll do my best to keep you as a friend."

He laughed and shook his head, then his expression turned hostile. "Don't make mistake of thinking I'm friend." A couple of seconds later his scornful smile returned. "I'm just more disciplined about following orders than the others. When boss is happy, she's very generous, but bad things happen to people who piss her off." He studied her again then picked up the empty bottle. "Make yourself comfortable. Boss will be here soon." He laughed again and walked away.

Jazmin assumed the mercenaries all worked for Senator Jiang. Over the past months she'd wondered how far Jiang was willing to go. Now she had her answer. Sinking an aircraft carrier. Why was it so important to the senator that Jazmin be delivered in chains instead of just being killed? Jiang clearly wasn't squeamish about murder, so why had this nightmare become so personal?

Chapter 56
Harry Dexter

Naval Air Station North Island
San Diego, California
20 July

From their private hangar, Harry had monitored the final attack wave against the aircraft carrier and merged Jazmin's radar and transponder tracks seamlessly into the electronic picture to finalize the clandestine mission. All had gone according to plan, until things went sideways. The last-minute addition of six replacement aircraft from Aggressor Aviation felt off. The timing had been too perfect, and the mandatory safety checks had been bypassed. Harry was powerless to intervene. All he could do was track the action and hope Jazmin escaped the melee.

His initial elation at her downing two of the aggressor F-15s turned to horror when her plane lost power and flight control, ending in a flat spin and Jazmin ejecting. Despite a flood of location information from her ejection seat, Jazmin wasn't found. With a sinking aircraft carrier, crippled carrier task force ships, and at least a dozen other missing pilots, finding the lone pilot from Truax Field was low on the Navy's priority list.

Worse yet, there was a report that two Coast Guard helicopter pilots had been attacked, and their aircraft stolen. There were conflicting reports of sightings after the air-launched anti-ship torpedoes hit the aircraft carrier, although no two eyewitnesses gave the same account. Once distress calls went out from the carrier task force group and the exercise aircraft, multiple units responded. The oversaturation of electromagnetic signals in the area, the signal distortion from the directed-energy weapons attack, and the lack of radar coverage out over the Pacific made it impossible for Harry to track the stolen Coast Guard helicopter. Once it was confirmed that the carrier had been attacked with multiple directed-energy weapons, Space Command was afraid military satellites would be caught in a residual energy wave. The orbital path of satellites in the region were changed to limit the damage. Harry was a bundle of frustration and felt an overwhelming sense of failure. He didn't know what had happened to Jazmin, just that she was gone. Could he still help her, or was she beyond his reach? She wasn't the only pilot missing, so the Navy simply added her to the list. The Navy's number one concern was the loss of the aircraft carrier.

Gadget nudged Harry's shoulder. "The octocopter is packed, and I signed us out. We need to leave before our cover story falls apart."

Harry looked around the hangar. The array of tool carts, specialized repair tools, spare parts, and munitions had all disappeared back inside the octocopter. He checked the time, realizing he'd lost the last twelve hours. Resigned he couldn't accomplish anything more by staying, he let out a long breath. "Agreed. We need to head back to the militia base."

In the octocopter, Harry sat in the copilot's seat with Gadget in the pilot's seat. The entire flight would be handled by the copter's autopilot. If things went wrong, Gadget knew the flight systems far better than he did, and she'd passed the pilot proficiency exam on the simulator. The robot tugger pulled them outside, detached, and scurried back inside the hangar. The large door closed with a resounding thud, a final depressing note on the mission.

The octocopter executed an automated checklist, and the engine generator started. A minute later the eight rotors spun up to idle. The variable pitch rotors were almost flat, providing no appreciable lift. Once their aircraft received clearance from the tower, the rotor pitch changed and bit into the air with every rotation. The octocopter lifted off into the remaining afternoon sunshine. Drowning in a wave of failure and exhaustion, Harry didn't even register the view outside the copter as they headed along the coast. The worst part was not knowing what happened to Jazmin.

Chapter 57
Ling Chen Jiang

Situation Room – The White House
22 July

Ling Chen sat in the situation room next to Trabago. Normally, she wasn't included when the President was briefed. She was only present today because she had information Navarro wanted. Her restraining order from the White House had been suspended for today only.

Chief of Naval Operations Admiral Bizander said, "The Navy held live wargames to test the updated systems on the USS *Theodore Roosevelt*. During the final aircraft attack wave, the carrier task force was attacked with directed-energy weapons, and two air-launched torpedoes were deployed against the carrier."

Looking like the angry underdog in a cage fight, Navarro growled, "Admiral, this cannot go unchallenged. I won't allow one of our carriers to be sunk in US waters without retribution."

Stone-faced, the admiral said, "Understood, ma'am."

Navarro glared at Ling Chen. "Senator, present your findings."

Ling Chen projected satellite video of the F-15s dive-bombing the carrier with directed-energy weapons, the two fighters launching anti-ship missiles, and the air-launched torpedoes detonating below the carrier's waterline. The final image was of the huge ship on fire and sinking. The screen froze on this image. "This was a brazen attack by China. They wish to be the sole superpower."

National Security Advisor Mahira Patel shook her head. "While the Chinese have made provocative actions over directed-energy weapons, this is an insane escalation. There's no indication China wants to attack the United States."

Ling Chen glared at Patel and pointed to the screen. "Look at what just happened. This is an act of war. A war that China has started."

Patel let out an exasperated breath. "Where is the evidence? The planes that attacked the carrier were approved military contractors with no ties to China."

Ling Chen's face turned into an ugly mask. She leaned forward and opened her mouth for an angry retort. Before she had a chance to make a blistering comment, Trabago placed a large hand on Ling Chen's arm to stop her. She turned her angry glare to the general. Everyone around the table watched the tension ratchet up but said nothing.

Trabago turned to Patel. "As soon as the incident happened, I directed DIA investigators to do a deep dive into every one of the suspect pilots. Their initial background checks cleared, but a more thorough investigation revealed all had ties to China. This appears to be a deep cover operation that took years to come to fruition."

Navarro said, "I thought all of these pilots were US citizens."

Trabago said, "That's correct, Madam President, though in this case they were naturalized citizens originally from China."

Navarro flashed an irritated look at Patel, who withered under the President's angry eyes. "General Trabago, did your investigation turn up any other relevant information?"

Trabago studied his tablet for a moment, then projected an image of an F-22 with a missile launching from its weapons bay. "Note the missile being fired from this aircraft." He zoomed out to show the scene with the F-15 with anti-ship missiles. "This is an electronic-weapon-only wargame. Each aircraft is checked for live weapons prior to takeoff. This F-22 was painted to match the Air Force squadron at Truax Field in Madison, Wisconsin, but was flown by known terrorist Ex-Navy Commander Jazmin Hassani. We know this because the entire squadron's aircraft and pilots based at Truax were participating in another exercise. The F-22 was flown from Bayfield, Wisconsin, not Madison. In addition, the F-15s that attacked the carriers were replacements at the last minute due to the original aircraft having maintenance issues. The attacking aircraft, other than Hassani's, were never on base but joined the exercise in the final minutes before the attack."

Navarro asked, "What happened to all of these fighters?"

Trabago said, "Two of the attacking F-15s went down along with the F-22 piloted by Hassani. The pilots weren't recovered. The remaining four F-15s escaped but went immediately dark. The search continues, though with each passing hour finding them becomes less likely."

Ling Chen said, "Madam President, we should declare war on China."

Navarro glared at her. "That's for Congress to decide." She looked at each of the service chiefs and seemed to be weighing a decision. "I want the Navy at DEFCON 2 and all other services at DEFCON 3, effective immediately." The President scanned the room. "Is there anything else I need to know right now?"

Everyone remained silent until the National Security Advisor said, "Madam President, we'll brief you with further updates as events unfold."

Navarro stood. "My next call is to the Chinese ambassador." Navarro headed to the door flanked by her Secret Service detail.

∗∗∗

Ling Chen and Trabago sat in the living room of her condo sipping an excellent single malt scotch. "General, you were superb briefing the President today, especially when you stopped me from my feigned fight with Patel."

He took a sip of his scotch. "I'm worried you overplayed our case by pushing the President to declare war on China."

She shook her head. "The President despises me, so she'll discount anything I say. She doesn't have the power to declare war, but as commander in chief, she can order the military to take any action she likes."

"But did we go too far?"

Ling Chen knew Trabago was driven by personal greed and his own issues with the country due to an investigation of his foreign-born wife before she died mysteriously, but he wasn't ready to go as far as she was to seek revenge. "I think we went just far enough. Navarro put the military on alert, and she'll press the Chinese ambassador, who will deny everything."

Trabago refilled his glass. It was his third, which was unusual. He was losing his nerve, so she'd need to watch him. She said, "Commander Hassani won't be a problem for us anymore. She's stashed in Canada for the moment. We can deal with General Suresh and the rest of her gang another day."

"What are you going to do with Hassani?"

Ling Chen smiled. "Turn her over to some friends in China."

Trabago downed the rest of his scotch and stood. "I need to check on the investigation and make sure my staff are achieving results."

Ling Chen put down her drink and stood. "Keep up the good work, General. We're almost there."

As he headed downstairs, she thought: The minute he was no longer needed, Trabago would need to be terminated.

Chapter 58
Jazmin Hassani

Masset Island off British Columbia
Western Canada
22 July

"Wake up, sleeping beauty." The words were slurred together. Her captor's Russian accent was thicker than before. His breath stank of vodka. Jazmin had slept fitfully and still had no idea what time or day it was. Sunlight didn't penetrate the hangar, and the overhead halogen fixtures were always on. She was so dehydrated she wasn't urinating. Not realizing how hungry she was, the smell of food brought her fully awake. Her nameless abductor had a tray with meat, rice, and steamed vegetables. The tray also had a large bottle of water with a straw. She inhaled the aroma of the food, though her mouth was too parched to water.

"Boss wants you in good condition for her visit, so I brought you something to eat." He placed the tray in front of her. Jazmin didn't move. She was so thirsty and hungry she wanted to pounce on the tray like a starved animal, but it wouldn't be that simple.

He leered and gestured. "Go ahead. It's for you."

She looked up at him hesitantly, then leaned forward to reach the straw. Her lips got to within an inch of the tip of the straw, but she was at the very limit of her restraints. No matter how hard she pulled, she couldn't reach it. The food was even further away. She'd been exposed to this type of psychological torture in her SERE training. Her captors then were military instructors, and they had limits. The man in front of her was a mercenary and she didn't know the depths of his depravity. Jazmin sat up and glared at him. She wouldn't give him the satisfaction of yelling or pleading or crying.

He pulled up a chair just out of her reach and sat down. "You seem to be having difficulty. Perhaps I can help you." His eyes held a hint of kindness, though Jazmin doubted it was genuine. His charade stank of psychological manipulation. "I trust you are smart enough not to bite the hand that feeds you, or the hand might lose control and beat you instead, despite boss's orders. Now you'll be good girl, eh?" He nodded repeatedly until Jazmin did the same. "Much better." He held up the bottle with the straw to her lips and she drank greedily, gulping the cool water as fast as she could, not knowing when or if she'd get more. "Slow down," he commanded. "I don't want you sick." He pulled the bottle away. A few drops dribbled down her chin and she licked them up. He watched with an amused expression.

"I bet you're hungry. Fang is very good cook." He gestured to the steaming food on the tray. He made a show of searching the tray then brought up his hands in bafflement. "Usually, Fang includes chopsticks, but I don't see any. You'll need to eat with your hands." He feigned a shocked expression. "Your hands are shackled behind you and that's a problem. Maybe I can help."

Jazmin remained impassive, reminding herself it was just a psychological game, but she was so hungry. He sat across from her not saying a word. Jazmin thought of what her Aunt Carmen said right before she headed to the Naval Academy. "Don't let the bastards grind you down." That mantra had gotten her through the worst parts of her academy, flight, and Special Ops training. She had refused to die when her octocopter went down, and she had made it through the darkest days of rehab. She'd survive this too. Jazmin sat up straight and looked her captor in the eye. "Please feed me."

He looked at her approvingly, like someone training a puppy who crapped outside for the first time instead of on the carpeting. "I only have my hands, so I trust you'll treat them gently." She nodded. He tore open the moist towelette on the tray then meticulously wiped his thumbs and each finger. "Hygiene is so important, especially on missions."

He picked up a large chunk of chicken and pushed it deep into her mouth, almost shoving it down her throat. She tried not to gag and accidently bite him as he slowly pulled his fingers around her closed lips. It felt like oral rape in its violation. She forced the meat forward so she could chew it before swallowing. He repeated this until the chicken was gone. By the end, Jazmin was more adept at constricting her throat when he shoved in the food. She kept reminding herself it was just a sick power game. She won every round by staying alive.

The rice and vegetable courses were exercises in choking her with the sheer volume of food. In between stuffing her mouth with food, her captor downed shots of vodka. He grew meaner as his blood alcohol level increased. Jazmin got better at allowing small amounts down her throat, even as he stuffed her mouth with more food. When the food was gone, he waved the straw near her lips but kept jerking it away. He finally let her catch it, and she gulped down the rest of the water, not trusting him to let her drink it more slowly.

Grains of rice, bits of chopped vegetables, and meat drippings trailed down her face and neck. Food she'd coughed up cascaded down her flight suit. He looked disgusted. "You eat like animal." He picked up the used towelette, now mostly dry, and wiped away the food trail from her face with coarse strokes. "That's better." He threw the towelette on the tray. "Now I've made boss happy." He looked at her with disdain, picked up the tray, and stomped away.

Jazmin felt dirty and violated. She wondered if this man would rape her. The other pilots were women, but would they stop him or cheer him on? She closed her eyes and tried to calm herself. Now that she'd eaten, she wondered if they'd let her use a toilet or if she'd have to let her bladder and bowels go, then stew in her own stink. The voices grew quiet. Jazmin's mind wandered in and out of dark places populated with surreal images, and the familiar grew distorted. The faces of her friends and family stretched into horrifying caricatures. Rooms in her parents' home rolled end over end with furniture sliding down walls that were floors, or maybe ceilings. A part of her brain wondered if she'd been drugged again, or was she was just going insane? The bizarre images sped up in their number, rotation, and intensity until everything turned black.

Chapter 59

An electric jolt surged through Jazmin's body. Every muscle seized. The pain rivaled the worst of her aircraft crash and jarred her awake. Her mind was foggy, and she didn't know how long she'd been unconscious. She tried to orient herself to new surroundings, now lying on her back in a bathtub staring up at the ceiling. Her arms and legs were no longer shackled, though her muscles ached from the electrical punishment and previous bondage. Her head throbbed and she stank horribly from rotting food and stomach acid splattered down the front of her flight suit. To add to her misery, she lay in a pool of her own urine and diarrhea.

Jazmin was in a much smaller room than previously. She didn't see any exits. It was as if she were sealed inside. Before she could study her new cage for a possible escape, a holographic screen opened. One of the Chinese fighter pilots glared at her. "You stink. Clean yourself up. The boss wants to see you." Jazmin's mind wasn't working fast enough to formulate a reply before the holographic screen closed.

The tub she lay in had a faucet at one end. There were liquid soap, towels, and clean clothes. She sat up and willed the room to stop spinning, then removed her filthy flight suit and tossed it into the waste chute. While undressing, her hand brushed against a snug collar encircling her neck. When Jazmin probed the collar with her fingers to see if she could remove it, a holographic screen opened again, and the same angry pilot's face glared contemptuously at her. "Training device for dog." Another surge of pain slammed Jazmin. "Don't touch again." The screen vanished. After taking several minutes to recover from the electric shock, Jazmin focused on making herself feel human again.

Using the spray wand, she hosed herself off with cold water and lathered with industrial detergent. A chemical smell like a janitor's closet clung to her, though this was an improvement from stinking like a sewer. Using a thin towel, she dried herself off and dressed in the ill-fitting clothes. She looked like a private on their first day of boot camp in the Chinese army, minus combat boots.

A wall slid open, exposing an elegant room with thick carpeting, furniture upholstered in ornate fabrics, and a polished teak table. A linen napkin-lined basket with warm plain and chocolate croissants sat in the center of the table, along with carafes of sparkling water and orange juice. Crystal glasses, porcelain cups, and pots of tea and black coffee were placed to one side.

Senator Jiang gestured to the chair opposite her. "Commander Hassani, please join me and enjoy some breakfast." The senator wore a perfectly-tailored silk dress and looked as if she were hosting a party at her home. Her smile was warm, controlled, and well-rehearsed.

The games continue, thought Jazmin. She wasn't sure how long she'd lost consciousness, though her stomach was empty. The pastries smelled fabulous, and the aroma of fresh coffee called to her. She desperately wanted to clear her head.

Using serving tongs, Jiang filled a plate with fresh pastries and placed it in front of Jazmin along with a white linen napkin. She poured coffee into an ornate porcelain cup and added two sugar cubes.

"I believe you take it black with sugar." It wasn't a question. Jazmin eyed the pastries and coffee suspiciously.

Jiang said, "It's not drugged, Commander. I want you to remember this conversation." Jiang served herself a croissant from the basket and refilled her cup of tea. She tore a piece of croissant off one end and crumbs fluttered down to her plate. She placed it in her mouth and savored the pastry. "I do love croissants." She dabbed at her mouth with a napkin. "Savor this breakfast. It's the last one like it you'll get for a long time. They don't serve this in North Korean prison camps. However, you'll only make it that far if you survive interrogation by Chinese Military Intelligence and prove yourself useful."

Jazmin reminded herself that the only way she'd ever get retribution was by surviving. She picked up a chocolate croissant and took a large bite. "These are fabulous. You'll have to give me the name of the pâtisserie that made these. It was so thoughtful of you to stop by and bring such a wonderful breakfast."

Jiang looked at Jazmin with a mix of amusement and irritation. "Commander, you're more resilient than most of my enemies, but I always win. If you think the last few days were rugged, wait until I turn you over to the professionals. You'll have no end of misery."

Jazmin didn't think about what was coming. Instead, she focused on learning everything she could from Jiang. The senator's words and facial expressions were being permanently recorded by her bionic eyes and ears. Jazmin wouldn't get this opportunity again. She took another bite of the chocolate croissant and took several sips of coffee hoping the caffeine would clear her head. "I'm sure your constituents would love to find out about your close ties to Chinese Military Intelligence. It's certain to motivate your voters for your upcoming election."

Jiang laughed. "The sheep who vote for me will only know what I tell them to believe. They think everything else are lies. Voter suppression will take care of the rest. The ruling party of China has been an outstanding role model." Jiang leaned forward, her angry stare drilling into Jazmin. "Dissidents will be reeducated, their confused thinking beaten out of them."

Jazmin shuddered inside and did her best not to react. "Why start a war with China? Win or lose, it will be devastating for both countries."

Jiang tore a croissant in half, crumbs scattered everywhere. "Americans are pompous and arrogant. They need to be taught a lesson."

Jazmin drained the rest of her coffee. "You're an American citizen."

Jiang flashed an icy smile. "I'm Chinese first, and China will prevail."

Jazmin leaned forward and spoke in a whisper. "Remember that when hypersonic missiles fill the sky over China, and everything you love is vaporized."

Jiang wiped the buttery crumbs from her hands and stood. "We're done."

A panel behind Jiang opened and two of the Chinese pilots marched in. The shock collar around Jazmin's neck surged with a jolt of electricity that paralyzed her, and she fell to the floor in agony as her muscles spasmed uncontrollably. The two pilots wrenched her arms behind her back, handcuffed her, and hauled her out of the room. A third pilot joined them and carried Jazmin to a waiting cargo plane. They chained her to a cargo tie down ring in the back of the jet. Then the three pilots disappeared into the crew compartment and sealed the door.

A few minutes later the aircraft spun up its jet engines and taxied to the runway. Once they were wheels up, Jazmin thought about what was coming. She steeled herself for a brutal interrogation. It wasn't a question of whether they'd break her, only how long it would take and how much she could endure before she gave in to the hopelessness of her situation.

Chapter 60
Mei Chan

Chinese Military Intelligence Headquarters
23 July

Mei saw the incoming encrypted video call from Ling Chen and was both relieved and infuriated. She cleared her subordinates from her office and accepted the video call. Mei was in no mood for pleasantries. "Where the hell are you?"

Ling Chen smiled. "Not in the US and not in China."

"Are you trying to start a war?"

Ling Chen's expression turned sour. "You should be congratulating me. I achieved the objectives of our war games with the added bonus of blaming it all on a domestic terrorist, Jazmin Hassani."

Mei said, "The US government will blame China. Your stunt was an insane act of brinkmanship. It can't end well, which is why I forbade it."

Ling Chen's face lit up in a mischievous smile. "Too late now."

Mei vowed to find Ling Chen and terminate their relationship. She bit back her anger. "How does Hassani play into this?"

Ling Chen laughed. "Hassani was involved in the attack on the carrier but was shot down. I had her in custody outside the US, along with the three mercenary pilots who actually carried out the attack on the carrier. The hired pilots were previously officers in the Chinese Air Force. I'm sending all four to you. They're in the air now. You're the spymaster. I'm sure you'll find a way to use them to your advantage. Better with you than in American hands."

Mei knew Hassani and the three mercenary pilots wouldn't solve her problem, though they could be used as bargaining chips to buy time with her superiors until Ping Zhao could make her move. As long as Mei was doing something positive to resolve the situation with the Americans, her boss would give her a free hand. "Reroute them to the American black site. I'll arrange a transfer there. Also, I want you here. Be on the next plane."

Ling Chen shook her head. "That's not going to happen."

"There will be a reckoning."

"At the time of my choosing." Ling Chen ended the call.

Mei knew there was nothing to be gained by calling back. She wanted to call Ping Zhao but restrained herself. She had to wait until Zhao was ready.

Chapter 61
Francesca Navarro

Oval Office – The White House
23 July

Francesca Navarro barely kept her rage in check while waiting for the Chinese ambassador to arrive in the Oval Office. She wanted quiet time before the coming confrontation, afraid she'd lash out at her staff when she needed them most. She'd already spent hours making condolence calls and meeting with families of the service members killed in the attack. She owed a debt to the people who had lost their lives defending their country. Meeting with their families was only a down payment. After the latest briefing on the aftermath of the aircraft carrier sinking, Navarro had decided that her response needed to send an unmistakable message to the country's number one rival. While the size of China's military now surpassed that of the United States, America was still a global superpower that didn't back down from a fight.

The National Security Advisor, Secretary of State, and Chairman of the Joint Chiefs entered the Oval Office. Navarro came out from behind her desk. "This will be a standing meeting." Her three top advisors looked as grim as she felt.

The head of her Secret Service detail knocked on the open door. "Madam President, the Chinese ambassador is here."

Navarro said, "Bring her in."

A moment later the Chinese ambassador, Wei Kuang, entered the Oval Office. A career diplomat, Kuang had been China's ambassador for the last nine years. Educated in China with advanced degrees from Harvard and Stanford, she spoke flawless English and had an excellent grasp of US politics. Kuang scanned the angry faces in the room, then her gaze locked onto Navarro's. "Madam President, on behalf of the Chinese people, we offer our sincere condolences on the recent naval attack and loss of life of the service members and civilians involved. We will do everything in our power to assist the US in finding the source of this unprovoked attack."

Navarro glared at Kuang. "You can start by looking in the mirror."

Kuang recoiled like she'd been slapped. After taking a deep breath, she regained her composure. "Madam President, I assure you, China was not behind the attack on your carrier group."

"Ambassador Kuang, we have credible evidence that shows otherwise. I've ordered our nuclear arsenal to an increased readiness status. In addition, I've requested that Congress approve a declaration of war against China. There will be a cost for attacking the United States of America."

"Madam President, I state again, China was not responsible for this attack. A war with the US would be devastating for both our countries. All appropriate Chinese government agencies are investigating this senseless attack, and we will openly share our findings. It's in both of our nations' best interests that the world's superpowers remain allies."

Navarro narrowed her eyes and clapped. "Bravo for your impassioned speech, Ambassador. I don't believe a word of it, starting with China openly sharing anything except state propaganda. Our countries have never been allies. You're welcome to investigate from China. The Chinese embassy is officially closed. The entire Chinese delegation has forty-eight hours to leave the United States or face arrest for espionage."

Blood drained from Kuang's face, and her light complexion went even whiter. The ambassador stiffened like a soldier coming to attention. "You will regret this decision, Madam President." Kuang turned and left the Oval Office. Navarro had no regrets about today's outcome. She'd wanted to kick out China's ambassador and their entire delegation long ago.

Chapter 62
Jazmin Hassani

Cargo Jet Flying over the Pacific Ocean
23 July

Shackled to the floor, Jazmin lay face down in the cold cargo compartment of the jet. Everything hurt. It was a long flight from Canada to China. Pain kept her angry and focused. The three pilots were in the crew compartment, leaving Jazmin alone to imagine the horrors that awaited her at the end of the trip. Time to think was worse than being tortured, as her mind wandered to ever darker places. Once she arrived in China, her chances of escape or rescue by the United States were effectively zero. No US president would spend their political capital on rescuing a terrorist from a foreign government. Even if the Wisconsin Militia figured out what had happened to her, they didn't have the resources to mount a rescue operation. She was on her own.

Jazmin rolled over onto her back and sat up. Her hands were shackled behind her but the chain between her wrists was longer than on standard handcuffs. This allowed her to contort her bionic legs and maneuver her hands in front of her. The electric jolts from the shock collar had wreaked havoc on Jazmin's muscles, though her neurotech and bionic parts weren't impacted. She resisted the urge to touch the collar and test for a release. The last time she had done that, the collar detected her touch and automatically shocked her. She closed her eyes for a moment to think. When she opened them, she stared at the names tattooed on her right arm and reminded herself of her debt to them. She'd have to find a way out before the jet landed.

The cargo compartment was filled with special ops gear, including parachutes, assault rifles, handguns, grenade launchers, explosives, and laser cutters. The controls for the rear cargo door and ramp were halfway back on the jet's sidewall. Jazmin studied the interior of the aircraft to determine its model and manufacturer. It was a commercial aircraft, as these were more readily available on the open market than military versions. The jet was likely owned by a shell company to hide its use by a mercenary group controlled by Senator Jiang. Since the American government was ultimately supporting the black ops contracts, the plane was manufactured in the US. Thanks to Harry's magic, her special ops security overrides still functioned, and the plane's powerful radios connected her to the military network. Jazmin scanned the jet's control systems and autopilot with her neurotech. Unlike military assets, pilot in command control protocols weren't in place, so she easily bypassed the civilian biometric security system. She verified the autopilot had control of the aircraft, then locked out the manual flight controls.

The plane was capable of both remote and independent AI control. Since it could fly without a human crew, the fire suppression systems were automatic. The jet had two independent synthetic halon fire extinguishing systems, one for the cargo area and one for the flight crew cabin. The chemical didn't conduct electricity, was effective on all types of fires, and left no residue behind. It was also fatal to humans. Jazmin locked the crew compartment door and disabled the emergency oxygen masks. She checked the cockpit video cameras. One pilot was sleeping, the other two were listening to music. Jazmin triggered the fire alarm, and all three pilots were jolted from their restful states. They frantically searched the control panel for warning messages and found nothing. Next, she flooded the crew compartment with synthetic halon. Within seconds the pilots were gasping for breath and began to asphyxiate. Panicked, they tried to shut down the fire extinguishers and get oxygen flowing through the masks that had automatically deployed, but no life-giving air came out. One of the pilots tried to force the aircraft into a dive, but the plane wouldn't respond. Desperate to breathe, one tried to exit the crew compartment, beating on the door, but the latch wouldn't open. She pounded on the door to no avail, her feeble slaps stopping when she passed out. Jazmin waited ten more minutes to ensure the pilots were dead, then stopped the halon. She was the sole survivor.

It was time to free herself. She took manual control of the aircraft and banked it violently several times until one of the laser cutting tools slid out of its mounting bracket and dropped to the floor. Using more controlled maneuvers and nosing the aircraft downward, Jazmin slid the laser cutter to within reach. She fired it up, removed her handcuffs, and routed the cargo jet back toward the US. She didn't have a plan yet, but at least she was heading in the right direction.

Her next priority was to remove the shock collar. She grabbed a handgun and chambered a round, just in case one of the Chinese pilots had survived. The residual halon would be toxic, so she picked up a portable oxygen tank, slipped on the mask, and turned the handle to start the air flowing. She moved to the front of the aircraft, unlocked the door with her neurotech and pushed the door inward. Two of the dead pilots were still strapped in their seats. The third lay on the floor with bloodied knuckles. Jazmin removed the shock collar control from the woman's belt, backed out of the cockpit, and closed the door. Their faces would be added to ghosts haunting Jazmin in her darker moments.

She studied the shock collar control and consulted the military database. After locating the unit's instructions, she pressed a series of Chinese characters to deactivate it, then felt for the release on her neck. As soon as the collar dropped to the floor, she knelt and repeatedly smashed it with the butt of her gun until it was pulverized. Jazmin sat on the floor and leaned against the front wall of the aircraft, taking a few deep breaths to calm herself. She had to get off the cargo jet undetected, and that would be impossible any place with a long enough runway to land. The parachutes onboard might provide an escape route, but she'd need to fly considerably lower before she could safely use them.

Using her neurotech, Jazmin updated the jet's flight plan to Bellingham International Airport in Washington state. It was just over the border from Canada and a common destination for international flights, so she wouldn't trip an immediate NORAD alert. The autopilot system would handle communication with the tower systems and fit her into the approach pattern.

She went to the rear of the plane and found a parachute, wrist altimeter, flight suit, helmet, goggles, and jump boots that fit. She also located a leg holster and spare ammunition for the 9mm handgun. She updated the flight plan to reroute her aircraft to Harvey Field, a non-towered airport about seventy-five miles south of Bellingham. The airstrip was adjacent to a skydiving area with a skydiving school. Using her neurotech, she programmed a series of actions for the jet to execute once she bailed out. The rear cargo door would close behind her. The aircraft would declare an inflight emergency. Communications would cease. The jet would turn west over the Pacific Ocean, go into a steep dive, and level off at 150 feet above the water. When the jet ran out of fuel, it would crash into deep water.

The autopilot flew the cargo jet over the drop zone northwest of the airfield at an altitude of 14,500 feet and slowed her airspeed to 150 MPH. This was the highest she could parachute from without supplemental oxygen. Once air pressure equalized in the cabin, Jazmin lowered the rear cargo door ramp. She looked out at the expanse below, jumped off the ramp, and remained in freefall using her arms, legs, and body position to keep her in the parachute drop zone. At 3,000 feet, she opened her chute and steered to a grassy area. She touched down and rolled, then collected her chute and headed to the skydiving school.

***

The skydiving school specialized in students taking their first jumps, so the few people who saw her would probably assume she was an instructor. She tossed her parachute, helmet, and goggles in a dumpster, then checked the parking lot for a car she could steal. Using her neurotech, Jazmin unlocked a car from a self-driving fleet and set the destination for Bellingham International Airport, where she would search for an aircraft she could use to fly to Wisconsin.

Forty minutes later she ditched the car in long-term parking on the general aviation side of the airport and set the log to overwrite the trip record. She headed to the plane parking ramp. Most of the aircraft were single or twin-engine piston planes which would require multiple fuel stops. Then she saw a freshly washed Cessna Citation private jet; it would have plenty of range to get her home. She used her neurotech to learn it was owned by Pulse Weapons Labs and used by one of the senators from Washington who was on the Armed Services Committee with Senator Jiang. Jazmin checked the jet's flight log. The aircraft had flown multiple trips between Bellingham, DC, and Chicago. It would be a good addition to the militia's fleet and help appease Gadget for the loss of the F-22.

The commercial security was easy to bypass with her military overrides. Jazmin entered the cockpit, then projected a holographic screen showing the pilot handbook. She memorized key data including takeoff and landing speeds, stall speed, landing roll, and max rate of climb. She checked the fuel level – the gas tanks were full. She filed a flight plan for Chicago, planning to change it midair to Bayfield and have Harry erase both flight plans from the national system. She called the tower for takeoff clearance, and ten minutes later she was airborne.

***

Once she was in range of the Bayfield base, Jazmin opened a full hivemind connection to Harry. He immediately accepted and his emotional relief flooded over her.

I thought you were at the bottom of the ocean or worse.

I was both.

Once you disappeared Gadget and I stayed as long as we could, but we had to head back to Wisconsin before our covers were blown.

Jazmin fought to keep dreadful images of the last several days from overwhelming her senses. She had to focus on flying the unfamiliar plane. She'd deal with her trauma later.

Where are you? What's your status?

Open the base runway. I'm in a business jet coming in dark. I need to disappear.

Understood. We'll be waiting.

Jazmin closed the hivemind connection. She had to land an unfamiliar aircraft and needed to concentrate. After checking TCAS, Traffic Alert and Collision Avoidance System, for any other air traffic, she lined up her approach and aimed for the runway apron. She lowered the landing gear and flaps, then throttled back to 200 knots. As soon as she touched down, she brought the engines to idle and braked. She shut down the engines and let out a long breath. She'd made it home.

Using her neurotech to connect to exterior militia cameras, Jazmin watched as a robot tugger connected to the plane's nose gear and pulled the jet down the ramp into the underground hangar. As soon as the jet had cleared the ramp, the ground opening was sealed. Ground cover pulled over the runway with an audible whir, making it invisible from the air.

Stepping down from the door of the aircraft, she was engulfed by Harry's arms. He took her face in his hands and kissed her like he had when they'd made love a lifetime ago. He hugged her tightly. "Thank God you made it back." Part of Jazmin wanted to feel for Harry like she had in the past, but she was too much of an emotional train wreck right now to deal with her feelings for him. She was relieved to be alive.

Jazmin's mom ran up and wrapped her into a crushing hug. "I was so worried." Her mom held her with tears running down her face. Jazmin was numb. She wasn't ready to deal with her mom, either. She extracted herself from her mother's iron grip. The older woman looked stricken and finally let go. Suresh stood back from the plane with Gadget by her side. The general said, "Welcome back, Commander. Glad you made it home. When you're ready, we'll need a debrief for senior staff." Her face morphed into a worried expression mirrored by Gadget.

Jazmin looked at Gadget. "I brought you a new plane to add to your collection. Sorry about the F-22." She pushed past them and headed to her quarters. All she cared about was a hot shower, her own clothes, and drowning herself in a case of bourbon.

Chapter 63

Wisconsin Militia Base
Bayfield, Wisconsin
23 July

Jazmin stood under the cascading water as steam swirled around her in the cramped shower stall. She scrubbed herself with her favorite scented soap, lathered her hair with shampoo, then rinsed thoroughly. She'd lost track of how many times she'd repeated this cycle. The parts of her still covered in human skin were wrinkled from long exposure to hot water. She felt less soiled and smelled like herself, though she feared she'd never be clean again. When the water turned cold, she turned it off, stepped out of the shower, and stared blankly at the woman in the mirror. The reflected image resembled her but felt like a stranger, both familiar and unrecognizable at the same time. She'd kept her new face after the changes required to break her mother out of prison. She saw a family resemblance, but it wasn't who she'd been her whole life.

Tired of the confines of her quarters, Jazmin went to the dining hall to eat a meal she chose, instead of whatever was forced down her throat. She picked out a New York strip steak, fried onion rings, and a chocolate tart. She cut the rare steak into small pieces and chewed slowly. Harry, Derez, and Gadget were across the room. They didn't invite her to join them or intrude on her table of one.

She could tell by the sad look in Harry's eyes he wanted to be with her, to save her, though she felt beyond saving. Thankfully he kept his distance.

Jazmin's mom appeared and, without asking, sat across from her. No one could help her now. Her mom reached out for Jazmin's hand, but she just pulled away. She didn't want to be touched by anyone, including her mom. Tears rolled down her mother's face. A moment later she stood and backed away.

Jazmin finished her meal in silence and headed to the lounge. She wanted to curl up with a bottle of bourbon, but militia rules forbade private drinking. Alcohol could only be consumed in the lounge. It was tracked to make sure no one abused it, though some alcohol abuse was what she needed right now. The room was unusually empty. She sat at the bar and waited for Oscar, the bearded, barrel-chested android bartender. Normally he would appear seconds after she sat down. She needed a drink. Impatient, she called out, "Oscar, there's a customer at the bar." Silence. Frustrated, she stood and peered over the counter. Everything was in order except no bartender. Bottles filled the back wall of the bar, but this was all for show. Anything that went into a glass came out of the bartender's drink nozzle, was precisely measured, and assigned to a militia member's tab.

Jazmin was about to leave when Monty walked in. He sat at a high-top table and waved. "Join me for a drink?"

"Sure, if you can find the bartender." She sat across from him and a moment later Oscar appeared.

"Good evening, doctor. What can I get for you?"

Monty said, "Two of my usual."

"Coming right up." Oscar went behind the bar and returned with a tray. He set down two highball glasses filled with a clear liquid and several ice cubes. Jazmin craved a glass of bourbon, but vodka would be a fine start. As soon as the barman disappeared, Monty picked up his drink. "Cheers." They clinked glasses. When Jazmin tasted her drink, disappointment bloomed into anger.

"It's water." She slammed her glass down onto the table. A wave of water and ice cubes flew out, landing on the high-top's polished surface and dripping on the floor. "I thought we were having a drink together."

Monty feigned surprise. "We are. This is my favorite bottled water from a mountain spring in Colorado. No purifying chemicals.

I think it tastes wonderful."

Jazmin glared at him. "Why are you here?"

Monty took a sip of his drink and set it down on the table. "Just enjoying a drink with a colleague."

"Cut the crap, Doctor. We're alone and I'm barred from ordering a decent drink. What's your real agenda?"

Monty's expression hardened. "I've read your file, and we both know exactly what's going on. I'm a retired military doc who'd rather be fishing at my mountain cabin, but I have too much respect for your commander to let one of her senior officers self-medicate her well-documented PTSD symptoms. You've been down this rabbit hole before, and you know exactly how it works."

She knocked her glass sideways. It spun in the air and arced to the floor, erupting in an explosion of glass shrapnel. "I'm no longer in the military. You can't drug me."

Monty leaned forward and lowered his voice. "The same rules apply here. We can do this the easy way or the hard way." He pulled a pill bottle from his pocket and placed a single tablet in her hand. "You stop by the clinic every twelve hours for another pill. Your alternative is I inject you with drug nanobots."

Jazmin shuddered at the thought of nanobots running around inside her and changing her brain chemistry. In rehab the people who took oral medication usually had better outcomes than those who were injected with nanobots. She stared at the pill in her hand, trying to delay the inevitable. Oscar appeared by her side with an encouraging expression and handed her a shatterproof glass of cool water. She hated happy dust, but this was the least unpleasant of several lousy options, the worst being thrown out of the militia and subjected to a memory wipe. She popped the pill in her mouth and drank the entire glass of water. Within a couple of minutes her anger dissipated, and she felt more relaxed and focused than she had in a long time.

Monty sat quietly and watched her. "I prescribed a seven-day run. A three-day frontload followed by a four day taper. The goal is to stabilize your brain chemistry. No alcohol, not a single drop. You're cut off from here. Don't make the mistake of swiping someone else's drink. This drug doesn't play nice with booze."

Jazmin closed her eyes, took a deep breath, and let it out slowly. "I saw what happened to soldiers in rehab who violated that order. It wasn't pretty, and they never got right in the head."

He looked at her like he was measuring her resolve. "This isn't a cure. You need more help than I can give you. My job is to keep you from self-destructing." He reached out and put his hand on her arm. "You know Dexter's in love with you. It would kill him if you came to a bad end. He was a mess when your plane went down in the Pacific."

Jazmin looked away for a moment then back at Monty. "I know. Harry and I have a complicated history."

"I hope you can hang in there and get yourself straight so you can figure it out."

Jazmin was silent as she wrestled with her messy relationship with Harry. Quietly, almost to herself, she said "Me too."

Chapter 64

Wisconsin Militia Base
Bayfield, Wisconsin
30 July

After the seven-day drug treatment and time to decompress, Jazmin felt stable again. She was functional, but she had even more to compartmentalize and shove into sealed containers. Jazmin stayed out of the lounge, not trusting herself to handle alcohol even if she was past the danger of a nasty drug interaction. Monty had cleared her for duty, except for flying and combat operations. She spent time with Harry, though she wasn't ready to deal with how she felt about him. Their conversations were superficial, and it was obvious Harry wanted to say more, though he held back.

Despite being surrounded by people who cared for her and protected her from frightening enemies, the militia base felt like a cage. Her life was no different from that of a zoo animal who hated confinement but wasn't safe in the wild. She knew her mom was desperate to help her but didn't know how. Catarina provided the solution. As her mother's android copy, Catarina knew Mercedes intimately and embraced her love of family. By spending countless hours with Mercedes, Catarina had also evolved. The two women treated each other like sisters. Their relationship created an interesting dynamic that Jazmin was still processing and that her dad would eventually need to accept. With access to the most effective PTSD treatments and the combined professional knowledge of the best practitioners in the field, Catarina was a superb counselor.

Jazmin sat across from Catarina in one of the small conference rooms they used to talk through all of her mental health issues. As always, Catarina dressed differently for these sessions than she did while working on aircraft in the hangar. She looked the part of a professional counselor, wearing a tailored suit with a silk blouse instead of a grease-stained jumpsuit.

Jazmin said, "Thanks for all of your help talking through my issues. My mom wants to help me, but she's too close. You have all of her personal knowledge and care without all the baggage. You can keep your professional distance. I appreciate you keeping my mom informed, so I don't have to face her."

Catarina smiled. "I'm glad I could help. I've grown really close to Mercedes, and I know how much she loves you. This whole process has been good for me, too. I'm becoming more human."

Catarina's last statement was a little jarring. Jazmin still hadn't come to terms with how she felt about androids. So much of herself was indistinguishable from an android, and those were the parts she had the hardest time accepting. Working with Catarina had blurred the lines between androids and humans.

Jazmin said, "Thanks for being there for the debrief sessions with senior staff. It was tough being questioned by the general, Harry, Gadget, and Derez. I know they weren't trying to gang up on me, but sometimes it felt that way."

"They were just trying to understand what you experienced, especially when you were captured. Remember, you have a joint enemy. They want to help you."

"They'll never hate that enemy the way I do." Jazmin stared at the names tattooed on her arm. "I still have a debt to pay."

Catarina said, "Let them help you. Have you thought about how to use the recording of the last conversation you had with Senator Jiang?"

"I need to release it to people who will believe it's authentic and not a deep fake."

"General Suresh can do that."

Jazmin shook her head. "It can't be done in a vacuum. I need to put together a more complete package. I'll give it to the general when that's done."

"Don't wait too long."

Jazmin nodded. "I won't." She checked her watch. Their time today was done.

Chapter 65

Wisconsin Militia Base
Bayfield, Wisconsin
10 August

For the first time since she had escaped the senator, Jazmin started quadcopter flight training on the simulator. It was one of her favorite aircraft, and she wanted to feel the joy of flying again. During flight training, she received an alert on her tablet from General Suresh. *Senior staff to the ops center.*

***

Suresh paced along the top level in the ops center. The normally cool flag officer looked more agitated than Jazmin had ever seen her. A minute later Harry, Derez, and Gadget arrived. Once they saw the general's demeanor, concerned looks flashed between them. Everyone took their seats. Suresh said, "Congress just passed a declaration of war against China, and the President plans to sign it later today. All the services have been moved to DEFCON 2."

Harry asked, "Have there been further combat operations on either side?"

Suresh shook her head. "Neither side has pulled the trigger yet, though there's lots of posturing. China insists they didn't sink our aircraft carrier."

"That's because they didn't," said Jazmin.

"Knowing that and proving it are two different things," said Suresh. "We have a credibility gap. Jiang and Trabago have done a masterful job of convincing Congress that China attacked and sank our aircraft carrier, and the President's out for blood after the earlier attack on Marine One, which she also blames on China."

Derez asked, "What military attack plans are in place?"

Suresh said, "As a geopolitical rival, all the services have extensive attack plans for China, with nuclear war always the last option. The President is demanding an equivalent response for the attack on our carrier group. Even if we stop at sinking a Chinese aircraft carrier, China's response would result in a further escalation."

"General, what's the mood of the flag officers you're in touch with?" asked Harry.

Suresh pursed her lips. "Their pucker factor is higher than I've ever seen it. Peace is a fragile thing. There are so many military alliances, they're terrified of starting a third world war. The military leaders are trying to keep the President from initiating a reckless attack."

Jazmin said, "Is there any meaningful dialogue with the Chinese? While they didn't initiate the attack, they've sponsored Jiang for years."

Suresh stopped pacing. "Now that the Chinese diplomatic corps has been sent home and the embassy and consulates closed, no one's talking. Certainly not officials high enough up in either government to put the brakes on."

Gadget asked, "Can we use the three dead Chinese pilots to prove the case against Jiang?"

The general shook her head. "They're at the bottom of the ocean. Any evidence we provide will be written off as AI fakes. Even if the Chinese acknowledge they were former military pilots, they'll claim they were rogue assets working for the US."

Jazmin said, "I have a contact in the Chinese Navy, Daiyu Teng, an intelligence officer. We met years ago when I was stationed in East Asia and our militaries were on better terms. She's a captain and well respected. I was in contact with her a couple of times a year until recently. She's smart and an independent thinker. I can reach out to her with what we know."

Suresh sat on the edge of the workstation table while competing emotions flashed across her face. "It's a risk, though doing nothing is a bigger risk. Captain Teng would be jeopardizing her career to help us. It's a lot to ask."

Derez said, "It's a better option than being vaporized by a missile attack."

"General, can I contact Captain Teng?"

Suresh said, "Yes. Proceed carefully."

Jazmin located the dossier she and Harry put together on Jiang which they had sent to the news agencies and projected it on the main holographic screen. "It's time to update and expand this report, along with cockpit video I shot of those F-15s when I was in Mexican airspace. President Navarro needs to see this. I'll also send the recording of my conversation with Senator Jiang."

Suresh said, "That will certainly get her attention. How do you propose to get it in front of her?"

"We send it to cabinet members and agencies that work for her. The press corps will also force the issue."

Suresh nodded. "Jazmin, Harry, make sure I see it before it goes out. We'll need help from my network." The general stood. "That's it for now."

Jazmin waited for the others to leave the conference room. She wanted time to think. If it were up to her, she'd drop a thousand-pound bomb on Senator Jiang's condo and a second one on her house. Suresh would never authorize that course of action, so a less direct approach was needed. Jazmin's only requirement was that it ended Jiang's life.

Chapter 66

Wisconsin Militia Base
Bayfield, Wisconsin
11 August

Jazmin made an encrypted video call to her friend, Daiyu, in Chinese Naval Intelligence. She hadn't spoken to her in over a year. The two had met as part of an exchange program for US and Chinese junior officers. The program ended a year later as relations between the two countries deteriorated. Jazmin and Daiyu, both planning on military careers, had stayed in touch.

Daiyu's familiar face appeared on the screen. "Jazmin, it's been too long, especially in these uncertain times."

Jazmin said, "Uncertain times require strong friendships."

"Is this a secure line?" asked Daiyu.

"Trust is the golden key." This question and response were the same on every call. This ensured the other wasn't under duress and the line wasn't monitored.

"I'm happy to hear from you, my friend, especially on the eve of war. We live in fear our skies will fill with American missiles and each day will be our last."

"I need your help to stop this insanity. It's a war neither country wants, but our leaders can't back away."

"Tell me how I can help," said Daiyu.

Jazmin sent the names and photos of the three Chinese pilots. "These three flew the planes that attacked and sank the American aircraft carrier during the training mission."

"Give me a minute to check a military database." The screen went blank while Jazmin waited. Each second seemed an eternity. Her friend's face returned to the screen, though Daiyu's expression was grim. "All three were Chinese Air Force pilots, but they had resigned their commissions and disappeared over two years ago. We suspect they left to join mercenary companies, but none of them have been seen in China or anywhere in Asia."

"I was part of the military exercise when the carrier was sunk. I shot down one of the attacking aircraft, then was shot down myself. I was rescued, taken prisoner, and held by these three pilots. Others were part of this attack. They are tied to a mercenary group under the control of a Chinese American, US Senator Ling Chen Jiang."

"How did you get away?"

"That's a story for another day and several glasses of bourbon."

Daiyu laughed and shook her head. "You Americans love to drink and tell crazy stories." Her expression turned serious. "Where are the pilots now?"

"They're dead and their bodies will never be found." Jazmin waited a moment before asking her next question. "Did the Chinese government sponsor this attack?"

Daiyu's nostrils flared. "That's an insulting accusation."

"I'm sorry. I don't mean to insult you. Let me explain."

Daiyu narrowed her eyes. "Go on."

Jazmin shared a photo of Senator Jiang and her senate website. "We have credible evidence that Senator Jiang is supported by the Chinese government. Jiang has been helped over her entire political career by Chinese Military Intelligence, and she's now head of the Armed Services Committee. No doubt China has benefitted from this arrangement."

"Even if what you say is true, why would China start a war with America?" asked Daiyu.

"They wouldn't. Our guess is Jiang has her own agenda. China is far from innocent, but war was never intended. The Chinese embassy is closed, and the diplomats have been sent home. With the normal channels shut down, I hope there's still time for a back-channel solution. Can you find out?"

Daiyu let out a long breath, and her angry expression dissipated.

"I've heard rumors about Senator Jiang, but your question can only be answered by those above me. I served under a general in military intelligence, Mei Chan. I'll need to see her in person. I can't put any of this in writing."

Jazmin felt relieved. "Thank you, old friend. I hope peace can be restored between our countries."

"We will speak again. Hopefully for many years to come." Daiyu ended the call.

Jazmin was glad Daiyu was willing to help her. Had the Chinese captain known her American friend was now a terrorist, it would have been a very short conversation. Even now it was a long shot at best to keep war from coming. She summarized the call and sent off a message to General Suresh, copying Harry, Derez, and Gadget.

Chapter 67

Wisconsin Militia Base
Bayfield, Wisconsin
12 August

In the ops center numerous open holographic screens surrounded Jazmin and Harry. The collection of damning evidence documented the case against Senator Ling Chen Jiang, whose web ensnared numerous associates. The inner ring consisted of General Anton Trabago and Sanjay Guptarian, the CEO of Pulse Weapons Labs. The next ring contained the black ops mercenary companies, the secret black ops overseas sites, and Chinese Military Intelligence. The outermost ring was the army of defense company lobbyists. Every name was tied to evidence links on the screen, most on the dark web.

Another section of the report focused on specific events, starting with the octocopter attack at Fort McCoy, continuing with the murder of Ajax Papadakis, the attack on the Truax fighter pilots, the downing of Marine One, and ending with the sinking of the aircraft carrier. The last step for completing the report was to finalize the distribution list including the President, vice president, members of congress, three-letter agencies—NSA, CIA, DIA, FBI—the service chiefs, and the major news organizations. There was something for everyone.

When the package was complete, General Suresh, Derez, and Gadget joined Jazmin and Harry in the ops center. They took four hours to walk through each section of the report and test every link. When they finished, General Suresh said, "I'll inform my network. Then we wait for the chokehold on Jiang's neck to finish her off."

"How will the Chinese respond?" asked Harry.

Suresh said, "A lot depends on how conciliatory the Chinese are feeling." The general stood and stretched. "While the Chinese didn't attack the carrier directly, they supported Jiang for years and bear some responsibility for her actions."

"Will Navarro back away from the declaration of war?" asked Gadget.

Suresh began to pace. "Only if the Chinese offer reparations and provide lots of transparency. It could go either way."

Jazmin said, "Both sides are playing a dangerous game of brinkmanship."

Derez snorted. "Arrogance knows no bounds."

Suresh said, "Jazmin, Harry, keep a close watch on Senator Jiang. I want us to know where she is at all times, especially if she leaves the country."

"What if she does?" asked Jazmin.

"We make sure she has her day in court." Suresh picked up her tablet. "Give me one hour to contact my network, then blast out the dossier. Let's see if we can stop this war before it starts."

Jazmin was exhausted from all the research and review. At the same time, she was buzzing with nervous energy. She wanted Jiang's severed head mounted on a pole outside the White House and to be the blood-covered warrior who mounted it there.

Chapter 68

Wisconsin Militia Base
Bayfield, Wisconsin
13 August

Jazmin's tablet lit up with an encrypted video call originating from China. The ID only showed it was a government line. She answered the call and was relieved to see Daiyu Teng, though her usual cheerful expression was gone. "You lied to me. I was a fool to believe a terrorist. I went to a general officer with your incredible story and put my reputation on the line. Now it's in tatters, and I'm being watched. I was lectured by Mei Chan for my stupidity."

Jazmin felt hope fall away and shatter on the rocks below. She struggled for something to say to mitigate this disaster. "You have every right to be mad. I should have told you when we spoke the first time."

Daiyu's face reddened. "Did you think we were stupid? That we wouldn't know? You underestimate our intelligence services. You're not the officer and friend I knew."

Jazmin had lost her toehold in Chinese Military Intelligence. She hadn't planned to share the complete dossier on Jiang with China. Given the wide circulation already, especially to news organizations, there was a good chance they already had a copy. "My situation is complicated, and I have no right to expect you to believe anything

I say. I'm sending you a dossier on Senator Jiang that was shared with government agencies and news organizations. Review the evidence yourself and share it with your intelligence service if you see fit." Jazmin attached the full document to the video call link.

"I will look at it on an isolated system, because I'm curious about your lies and how you Americans think. Goodbye, Jazmin. Don't contact me again." The call disconnected.

Jazmin knew Daiyu would have her team dissect the dossier. She had no way to know whether it would be passed on, written off as an elaborate fake, or ignored as an exercise in American deception. Only time would tell. Since Jazmin had no other back channel contacts in China, she'd just have to wait.

Chapter 69

Wisconsin Militia Base
Bayfield, Wisconsin
14 August

At 0300 hours, automated alerts woke Jazmin. She rushed to the ops center. Suresh, Harry, Derez, and Gadget joined her, and they reviewed the threat warnings together. All were generated by AI programs tracking the mercenary groups tied to Jiang.

Suresh said, "Harry, what's your assessment?"

"The AI algorithms focus on communication traffic at mercenary group locations or cells tied to the core groups. There's been a massive increase in transmissions similar to what we've seen just prior to ops. People and equipment are moving."

Suresh studied the screens. "What story do the geolocation patterns tell?"

Harry said, "Not a good one." He opened two additional holographic screens. The first showed comms traffic over time. "The patterns show they're in the pre-attack phase. There's a high probability teams will carry out operations in the next twelve to twenty-four hours." The second screen showed a heat map of mercenary assets active in northern Wisconsin. "Our base is the epicenter of all the mercenary activity."

Suresh turned her gaze away from the screens and focused on

her senior officers. "Jiang and her minions are lashing out. It's time to end this. All options are on the table. I want specific action plans from each of you."

Derez spoke first. "I'll recall all militia members who can be on station within eight hours, activate perimeter weapons systems, and set up a manned defensive perimeter around the base. My team will reroute all civilian ground traffic in the area."

Gadget was next. "I'll head to the maintenance hangar and have my team fuel and load weapons on all combat ready rotorcraft and ground vehicles. It's time to lower the trip warning threshold for external sensor arrays and activate android sentries."

Harry said, "I'll update real-time AI predictive models to show likely engagement points. My team will track assets and outcomes in the ops center. I'll also generate a barrage of simulated comms traffic to the mercenary groups, with constantly changing directives from Jiang."

Jazmin said, "I'll have the FAA declare a no-fly zone for a fifty-mile radius to limit collateral damage. Then I'll start combat air patrols with drones and our quadcopter. Catarina is an excellent pilot. She can control the drone fleet while I fly the fast-attack quadcopter."

Suresh said, "Execute all your plans. I'll warn my network that Jiang started a war she can't win. My contacts will send the message to the military and clandestine services to stay clear, so they can avoid the crossfire. We reconvene in four hours for a status update."

The others exited the ops center, leaving Jazmin alone in the room. She was still battling too many mental health issues, and it was a struggle to get through each day. A sense of dread gripped her as flashbacks from her accident, rehab, and incarceration in Canada flooded her mind.

She closed her eyes, wanting to be anywhere else, but she knew this was a fight she couldn't run from. After a moment, she opened her eyes and forced herself to focus only on what she had to do next. She didn't have the authority with the FAA to declare a temporary no-fly zone, so she'd have to work through Ebony Diamond. She hoped the captain was still an ally.

Chapter 70

Wisconsin Militia Base
Bayfield, Wisconsin
14 August

Jazmin contacted Captain Diamond on an untraceable encrypted line. Diamond accepted the call. "Identify yourself."

"The zombie pilot is back. Others died instead."

"I'm not surprised. I read the dossier you and Harry put together. There's nobody in Washington brave enough to go after Jiang in the open. The senator is radioactive, and most people are locking themselves in their panic rooms. Only a select few are brave enough to line up a kill shot from the shadows."

"Jiang is rallying her flying monkeys and they're enroute to Bayfield. This place is about to be a warzone. We need to declare a no-fly zone with a radius of fifty miles of the underground militia base that isn't on any maps, or civilians will get caught in the crossfire. Can you convince the FAA? My designation as a terrorist would derail the conversation."

Diamond laughed. "I've been monitoring activity around Bayfield too. Lots of all the wrong kind. Would you like a little extra aerial firepower?"

"Only if you can flush out the tourists first."

"I'm planning a live fire, fast-attack quadcopter exercise.

Lieutenant Commander Jack Macy will be joining me, and he's especially motivated. He's the brother of the pilot you interviewed at the Milwaukee Joint Military Rehab Facility."

"Sounds like a great opportunity to practice reverse maglev captures. Can you get here in the next twelve hours?"

Diamond hesitated. "That's a little tight. Maybe sixteen. It will be a good test for Commander Macy."

"I'll have Gadget arrange quarters for the two of you. Contact me when you're enroute. We'll boot the locals out and lock the base down tight. We'll make the dead mercenaries disappear, but we can't do the same for any locals caught in the crossfire."

"Macy will send you updates. His callsign is Sniper."

"Good hunting, Shockwave." Jazmin ended the call. It was time to reconvene in the ops center with an update. She felt the adrenaline buzz of combat, the potent mixture of excitement, resolve, and fear that kept her wired for action. The familiar buildup was back, and she welcomed the high. Her sense of dread was shoved aside for now, but when the fighting was over, she'd need Catarina's help to manage her unresolved issues.

Chapter 71

Wisconsin Militia Base
Bayfield, Wisconsin
14 August

Jazmin, Harry, Gadget, Derez, and Suresh were in the ops center, ready for war. All wore camouflage uniforms with their former military rank and carried holstered sidearms. They also wore tactical vests with extra 9mm 15-round magazines. If they ran into civilians while outside the militia base, they'd look like active-duty military and carry the authority to move people away from the coming danger. Derez would lead the outside patrols, so in addition to his sidearm, he carried an assault rifle and four anti-personnel grenades.

Suresh said, "Washington is buzzing from the fallout of the dossier on Senator Jiang. All the service chiefs are on a knife's edge from the declaration of war on China, and the clandestine services are tracking a heightened level of activity. Everyone is chasing shadows or running from them. I've never seen it this bad."

Harry again projected his two charts showing mercenary communication and movement in the area. "All indicators are accelerating. Our enemies are tightening the circle around us."

"How soon before they're in position?" asked Suresh.

Harry projected a time stamp on one of the charts. "They'll hit us tonight in the wee hours."

Derez cradled his assault rifle. "The after-hours welcoming committee will be waiting for them." With an evil smile, he touched the grenades on his belt. "We have incentives for early checkouts."

"How is our personnel count?" asked Suresh.

Derez said, "We're at eighty percent and expect a full complement by nightfall."

The general turned to Gadget. "What's our vehicle and airborne equipment status?"

"Ground vehicles, aircraft, and drones are all fueled with weapons loaded."

Harry said, "All personnel have checked out weapons from the armory. We have plenty of stock if things go longer than expected."

"Let's hope they don't," said Suresh. "Has anyone checked in with Monty? Are we ready for casualties?"

Derez said, "The other combat medics are coordinating with Monty. There's an additional trauma surgeon, three triage nurses, and four operating room nurses inbound."

"How are we on air power?" asked Suresh.

Jazmin said, "Catarina is coordinating the drone assets, and Mercedes is leading the aircraft repair teams. I'll fly combat air patrols with a fast-attack quadcopter. Two more quadcopters are inbound. One piloted by Ebony Diamond and the second flown by one of her officers, Lieutenant Commander Jack Macy. The three of us will protect the skies over the base."

Suresh stood. "Take care of your areas, communicate with each other, and improvise as needed. We've all been in combat and know the second the shooting starts, plans go to hell. There's a fine line between brave and stupid. Let's all stay on the right side of that line." She briefly made eye contact with each of her officers. "I'll be in my office."

The general exited the ops center. The rest of the group took a collective deep breath, then exited one by one. Other than Jazmin, Harry was the last to leave the room. He hugged her tightly and said, "When this is done, come back to me, *mon amour.*"

She caught his hands as he pulled away. "Be safe." A moment later he was gone. She stayed behind and relished the silence, knowing things would get crazy tonight. If she kept her head in the game and her luck held, she'd get the chance to go after her real target. She resolved to finish this with Jiang, no matter what.

Jazmin headed for the aircraft repair hangar in search of her mother. When she got there, Mercedes was explaining an avionics upgrade to one of the aircraft technicians. When she saw Jazmin, she broke away. Her face lit up with a smile that was a combination of pride and worry.

Jazmin said, "Mom, it's going to be chaotic tonight. I'll be guarding the base from the air."

Her mother pulled her into a crushing hug. "Be careful. It's hard enough being here without your father. I can't lose you." Tears rolled down her face.

Jazmin said, "I'll be fine. I'll find you when the fighting is over." She gave her mom another squeeze and pulled away.

Chapter 72

Wisconsin Militia Base
Bayfield, Wisconsin
15 August

On hour number four of Jazmin's combat air patrol over the Bayfield base, there were a few skirmishes with small arms fire below, but nothing requiring an airborne platform with serious firepower. The intrusions so far were handled by Derez's teams and were likely just scouting missions looking for weak spots or entry points. No doubt heavy weapons were on the way. Jazmin shared a common encrypted radio channel with the other senior staff and the ops center. She also kept an open hivemind connection to Harry. They both had an unspoken sense of foreboding.

Long-range radar showed two fast-attack quadcopters on an intercept course. Jazmin reflexively checked her weapon status. All systems armed. She did a range check on the two copters but didn't lock weapons. Diamond's voice burst through Jazmin's headset on an encrypted military aircraft radio channel shared with Catarina. "Hell of a greeting for friendlies who've come a long way. We were expecting warm cookies and turn-down service, not having our threat radar lit up."

Jazmin was relieved to hear Diamond's voice. "I'll alert the concierge you've arrived. Sorry for the electronic frisk. We've had some unwelcome visitors trying to check in. Suddenly we've become a very popular destination, though the level of clientele has dropped precipitously."

"We've heard rumors of security concerns in the neighborhood," said Diamond.

"We're expecting some unruly party guests. We hope your live fire training conference will dampen their enthusiasm."

"Can we land and review plans?" asked Diamond.

"As long as your landing permits are up to date."

Lieutenant Commander Macy spoke for the first time. "We completed our training for landing on top of a drinking straw and getting sucked inside."

"Catarina, can the drone fleet handle eyes in the sky?" asked Jazmin.

"No problem, Commander. I'll let you know if aerial guns are needed."

Jazmin did a quick three-sixty ground sweep. "I'll land first, then Macy, then Diamond. We need thirty seconds to clear the pad between captures."

"Roger that," said Macy.

"Copy," said Diamond.

Normally, Jazmin would have covered the other two copters while they landed, but the drone fleet controlled by Catarina was capable of doing so. Jazmin wanted to monitor the reverse maglev captures from inside the base in case anything went wrong. She hovered over the capture point. Once the maglev system locked onto her, she set power to idle and set her props to rotate freely. She floated down the launch tube and touched down, then a robot tugger towed her copter into the hangar. She tapped into the external monitors to watch Macy, and he performed a perfect reverse maglev capture. A tugger pulled his aircraft clear, then Diamond landed.

Macy exited his quadcopter, walked up to Jazmin, and stuck out his hand. "I'm Jack Macy. I've heard a lot about you, Commander."

When Diamond had first suggested Macy, Jazmin checked his official record and also ran a deep background check on him. His pilot and officer reviews were excellent, and no red flags turned up. He looked back at Jazmin with an unusual intensity, even for a Navy Special Ops pilot. "I want retribution for the people who killed my sister."

"I thought your sister was Lieutenant Kristin Macy? I saw her at the Milwaukee Joint Military Rehabilitation Center."

"She died in surgery to replace her neurotech. After you spoke with her, she was determined to get back to flying."

Jazmin let out a painful breath. "I'm sorry, Jack. I met your sister only briefly, but her intensity and fire had an impact on me. I can see it's a family trait."

"That's why I told Captain Diamond I was flying as her wingman, invited or not."

Diamond overheard most of the conversation. "Glad to have you covering my six."

Jazmin said, "Let's go to the ops center and check on overall status. We can plan our combat air patrols." She led the way through the hangar, down two corridors, and into the ops center. There were half a dozen people whom Jazmin didn't recognize, and she assumed they had just been called up. Harry and Catarina came over. Harry said to Diamond, "Hello, Captain, welcome back." Diamond nodded but said nothing. He faced Macy and stuck out his hand. "I'm Harry Dexter."

Macy smiled and they shook hands. "It's a pleasure to meet the mysterious Harry Dexter. I've heard rumors about you for years." Harry didn't respond, though Jazmin felt his darkness through their hivemind connection. His outsized reputation, most of it negative, was a sore subject for him.

After Catarina introduced herself, Harry pointed toward multiple holographic screens circling the room. "Inbound signal traffic has picked up over the last several hours." Using a red laser pen he circled several areas around the base. "Derez and his assault teams are in these areas. They're all chokepoints. He's deployed android infantry assets, too."

Catarina used a blue laser pen to circle several key places around the base, including the NAVAID sites. "Drone coverage is solid. These areas are the weak points the quadcopters need to protect. The drones are light and fast but have limited directed-energy weapon shielding. If we get blanketed with PWL weapons, we'll lose the drone fleet along with our NAVAIDs. The militia quadcopter has a special nanotech coating that offers additional protection. Captain Diamond, we're coating your two quadcopters right now. Mercedes is overseeing the operation."

Diamond said, "Thank you. Any edge in combat is welcome."

Jazmin said, "That nanotech coating saved my life when my F-22 was shot down with a directed-energy weapon." Jazmin used a yellow laser pen to draw three circles over the base, all overlapped in the center like a Venn diagram. "I'll cover the southwest. Captain Diamond, I'd like you to cover the southeast. Lieutenant Commander Macy, you'll patrol the north and watch for threats from Lake Superior. The base has a submarine pen so we're susceptible to an underwater attack. The overlap area is our catapult launch point, so that needs extra protection."

Catarina said, "I have a couple of underwater drones patrolling the area. The big concern for a water attack is shipboard cruise missiles." Macy studied the area map, then stared at Catarina. Jazmin wondered if he knew it was an android. Most of the people on base didn't know. Macy would figure it out when Catarina took over air traffic control, coordinated the forward air controllers, and piloted both airborne and seaborne drone fleets.

Without warning, the ops center went completely dark and silent.

And so it begins, thought Jazmin. The opening salvo. Nobody moved or said a word, no doubt thinking the same thing. She silently counted to ten, and the emergency lights bathed the room in a faint yellow glow.

Harry said, "It's a Zero hit. Gadget and I reinforced shielding and installed rapid power back-up systems for all critical areas after the last attack. In another thirty seconds we'll be back to full power."

Diamond said, "Impressive. I've never been on a base that recovered that fast after a zero hit."

Harry turned to one of the techs monitoring the ops center. "Samantha, let the general know the fun is starting."

"She probably already knows, sir."

"Tell her anyway."

Jazmin turned to Diamond and Macy. "Time to kick up our hooves and fly." She exited the ops center and headed toward the hangar with Diamond and Macy right behind her.

Chapter 73

Wisconsin Militia Base
Bayfield, Wisconsin
15 August

Jazmin, Diamond, and Macy arrived in the hangar just as Mercedes finished curing the nanotech particle coating on the second quadcopter. Gadget rolled the nanotech equipment away from the aircraft. "All birds are fueled and pre-flighted. Commander Macy, your quadcopter's in the chute. Get airborne."

Macy hesitated and looked at Diamond. "Sniper, you heard the chief. Launch." Macy hustled to the copter, strapped in, and fired up the engine generator. Fifteen seconds later he was catapulted skyward.

Gadget said, "You're up next, Captain." A robot tugger pulled the copter into the launch tube, then scurried away.

Jazmin said, "Good hunting, Shockwave."

Diamond jumped into the pilot's seat, strapped herself in, and fired up the engine generator. She flashed a thumbs up and shot skyward.

Jazmin waited for the robot tugger to pull her quadcopter into the chute. Her mom had stayed in the area and her expression was a combination of pride and poorly disguised fear. She mouthed "I love you" and Jazmin did the same back. As soon as the robot tugger exited the chute, Jazmin strapped in, hit engine start, and waited for the flight indicators to glow green. The automated checks cleared, and the maglev catapult threw her skyward. She engaged power at the top of the magnetic push and flew south.

Her eyes went into night vision mode with flash suppression. Everything below had a light green hue. Activity had jumped tenfold in the last hour. Eight different groups were involved in small arms exchanges but Jazmin didn't intervene, afraid she'd kill militia members. Several enemy ACVs were in the area; the militia ground teams could dispatch them using RPGs. The enemy target behind the ACVs chilled her: a battle tank. That presented firepower Derez's teams couldn't combat.

Jazmin targeted the tank with her 30mm cannon and fired. The armor-piercing shells damaged the front end of the tank, but it kept moving. It spun hard left on its tracks and disappeared behind a grove of mature trees. She pulled up and was making a second pass when her threat alert radar screamed a warning and a surface-to-air missile shot past her, barely missing her front windshield. It arced over, and the heat-seeking missile headed back.

Jazmin deployed flares to confuse the missile with multiple white-hot heat sources. It exploded high and to her right, but the shock wave knocked her aircraft sideways and downward. She recovered, she was flying so low machine gun fire pinged off her windshield. She rolled hard left, then climbed. Multiple damage alerts flashed on her heads-up display, but there were no critical warnings. She searched the ground for enemy forces with shoulder-mounted weapons and spotted two combatants near an ACV. She strafed the area with her .50 caliber guns and killed the two black-clad enemies. A short burst from her 30mm cannon tore through the ACV, and it was engulfed in flames as its onboard weapons exploded. Next she needed to locate and destroy the tank. Jazmin spoke over the shared aircraft channel. "Catarina, I'm trying to locate a battle tank in my sector."

"Drone swarm shows two. Sending coordinates."

"Engaging enemy." Jazmin's flight computer temporarily took control of the quadcopter, and she made a low pass over the target. She set the anti-tank cannon to full automatic. At the optimum angle and distance, the 30mm cannons pummeled the tank. The munitions and fuel ignited, the explosion lighting up the night sky as the fireball shot skyward. Everyone onboard and nearby would have died instantly.

Jazmin rolled right and climbed to avoid the residual exploding ordnance. She'd barely cleared the area, her eyes adjusting back to standard night vision mode, when her flight computer took control of the copter again. The second tank was visible in a clearing. In a desperate attempt to defend itself, the turret spun and aimed skyward, but it was too late. Jazmin's 30mm cannon blasted through the tank's armor plating, killing the crew. The tank's tracks were blown off and uncoiled. The deadly war machine died like a pulverized loser in a demolition derby. The nearby ACVs scattered and headed for cover.

Over the radio Jazmin said, "Tanks neutralized. Shockwave, Sniper, what's your status?"

Sniper said, "Small arms fire in my sector. Friendly forces holding ground. Breaking away to edge of sector to check threats from Lake Superior. Unusual watercraft activity."

"Copy. Keep us informed," said Jazmin.

Shockwave said, "Enemy robot infantry on east flank sweeping toward the base. Friendly forces outgunned and falling back. Holding off on a strafing run while friendly forces retreat."

"Copy." She checked her sector. After the second tank and multiple ACVs had been destroyed, no additional assets engaged. "Shockwave, quiet in my sector. Coming to assist." Jazmin gained altitude and headed east. Her helmet display showed enemy robot infantry mixed with friendly assets. She was out of range for effectively using her .50 caliber machine guns and wouldn't risk hitting militia personnel.

Shockwave said, "Robot infantry halted advance and is aiming shoulder-fired weapons skyward. Weapons launched but no obvious target." There was static, then the radio transmission went silent.

Jazmin's threat radar alerted in her helmet display. *Directed-Energy Weapons deployed. Avoid red zone.* She was flying through the yellow zone just at the edge of the red zone. Jazmin rolled hard left to stay in the yellow zone, but even with the additional nanotech shielding, she couldn't stay for long before she would lose flight control. The copter's control response was sluggish, and she had a hard time staying on course. Once she exited the yellow zone into clear airspace her control response improved, though it was still compromised.

She zoomed out on her helmet map display and saw the red zone wasn't stable. It was still spreading outward. Diamond had been in the middle of the red zone, and her aircraft was no longer on radar. Jazmin tried the shared aircraft radio frequency. "Shockwave, what's your status?" No response. "Catarina, what's happening in the eastern sector?"

"Directed-energy weapons blanket attack by infantry robots. Drone network and comms lost. Residual radiation present. Redirecting remaining drone assets to monitor sector." Jazmin's helmet display showed the red zone receding and turning yellow. It was still dangerous to fly in that area. She'd have to avoid it or risk losing her aircraft.

She engaged her hivemind connection to Harry. *What's happening in the eastern sector? There was a directed-energy weapons blanket discharge and signal intelligence blanked out.*

Harry said, *Derez's teams headed to protected tunnel systems when enemy infantry robots overwhelmed the area and launched directed-energy weapons. Diamond's quadcopter down. Hard landing. Team dispatched. No more info.* Harry's communications were choppy. He was multitasking, so she didn't press him further.

The yellow zone expanded, but radiation levels were showing too high for Jazmin to enter the area. She zoomed out her helmet display to show all three sectors. The western sector was still quiet, though the northern overwater sector had increased activity. She hadn't heard anything from Macy. She vectored north, well out of the yellow zone, when her radio activated.

A blast of static then Macy's voice. "Mayday. Mayday. Mayday. Engine out. Flight controls INOP."

Jazmin yelled, "Eject, eject, eject." She hoped this would spur him to make the hard call to pull the handle. If Macy's flight controls were inoperative, he couldn't autorotate for a survivable hard landing. Whether he hit the ground or the water, the result would be the same – the impact would kill him, and his copter would be destroyed. If he went down in the lake and he didn't die instantly, hypothermia would finish the job.

Jazmin pushed her quadcopter to full power and set her flight computer for the shortest intercept course. She arrived in time to see Macy spiral downward and impact the roadway along Lake Superior. The impact crushed the copter, and the fireball incinerated what was left. At best they'd recover Macy's ashes.

Jazmin hovered for a moment, then her threat alarm triggered.

Two octocopter gunships hovered over the water. They targeted her aircraft, but they hadn't locked weapons. It was as if they were cats taunting a mouse. Jazmin had spent thousands of hours flying identical gunships and knew their strengths, as well as their weaknesses. She would be outgunned in a straight-up match, but she'd take them out anyway. This was her turf, and she'd set the rules for engagement.

Jazmin spun her quadcopter and shot through an opening in the trees. She had hundreds of hours of low altitude flying experience in these woods. Her fast-attack quadcopter was smaller than an octocopter gunship designed for carrying troops. She could squeeze through openings in the trees at ground level where a bulky octocopter wouldn't fit. If they tried following her from above, they would lose her in ground clutter. She zipped through the woods to put distance between herself and her pursuers.

She spoke over the aircraft channel. "Catarina, I need eyes in the sky. Patch radar on enemy octocopter gunships to my helmet display."

"Radar feed confirmed."

The enemy octocopters were flying low but well above the treetops. She could tell one pilot was more skilled than the other, taking more aggressive actions and dipping below the tree line through larger openings. Jazmin slowed and hovered at the edge of the woods, unseen in ground clutter. She'd dispatch the weaker pilot first. When the two octocopters closed in on her, she fired a burst from her 30mm cannon. One pilot flew upward to get away, giving Jazmin a clear shot with an air-to-air missile. She locked on and fired. Not waiting for impact, she took immediate evasive action. The other octocopter fired on Jazmin's location, but she was already gone. Her attack on the octocopter was rewarded with an explosion that rocked her quadcopter. One less enemy aircraft showed on her helmet display.

She found another opening in the tree line and flew into the forest. The octocopter pursued. When the trees closed in, the pilot halted and hovered. Jazmin activated her hivemind connection with Harry. *I need to set a trap for an enemy octocopter gunship. Dispatch an android infantry team to tunnel hatch 33 with an EMP grenade launcher. I'm the bait.*

Team dispatched. She could tell he wanted to say more. So did she.

Jazmin thought of General Suresh's admonition about staying on the right side of the brave-stupid line, but in battle, luck determined more outcomes than skill or bravery. On her helmet display, Jazmin brought up the area map showing the tunnel hatch openings overlaid with woods. Her quadcopter was lighter, faster, and more maneuverable than her enemy's octocopter. However, an octocopter gunship was more powerful and stable, so she couldn't let her enemy get a clear shot.

Go time. Jazmin climbed above the treetops long enough for the octocopter to spot her and fire a burst from its guns. A couple of rounds hit, causing only minor damage. She flew at ground level and kept to openings large enough for the octocopter to follow her. The pilot took the bait, and Jazmin led the enemy aircraft on a zigzag course through the woods. She fired her rear guns often enough to keep her pursuer off balance but avoiding direct hits to keep the chase going. She approached hatch 33 and caught sight of the two-android infantry team with shoulder-mounted EMP grenade launchers as she zipped by.

A flash in her peripheral vision signaled the grenade detonation on impact with the octocopter. Trees snapped off as the octocopter gunship lost flight control and careened into the heavy woods.

Jazmin turned and hovered, taking in the scene. She waited for the android team to head back down into the tunnel and seal the opening. The enemy pilot and two crew members staggered out of the broken copter. All were armed with assault rifles, with one shouldering an RPG. The brutal reality of war was that the fight doesn't end until your enemy couldn't get up. Jazmin targeted the three assailants with her .50 caliber guns and turned the trio into hamburger. She hovered long enough for the grim images of the dead bodies to be seared into her memory, then picked up altitude to get over the tree line.

She climbed to three thousand feet and was making a three-sixty turn to assess the remaining action when her threat alarm warbled, followed by an audible alert. "Cruise missiles inbound. Take immediate evasive action."

Her helmet display showed four inbound cruise missiles targeting all four quadrants of the underground base. The flight computer took control of her copter. Her aircraft rapidly rolled right and climbed at full power to avoid the path of one of the missiles. None of her onboard weapons could stop a cruise missile. Jazmin watched all four impact the ground with shuddering explosions. Clouds of smoke rose while dirt, boulders, and massive pieces of broken concrete flew upward, then crashed to earth. Holes and scorch marks remained, and building debris lined two of the craters.

On the aircraft frequency, Jazmin said, "Catarina, what was the origin of the cruise missiles?"

"Missiles were ship-launched. Underwater drones five minutes out on an intercept course. The militia's remaining aerial drones are capturing video of enemy activity."

Jazmin's helmet display showed a Great Lakes freighter with a missile launcher. The ship was designed for stealth, as the launcher was on a lift to hide it under the deck until deployed.

"Heading to area to engage." Jazmin went to full power and set an intercept course. As soon as she was within range, she locked onto the ship with an air-to-ground missile and fired.

Exhaust left a visible smoke trail like a rope line all the way to the ship until the missile slammed into the deck. The bridge exploded, and the ship listed to starboard with equipment and a few of the crew sliding off the deck into the frigid lake water.

Jazmin locked onto the ship and fired again. The second missile tore a gaping hole at the waterline, and the ship started sinking. Fire engulfed what still remained above water. In a few minutes the flames were extinguished as the ship disappeared below the surface of the lake. On the aircraft channel she said, "Enemy ship sunk. Any remaining targets?"

Catarina said, "None detected, but remaining drone coverage is spotty."

Jazmin opened her hivemind connection to Harry, though she only listened. He was consumed with damage control actions on the base. His fear and weariness added to her own. She was glad he survived the attack, and she closed the connection. She headed back over the base to do her own aerial assessment and finish off any remaining enemies.

Chapter 74

Wisconsin Militia Base – Bayfield, Wisconsin
15 August

Flying the sole manned aircraft in the area, Jazmin systematically checked each of the three sectors for combat activity. A sliver of early-morning sunlight peeked above the horizon, and the sky went from black to light gray. Nothing on the ground moved. All she could see was combat wreckage, charred earth, and dead bodies. She welcomed the silence. No radio chatter, no open hivemind connections, just her own conflicted thoughts and feelings. She stuffed them into sealed boxes and vowed to unpack them when she had settled the score with Jiang. Jazmin owed retribution for her lost teammates. She owed herself time to heal her emotional scars.

After completing two circuits of the area and seeing no changes, she headed to the maglev capture point. It was offline. She set down next to the access hatch for the underground aircraft ramp and got out of the copter. She triggered the ramp control, but it stubbornly stayed in place. She found no indication it was still connected to power. Jazmin inspected the lift mechanism and saw the extensive bomb damage. She located the emergency entrance and climbed down the ladder to the hangar. The normally pristine space was now a scrapyard of mangled vehicles and drones. Damage ranged from small arms bullet holes to armor plating destroyed by land mines.

Gadget's team would have years of work to restore the fleet. Not a single person was in the usually bustling hangar. The silence was eerie. Everything looked and felt wrong, as if she were the last survivor in a ghost town. Where was everyone?

The automatic doors no longer worked, so she forced her way into a debris-strewn hall. Sparking overhead lights hanging by pieces of conduit, smashed ceramic tiles, and rebar jutting out of broken concrete blocked her path. She carefully made her way down the hall to another one more centrally located in the base. There was less building damage here, but wounded soldiers with bandaged heads and limbs lined the hallway. Jazmin recognized one of the avionics techs who worked for Gadget. "Did Gadget survive the missile attack?"

The young man looked at her but seemed to be in shock. "I think so. Everyone ran for cover."

"Did the other techs make it to safety?"

"I don't know. We were all spread out. The medics pulled us out one by one. After treating us, they brought us here so the clinic could deal with people in worse shape."

The tech looked dazed, so Jazmin moved on, hoping to find someone more alert. Further down the hall she saw a combat medic checking on a soldier with a head wound. When she reached him she asked, "Is the general still in charge after the attack? Did the rest of the senior staff or Captain Diamond survive?"

"I don't know who's in charge. You'll need to go to the ops center. Diamond's in the clinic, but I don't know her status. Derez is in bad shape and was rushed into surgery. That's all I know, Commander."

Jazmin patted his shoulder. "Thanks." She made her way down the hall and greeted those she knew. After shaking hands and letting them know she was glad they survived, she arrived at the ops center. Harry and Catarina were the only ones still there. The room was a mess. Abandoned coffee cups, food wrappers, and loose items from workstations were scattered across the floor. The stink of burned electronics and residual smoke hung in the air. Several of the workstation monitors flickered.

In a monotone Catarina said, "Most of the drone fleet is gone. A few assets are patrolling and everything is quiet. I will inform Mercedes you have returned." Catarina spoke as if her personality had been erased. The android sounded the way she had when Jazmin and Gadget first pulled the electronic brain out of its box for initial programming. Jazmin wondered if the android had been damaged by the residual radiation of the directed-energy weapons.

Harry looked exhausted and lost. He'd always been cool under fire, but today his calm under pressure had been burned away. He went to Jazmin and hugged her for a long time. "We didn't win today, we just survived."

"How's my mom?"

"She's okay. Gadget pulled her under an armored vehicle right before the missiles hit. They're both all right."

Jazmin let out a long breath. "Thanks for letting me know."

***

The base clinic was mobbed. Jazmin learned that Diamond had survived the hard landing in her quadcopter. She had a concussion and numerous contusions, and was cut up by flying debris. She was sedated and being held overnight for observation. Derez was in surgery and, assuming he survived, had a long road to recovery. The triage nurses were swamped with injured patients, so Jazmin left.

She was exhausted but so wired from combat she couldn't sleep. Too much to process. She hunted down Gadget and found her with a small team repairing the main vehicle ramp. Jazmin said, "The base took more of a beating than I could see from the air."

Gadget scanned the hangar and let out a long breath. "The tanks and the cruise missiles did a lot of damage. I'm working on critical repairs so we can function."

"Where's Suresh? I didn't see her in the ops center."

Gadget said, "She's pulling in every political favor she can to keep the feds and the military from pouring in. Our underground base used to be an open secret. The last twenty-four hours tore away any veil of secrecy. Too many people knew where we were located, and obviously the mercenary companies got to them. We need to clean things up in a hurry and disappear from view."

Jazmin thought of the wreckage outside. "Have any teams been dispatched to collect the dead and clean up the destroyed equipment?"

Gadget's tired expression hardened. "Militia teams don't leave anyone behind but there's no one left to pick up the mercenaries."

"It's grisly work, but we need to do it. Can you spare a couple of infantry robots and a truck? I'll ID and collect the bodies."

"I'll be right back with the robots and a reefer truck. I need my best techs on repairs. I can spare one of my guys to drive a wrecker to pick up destroyed equipment." Gadget shook her head. "The hangar already looks like a damn junk yard." She headed off.

Jazmin ran a mental checklist for identifying bodies and collecting critical evidence to use against Jiang and Trabago. She went to the clinic to obtain body bags. When she got back, Gadget was waiting for her with two infantry robots and a refrigerated box truck. Next to it was a wrecker big enough to haul a battle tank. Jazmin recognized the tech behind the wheel of the giant wrecker. She waved hello, and he nodded back. She and the two robots climbed into the reefer truck. The two vehicles headed up the ramp to the outside. The remaining drone fleet identified enemy casualties to pick up. Jazmin hoped they were all dead. She was afraid she'd shoot them if they weren't.

The truck stopped at the first pile of dead bodies. The two robots laid them out, then Jazmin took photos with her bionic eyes and scanned their biochips with a handheld reader. One robot collected weapons and personal effects while the other bagged the bodies and stowed them in the truck, stacking them in neat rows. The robots had superhuman strength and dexterity, so the work went quickly. Unlike Jazmin, the robots felt nothing. The toughest body retrieval of the day was the trio who had climbed out of the octocopter after her EMP grenade ambush. A single .50 caliber round would mutilate a body. The number of rounds she unloaded into this crew and their war machine had been excessive by any standard. So little was recognizable that all she could do was scan the biochips and have the robots mop up the rest into a single body bag. Jazmin took in the grotesque images of combat death, recording it all with her bionic eyes for later download. The downside of having bionic eyes was that she could never forget the indelible high-resolution images. One more episode she compartmentalized, wondering when her inner storage capacity would run out. One day the horrible things she locked away might rush out and overwhelm her senses and what was left of her sanity. While selective hardware wipes of digital images collected by her bionic eyes were an option, only total detailed recall would be eliminated. Residual memories in her brain would likely remain.

It was nightfall by the time the now full truck drove back down the ramp into the hangar. Jazmin had been fueled all day by adrenaline, bottled water, and a couple of energy bars, but now she was spent. Not trusting herself with a hivemind connection, she went looking for Harry in the last place she had seen him, the ops center. He was with two other techs, and he looked even more exhausted than when she had seen him earlier in the day. She sank into a chair next to him. "Have you been here all day?"

He nodded. "I spent the day erasing electronic evidence of what happened. If I couldn't erase the trail, I created enough noise to hide it. General Suresh is doing her best to keep anyone official away, and I'm trying to make sure there's nothing to find if someone does shows up. I'm done for today. It's as clean as I can make it, and I can't think straight anymore. I'm more likely to create problems than cover them up." Bleary-eyed, he looked at the two techs. "Thanks for everything today. Let's get some sleep and do a final scan tomorrow when our heads are clear." The techs struggled to their feet and trudged away.

Jazmin put her hand on Harry's. "I need something to eat and a hot shower." She squeezed his hand. "I don't want to be alone tonight."

Chapter 75

Wisconsin Militia Base
Bayfield, Wisconsin
15 August

The cafeteria was busier than usual for this late in the day. Fortunately, the automated cooking equipment had survived the battle. The aroma of roast chicken, fresh baked bread, and stir-fried vegetables was wonderful. Jazmin sat at a table with her head down while Harry got food for both of them. She barely had the energy to eat, though she felt better afterward. Stomachs full, she and Harry went back to her quarters. They both undressed, dropped their clothes on the floor, and squeezed into the shower stall. It was a cozy fit as hot water cascaded down on them while they lathered each other. They dried off and fell into bed naked.

They lay next to each other and held hands. The sexual tension between them would have to wait for another night. Both were too exhausted and emotionally drained to act on their feelings. Battered by the last twenty-four hours, they just needed someone they trusted to hang on to.

Before drifting off Jazmin said, "This isn't over."

"I know, my love." A moment later, his hand relaxed and Harry was asleep.

Jazmin squeezed his hand then let go, though his arm still grazed hers. She was starved for his touch and human connection. Despite his many ethical failings, Harry had never wavered in his love for her. When she had settled the score with Jiang, she'd have to resolve her feelings for him. They both deserved an answer on their future together.

Chapter 76
Mei Chan

Chinese Military Intelligence Headquarters
16 August

After the attack on the American aircraft carrier, Mei had directed her staff to closely follow all mercenary teams controlled by Ling Chen. The US senator was no longer considered an asset, only a liability. Mei's once-close relationship with her had ended, and all communication between them had ceased. Given the status of US-China relations, Mei had hoped the attack on the Wisconsin Militia base would have provided a distraction for President Navarro and deflected blame toward Hassani. Unfortunately, it had turned into another disaster. Mei had spent twenty hours straight in the ops center monitoring the battle, as well as reading her staff's analysis of potential fallout.

Now late at night, Mei sat in her darkened office illuminated with just a single lamp. Exhausted, head pounding, she sipped green tea hoping the caffeine would energize her, but it had no effect. It couldn't overcome her lack of sleep. Even in her current brain fog, Mei knew she had to take drastic action. All ties to Ling Chen had to be terminated.

Chapter 77
Jazmin Hassani

Wisconsin Militia Base – Bayfield, Wisconsin
16 August

Jazmin and Harry spent the morning identifying the dead operators, tracing their mercenary company connections, and tying the groups back to Jiang and Trabago. After searching the dark web for background information, they found their assailants originated from a number of countries. All had elite special forces experience. Jazmin pieced together dossiers on all of them. Many had ties to Chinese Military Intelligence from their military experience or mercenary operations.

*** *

General Suresh met with Jazmin, Harry, Gadget, and Diamond in the damaged ops center. Years of command responsibility had etched every line in Suresh's face. She said, "Derez survived surgery, but his commando days are over. He'll need multiple invasive medical procedures to restore function for both legs and his left arm. His neurotech implants also need to be replaced. Monty did what he could, but Derez needs the help and expertise of a military rehabilitation hospital, something unavailable to him."

As difficult as her military rehabilitation hospital time had been, they'd replaced her legs and accomplished dozens of medical miracles for her. It was terrible that Derez wouldn't get that kind of care. "What happens to him now?" asked Jazmin.

"We take care of our own. Monty is researching private offshore facilities with no ties to the US government that can handle Derez's needs." Suresh looked at Harry. "You'll need to obtain some additional donations from the Cayman Islands bank customers who have been so generous in the past."

Harry said, "I'll make sure there's plenty of money for whatever Derez needs."

"I'm sure he'll appreciate that." Suresh looked at everyone around the room. "We survived the attack, but we have a lot of rebuilding to do. Gadget, how long before the base is operational again?"

Gadget sighed. "Critical repairs so we can function will take at least two weeks. Structural damage and systems repairs will require months of work, and the vehicle fleet and aircraft will take years. Obtaining or fabricating parts to rebuild will be the biggest challenge."

Suresh closed her eyes for a moment while she took in the full impact of Gadget's report. Then she focused her gaze on Gadget and Harry. "We've come to the attention of too many people with entrenched interests that aren't aligned with ours. Buying surplus military gear will get much harder. Let's focus on expanding our 3D printing capabilities and electronics fabrication."

Jazmin asked, "How is Washington reacting to our war zone?"

"Not well. I called every politician and flag officer I know begging them to keep anyone official far away. In return, I had to make promises we can't possibly deliver on." Suresh's whole body sagged as if she was crushed by a debt she could never repay. "We need to keep a low profile for the foreseeable future. The only thing pulling attention away from us is that General Trabago was found dead this morning from a gunshot wound to his head. Rumor is that it was suicide, but details are sketchy."

Diamond said, "My boss, Rear Admiral Jameson, was livid when I told her I lost my executive officer and two quadcopters in the battle. Unless I can provide actionable intel to justify these losses, my career is over. I'll be lucky to avoid jail time after my court martial."

Jazmin said, "Harry and I spent the morning creating dossiers and tracking the raiding party back to Senator Jiang. We also found ties to Chinese Military Intelligence."

Diamond said, "Thank you. I need something to appease Jameson so she can justify protecting me. I need to know this was worth losing Macy over. I owe that to his wife and parents."

Jazmin said, "Now that Trabago is out of the picture, I want Jiang's head."

"Jaz, you're not alone, but she's vanished. I checked with my network. NSA and the clandestine services have lost her."

Jazmin said, "We can send her a message."

Suresh looked skeptical. "Go on."

"We send the refrigerated truck with the bodies to Jiang's condo. Her security team will know how to find her. If Jiang doesn't deal with the grisly fallout of a failed raid, they'll turn on her." The room went silent for an uncomfortably long time.

Finally, Suresh said, "I agree. That's a message the senator can't ignore. Make sure the truck is untraceable, and send it today."

"When Jiang comes out of hiding, I can take over her neurotech. It's something I learned from a rogue government tech on an NDA case. I have to be close, and I need to do it alone."

Harry whirled on her. "How come you never told us before?"

"The legitimate NDA techs said it was impossible, but I saw it done once. It's dangerous. The feedback loop can kill the person trying to take control, along with anyone nearby."

Harry glared back at her, a mix of anger and fear etched into his face. "How's it done?"

"There's a government registry for all neurotech users, allowing them to interface with other technology. Fifteen levels deep there are two undocumented flags. You set one for the controller and one for the target. Both people have to be physically close, as the signals won't survive network handoffs. I was ordered to leave the technical details out of my NDA final report. If it was true, and my bosses weren't convinced it was, this knowledge would upend peoples' trust in the government neurotech registry system." Jazmin paused, waiting for everyone to process the implications of this power. "Jiang is a US senator, so she's in the government system."

Suresh's eyes bore into Jazmin. "Are you certain you can do this?"

"Yes, the rogue tech showed me exactly how to do it, right before he blew his brains out. I've never shared it with anyone else."

"What support do you need to make this happen?" asked Suresh.

"I need a new identity so I can move unmolested on the streets of Washington. Since I'm going after Jiang, I'll need a new face. Gadget, how long will it take for the 3-D printers to make me unrecognizable?"

"A few hours. We can darken your skin tone a little more, make a slight change around your eyes, and make your lips a bit fuller. It doesn't take much to throw off facial recognition software."

Jazmin asked, "Harry, how soon can you create a new identification for me?"

"I thought you might need one after the prison break was covered on the news, so I took the time to create a new military identity and generated history for it."

"We can send the bodies today. Then I can go to Washington and wait for Jiang to turn up. She can't stay away long. She has to bury the evidence."

Harry said, "I'll go too. You'll need someone to watch your back."

Jazmin shook her head. "I need to do this alone. I'll blend in more easily by myself, and we've shared a hivemind connection. You'd get caught in the feedback loop, and your implants would overload." She ignored Harry's angry stare.

Suresh said, "Harry, help Jazmin send the rolling message to Jiang. Make sure the truck is clean of every trace of us. Stay on base and monitor the op from here. Jazmin, see me before you head out."

Diamond said, "Jazmin, if you need backup, you know how to find me. Otherwise, I'll stay clear."

Jazmin stood. "I'm going to end this for all of us."

Chapter 78

Wisconsin Militia Base
Bayfield, Wisconsin
16 August

In the maintenance hangar, Jazmin and Harry stood near the refrigerated truck packed with enemy corpses. She ran a final systems check to make sure the truck was ready for the trip to Jiang's condo. "Is there anything linking this vehicle to the militia?"

He glared at her. "Does it matter? Jiang will know who sent it."

"It matters to Suresh."

"The truck is clean, and there's nothing anyone can trace. You've followed the general's orders, so now you can be a hero or a martyr or whatever the hell it is you're doing."

Jazmin closed her eyes and bit back an angry retort. Harry had been sullen since she announced her plan to go after Jiang. After the battle they'd been physically and emotionally close, though now they'd drifted apart yet again. An unfortunate pattern they kept repeating.

They stood in silence for a few moments, then Harry lowered the ramp to the outside. He said, "The truck is ready. Time to launch." The vehicle's lights came on, and it pulled away from the parking spot and headed up the ramp. When it was out of sight, the ramp lifted and sealed the opening to the outside.

Harry's expression lost its anger, though any trace of warmth was gone. "Let's go over the neurotech flag registry process one more time."

"We've done this dozens of times already. I know the damn process."

"You only have one shot. You won't have time to think in the moment."

She was annoyed, but she knew he was right. She recited the process checklist. "Verify proximity to Jiang won't require a network handoff. Peer-to-peer signal strength at eighty percent or better. Open the government neurotech registry interface. Drill down fifteen levels to access the hardware keys. Reverse two unlabeled flags, one for the controller and one for the target. Test hivemind connection. Upon mission completion, reverse flags and close the interface."

Harry's expression changed from irritation to concern. "Wait here. I'll be right back."

She was about to argue but let him go. Jazmin was glad she hadn't shared the rest of her plan with Harry or anyone else on base. As a Special Forces pilot she had also flown CIA Psyops teams on missions. Though illegal and in violation of US policy, they had rigged dead soldiers' neurotech for launching hivemind overloads. A small external power source was all that was needed. Legitimate government techs swore it was impossible, though Jazmin had seen in done on multiple missions. She had already installed a stealth power source in the reefer truck. The results were sickening and, once triggered, they weren't reversible.

A few minutes later Harry returned with a weapons case from the armory and set it on the floor in front of Jazmin. She crouched and opened it. The black case contained two 9mm handguns, spare magazines, and several boxes of hollow-point ammo. Also inside was a combat shotgun with several boxes of 12-gauge shells. She latched it shut and stood. "Thank you."

He reached out his arms and pulled her in for an awkward hug. "Be careful, Jaz."

She pulled back but still held his hands. "Were you able to get into the PWL targeting system?"

Harry yanked his hands away. "Yes. Are you sure you want that on your conscience?"

She looked at the names on her forearm. "I made a promise."

Harry shook his head, his face covered in disappointment and sadness.

After a moment she backed away and climbed into an ACV. The exterior ramp lowered, and she pulled away. It took a few hours to drive to Truax, and her inner turmoil took her to dark places in her mind.

Shortly before arriving at Truax, she checked her new ID. Jazmin was now Commander Shantell Cirocco, a DIA investigator. Having changed her face and height, no one at the base recognized her. From Truax, she took a military transport to Joint Base Andrews, then a military car in stealth mode into Washington.

***

The next morning, Jazmin checked into a hotel near Jiang's condo, then scouted the area. She found a coffee shop within sight of Jiang's condo, purchased breakfast, and sat at an outdoor table where she had good sightlines. She sipped a mug of dark roast coffee, slowly ate a fresh croissant, and waited for events to unfold. A short time later, the refrigerated truck pulled up to the condo. Jiang's security team investigated. Sensing human intrusion, the truck locked down in place, and the door rolled up to reveal a mountain of body bags stacked inside. A small charge inside the refrigeration unit exploded, rendering it useless for further cooling the inside of the truck. The warm day accelerated the decay of the already decomposing bodies. Within a few minutes, the pungent stench of death overwhelmed the area. The other coffee shop patrons retreated indoors, though Jazmin remained riveted in place.

Panicked, the security team hauled the bodies inside the condo to get them out of the hot sun and the view of the neighbors. A patrol car stopped, and two police officers spoke with Jiang's security team. The officers were convinced, pressured, or possibly bribed to leave.

On her tablet, Jazmin monitored the condo's security systems. She also had access to audio and video inside the condo, as well as tablets, and biochips of everyone present. She forced herself to be calm and to bide her time, knowing Jiang would be there soon.

Chapter 79
Mei Chan

Washington, DC
17 August

After her last visit to Ling Chen's Washington DC condo, Mei expected a more robust security presence and additional measures to block her entrance. Instead, building heat signatures and electronic traffic showed the opposite, a vastly reduced security presence. Mei bypassed the alarm and surveillance systems, entered the building, and stayed hidden in the basement. Her team was keeping her abreast of all activities at the Wisconsin Militia base and of the grisly cargo that had just arrived. The refrigerated truck filled with dead bodies meant an ignominious end for Ling Chen, and its presence would destroy any shred of respect her security team had for her.

Ling Chen needed to be terminated – she was too dangerous to be left alive. Mei would prefer it if others did the job, but if that didn't happen she'd do what was necessary. If Mei's gamble with Ping Zhao paid off, she might survive, though the odds were slim. More likely her career was over and possibly her life. Either way, Mei had to clean up the mess she had allowed to happen.

Mei tapped into the building's surveillance system and watched in both horror and fascination as the show unfolded. She took advantage of the chaos to find another hiding spot inside the condo, closer to the action.

Chapter 80
Ling Chen Jiang

Washington, DC
17 August

Ling Chen saw the incoming call from Danica and let it go to voicemail, though she read the real time transcription. "Senator, we have a dire situation at the condo. Call me immediately." She was in no mood to respond. Danica would have to deal with whatever was happening, so she blocked the number. A moment later, another call went straight to voicemail. "Call me right fucking now before your entire security team walks out and you have to clean up the mountain of dead bodies yourself." Ling Chen checked the video at her condo. The grisly images unnerved her. She took a couple of deep breaths to calm herself, then called Danica.

The security agent picked up on the first ring. "Where the hell are you?"

"I'm on my way. I'll be there soon. Get the bodies inside and out of sight. Crank the air conditioning as cold as it will go. Take charge of the team, and we'll deal with it when I get there."

"Get here fast or there won't be a team when you arrive."

Ling Chen's irritation spiked, though she said nothing. In the background she heard Danica address the others, "The senator is on her way," then ended the call.

It took Ling Chen ten minutes to get to the condo. Her ice-cold composure wilted as she took in the scene. Leaking body bags covered with flies lay everywhere in the normally pristine living space, and it was impossible to move without stepping over the dead. She coughed at the stench of decaying flesh and covered her mouth with a handkerchief. Her angry security team surrounded her, and she glared back with rage. "Why are you standing around? Get these bodies to the basement. Why isn't the air conditioning blasting cold air?"

The older male guard opened his mouth to argue, but Jiang cut him off. "There's nothing to discuss. Do your damn job. That's what I pay you for."

He scowled at her. "I didn't sign up for this."

They stared at each other with contempt. Eventually, he picked up one of the bodies and headed to the basement.

One of the computer techs fixated on the fluid leaking from one of the body bags, then threw up. "I can't do this." He backed away and locked himself in the security room.

Danica looked rattled as she stared at the body bags arrayed around her. "Senator, we can't keep the bodies here."

Jiang felt demoralized at the situation. "I know. We need to find a discreet way to make them disappear. This might take a little time."

Danica closed on Jiang. "You need to find a solution fast, or the few of us left will leave."

Ling Chen knew if that happened, she was done.

Chapter 81
Jazmin Hassani

Washington, DC
17 August

Jazmin felt an adrenaline buzz as she watched the scene at the condo unfold on a holographic screen only she could see. Now was the time to strike. With well-practiced keystrokes, she reset the hidden registry flags. She now had an intimate hivemind connection to her enemy's thoughts and the ability to control Jiang's neurotech. The condo's security cameras and hivemind connection gave Jazmin a front row seat to the show.

She headed to the condo on foot. Testing her new power, Jazmin dimmed the lights in the condo, then adjusted the thermostat. She killed the AC and turned on the heat. Using her personal holographic screen she watched flies scatter as hot air blew out of the floor vents.

It took Jiang a few minutes to realize what was happening. Sweating and irritated, she stormed into the security room. "Why is there hot air blasting out of the vents? You need to get the AC working again."

The tech gave Jiang a withering look, then he stomped over to the electronic thermostat and reprogrammed it for AC. Every time he made an adjustment, Jazmin negated the command, forcing the unit to max heat. After several unsuccessful attempts to get cold air blowing, the tech took out his gun and smashed the control unit off the wall. The heat remained on. Without saying a word, he holstered his weapon and walked out the door.

Jiang said, "Where the fuck are you going?" The man kept walking. Jiang was in such an emotional state, she didn't realize she was in a hivemind connection with Jazmin. Jiang tried to open a window, but all were locked shut to maintain security. She even headed to the balcony door, then forced herself back. She had to remain in hiding. Just outside the building, Jazmin watched the condo's security cameras showing-closeups of Jiang unraveling.

Now, only Danica and a single security team member remained. The two of them carried another body to stack in the basement. After setting it on the pile, they exited the condo. Jazmin entered the condo's front door and headed up the steps. Jiang stayed upstairs and sat sullenly on the couch, making vain attempts to swat flies away.

Through her hivemind connection, Jazmin said, *I have control of your neurotech and I'm going to destroy you.*

Jiang jumped to her feet. Her eyes darted around the room. It took her a moment to realize Jazmin was across the room at the top of the stairs. The senator's eyes went wide in fear, seeing a gun pointed at her chest. "Danica!"

"There's no one here to save you."

Jiang looked around wildly. She lunged for a handgun on a nearby table but tripped over a body bag.

Holding her gun on Jiang, Jazmin closed the distance between them, stepping carefully over the dozen bodies stacked up. "I don't plan to shoot you. I have something more insidious in mind."

Jiang glared at her from the floor. "There's a price on your head. If I don't kill you, someone else will."

"Have you ever experienced a hivemind overload? It's a miserable experience." She didn't wait for a response and triggered the neural onslaught using the same illegal technique she learned from the psyops teams she'd flown.

The voices of the dead mercenaries chanted, *It's your fault we're dead. We'll see you in Hell.* After several choruses, Jazmin severed her hivemind connection with Jiang and reversed the neurotech flag settings. The evil woman moaned, and her face contorted into a hideous expression. She panted so hard she couldn't catch her breath, and her eyes bulged with fear. Jiang was too debilitated to climb off the leaking bags of decaying bodies. She vomited on herself until her stomach was empty, then convulsed with dry heaves.

"You'll get weaker and weaker, and your heart will race until it fails, and then you'll die." Jazmin had waited a long time for her revenge. She considered putting a bullet into Jiang's head, but she was in no hurry. She'd wait patiently for as long as it took for the monster to die. It had taken years to catch up with her.

Movement in her periphery caught Jazmin's attention. She swung her gun toward the black blur. Before she could lock onto the target, a muzzle flash erupted with two quick shots. Jiang crumpled to the floor and blood gushed from two chest wounds. The rounds hadn't exited her body, so Jazmin assumed they were hollow point. The senator would bleed out in a few minutes at most.

The intruder pointed her weapon to the ceiling, dropped the gun's magazine and ejected the bullet in the chamber. With the slide locked back, she placed the firearm on the floor, stood, and put her hands behind her head. "Commander Hassani, my mission was to terminate Ling Chen Jiang. I see you beat me to it."

Jazmin kept her gun centered on the woman's chest. "Who are you?"

"I'm Lieutenant general Mei Chan, Chinese Military Intelligence. I'm here to clean up a mess."

"Were you Senator Jiang's sponsor?"

"Yes. Ling Chen got arrogant and dangerous. None of what's happening now was sanctioned by the Chinese government. I came to terminate our association with her."

"How do we stop the madness between our countries?"

"This is the first step. No one wants war. Please deliver that message to your president."

Jazmin laughed. "What makes you think I have the President's ear?"

"We've been watching you for a long time. You've proven yourself to be amazingly resourceful." Mei lowered her hands to her hips. "I'm unarmed and have no interest in hurting you. I'd appreciate it if you'd holster your weapon."

Jazmin lowered her gun but kept it at the ready. "So what now?"

"We walk away. Perhaps we'll meet another day."

Before Jazmin could respond, Mei tossed a micro flashbang grenade at her. Normally flashbangs had a limited effect on Jazmin's bionic eyes and ears, but this one was designed for maximum pain for bionic devices. She couldn't see or hear anything for close to a minute. When Jazmin recovered, Mei, her gun, magazine, bullet casings, and ejected round were all gone.

Chapter 82

Chicago, Illinois
18 August

Jazmin entered the Girl & The Goat restaurant in Chicago's famed Restaurant Row in the West Loop. She walked past the hostess counter in the Michelin-starred restaurant and entered the dining room. At a table near the window, Sanjay Guptarian and Rogo Blozard sat across from each other, sipping scotch. Jazmin pulled up a chair and sat, saying nothing.

After a moment Guptarian said, "I think you have the wrong table."

Jazmin looked at the tattoo on her forearm, then back at Guptarian. "I kept my promise to my SEAL team and settled the score with Jiang. You two are next on my list."

Fear flashed across Guptarian's face. Despite her changed appearance, Guptarian knew exactly who sat across from him. He recovered his composure and his eyes went cold. "Are you threatening us?" He gestured at the full restaurant. "If you're going to shoot us, there are lots of witnesses."

"Enjoy your drinks. They'll be your last." Jazmin stood and nodded toward the two-person security detail at a nearby table, their hands poised to pull concealed weapons. "They can't save you."

Jazmin left the restaurant and jumped onto the fire escape

attached to the building next door. She climbed to the rooftop and waited. From her perch, she had a clear view of the front of the restaurant. A few minutes later Guptarian and Blozard, flanked by their security team, left the restaurant. A self-driving armored Bentley picked them up and sped away.

Jazmin opened her tablet and initiated the PWL targeting system. A demonstration for a terrorist organization had been scheduled this evening to show what PWL's system would do in an attack on an armored car. Instead of the prearranged empty vehicle, Jazmin changed the target to the Bentley carrying Guptarian and Blozard. She opened a holographic window showing an aerial view of the armored car. She watched as the vehicle sped up on the on-ramp and entered freeway traffic. It drove in the far left lane reserved for self-driving cars and accelerated to 200 MPH. The PWL weapon fired just after the car entered a low area of the freeway with cement walls on both sides. The Bentley careened out of control, hit the wall, flipped over multiple times, and exploded. There were no survivors.

Jazmin went cold inside. She felt neither relief nor elation. She'd been judge, jury, and executioner. She'd kept her promise, though it was one more savage act on her long list to reconcile before she'd ever find peace.

Chapter 83
Mei Chan

Chinese Military Intelligence Headquarters
19 August

Upon her return to China, Mei learned of seismic changes in the country's leadership. The seven members of China's most powerful political body, the Politburo Standing Committee, was in complete agreement: The Paramount Leader needed to be replaced before he did irreparable damage to the country. They removed Yulong Qing as the General Secretary of the Chinese Communist Party, Chairman of the Central Military Commission, and President. To save face, the official reason for Yulong Qing stepping down was his rapidly declining health, which made him unable to perform his official duties as the leader of China. The news organizations were told he was suffering from an aggressive, untreatable cancer and that he was retiring to his country home to live out his remaining days. The Politburo Standing Committee promoted Ping Zhao to all three positions. She was now the Paramount Leader of China.

Zhao sacked the head of Chinese Military Intelligence and promoted Mei to replace him. Along with Mei's new job as head of military intelligence, she was promoted to general. Ping Zhao called Mei into her new office, where the Paramount Leader shared her happy news. Mei was both relieved and terrified at the swift changes in the seat of power and at her own incredibly good fortune. She could not have hoped for a better outcome. Mei rewarded her most trusted officers with promotions. A few officers loyal to the previous head of Chinese Military Intelligence, Fenhua Tian, were silenced and forcibly retired.

Having never served in the military, Zhao was at a disadvantage. She had to decisively take command of China's powerful armed forces. If she could control the generals, she had the might of the country's military at her will. She wasn't worried about ordering the generals to attack; it was ordering them not to. Therefore, Mei's first priority was to provide the new Paramount Leader with leverage to control the generals. Mei had dossiers on all Chinese flag officers, and she immediately put her most trusted and discreet staff members to work scouring their backgrounds. Mei had private conversations with the most bellicose officers letting them know the new Paramount Leader expected their full support. Mei knew things about them Ping Zhao didn't, but as long as they supported Zhao, Mei would keep quiet. The old men bristled at her threats, but since Mei was a senior general, they took her seriously. As a final step, Mei coached Zhao on how to speak to the generals. Zhao needed to maintain her authority while conveying respect for their experience.

***

Mei met alone with the new Paramount Leader. Zhao said, "Our rapidly deteriorating relationship with the United States is my biggest concern. The US will surely respond after the sinking of their aircraft carrier. Minimizing China's response is the key to keeping peace with our superpower rival. I need your help predicting how the American president will respond. If China goes to war with the US, there will be no winners."

Mei said, "Compared to China, the Americans have a superior nuclear arsenal, though they will be hesitant to use it against us. They are worried about a retaliatory nuclear strike on US soil and being vilified by the other advanced democracies. However, the US is far behind China on directed-energy weapons, which don't have the stigma of nuclear arms."

Zhao asked, "Short of an American nuclear strike, how else might the US attack?"

"An EMP strike. They could launch ballistic missiles and air-burst atomic weapons, resulting in an electromagnetic pulse destroying anything run by a microchip."

Zhao put down her teacup and leaned forward. "What would that mean for China?"

"The remaining rural areas of China would fare the best, as they have limited technology and grow their own food. Large cities would stop functioning, and chaos would overtake them within days. With no transportation, communication, or electric power, society would break down and the government would be powerless to control it."

Zhao looked horrified. "Instead of a quick death from an atomic blast and radiation, we'd have starvation, riots, and loss of control."

Mei nodded. "If we want to save China, we must keep the generals from attacking."

Obviously shaken by this reality, Zhao said. "Thank you, General. I will carefully consider your advice."

Chapter 84
Francesca Navarro

Situation Room – The White House
30 August

Francesca Navarro sat at the head of the large conference table in the Situation Room, joined by the Secretary of State, the National Security Advisor, military chiefs, and commanders of both Indo-Pacific Command and Strategic Command. Live satellite images of the destroyed Chinese Naval base on Mischief Reef in the South China Sea filled the large wall monitor. The assault by US Navy fighters and the cruise missile attack by a navy destroyer had left the base in smoking ruins. Several ships docked at the Chinese base were gashed open and sinking. A second screen showed a burning crater where the secret American black ops base in Yunnan Province had launched the attack on Marine One.

Admiral Lynn Stetson, Commander of Indo-Pacific Command, said, "Madam President, we can still attack their aircraft carrier group. We have assets in the region to handle that mission. The assault teams are still in the area awaiting further orders. Chinese forces are closing in but have not yet engaged."

"America has responded; we've sent a message to China. Let's hold off on further action."

Colonel Sandling, the senior communications officer in the room said, "Madam President, I have the president of China, Ping Zhao, on the red phone. She urgently wishes to speak to you."

"I expected her call. As the newly elected president, she has to react to an attack. Put her through."

As soon as the call connected, a life-sized image of Ping Zhao filled the holographic screen, her face a mix of rage and panic. Elderly Chinese generals filled the background. "Madam President, you must stop this unwarranted aggression against China immediately, or there will be drastic and deadly repercussions."

Navarro stared at her most powerful rival. "America's aggression was a restrained response to China's attack on the US and its president."

"Both unfortunate incidents, but neither perpetrated by China. A US senator is responsible."

"One supported every step of the way over many years by Chinese Military Intelligence. Your country's long con paid off, but not without consequences."

Zhao looked nervously at the generals, then back to the screen. "All of this was done by my predecessor. We all play the espionage game, and America can't claim innocence. Let me be very clear, the attack on your aircraft carrier was neither sanctioned nor carried out by China. We have not declared war on our most powerful rival, as it's not in our best interest. Neither has our military engaged with the perpetrators of your brutal military attack on Chinese soil. I insist on an immediate ceasefire. Like the US, China is a superpower. Even a limited war would be devastating for both our countries. As heads of state, our primary job is to protect our people. Hundreds of millions of lives are at stake. Madam President, is this the legacy you want?"

Navarro took a deep breath and fought off horrifying images of bombed out cities, something the US hadn't experienced since the Civil War two hundred years ago. "No, it's not."

Zhao looked relieved. "It's not the legacy I want, either. Let's stop now and declare a ceasefire. Order your Navy out of our national waters and reopen the Chinese embassy. We disagree on many things, but we must always find a way for peace between our nations."

Navarro had to be strong with her rival superpower. She'd succeeded in a retaliatory attack with no American casualties and settled a personal score. A war with China wasn't something she wanted to pursue, especially when her rival didn't. "President Zhao, I agree to a ceasefire. Further military aggression serves neither of our nations. The US has many grievances to settle with China. They would be best dealt with by our diplomats, but only if China can do so in good faith."

Zhao said, "Let both of our governments act in good faith and our people sleep in peace."

"President Zhao, I will order US forces back to international waters. I expect they will move freely and remain unmolested by Chinese forces." Navarro made eye contact with each of her military chiefs and functional combatant commanders. All nodded agreement.

Zhao exchanged similar looks with the dour-faced generals surrounding her. "Agreed. After today's events it would be best to keep our militaries apart. Emotions on both sides remain high."

Navarro said, "Let both of our nations sleep well tonight and keep our most vigorous exchanges between our diplomats instead of our armed forces."

Zhao said, "I look forward to speaking again. Goodbye, Madam President."

"Good night, President Zhao." Navarro signaled the colonel to end the call, and the screen went blank. Navarro's worst fear was a nuclear attack on US soil, and that hadn't happened. Peace was always a welcome option, especially when initiated by the enemy. "I want all military services to remain at DEFCON 1 for the next forty-eight hours. We need to make sure Zhao keeps her word. If she demonstrates firm control of her military, then I'll consider moving to DEFCON 2. If she can deliver on what she proposed, peace is always a good outcome."

Navarro turned to her Secretary of State and National Security Advisor. "Reach out to your Chinese counterparts and get a read on how securely Zhao has her grip on power. If your assessment of Chinese intent looks promising, then develop a plan for a minimally-staffed Chinese embassy." She scanned the faces around the room for disagreement and saw none.

Navarro stood. "Let's do our best to keep the peace with China." She turned to her chief of staff. "Feel out Congress for officially terminating our declaration of war with China. It's too early to act, but I want to be ready."

Navarro headed back to her office and closed the door. From a bottle she'd been saving for a special occasion, she poured a glass of Macallan 30-year-old scotch over ice. Avoiding a war with China was as good a reason to drink premium Scotch aged for three decades as she'd ever see. She kicked off her shoes and let the alcohol ease away her stress.

341

bottle she'd been saving for a special occasion, she poured a glass of Macallan 30-year-old scotch over ice. Avoiding a war with China was as good a reason to drink premium Scotch aged for three decades as she'd ever see. She kicked off her shoes and let the alcohol ease away her stress.

Chapter 85
Jazmin Hassani

Wisconsin Militia Base – Bayfield
21 September

After returning to Bayfield, Jazmin reported to General Suresh, who insisted on a thorough debrief for the remaining senior officers. Once that was done, Jazmin kept to herself. As the base's chief pilot, Jazmin focused her efforts on aircraft and drone rebuilding, working alone whenever possible. She relished the quiet and solitude.

Everyone on the militia base was relieved when President Navarro announced an end to hostilities with China. The President's popularity shot up after peace was restored, giving a boost to her reelection campaign. The two countries were now in the process of restoring normal diplomatic relations.

Jazmin's life over the last several months had been laser focused on bringing Jiang to justice. She finally had closure for the event that had changed her life and cost the lives of her SEAL team, though the peace of mind she'd longed for was still elusive. Now that Jiang, Trabago, and Guptarian were dead, Jazmin was at a loss as to where her life would go. She was still on the wanted terrorist list, so remaining at the Wisconsin Militia base felt like her only viable option. She'd seen Harry a few times, but always with other people around. They needed privacy to resolve what was left between them, though neither was willing to initiate that difficult conversation. She still had feelings for him, yet she wasn't clear what she wanted to do or even what their future might look like. To work through the mess of her feelings, she opened up to Catarina, as the android had no preconceived biases or agenda about what Jazmin should do.

***

Jazmin was in the middle of testing the rebuilt flight controls on one of the quadcopters when she was summoned to the general's office. When she arrived, a man and a woman she didn't recognize were with the general. They wore dark suits, earpieces, and shoulder holsters. Harry was there too, dressed in a suit Jazmin had never seen. The odd cast of characters, along with Harry's unusual clothing choice and stoic expression, made Jazmin uneasy.

Suresh smiled. "I spoke with Ebony Diamond this morning. The President wants to see you and Harry in the Oval Office." She gestured to the two strangers in dark suits. "They're from the President's Secret Service detail, here to escort you to Washington." The two nodded at Jazmin, though said nothing. Suresh took a garment bag from a hook on the wall near her desk and handed it to Jazmin. "The President wants you properly dressed." Suresh pointed at the private door in her office. "Change your clothes. You're leaving now."

Jazmin took the bag from Suresh, then went into the private room. She was surprised to find a Navy dress white uniform with all of her medals. She changed out of her flight suit and into her uniform, which had been altered to fit her latest body specifications. In the mirror she checked that her badges, name tag, and medals were on straight. She left the garment bag and her other clothes behind. When she reentered the office, the female Secret Service agent said, "Let's go." A few minutes later, Jazmin, Harry, and the two Secret Service agents were flown by helicopter to Truax, then the four were hustled onto a private jet. They were flown to Joint Base Andrews, where a motorcade of black SUVs picked them up. The whole experience was surreal.

On the way to the White House, Harry asked the Secret Service agents, "What is the meeting with the President about?"

The female agent answered, "The President wants to see you. That's all you need to know."

Jazmin wanted to know what was going through Harry's mind,

but she didn't want to talk in front of the agents. She considered a hivemind connection, though the Secret Service was rumored to have equipment capable of monitoring their wordless conversation. That was a risk she wasn't willing to take. Harry remained silent for the rest of the journey. Without a hivemind connection, she couldn't read his thoughts. His facial expression gave up nothing, but he had a dark, brooding look in his eyes. All she could fathom was he expected a bad outcome. Her own thoughts were all over the spectrum. Despite Suresh's smile and mention of Ebony Diamond, Jazmin didn't know what to expect. She'd been AWOL from the Navy for months and was on the terrorist watch list. She had a hard time imagining anything positive resulting from a presidential summons.

When they arrived at the White House, they were taken to a waiting area outside the Oval Office. The minutes ticked by slowly. After almost an hour went by, a well-dressed admin came for them. "The President will see you now."

Jazmin and Harry followed the admin into the Oval Office, trailed by the two Secret Service agents who then stood by the door. The admin left and closed the door. President Navarro came out from behind the Resolute Desk. "Thank you for coming to Washington on such short notice."

As if we had any choice, thought Jazmin. Navarro's icy smile was creepy. She stood in front of Harry, then looked him up and down. "Mr. Dexter, I've heard so much about you. I'm glad we were finally able to meet face to face." Harry didn't respond, and the unnerved feeling Jazmin had felt since the agents showed up in Bayfield spiked.

Navarro stepped back, her expression more serious. "Mr. Dexter, I want to thank you for everything you've done recently, both for the country and for me personally. As president I can issue pardons. However, I grant them sparingly and only to people I'm convinced won't break the law in the future. Given your track record of committing countless felonies, including murder, both as an Air Force Cyber Command officer and in all the years since as a member of the Wisconsin Militia, I can't in good conscience grant you a full pardon."

Navarro began to pace, though Jazmin sensed it was for theatrics rather than to allow the President time to think. Navarro faced Harry again and her eyes burned into his. "Here's what I'm going to do. My best offer is a get out of jail card good today only. You have twenty-four hours to leave the US and disappear. As long as you stay out of sight and give me no reason to find you, I'll let you enjoy your freedom. If you make the mistake of violating US laws or interfering with legitimate government operations, I'll send a black ops team to hunt you down. If that happens, there's a distinct possibility you'll be repatriated inside a body bag. I can't guarantee what my successor will do, as they might not feel as magnanimous as me." She looked at her watch. "Your twenty-four-hour time limit starts now. I suggest you take advantage of every minute." She glanced at the two agents by the door, who snapped to attention. "My Secret Service detail will escort you out."

The Oval Office doors sprung open and two agents carrying compact submachine guns charged in. Harry's eyes hardened, though otherwise his neutral expression didn't change. He avoided eye contact with Jazmin. The two agents who had escorted them from Bayfield grabbed Harry by his arms and marched him out the door, with the two additional agents bringing up the rear. In seconds he was gone, and the Oval Office doors closed. Harry's sudden disappearance clawed a hole inside Jazmin; their unresolved relationship was now decided for them.

Now alone with the President, Jazmin feared a similar fate, or one even worse than being banished from the country she loved.

Navarro studied Jazmin for a moment. "Commander Hassani, in the future you should choose your associates more carefully, especially your intimate partners."

Navarro's words chilled her and drove home the power and knowledge of the American presidency. Jazmin didn't know how to reply, so she remained silent. Ebony Diamond might be the only safe person to have a conversation with about the President's admonishment. Navarro's penetrating gaze lasted a few seconds longer, then her face lit up in a warm smile. It was an entirely different look than the icy grin she'd had for Harry. Jazmin didn't know what to think or how to respond to this mercurial woman.

Navarro gestured to one of the couches. "Please sit, there's something I'd like to discuss with you." Jazmin hesitated and Navarro pointed to the couch again. "I'll be right there."

Jazmin sat, and Navarro took a small box from her desk drawer. She sat across from Jazmin and held the mysterious box on her lap. "I had the pleasure of pinning a star on Ebony Diamond this morning. Rear Admiral Diamond and I had a long talk about you." Jazmin wondered where this conversation was going. She feared it sliding sideways and tried not to react.

Navarro said, "I want to thank you for everything you've done over the last several months and for what it took for you to take down Senator Jiang. I'm also aware of your role in the attack on the founders of Pulse Weapons Lab. Their ending was no accident."

Jazmin tried not to react to the President's knowledge that she had killed Sanjay Guptarian and Rogo Blozard. A chill washed over her while she waited for her fate.

Navarro's icy smile returned. "They came to a fitting end. All of PWL's intellectual property has been confiscated by the government for national security reasons, and the company is permanently shut down. Senators who were secretly on their board of directors have been sanctioned." The President cocked her head at Jazmin and silence hung in the air. Navarro continued, "When the government agencies that should have supported your efforts instead hunted you, along with countless enemies of the state, you never quit. Your bravery and perseverance are commendable."

Jazmin waited for the blade from a hidden guillotine to chop off her head, but Navarro said nothing more. Stunned, Jazmin said, "Thank you, Madam President."

"Commander, you're out of uniform, which is no way to be, especially in front of your commander in chief." Navarro tapped the box in her lap. "Allow me to fix that for you." The President stood and Jazmin jumped to her feet. Navarro opened the box containing captain's shoulder boards. She unfastened the commander shoulder boards and replaced them with her new rank. "That looks much better, Captain."

Jazmin grinned, then saluted. This was the last thing she expected.

Navarro returned Jazmin's salute then motioned her to sit again. "Rear Admiral Diamond is taking command of the *Enterprise* aircraft carrier group to keep an eye on our interests in Asia, especially China. She wants you to take command of the special ops pilots and aircraft for the carrier group. You have two weeks to get your personal affairs in order and report to the *Enterprise*."

Jazmin was excited and terrified by this change of events. "What about everything I've done over the last few months since going AWOL?"

Navarro waved her hand dismissively. "Your military record's clean, and you've been removed from the terrorist wanted list. Officially you were under Top Secret orders from the President."

"What is the status of the Wisconsin Militia?"

Navarro pursed her lips. "We're still straightening that out. We're looking at everything General Trabago touched, especially anyone involved in what the DIA deemed to be terrorist activities."

"What about my mom?"

"Mercedes' record has been cleared and everything that happened is sealed. She's welcome to return to her job as VP of Engineering at Defense Air Systems, and her security clearance has been reinstated. She's on her way to be reunited with your father right now." Navarro laughed. "Your mother insisted on agency for her android twin, Catarina Silvado. My staff fast-tracked android permanent residency certification for Ms. Silvado. She's now officially an independent sentient being and is no longer anyone's property. We also provided her transport with your mother."

A knock on the door interrupted their conversation. Navarro said, "Enter."

The admin who had brought Harry and Jazmin stuck his head in the office. "Madam President, the Secretary of State and National Security Advisor are here."

Navarro stood, and Jazmin did as well. "Captain, I hope one day I'll get a chance to pin a star on you as well. On behalf of our entire nation, thank you for everything you've done."

Jazmin left the Oval Office still trying to wrap her head around what had just happened. She'd have to get used to being addressed as Captain Hassani and to the protocol that went with her new rank. Her tablet chirped. A message from Rear Admiral Diamond. *Congratulations Captain. We need to discuss your new command.*

A second message appeared and stayed on the screen just long enough for Jazmin to read it before it vanished. *Congratulations on your promotion to captain. Daiyu Teng is now on my headquarters staff. A back-channel is always open. General Mei Chan.*

Epilogue

EAA AirVenture – Oshkosh, Wisconsin
25 July

It had been almost a year since President Navarro placed captain's bars on Jazmin's shoulders. Her new job commanding the special ops air assets in Asia was endlessly challenging, exhilarating, and exhausting. Jazmin loved it, but the Navy was her entire life. Even on one of her rare leaves, she agreed to help recruit young people for naval aviation, so she was at her favorite air show, EAA AirVenture in Oshkosh, Wisconsin. The Blue Angels roared by in a low pass breakaway formation, then arced skyward. She relished that sound, as jet fighters would always be her first love.

Jazmin had wonderful memories of going to AirVenture every summer with her mom. For most of those years, her mother had worked for Defense Air Systems, but after leaving the Bayfield militia base she hadn't wanted to return to her old job. Instead, she and Catarina opened their own company, Twin Engine Warbird Restoration. Within a few months they had more business than they could handle. They rebuilt everything from WWII rotary engine planes to military surplus jet fighters. They developed a loyal customer base of wealthy warbird enthusiasts and had a cadre of retired military fighter jocks on their advisory board. Their booth at the air show was packed with customers, and Jazmin's mom was even one of the keynote speakers.

Jazmin was thirsty on this hot, sunny July day as she walked the grounds admiring a hundred and fifty years of aviation history. An older guy dragging a wagon filled with bottles of lemonade on ice strolled up to her. Everything about him was an anachronism, from the old-fashioned child's red wagon, real ice instead of blue synthetic ice packs, and glass bottles. He had a craggy, weatherbeaten face, though he moved like a much younger man. There was something familiar about him, but she couldn't place what. To keep off the sun, he wore a floppy hat covered with buttons and patches from prior year's shows. In a squeaky old man's voice he said, "Hey Captain, you look thirsty. How about an ice-cold lemonade?"

Before she could answer, he pulled a bottle out from the ice and thrust it into her hands.

"Thank you." She twisted off the top and drank half the bottle. "What do I owe you?"

"Five bucks for most people but I have a soft spot for women in uniform." He grinned at her with crooked teeth. "For you it's free."

He seemed harmless but she didn't want to encourage him. "Thanks again."

She was about to walk away, when a different voice from the old man stopped her cold. "I've missed you, Jaz."

Now she knew what was familiar. It was the way he looked at her. "Harry?" He nodded. Today she didn't hesitate. She whispered in his ear. "I have a suite at the Pfister hotel in downtown Milwaukee overlooking Lake Michigan. Meet me there in two hours." She backed away as an ear-to-ear grin took over his face. She turned and walked away, thinking people strolling by must have wondered what the Navy captain said to the old guy that made his day.

Jazmin was due back to her command responsibilities in two weeks and couldn't extend her leave. Any time Harry spent in the US was a huge risk. Over the last several months he'd sent encrypted texts that vanished as soon as she read them. He'd been supporting the Wisconsin Militia from his various hideouts and data centers throughout the world.

They had no long-term future, but life was short and violent. She was determined to enjoy every minute of the time they had together.

THE END

Acknowledgements

Writing and publishing a book is a team effort. I want to thank the many people who were key to getting Electromagnetic Assault completed and published. The first person is my wife, Barb. She's been super supportive through the ten plus years I've been writing. She graciously allowed me the time to read bookshelves of writing craft books, go to writers' conferences, and spend countless hours locked up in my office writing and working on social media.

Learning to write well has been a long process. I've worked with some great teachers along the way including Christine DeSmet, Tim Storm, and Sue Burke. All three of these wonderful teachers made me a better writer.

Lisa Lickel, my developmental editor, did a fabulous job identifying numerous issues with the manuscript. From a story standpoint, she provided clear guidance on what needed to be fixed and why. Lisa reviewed the novel a second time focusing on line editing. She found many smaller issues and challenged me to make all the story elements work. The book is so much better because of her efforts. More importantly, she taught me to be a better writer. Lisa also recommended the hybrid press I'm working with, Sisyphus Triumphant.

My wife, Barb, graciously volunteered to proofread the novel, but she determined it needed copy editing as well. Barb has been fascinated with languages her entire life, learning Latin, French, Russian, and some German. She's also a historian and voracious reader, and she knows how languages are constructed. Because of this knowledge, she understands precise writing in ways I never will. Barb made sure I wrote what I intended and that it would be clear to readers. One of my top priorities as a writer is to create well-crafted stories. She helped me bring that vision to life. After working with such fabulous editors, any remaining errors are mine.

I had the pleasure of working with three phenomenal military experts, each with decades of experience. Collin "Gator" Coatney, Colonel, US Air Force (Retired) provided military fighter jet expertise. He has many years of experience as an F-16 Fighter Pilot instructor and was the former Senior Advisor to the Commander of Air Education and Training Command (AETC). He's now an Airbus A320 First Officer with American Airlines. Collin corrected numerous mistakes in air traffic operations and communications, fighter jet battles, and had creative ideas for fixing a chapter he felt wasn't credible late in the book. The book is not only more believable but also more exciting because of his help.

For Special Operations expertise I worked with Sean Haggerty, Sergeant Major, US Army (Retired). Sean spent 25 years in Special Forces and up until recently, worked for the Department of Defense Science Board as a Senior Advisor. He corrected a number of issues involving Special Forces, weapons, and command hierarchy. Sean is also the author of two novels featuring a Special Operations soldier as the protagonist, Jones Point and Cabal. You can learn more about him on his website. https://authorseanhagerty.com/

Helicopters and rotorcrafts were used extensively in the book. The expert I worked with was Karl Metz, Chief Warrant Officer 5, US Army (Retired). Karl spent over 20 years on active duty, flew numerous combat missions, and spent thousands of hours in the air. Karl flew AH-64 Apache attack helicopters, the deadliest helicopters in the world, along with other helicopters. Later in his career he was an instructor on AH-64 Apache and other rotorcraft. His military service was followed by various roles with government contractors as an Army Aviation expert.

All of my military experts pointed out numerous technical errors, and all made the story stronger and more realistic. I corrected as many details as I could, though some stayed in to make the story work. In a few cases I ask readers to suspend disbelief as the story world is set in the future. Any remaining errors or inaccuracies are solely mine.

A number of beta readers reviewed early drafts of the book and provided insight on what was working and what needed to be improved. The following people were especially helpful – Brad Banks, Randy Cleven, my daughter, Karen Landay, Kristin Oakley,

Emilie Smith, Joshua Shepherd, Greg Thurston, Linda Whitaker, and Kristin Workman.

Finally, I'd like to thank Steve Strackbein, the owner of Sisyphus Triumphant Publishing https://sisyphustriumphant.com, the hybrid press I'm working with. It's been a great experience working with a small press focused on science fiction and fantasy where my book fits squarely in the market they are serving. I enjoyed having more control than I would be allowed at a traditional publisher while getting expert advice and guidance to create a book with the highest professional standards. I really appreciate how collaborative the entire process has been.

About The Author

Bruce Landay is a former US Air Force Officer and a current member of the Experimental Aircraft Association (EAA). He lives in Madison, Wisconsin.

You can learn more about him at https://brucelanday.com/ Landay also writes a weekly Substack column, Future Trends and Science Fiction. https://brucelanday.substack.com/